Praise for Janet Lynnford's novels

Firebrand Bride

"Lush and sexy, *Firebrand Bride* is a compelling read that brings the romance of the Scottish countryside to life."
—Tess Gerritsen

"Lively action . . . vividly rendered scenes, and a dash of the paranormal recommend this fast-paced, intricately plotted tale."

—*Library Journal*

"Remarkable . . . a treat . . . Black Graham is exactly what women want in a hero: a strong, sensitive, and courageous person. The firebrand Lucina is an intrepid heroine, who when she loves, really loves . . . a refreshing saga."
—*Under the Covers*

"Rich in historical detail and personages, *Firebrand Bride* is a delicious banquet for Scottish history/romance fans. A strong heroine and an equally powerful hero, an exciting backdrop, colorful details and fascinating characters make this a not-to-be-missed read."

—*Romantic Times*

Lady Shadowhawk

"Breathtaking."
—Connie Reinhold

"A provocative tale with intense characters and some heart-pounding twists that leave the reader wanting more."
—*Rendezvous*

Continued on next page . . .

Lord of Lightning

"Intriguing. . . . The story of a strong-minded woman who seeks to dominate the pattern of her life . . . and the brave man who has the strength to let her be strong."
—Edith Layton

"Janet Lynnford has a magical gift for drawing readers into the story, and into the hearts of her characters. . . . *Lord of Lightning* is a captivating tale, rich with detail, brimming with adventure, and spellbound with a love not to be forgotten."
—Patricia Rice

Pirate's Rose

"An impressive debut that captivated me from the very first page. Ms. Lynnford captures the lush sensuality of the Elizabethan period with effortless skill. Rich in passion and intrigue and blessed with a bright, vibrant heroine and a winning hero, *Pirate's Rose* is a delightful romantic adventure that kept me turning pages long past my bed-time."
—Teresa Medeiros

"Just the kind of dynamic, spirited, richly detailed romance I love to read. I expect great things from this author."
—Linda Lael Miller

"Makes the battle of the sexes fresh and exciting. . . . Sweeping in scope and intimate in detail. . . . A book to treasure."
—Karen Harper

"A vivid tale. . . . Enjoy!"
—Kat Martin

Bride of Hearts

Janet Lynnford

A SIGNET BOOK

SIGNET
Published by New American Library, a division of
Penguin Putnam Inc., 375 Hudson Street,
New York, New York 10014, U.S.A.
Penguin Books Ltd, 27 Wrights Lane,
London W8 5TZ, England
Penguin Books Australia Ltd,
Ringwood, Victoria, Australia
Penguin Books Canada Ltd, 10 Alcorn Avenue,
Toronto, Ontario, Canada M4V 3B2
Penguin Books (N.Z.) Ltd, 182–190 Wairau Road,
Auckland 10, New Zealand

Penguin Books Ltd, Registered Offices:
Harmondsworth, Middlesex, England

First published by Signet, an imprint of New American Library,
a division of Penguin Putnam Inc.

First Printing, August 2000
10 9 8 7 6 5 4 3 2 1

PUBLISHER'S NOTE
This is a work of fiction. Names, characters, places, and incidents either are the
product of the author's imagination or are used fictitiously, and any resemblance to
actual persons, living or dead, business establishments, events, or locales is entirely
coincidental.

This book is dedicated to:

My beloved family,
who missed me greatly
while I agonized my way through this work.

My friends in
Central Ohio Fiction Writers.
Thank you, ladies, for all your kind support.

Connie Rinehold, who writes as Eve Byron
and is as inspiring a mentor as ever drew breath.

Cecilia Malkum Oh, an editor who genuinely cares
first and foremost about honing a work
into a splendid final creation.

PART 1

~~~~~

Chapter 1

Midnight. Cordelia Hailsworthy, Viscountess Wentworth, pushed back the silk-lined hood of her cloak as she hurried along the Thames River path, away from Queen Elizabeth's other maids of honor. She had agreed to visit the midsummer eve's fair with them, but they irritated her, their constant prattling grating on her nerves. Grateful as she was for her new position serving the queen, she wasn't used to the lack of privacy at court. She worked, ate, and slept in the company of women. What a relief to escape, if only for a while.

Patches of mist rose from the water as she glided along the foliage-lined path, and she raised her chin to let the fine veil of moisture kiss her cheeks. The rain hadn't closed the fair, nor was she daunted by the damp. Drinking in the freshness, so welcome after the dank chill of the palace, she caught the scent of roasted chestnuts wafting from the fair she'd left behind. But if she turned back to buy some, the others would find her, and she wasn't ready yet. She needed the solitude of the rain-washed night.

Cordelia halted on the path, and looked back over her shoulder. The lights of smoldering bonfires twinkled through the mist. Dim shapes of tradesmen moved along the riverbank near Hampton Court Palace, offering food, trinkets, and knacks, eager to serve the wealthy who thought it fashionable to come out into the enchanted night.

It did seem enchanted. Magic flowed around Cordelia as she stripped off her cloak and draped it over a tree limb. Her kirtle skirt and long-sleeved bodice followed, though after a moment's thought, she restrapped her purse at her waist. Shoes and stockings dropped at the foot of the tree before she moved on bare feet to test the crystal clear water of the Thames. She was going to wade in the life's blood of London, west of the city where the water flowed so clean it sparkled. Never in recent memory had the river swollen so high in its banks, but on her first visit to court, summer storms brought an unprecedented wealth of water. Was it an omen? Promising what?

Hugging her solitude to her like a protective cloak, Cordelia stepped into the river, lifting her single petticoat above her knees. Tiny wavelets lapped her toes with cool, eager tongues. Above her, the full moon pierced the mist, its reflection on the water's cobalt surface like a jewel reflected in a magic mirror.

Some yards ahead, a bonfire smoldered beneath dripping trees, another feat of magic. Its intimate light made her think of her mother, who had died when she was twelve. Twelve years later she still longed for her beloved mother's warmth, for the strength of her arms holding her close as they drifted on her swing beneath blossom-ladened trees.

The peace of Cordelia's solitude fled, chased by the memory of what had come after her mother's death. Bound in the cradle to Viscount Wentworth, the Earl of Whitby's son, she'd gone to live with his family, consigned to the care of her young husband's grandam.

The loss of her mother had ached like a wound, though over time the old lady's nurturing had helped fill the gap. Then, six months ago, on a whim, her father-in-law parted them as easily as peas popped from their pod. Once more her circle of love had been destroyed.

Hating her desolation, Cordelia moved along the riverbank. The shimmer of the moon beckoned, as did the fairy-tale quality of the soft ground mist that transformed the woods into a mysterious grove, fit for sacred rites.

"God'den, m'lady." A bent, wrinkled peddler woman darted from the bonfire to hail Cordelia, nodding and bowing. Her big pack was stuffed with fairings—pretty laces, scarves of gauze, carved pomanders of wood.

Wanting to be alone, Cordelia prepared to move on.

"Woulds't care for a trifle, m'lady?" With a withered hand, the woman reached into her pack and plucked out several scarves. "A pretty knack to remind you of this amazing night?"

One of them arrested Cordelia, its startling green a perfect mirror of the rain-freshened woods. It whispered of spring and of dew on new-sprung grass. Without meaning to, she stepped from the water, one hand outstretched.

The scarf came eagerly into her grasp, as if it had chosen her and not the other way around. Dropping her petticoat hem, Cordelia threaded the scarf through her bare fingers, letting it weave itself around her palm.

"A shilling," she offered impulsively, feeling in the purse still strapped to her waist. It was too much for a scarf, but she would have it. Pulling out the coin, she offered it to the woman.

"M'lady's got taste, she does." The woman's gnarled claw nipped the coin from Cordelia's hand. "This silk is the finest from Genoa." She reached into her pack again. "Care to have a spin of Dame Fortune's wheel?" She waved the bauble on a stick and laughed, the coarse sound grating on Cory's ear. "I can guess your fortune without the wheel, though. Eyes like yours, and that face. Made for love, aren't ye?"

Cory gazed into the woman's small dark eyes and had the eerie sense that she faced Dame Fortune herself. A shiver rushed up her spine as she clutched the scarf. She wasn't made for love. Life had given her quite the opposite.

At thirteen, her husband had tried to bed her, despite both their fathers' orders to wait. She had spent three years fending off Thomas's advances and watching him seduce every female he could lay hands on. Then, when they both turned sixteen, before they had consummated their marriage, a fever had carried him off. Should she thank Fortune for any of that?

Cory stepped away from the peddler woman. "No, thank you, I know my fortune already. It needn't be told." Fighting despair, she gathered up her soaked hem and fled, the scarf looped around her throat, a silky wisp floating in her wake.

Mist as fine as a fairy's veil ebbed and swirled as Cory forged along the riverbank, parting the magical curtain that hid the rest of the world from view. Stands of rushes framed blooming water lilies. Their tightly closed buds glowed in the faint moonlight like beacons to serenity, but the dreamlike quality of the night no longer offered peace. Cordelia's fists tightened on her wet skirts. She was not made for the kind of love the peddler meant.

She walked blindly along the bank. Two snow-white swans nesting in the rushes startled as she approached, their heads popping up from beneath their wings. On impulse, she turned from the bank and waded deeper, the water swirling around her thighs. If only she could leave her sorrowful past behind and fly as swans did, skimming across the water, lifting in flight to soar on strong wings.

"Cory, wait. Wait for me."

Cory turned, her heart warming at the sound of the high, young voice. Thirteen-year-old Carew Cavandish raced after her, his shoes clutched in one hand, netherstocks flapping in the other. Having seen her wading, he'd decided to imitate her. Except that he looked as comical as a jester, racing through the water, spray flying in every direction as he lifted each foot high.

"Gracious, what are you doing still up and about at this hour. You belong abed." She grasped his hands to steady him as he splashed to a halt before her.

"I quarreled with my father," he panted, distress showing in his voice and face. "I told you I would. He sails around the world for almost two years, then decides it's time to come see me. Four hours back and he's shouting at me again. I hate him." He clung to her, pretending to lose his footing, but she knew why he looped his arms around her neck.

Giving in to the impulse, Cory hugged him to her, feeling his pain. "But Carew, bad storms blew his ship off course last summer. He couldn't get back to see you. Surely you don't hate him for that. He's your father. He loves you."

"I do hate him." Carew drew back, looking fierce. "He forbids me to see you ever again."

"Why? He doesn't know me." Cory blinked away droplets that had settled on her eyelashes. The mist verged on rain now, the droplets thickening into a fine curtain of beads.

Carew hung his head. "He heard about the trouble tonight over the card game."

Cory wrinkled her nose in distaste. Nothing was private at

court. She'd been having a quiet game of cards with Carew and some of the other palace children, getting them settled down before she sent them off to bed, where they belonged. But a parent had found them and raised a clamor. You would think she'd been teaching them to cut purses, not an innocent little sleight of hand. At least they'd been supervised. Everyone knew what the older boys and girls would have been doing in the absence of an adult. "I'll speak to him on the morrow," she said with more confidence than she felt. "He'll understand."

Carew tossed a hank of blond hair from his eyes. "He won't listen. He never does. And he's always said Grandsire Cavandish switched him and his brothers for serious offenses once they turned thirteen. I'm thirteen now."

"That doesn't mean he'll do what his father did," Cory insisted, hoping she was right. "And he may not listen to me, but he cannot ignore the improvement in your behavior." She put a hand on his shoulder in a comforting gesture. "You've been much steadier of late, Carew. Lady Russell is well pleased."

Carew averted his gaze and kicked at the water. "I don't need a nursemaid."

"She's a friend of the family, not a nursemaid." Cory pushed back the unruly lock that refused to stay out of Carew's eyes. "Your aunt and uncle chose her to travel with you from Dorset because they trust her. But you worried her terribly."

"Uncle Charles should have come with me instead. He understands when I want to be with a girl," Carew complained, splashing in the water with one foot.

"He understands, but he also keeps up with you better than Lady Russell can. He makes sure you don't misbehave," Cory reminded him with a stern expression.

"I haven't misbehaved," he vowed, passion brimming in his voice. "Not since you became my friend." He hung his head, as if remembering the things he'd done before she'd taken him in hand. "I like being with Sarah Vasavour."

"Which do you like more, her company or the opportunity to put your hand up her skirt?" Cory probed. His expression sheepish, Carew churned the water with both feet. "Carew, if you truly liked her, you would not do such things. You must not dishonor her else she'll be sent away." She should be anyway, Cory thought. Court was no place for a young girl, nor was it a healthy place for a young boy like Carew. A pity his father visited him only once a year, and then only at court. The child didn't have a home to call his own. Nor did Carew's father, it seemed. He was too busy sailing the Spanish Main.

"Come now, Carew. You should be abed. You said your father rises with the dawn. He'll expect the same of you." She felt in her purse for a small coin. "Buy some gingerbread or chestnuts and go to your chamber. I forbid you to say another cross word to your father until I've spoken to him."

He accepted the coin and flashed her a cocky grin. "Can I say a cross word *after* you've spoken to him?"

"No, you rascal." Cory stamped her foot for emphasis, making water fly. "I tell you he'll understand."

"He won't, but I don't care as long as you're here." Carew hugged her with such sudden ferocity, her ribs hurt. He released her just as suddenly and raced away, splashing through the shallows. Within seconds, the curtain of fine rain cut him off from view.

The desolation that had disappeared in Carew's affectionate presence returned, and Cory plunged deeper into the river, heedless of her clothes, her purse, or the scarf. Her smock and petticoat floated around her as the bottom dropped away, and she swam, the scarf trailing from her throat. It hurt more, not less, when young folk like Carew came to her, reminding her of all she'd been forced to leave behind.

She shouldn't take on Carew's cause. She should serve Her Majesty faithfully and mind her own business so her heart wouldn't be broken again. The queen hated her attendants to wed, so she was finally safe from her father-in-law's unrelenting efforts to marry her off. She should form no attachments of any kind. Life was safer that way.

Just ahead, marble watersteps rose from the river, lined by gleaming white balustrades on each side. Her wet linen clung to her body like a second skin as she rose from the water. The peddler woman had spoken the truth about the quality of her scarf. No dye stained her white smock as the scarf plastered itself to her breast and waist. Her single braid hung wet and cool down her back, and the smooth marble gleamed white beneath her feet. But she forgot all those things as she left the river mist. A clear view of what lay ahead halted her in midstep.

Water spilled from a high bank in a burst of silver, tumbling to a basin in a fern-adorned grotto. The silver moon hung full above, the symbol of Diana, the self-sufficient Queen of the Hunt. Why wasn't she like Diana, needing no one and nothing?

Warm vapor from her lungs formed clouds in the cool air as she held back tears. Tipping up her face, she let the silent rain soothe her cheeks. With chest heaving, she held out beseeching arms to the moon. A yearning swelled in her heart.

She wanted something sure in her life. A home that was hers, a cozy cottage or a huge palace, it didn't matter which. As long as the people she loved couldn't be taken away—Grandmama Hailsworthy, her foster children, Letty and Marcus . . .

Cory's arms dropped to her sides. Impossible wish. Her dreams had died with her mother. Nothing remained of her mother's love but a deck of cards tied with a red ribbon. And now, her life at Whitby Place with her foster family was gone as well.

Wanting to be brave, as her mother had taught her, she walked to the basin and stepped into it. Her calves forged twin trails in the pool as she approached the falls, arms outspread. The force of the water felt good as she stepped under the cascading torrent, pretending she could pass through its curtain into another world, leaving her troubles behind. Perhaps she could wash away her sorrow. Revive her parched soul in this plentitude of water. She must move heaven and earth to find a way to survive her loneliness.

Matthew Cavandish, Baron Graystock, sat on a marble bench screened by shrubbery, drenched from two hours of rain, and watched the graceful water fairy step in and out of the cascading waterfall. As she entered the falls, her lithe body became a silhouette of silver, so that he felt more than saw her beauty shining in the moonlight as she hovered just beyond reach, as ethereal as the mist.

Joanna, my love, is that you?

His rain-soaked brain insisted he saw his wife glide through the shining curtain, and he ached to reach out, to enclose her in his arms and know she was mortal once more. But he couldn't move. His heart was a lump of mud, dried and hard in his chest.

He had been wondering only moments ago if he might walk into the Thames and find eternal rest in the cradle of dark water when his son had emerged from the screen of trees and lunged into the fairy's embrace. Joanna, clasping the child she had never really known?

His gut had twisted as he had watched the impossible tableau of his wife with the nearly grown child she had borne. Matthew had wanted to rise and go to them, but he couldn't even blink. Carew had grown taller in two years. Not yet a man, but no longer a boy. Someone he neither understand nor could talk to.

I am trying, Joanna. I swore to guard our son with my life.

He hated leaving his son to make a living at the queen's bidding, but once he'd become successful, Elizabeth had insisted. Yet the last time he returned home, when he offered advice or guidance, Carew lashed out as if he'd been struck. Matthew only wanted the best for him, but within hours of arriving back in England, he'd quarreled with the boy. A young, rebellious male cub, Carew was much as he'd been at close to that age. At sixteen, Matthew had ignored his father's advice and taken his beloved Joanna to wife.

"Wait," his father had warned him. "She shouldn't bear children yet. She's too young."

Youth's arrogance had turned a deaf ear. Arrogance? he scoffed. More like ignorance. He'd believe he was charmed, that nothing ill could befall him.

Of course he'd lost what he loved most and, ironically, become a father in the process. Now, just as with his own father, his advice to his son fell on deaf ears.

As he watched, the water fairy stepped into the waterfall, vanishing completely from his sight. Carew had disappeared earlier, retreating into the mist along the river like an actor to the tiring chamber after his part. Would the fairy disappear as well?

As if in answer to his question, she emerged from the sparkling spray, a vivid trail of green molded to her body like a flare of water weed. Her alluring form, marble white in the moonlight, made him think of Titania, queen of the fairies, from a play he'd read last time he was here. Who was the fellow who'd written it? The single scene had been rough in its infancy, but eloquent with midsummer night's magic. Except in those pages, Titania had fallen in love with a monster, and he wouldn't wish that on anyone, especially this female, whether she were fairy or flesh and blood.

He wanted to watch her forever. Maybe he would rust in the rain like a metal machine, with her image etched in his brain, a rain-kissed fairy lit by the silver moon, banishing his loneliness for eternity.

The angel stepped among the violets bordering the basin, her form seeming to drip diamonds rather than mere water. Moving toward the grove of silvery birch some paces to his right, she paused beneath a tree. The rain had abated, and rows of shining droplets ornamented the branch above her head. With a graceful motion, she reached up and tugged.

With face and arms uplifted, she welcomed the rain of crystals that settled like jewels on her skin. A moonbeam lit her face, revealing the beauty of an angel, her eyes glistening as if full of sad visions others couldn't see. Her expression touched him deeply, reminding him of Joanna the night she'd died. But his gut twisted again as he admitted she wasn't Joanna. One dark, glossy braid fell over her shoulder as living proof. Joanna had been blond.

Water nymph. Rain fairy. Young and beautiful, as his Joanna had been. Who was this woman? His son had embraced her as if he loved her, though he didn't love his own father. He had heard her words as she ordered Carew home to bed, and his son had obeyed instantly, running off toward the palace. With his father, he would have argued. It wasn't right.

A twang like an untuned lute string sang in the air and a hot bite of pain clipped his arm. To his astonishment, blood stained his doublet.

Another missile streaked through the air over his head and struck something with a thud. A load of rain plummeted from the branches of a thick oak. Matthew stared at a crossbow bolt embedded in the trunk just above Titania's head. By God, someone had shot at him . . . or at her. Twice.

She stood frozen in place, gazing at the bolt as if dumbstruck. He leaped from his seat and raced to her, forcing his stiff limbs to move. "Get down," he shouted as he dragged her behind the tree and bore her to the ground, his mind racing over the possibilities.

He'd just returned to England after two years' absence, so how could he have an enemy so anxious to kill him? Despite a rousing quarrel with the Earl of Essex earlier that evening, he didn't think anyone intended to murder him. More proof—he'd been struck by the first bolt, but the second had missed him by a wide margin, coming closer to the woman. The evidence left no doubt in his mind. Titania had been the intended victim.

Chapter 2

Cory crouched on the ground, her stomach churning with fear. One moment she'd been alone, gazing dreamily at the moon. The next she lay flat on her belly among the trees, dragged there by a shrub that had leaped to life and attacked her. Or had it saved her life?

In the semidark, she studied what had to be a man, not a shrub. He was so close, his body pressed protectively against hers, she saw only an expanse of gray doublet, decidedly wet. He must have been out in the rain for a long time.

Shifting her gaze to the tree, she studied the deadly metal bolt that protruded from the thick trunk. Thank fortune Carew had returned to the palace earlier.

"Are you well?" Her protector rose and wrestled the bolt from the tree.

She was too stupefied to reply.

He tucked the bolt in his pouch and bent over her, concern in his eyes. "I asked if you were hurt."

"No, but you are." She pointed a shaky hand at his left arm. "You're bleeding. You must let me see how bad it is."

"Let me be. It's barely a scratch," he growled, the anger in his tone demanding she keep her distance. "Stay here. I must see who shot at you." He sped away, moving as quickly as when he'd borne her to the ground.

At her? Cory gazed after him, stunned at his assumption.

The shots hadn't been for her. She had no enemies except her father-in-law, and though he'd sent her from noble house to house, attempting to marry her off, he didn't want her out of his way so badly as to kill her.

She trembled as a single, chilling thought overwhelmed all others. If the shots had been meant for her, if someone wanted her dead, then her rescuer had been wounded in her stead. If not for his quick action, she would be the one bleeding, mayhap lying on the forest floor, her life slowly ebbing away.

As if that weren't enough, he tempted even greater danger by searching for her attacker. She heard him move through the woods, his footsteps growing fainter. Then she heard nothing as all sound of his movement died away.

Panic set in, its chill reaching deep into her bones. He took action while she crouched on the ground, fretting over what had happened. She must help him.

She started to rise, meaning to follow him, but sank back as he reappeared . . . alone. He'd found no one. The assailant had escaped.

She shivered like a kicked cur from cold and delayed shock as he clasped her hand and pulled her to her feet. Her gaze clung to him as she wondered why she accepted his aid without question. He was a stranger.

His full beard and mustache, thicker than fashion recommended, suggested he was a seaman. The rough quality of his doublet and leather boots agreed, as did his broad shoulders and well-defined thighs, which hinted at muscles honed to fighting strength. As their gazes locked, she studied his eyes. The irises were a rich brown like molasses from the wild Spanish Main. Mysterious eyes, with an intriguing intensity that hinted at deep secrets she couldn't and perhaps shouldn't understand.

An earthquake shimmered in her middle as his gaze slipped down her body, clearly outlined by her wet clothing. His eyes seemed to smolder as he sucked in a slow, deep breath. Awareness of him thundered through her veins as he stood stock-still and assessed her, like a jungle tiger, taut and poised to spring. She could hardly breathe.

Suddenly he tore his gaze from her and looked at a place just over her shoulder. "You're cold and wet. Come." He turned her and propelled her ahead of him, one hand firmly in the small of her back, the other gripping her arm.

Cory tried to read his expression over her shoulder but caught little detail in the semidark. If he had been aware of her near nakedness, he no longer showed any sign of it, taking her shiver for a chill. She stumbled ahead, feeling foolish at her unwarranted excitement. "Where are we going?" she asked.

"To take you home. You've been out too long."

She wanted to argue that she could find her own way, but she couldn't find the words. It had been so long since someone took care of her. And the thought of returning to the palace alone, in the dark, set her quivering with anxiety. Someone had tried to kill her. Might he come back? "I need my cloak and clothes. They're over here."

Common sense prevailed as she led the way back along the riverbank to where she had hung her clothing. She should stick to this man like a burr, at least until she was somewhere safe. "He wasn't shooting at me," she insisted, in a last attempt to banish the danger. "It must have been you."

"Do you have enemies?" he asked, the pleasant timbre of his voice hard with what sounded like disapproval. "I've none that I'm aware of."

"Nor I." She again wondered about her father-in-law but pushed the thought aside. They had never liked each other, but he was a miser, not a killer. "It might have been an accident," she suggested. "Perhaps he was hunting and didn't see me."

"He wasn't hunting at this hour." He lifted his eyebrows, as if he thought she were mad. Definitely for the idea. Perhaps for her waterplay. "Nor was he at target practice. He shot at you, and it was no accident, believe me."

His answer frightened her. Who would want to kill her? And why? She had harmed no one. Nor did she possess anything a thief would want.

Whatever the reason, she resolved to borrow this man's protective presence a little longer. It was only sensible, as was the need to know more of whoever had tried to take her life. "Did you find footprints?" she asked.

He nodded, looking grim behind the thick beard. "They led back to the fair, where they were lost in the crowd. Impossible to follow, which was probably his plan."

"I wish to see them."

He appeared irritated with her demand, but she persisted until he led her back to the spot. Now wrapped in her wool cloak, Cory bent over but could make nothing of the muddled tracks. "There's nothing here," she said in despair.

Silence met her statement, and she glanced up to find him studying the footprints with an intense gaze. The look on his face suggested they told him a secret about the culprit, but he wasn't sharing it with her.

"What do you see?" she demanded, annoyed by his refusal, unnerved by the mystery.

He ignored her, instead taking her arm and steering her back toward the fair. "Where do you live? I'll see you home." He looked determined though unenthusiastic, as if she were an unwanted responsibility foisted upon him. Well, she wasn't, nor did she want him to know she lived with the queen.

"You need not accompany me."

But he seemed determined she not go alone, and walking alone *was* unwise. As she slipped on a slick patch of mud, he clasped her around the waist and steadied her, his thigh pressed to hers, as if she weighed no more than a water drop. Tremors of excitement spun down her spine at his touch. A dangerous reaction.

Yet he seemed unaware of how he affected her.

Let him remain so. Men who knew they aroused women could use it as a weapon to hurt them. Thomas had taught her that.

In silence, she groped for composure and let him guide her back along the river. As they approached the fair, she shivered, suddenly freezing as she thought of the bolt nicking this man, then the second missile so nearly missing her. Her teeth rattled in her head like loose dice in a cup.

He glanced down at her and, without asking permission, changed course. What now? she wondered, too dazed to ask.

He led her to a small hut with a bonfire before it. After he flipped coins to the two tradesmen warming their hands, they obligingly withdrew, and he guided her into the hut, remaining behind. "Change," he ordered in a tone that brooked no argument. With his back to the hut, he stood guard, blocking the entry.

Chilled and glad to obey, Cory retreated deep into the hut and scrambled out of her wet things, rolling them into a bundle. Then she dried herself with her cloak and put on her kirtle skirt and bodice. Huddled in her cloak, she emerged from the hut and let him guide her into the bonfire's inviting ring of light. Parting her cloak, he held it wide to capture the heat. "Now we must get you warm."

Despite his plain clothing, he had all the finesse of a gentleman. Definitely of the upper class, she thought. She should ask his name.

But then she would have to give hers, and she was reluctant to lose her anonymity. She wanted to be purely female in the presence of this intriguing male, whose strength let neither the rain nor the blood on his arm have meaning. For one night, she wanted to be someone other than the landed heiress and widow, coveted for her wealth. Besides, she still shook with shock from the shooting. She needed to stare at the flames and let them sear away everything except the lazy warmth creeping into her bones. The crackle and hiss of the logs burned off her chill as the heat of looking at him warmed her inside.

Stealing a glance at him from beneath half-lowered lashes, she confirmed her first impression. He was built with a sleek strength and moved with the agile grace of a wilderness beast. Best of all, with his full beard and dashing figure, he fulfilled her fondest fantasy. As a girl, she had invented a fantasy of a lawless pirate prince sweeping out of the mist to rescue her from her woes. He fit the image of her dream pirate perfectly.

But as warmth seeped into her limbs, she realized that he did not return her interest. He scanned the milling crowd beyond the bonfire, one hand gripping his sheathed dagger. Far from giving up on the attacker, he was searching for him with barely veiled intensity.

No use being silly about his helping her, she thought as she held up her scarf to dry before the fire. He must be one of those men who never refused a challenge and thought nothing of courting danger. He wouldn't rest until he caught the culprit. Loving cards the way she did, she understood. She could never resist a challenge from an experienced player. Still, she wished she were something more than a hindrance to him.

"I'm warm enough now. I'll be off. My thanks." She jerked her dove gray cloak closed and set off, feeling unreasonably hurt that he wanted to be rid of her. Yet she must not expect anything from him.

His large, warm hand on her shoulder spun her around. "You're not going alone. Not after what happened. Did you come with friends? I'll escort you to them."

"I didn't come with friends." Relieved that he had stopped her, Cory contemplated her partial lie. In her six months at court, she had found faithful friends and followers, mostly among the children and servants of the palace, but only one maid of honor appreciated her outspoken ways. The rest were so young, they blanched whenever she spoke her mind—as she was about to do. "You're looking for *him*, and I'm in the way," she blurted. "I know you saw something in the footprints that I didn't. What?"

His dark gaze darted from her to the crowd, revealing his dilemma. He was unwilling to send her off alone, yet impatient to find the person who had shot the crossbow.

"If you won't tell me what you saw, at least let me help you search for him," she insisted. "Two can accomplish more than one."

"What can you do?" He continued to scan the crowd, never meeting her gaze.

She disliked the assumption in his tone that she was helpless. "What can you do if you don't know who you're looking for? And why are you taking this upon yourself? I don't understand."

"I know exactly what I'm looking for."

His confident but cryptic answer maddened her. He knew what he was looking for but he wouldn't tell her. "Let me accompany you," she urged. "We can appear to enjoy the fair as you search. That way, he won't know you're looking for him. I'll sleep much better tonight if he isn't roaming free to shoot at me again. Or at someone else."

His expression suggested he felt the same way, so without waiting for verbal agreement, she wedged her hand into the crook of his arm and smiled up at him, ready to play her part. They would not encounter the other maids, who would have returned to the palace long ago.

He responded with undisguised relief, guiding her into the crowd. The longer he waited, the more likely the assailant was to quit the fair. His reluctance to have her along was apparently overcome by necessity.

Cory tossed her head and smiled at a brace of jugglers as her companion studied one person after another. *You're too obvious,* she wanted to caution, but she said nothing. Instinct told her he would not welcome her advice.

She scanned the crowd, wanting to help, but saw only masses of people. People eating, people drinking small beer and fermented cider, people making asses of themselves as it grew late and strong drink muddled their wits.

"What are we looking for?" she demanded again, peeved that he wouldn't tell her.

He watched a skinny man march up and down on stilts, half his body clothed in shocking red, the other half in lime green. "A pair of boots," was all he said.

Marvelous. There were hundreds of boots here, Cory thought as a cluster of men roared with laughter at the stilt walker's antics. The pair they sought clearly had a special feature that showed in the footprint. What could it be?

"Your wound has stopped bleeding. You were right. It was a nick." She peered into the hole in his sleeve, wishing she could draw him out, make him tell her more about the boots, or even why he'd been sitting alone in the rain. "Dame Fortune was with you," she said aloud.

"I would like it better if fortune left me alone. She brings me little good."

The desolation of his words ran through her like cold rain. "Do you mean you have had misfortune, or that you have not obtained what you wanted in life?" she asked gently, wishing she could banish his dark mood.

He shrugged without answering and continued to search the assembly, seeming to forget she was there. The logs of a bonfire shifted as they passed. Sparks shot up, and she thought again of the peddler woman's fortune telling.

Made for love, she had said. She must be mad. Thomas hadn't known the meaning of the word. And tonight, she encountered an attractive man, but it was her rotten fortune that after one steamy gaze, his only interest was in being rid of her and finding a pair of boots.

Or did he suffer some unspoken torment? His expression seemed grim and drawn, and he'd been sitting alone in the rain, apparently for some time. A man didn't do that unless he was troubled about something.

How she would like to press his arm and murmur comforting words, though his manner didn't invite intimacy. That rarely stopped her if she saw someone in need, but instinct warned her to tread warily with this man. Her reactions to him were too intense, too disturbing.

"I would like to buy some chestnuts. Do you mind if we stop?" She reached for her purse, knowing the search was proving fruitless and she must soon leave him. An aching emptiness had grown in the pit of her belly, and she hoped chestnuts would fill it as well as help push all thoughts of being a victim from her mind.

He whipped out coins and paid for the nuts, making her further beholden to him.

Frustrated, she cupped the little muslin bag between her palms. The heat of the chestnuts penetrated the fabric, the same way looking at him lit a fire deep within her. Both could burn the unwary, and she still bore the scars of wounds from the past. She must have a care.

Yet a multitude of people pressed her tighter against his side, and she hugged his arm again. It was an unaccustomed luxury to rely on someone. She, who was usually so independent, might be dependent for a night on a capable stranger she would never see again. Couldn't she?

Yet what of him? Why was he so intent on finding the culprit? He hadn't even asked if someone else would help her pursue the matter. Was it merely his desire to stamp out evil, as she'd guessed?

Follow the other maids. Hurry home to bed, her mind warned. But a reluctance to part with him dragged at her willpower. Remembering her recent danger, she wanted to relive how he'd sprung to her aid without holding back, even though his daring suggested a disregard for his own safety. No one did that for her. She was the one who took care of others—children like Carew, or her friend Moll, the queen's tirewoman. No one leaped to her defense but this dashing pirate of a man, whose gaze had burned into her with what had momentarily seemed like desire.

A church bell chimed two, and Cory realized they had scoured the crowd for more than an hour. "He's probably not here anymore," she said, breaking the silence between them.

"No."

"He would have slipped away and gone home to bed."

"Umm."

His abbreviated replies frustrated her. "Are you always so cryptic?"

"People say I am."

Cory wanted to snap at him for dissolving her fantasy. He had been so concerned for her welfare, and now this. What an uncommunicative man. "I would like some gingerbread." She darted from his side and paid the pastry cook for a large slice before he could do it for her. She didn't want to owe him more. Not when she apparently owed him her life.

But she needed to fill the emptiness within her, and while she tried to do so with warm gingerbread, she would prolong their final moments together. Perhaps she could coax him out of his doldrums, the way she did the queen, who was more temperamental than he could possibly be. She would see if his desolation could be banished, hoping at the same time to recover some of the night's magic that had begun in a swirling curtain of lacy mist.

Matthew concentrated on scanning the thinning crowd along the riverbank, but he knew it was no use. The assailant's trail had grown cold; the trouble would not be solved tonight.

Feeling suddenly drained, he looked at the pure profile of the woman beside him. He should have escorted her home, but instead he'd dragged her around for over an hour in the damp night air. All because of the heat that had risen within him as he'd pressed her to the ground, shielding her with his body from the attacker. He shouldn't have let her linger, then or now.

But she was like the first heady scent of land after being at sea too long. One touch of her pearl-smooth flesh against his and he was consumed with a desire as driving as the need for fresh water and solid ground beneath his feet. In her wet garments, she'd been all but naked. Now, visions of Titania, naked in his arms, exploded in his imagination like gunpowder charges.

Praise heaven she didn't noticed his body's interest whenever he touched her. Or his displeasure at the uninvited response. No matter that she had offered to accompany him. No matter that she had *insisted* on helping. He must take her home. Except first, he must find out how she knew Carew. "I saw you with a young lad earlier," he said cautiously. "He appeared . . . fond of you."

She raised her eyebrows, as if wondering why he cared. "Poor child, he's newly arrived from the country and has plagued his chaperon nearly to death with his mischief. I have tried to be a friend and guide him. He belonged in bed, which is where I sent him."

So she was from the court, and in two short weeks, his son had grown attached to her. Resentment mingled with grudging interest as he watched her sample the gingerbread, her lips parting to bite with white, even teeth. Then she ate a chestnut, savoring it with an easy pleasure that sent pangs of longing deep into his gut. Imagine enjoying something so completely. As if sensing the thoughts behind his stare, she stopped in the shadows, forcing him to halt as well.

"Your turn." She held out a piece of gingerbread to him.

"I don't care for sweets." It was too crass a refusal. "But I thank you," he forced out.

She smiled for the first time that night, her grin impish and beautiful, reminding him again of Joanna. "Then 'tis time you learned. Everyone needs something sweet in their lives." Catching his arm, she held the gingerbread to his lips.

Her teasing words, coupled with her grip on his arm, sent a charge of lust through him. *Stop it,* he reproached his body. She was a lady of quality, despite her odd behavior in the river and waterfall. Her rich cloak and embroidered bodice told him so, as did her knowing Carew. He hadn't been near an English lady in almost two years; perhaps that explained his response to her.

But it didn't. The last time he'd been home, several beauties had offered themselves. He had been unaroused by their charms. But this female had seemed wrought in magic as she glided through the water, touching him with her loneliness. Then his son had embraced her. Yet despite the tenderness in her response, she had sent Carew home to bed—just in time before danger struck. Praise heaven for that. The idea of his child being caught in the path of the crossbow bolt was too ugly to be considered.

As he accepted the bite of gingerbread, he studied her more closely. Her luminous skin was moonlight pale, tempting him to touch her cheek, to discover if the magically elusive fairy felt as soft as she looked.

"Close your eyes," she ordered, "and hold the sweet on your tongue. Imagine you are a boy again, sitting in the warm kitchens of your home."

"How do you know I had a warm home?" he challenged. So she wanted to play with words, did she? Such games never lasted long around him.

"Just a guess. Do you have brothers or sisters?" She seemed untroubled by his contrariness.

"I have both," he relented, for no reason he could explain. "Angelica, Charles, and Lucina are younger. Rozalinde and Jonathan are older."

"Good. Then imagine you and the younger ones—Angelica, Charles, and Lucina—are together in the warm kitchens of your home on a winter's afternoon." She rattled off their names as if she knew and liked each one of them, rekindling his memories of the past.

A sudden image formed in his mind from his boyhood; of sitting before the blazing kitchen hearth on a cold day, a place of treasured warmth after they'd romped in the snow for hours. With so many siblings, someone had always been ready for a game or a story or a prank. The memory warmed him like the bonfire earlier. "There was also Roger, the baby," he offered before realizing he had joined her game.

"Of course there was." Her calmed voice circled around him, sweeping him back to his childhood days in Dorset. "The four of you *and* Roger are sitting snug and cozy in the kitchens. Your mother has just taken a great pan of hot gingerbread from the oven, and you are so ravenous, you think you might faint before you get a piece."

He opened his eyes. "How do you know my mother made gingerbread?"

She patted his hand and smiled. "I know because you're protective. You learned that from her. And from your father. Now close your eyes and listen to me."

He obeyed, realizing she was right. His parents had been fiercely protective of all seven of them, from the eldest on down. The distant memory of his father's love wafted to him across the years, as elusive as the scent of gingerbread on the wind. With a stab of pain, he remembered the boy he had once been.

He was a different person now. No longer the innocent youth, so secure in his parents' love.

"You simply cannot wait another minute for a taste, so you plead with your mother, and she serves you first," her tender voice continued, unaware of the pain needling through him.

The ginger tingled on his tongue as she painted the picture with words. He could almost smell the scent of the kitchens, the sage and thyme from the roasted capon eaten at noon mingling with the mouthwatering scent of gingerbread. Charles, at nine, would chuckle and tickle seven-year-old Lucina to tease her as they waited for the treat. Four-year-old Angelica's chubby little hands would be braced on his knee as she watched the hot oven, her eyes round with anticipation, and baby Roger would be a sweet bundle on his lap, sucking his thumb.

If only he could reach out and touch those days again. . . .

"You take your gingerbread on a wooden trencher," she whispered, leaning so close, her warm breath misted his cheek, "and though it is still piping hot, you take a huge bite. Your mother scolds you for being greedy, but you know she's worried you've burned your mouth."

She had it exactly right. He'd always been impatient, refusing to wait. In a flash of memory, he saw his mother's concerned face, felt her love and caring that were now lost in her forgetful old age.

"You talk around the mouthful of bread to assure her you're fine and earn another scolding for speaking with your mouth full. But your mother isn't really angry. She kisses your brow so gently, you feel entirely, completely loved."

Matthew's eyes snapped open as a strangled sob startled him.

The queen of the fairies was crying. The thick lashes framing her eyes were beaded with tears that shone like pearls. Her sorrow pierced him as he realized she'd been describing more than the scents and tastes and feelings of his lost past. They were hers as well.

Her pain, coming so swiftly after his own, disturbed him, urging him to take her in his arms and comfort her.

But he wasn't used to comforting anyone, not even himself. He put one hand on her shoulder and groped for words. None seemed adequate to soothe her obvious grief.

She choked and turned away, pulling out a handkerchief. It was the right moment to offer his own, along with his sympathy for whatever troubled her, but he couldn't move. He felt as mute as a mud clod.

Suddenly she stuffed the handkerchief into her purse and plunged into the crowd at a dead run.

Taken by surprise, Matthew lunged after her, but she disappeared within minutes. Damn it, why was she running away?

He never understood people. His son hated him. His brothers accused him of being morose and uncompanionable. His sisters scolded him when he didn't respond to their affection. He elbowed his way through the throng, a fierce resentment coursing through him. The wench was in danger and needed protection, but she ran off without giving her name.

"Ho, there, what's the hurry?" a burly man demanded angrily as Matthew trod on his foot.

A pretty but heavily painted woman caught Matthew's arm and pursed rouged lips at him. He wrenched from her grasp. The crowd thinned as he turned and headed up a new avenue of stalls. A trio of jugglers whirled onions in a golden blur. The clown on stilts chuckled and looked down his nose as Matthew sped past. Where could she be?

Hating to admit he'd lost her, he halted at the head of a street and leaned against a post, full of frustration. Why should he be sorry? She rekindled the pain of his deepest loss, then reminded him all too clearly of his failure to understand his son.

Drawing in a steadying breath, he glanced up and spied his reflection in a shop window. A dark wraith stared back at him with tormented eyes.

He was more than sorry to lose her. In her presence, he had felt drawn to the edge of a circle of warmth. No matter that he couldn't enter, that the warmth of love was lost to him. To be near was enough.

He turned back the way he'd come. As he walked, his gaze lit on a patch of green that reminded him of jonquils sprouting through the rain-ripened earth. But jonquils didn't grow in August.

Upon closer inspection, he discovered it was the green scarf that she'd carried. She must have dropped it as she fled, proving she had come this way.

He picked it up and smoothed the damp silk with rough

hands, seeing her in his mind's eye as she stepped from the cascading waterfall. Her face had been tilted upward to catch the spray, her eyes closed, her glossy braid pouring over her shoulder. Titania, emerging into the beginning of the world. And up close, her eyes, like the scarf, were the same haunting green of new beginnings brought by early spring.

Chapter 3

Matthew threaded his way through the courtyards and corridors of Hampton Court Palace where hundreds of courtiers lodged. His thoughts were as tangled and confused as the dark maze. The woman he'd met tonight was enough to drive a man to strong drink. She aroused such conflicting feelings in him, he hardly knew what to do with them.

At first, he'd judged her to be a lunatic, swimming alone at midnight. He often did it himself, especially in hot weather and at sea. But a gentlewoman? Unattended? In a part of the Thames where she could be seen by anyone . . . like him. He strongly believed in propriety for women, and she was improper in the extreme.

Then she'd usurped his place with his son. How it galled him that a stranger had succeeded with Carew where he had failed. The memory of her standing in the water, tenderly embracing his only link to his dead wife, infuriated him. How had she won his son's trust when he could not?

More important, how had he become so involved with her in so short a time?

Of course he'd done what he had to when danger came. He'd saved her from being skewered by a crossbow bolt. He'd gathered the evidence, as was necessary, assessed the fresh footprints in the soft soil behind the shrubbery, collected the two crossbow bolts. He'd even estimated the height and weight of the slight man he'd seen flee into the woods.

If only he hadn't been the sole witness, forced to act by default. She was too seductive. Too erotic, rising from the Thames like a water siren. As he'd covered her body with his own to protect her, he'd been acutely aware of every curve of her soft flesh, hugged by translucent, wet cloth. He had been aroused beyond bearing.

She hadn't seemed to notice a thing.

His experience with women said she was a true innocent. A woman bent on seduction would have handled their encounter far differently. Another woman would have tempted him to kiss or caress her as he bent over her on the forest floor. The fairy queen hadn't moved a muscle. She'd lain there until her teeth rattled from her shivering. Not exactly a device meant to spur him to amorous attempts.

Then there was the moment when she'd retrieved her clothes. Instead of flaunting her near nakedness, she'd put on her cloak, netherstocks, and shoes without comment. And when he'd shown her the hut, she could have lured him inside the intimate shelter. Instead, she'd simply changed into her dry clothes, as bid.

An innocent, indeed. She might look more erotic than the dozen promiscuous London beauties who offered themselves every time he returned home, but he didn't touch innocents. Joanna had been his first and only innocent, and he meant it to stay that way.

Except he sensed a struggle was at hand. Their brief, intimate contact had tantalized him in unexpected ways, which meant he shouldn't get further involved with her. But judging from the closeness Carew had displayed with her, he would have little choice. If he'd been thinking more clearly, he would have questioned her further about her ties with his son. Yet knowing who she was wouldn't have ended the need to see her again. He still had the information he'd collected about the assailant. And he still had her scarf.

He fingered the green silk tucked in his sleeve and was appalled at how his loins tightened at the mere thought of her bewitching green eyes.

Disgusted with his reaction, he forced his mind down more practical paths. He must at least turn over the evidence he'd gathered to the authorities. He had enough to deal with during this stay without worrying about what trouble the woman was in. Gold and other valuables from his voyage sat in guarded London warehouses, tempting thieves until he delivered them to the queen and his sponsors. His ships would sink without extensive repairs before he sailed again. A letter from his estate manager shouted for attention. His sister-in-law and mother wanted him to visit. His list of obligations went on and on.

As he rounded a corner and started down another corridor, he considered whether to tell the queen, the captain of the queen's palace guard, or the local sheriff about the shooting. The queen could order an investigation. The other two could look into the incident themselves.

Another consideration occurred to him. Carew's obvious closeness with the fairy queen indicated she lived at Hampton Court. If she was a member of the queen's household, then Her Majesty would have to be told what happened.

All the better. The queen's interest would add expediency to the investigation. He would be relieved of all responsibility beyond relating what he knew. A good thing, since he would only be here a month.

He shrugged as he rounded a corner and started down another corridor. He would pass the information to Captain Wells and forget it.

Still, he did wonder what Titania could have done to merit murder. Why would someone go to such lengths as to follow her at midnight and attempt assassination? He might find out if he went to a certain cordwainer's while about his London business. Based on the footprints, the man wielding the crossbow had worn an expensive pair of riding boots that left a clear heel impression in the soil, along with the mark of their maker—an H stamped in the sole.

He cut off the thoughts. He needed to stay out of this . . . except that the questions were maddening. Why was his son friendly with a woman who was shot at? Why had she been wading alone at midnight? For that matter, why had Dame Fortune put him there to see her rise from the Thames?

Matthew passed through a set of doors, wrestling with the dilemma. He shouldn't become involved with her, but he needed to know what kind of influence she had on his son.

Though that seemed rather obvious after the way she'd whisked him into the past with such uncanny ability, using nothing more than a bite of gingerbread. How had she understood so well what he'd felt as a boy, a time when he'd loved and been loved?

Her ability to tap his deepest emotions had been as inescapable as a dangerous tidal undertow. Did she have the same effect on his young, vulnerable son? Was she perhaps even responsible for Carew's hostility toward him?

Remembering his own youth and the pain of losing Joanna, he worried about Carew. Almost two full years had passed since he'd seen him. His son had changed so, he didn't know him anymore. Lady Russell had complained that he had sneaked out every night when they first came to court, despite her scoldings. Several courtiers had accosted Matthew as soon as he arrived, complaining that Carew wagered at cards, trifled with their daughters, and fought with their sons.

Once again, Matthew cursed the West Indies hurricane that had all but destroyed one of his ships last summer, delaying his voyage home. Of course Carew had been disappointed by their missed visit. Of course he had a right to vent his resentment. But Matthew hadn't expected such open hostility. Carew's intentional disregard of the rules of decent behavior also surprised him, as if his son didn't care whom he hurt or what anyone thought.

Matthew's head ached as he wondered if Carew would be in bed or out getting into trouble. Let it be the first, he prayed. The last thing he wanted was another quarrel with the child who had come from his and Joanna's love.

He nudged open his chamber door, half expecting to find the room deserted. To his relief, the bedclothes rose in a hefty mound, a head sunk into the pillow at one end. A quick scrutiny told him it was Carew, not a bolster, as Lady Russell said he'd left one night.

Grateful for the small blessing, Matthew tiptoed in and closed the door.

"Hello, Graystock. Have a good time at the fair?" The mound sat up and Carew reached for the tinderbox by the bed.

Matthew winced, hating the title on his son's lips. "Don't call me that," he barked more harshly than he meant to. Collecting his patience, he spoke more calmly. "Why aren't you asleep?"

A spark leaped in the lint and Carew lit a candle with it, his expression rebellious. "What should I call you? Papa? Like my cousins call Uncle Charles?"

His sarcasm lanced through Matthew. His son knew exactly how to hurt him. His brother was a far better father to Carew than Matthew had ever been. "I've told you before, Carew, I'm away so often out of duty to Her Majesty, not by choice. If I could—"

"If you could, you would stay home with me at Graystock Manor? I don't believe you." Carew's jaw jutted angrily. "You prefer sailing with the great Sir Francis Drake, the scourge of Spain. I know how unimportant I am to you."

"I always come home to you, son." Matthew tempered his tone with what he hoped would be recognized as concern.

"Why trouble? All you do is shout at me when you're here, like you did earlier."

Guilt cut into Matthew. He had shouted at his son, but it was for his own good. "I told you before. Wagering on cards is a bad habit that can only get worse. You've already seen what comes of it. Within two hours, you lost all that money I gave you for—"

"What if I did?" Carew interrupted. "You don't care about me, just the money." He flipped a stray lock of blond hair from his eyes and gazed at his father in defiance.

Matthew clenched his jaw and restrained the urge to smack him. This was why they had argued within hours of his arrival. Five whole pounds squandered on useless games of cards. The money had been for a new suit of clothes since Carew had outgrown everything he owned. But the lad threw the money away. God knew he tried to discipline his son, but the last time he'd returned from a voyage and attempted to guide him, he ran to ruin. Worse yet, Carew seemed to enjoy giving him pain.

The night of Joanna's death returned to him, the agony still fresh. Once her sweet body had filled his arms, and he had basked in the heat and light of their love. But as their child's birth had torn her from him, with her last breath, she had begged him to cherish their son.

He stared at Carew, seeing in his face the graceful bow of

Joanna's mouth, the blond of her hair. But her love hadn't lived on in Carew. His son hated him.

He dropped to a stool and tugged off his wet boots. "The money is gone," he said, determined to keep his temper. "I'll not punish you this time, but you must not wager again, Carew."

Carew's gaze was withering, as if he hated Matthew just as much for *not* punishing him. "Your advice is so sage, Father."

As he placed his boots outside the door to be cleaned by one of the palace servants, Matthew steeled himself against the boy's mockery. "Just tell me this. Who did you game with?"

"No one," Carew evaded the question. "A pack of fellows around court."

Matthew knew it was the pages and children of other nobles. The youngsters were regular nuisances when they didn't have duties or lessons. Court was no place for children, especially not Carew. Yet the queen required his presence when he returned from a voyage, so where else could he see his son? "I'll find out who took your money, Carew, even if you don't tell me." He hung up his cloak and unbuttoned his doublet. "He will be punished, as will you if it happens again."

"It's no one you know. Even if you did, you couldn't punish *her*," Carew said petulantly, seeming not the least intimidated by the promise of punishment. How well he knew Matthew's reluctance to follow through on his threats. Carew paused, seeming to debate saying more. "She's amazing, Father." He launched into a recitation with sudden enthusiasm. "She can slip a card from the deck without anyone seeing and put it back when she's done with it. I want to do that."

Facing the bed that dominated the tiny chamber, Matthew frowned. "You were gaming with a *girl*? I shall see that her father is told she was showing you how to cheat."

Carew's excitement faded like the wind in a calm at sea. Matthew met his gaze, wanting to show how much he cared, but the impotent fury in his son's eyes hurt as much as it surprised him. "Carew, wagering is bad enough among lads," he tried to explain, "but a girl should never, ever wager. Cheating is even worse. Both are unbecoming to the female sex." As the words left his mouth, Matthew saw Carew's body go rigid with resistance. Carew lay down, his back to Matthew, rejecting him and his attempts at reason.

Frustrated, Matthew stripped off the rest of his clothes and donned a sleeping shirt. All he wanted was for Carew to be respected for his integrity once he achieved manhood. Yet on his last visit two years ago, his son had seemed to search for ways to defy him. Now it was even worse. How was he ever to teach him correct behavior? As a lad, if Matthew had violated his father's rules for decent conduct, he had been punished. Yet he hated the need for punishments during these brief visits with Carew.

Checking the green scarf he'd stuffed in his doublet sleeve, he climbed into bed, wishing for affection and understanding such as his son seemed to share with the water fairy.

"Her Majesty was angry when you didn't attend her tonight," Carew muttered as Matthew settled into the featherbed. "She wants to speak to you first thing on the morrow."

Matthew stirred uneasily. The entire court tiptoed around Elizabeth, trying to avoid the royal wrath. He usually enjoyed praise and good humor from her, but on this visit Her Majesty seemed testy with everyone. The complaints about his son probably hadn't helped. "I'll speak to her when I get a chance."

"When you get a chance." Carew snorted with disdain, his back still firmly to Matthew. "Like you do with me. I guess I should be pleased, to be as unimportant as a queen."

Matthew sat up, furious at his son's disrespect. "The queen is important to me, and so are you, Carew," he snapped. "The only reason I come home at all is because of you and Her Majesty. How can you think otherwise?" He waited, wondering how his son would answer what seemed to him an obvious truth.

"I'm impressed by your touching declaration, Father," Carew drawled, his belligerent tone cutting off Matthew's hope of any meaningful communication. "I'm just impressed as hell."

A flutter of wings brushed through Cordelia's consciousness as she wandered blissfully in a jungle thick with exotic flowers and steaming with tropical heat. Brightly colored birds swooped overhead as she paused by a roaring waterfall. Her pirate prince burst through the veil of mist, his face clear to her for the first time.

It was the man she'd met on the river last night, except that unlike last night, this man would sweep her into his arms. All her life she'd dreamed of a pirate prince to carry her away to a paradise of love.

Wings swooped. Cory's dream dissolved into waking, followed by the realization that the wings belonged to Giordano. The parrot was after her toast.

Flinging back the quilt, Cory leaped for the tray on the nearby table. "Bad bird," she scolded the brilliant green parrot as he latched on to her toast before she could reach it. "I saved that bread to break my fast."

Giordano flapped back to his perch, settled, and munched on the treat with a great show of contentment.

Cory folded her arms and scowled at him. "Shame on you, Giordano. And after I shared my figs with you last night. You're an ungrateful rascal." Forcing her tired limbs into motion, she stirred up the fire and added a log. As flames blazed to life, she hurried back to her improvised bed on the settle, huddled under the blanket, and closed her eyes.

The queen's last parrot had died, supposedly from the chill of their summer nights compared to his native tropics. Her Majesty had ordered a fire at night to warm Giordano. Ordinarily old Thomasine took the "parrot watch," as the maids called it, spending the night on a cushioned settle. But the poor old woman had wheezed and coughed so from a summer head rheum, Cory had sent her home. The serving woman needed her own bed and an uninterrupted night's sleep.

Cory hoped her friend had gotten it, because she certainly hadn't. The settle was comfortable, but after being shot at and meeting the disturbing pirate prince, she hadn't fallen asleep for some time. Closing her eyes, she burrowed deeper under the covers, determined to catch a few more minutes of rest. Her Majesty wouldn't be up for another hour.

Sleep enveloped her in a swirl of veil-like mist. The pirate reappeared and encircled her with his arms, rescuing her from the loneliness that threatened to suck her down into the vortex of its powerful whirlpool.

A door creaked on its hinges. A muffled sob rang in Cory's ear.

The sounds didn't fit in her dream. Dragged back into waking, Cory opened one eye. Samuel, Lady Dorothy Fleming's little page boy, collapsed in a dejected heap on the floor beside her, his eyes red, his chubby cheeks streaked with tears. Her own sorrow at losing her mother returned to haunt her, reinforced by last night's bittersweet gingerbread memories. She held out her arms to gather him close. "What is it, dear?" she whispered, fighting back her own tears.

"My lady struck me with her crop last night, and it throbs so."

Anger boiled through Cory. "Show me the place. You should have come to me at once."

He displayed a chubby fist, the knuckles black and blue. "My lady made me go to my bed."

Her sympathy escaped in a sigh as she kissed the small hand. "Why did she strike you?" she asked between kisses.

"I-I delivered a letter from the queen to my Lord Essex yesterday, but it was for Baron Graystock. The letter was important. It was a bad mistake."

"The letters might have been important, but she shouldn't strike you for an honest error. People should tell you more clearly for whom letters are meant. I will speak to her."

"But Lord Essex quarreled with Baron Graystock over it," Samuel sniffled, tears oozing from his eyes. "He said the baron s-shouldn't be allowed near Her Majesty because he was born a filthy commoner. They're going to fight a duel, and Lady Fleming says 'tis my fault." A sob broke from him, and he buried his face in her shoulder.

" 'Tis not your fault, Samuel. Lord Essex is a hothead who issues challenges without thinking." Cory stroked his hair and rocked him. His little body was chilled from the damp night. "Slip off your shoes and doublet and climb under the covers," she urged. "We'll have you warm in no time." He obeyed, and she cuddled him, achingly reminded of her mother holding her the same way. "How did you find me since I wasn't in the maids' dormitory?" she asked.

"I asked your friend Ann." He yawned and wiggled into a more comfortable position. "She was awake."

He meant Ann Sims, the one maid of honor who was Cory's friend. "Did she say why she was awake?" Cory asked, worried that something had disturbed Ann's sleep.

"Yes, she's worried about Moll Dakins."

Cory said nothing about her own worry for the royal tire-

woman as Samuel dropped off to sleep. But as she rearranged
a strand of his curly brown hair, she tried to think what to do.
In the months she'd known Moll Dakins, Cory had judged her
to be hardworking and conscientious, using her wages to help
her mother feed her eight brothers and sisters. Yet she had
been absent for two full days, with no message or explanation
sent.

What could be wrong? It seemed so unlike the diligent, de-
pendable Moll. She hadn't mentioned any trouble at recent
gatherings. Rather, she'd seemed as eager as ever for Cory's
friendship, no doubt because she had no other close female
friends at court. Yet Moll's pallid coloring and apparent exhaustion had troubled Cory. Could she be lying ill somewhere?

In the meantime, the queen expected four tirewomen to
dress her under direction of the mistress of the robes, so the
position had been filled. How could Her Majesty do otherwise? Moll had given the queen no reason to hold the post for
her.

Cory also mourned the fate allotted to Samuel. How she
wished he could spend his days at lessons and games, with
healthy meals and hugs from a mother who loved him. Instead, Dame Fortune dictated he dress like a miniature soldier
and run errands from dawn often until midnight. All because
he was the bastard son of a servant girl who had died a year
ago. Most people at court considered Samuel fortunate. Lady
Fleming gave him a roof over his head and food to fill his
belly. Having his ears boxed or his hand beaten from time to
time was considered a small price to pay, but Cory's heart rebelled against such a spurious form of good fortune.

Closing her eyes, she burrowed beneath the covers, taking
comfort by giving comfort, as her mother had always advised.
As she drifted toward sleep, the enchantment of last night enveloped her once more.

In a moment of miracles, she had left the ordinary world
and entered a fairy-tale forest where she could hope—if only
for a moment—that magic might transform her life. True to
the night's promise, her pirate had emerged from the sparkling
mist, coming to her aid in her time of need.

Yet even her dreams reflected the dreary reality of life, for
as she reached up to encircle his neck with both arms, he van-

ished. She was left alone on the bank of the Thames. The fairyland disappeared. Dirty water churned between muddy banks, reminding her that the man she'd met wasn't interested in her. He'd wanted to know who'd shot at her. That was all.

There was no such thing as a pirate prince.

And her beautiful green scarf, the talisman from the fortune-teller who said she was made for love, was lost.

At a few minutes before seven of the clock, Matthew strode down the corridor of the queen's apartments and opened the third door on his left. He gazed into the darkened antechamber. Wrong room. Yesterday, the queen said her blasted parrot was in the third room on the left, hadn't she? Why did she insist he look at it? He didn't know a thing about birds, but she had it in her head that because he'd just returned from the tropics, he was an expert on parrot health.

He rubbed his chin, the flesh irritated from removing a year's worth of beard, and tried to remember what the queen had said. After his first quarrel with Carew last night, he'd forgotten all about the parrot. Now he couldn't recall the location. Must be third door on the right.

The new chamber proved to be the correct choice. Inside, a gaudy green parrot sat on a wooden perch near a blazing fire, contentedly munching a tidbit clutched in his claw. The old woman whom he'd been told would be watching the fire lay on a nearby settle, bundled in a quilt, sound asleep. He glided in silence to the bird.

The parrot regarded him warily but didn't protest as he ran two fingers down its back, then unfolded a wing and checked the inner folds. Nothing wrong with him that a good dusting with fleabane wouldn't cure. He would probably fuss like the devil, but it was what he needed.

We rarely get what we need.

The inner voice brought tormenting memories, and he turned to go. His eye lit on the sleeping woman. From this angle, he saw a length of glossy black braid lying across the cover, reminding him of the woman who had put him in such turmoil last night. Finding her right under his nose would be too ironic. It couldn't be her.

Even so, he held his breath as he moved closer to peer under the white quilt.

It *was* her . . . the fairy queen.

Stunned, Matthew stood riveted to the spot and stared his fill. She looked infinitely appealing in the dim flicker of flames from the hearth, one hand pillowed beneath her cheek, exactly the way Joanna used to sleep. A glimpse of her ivory throat, with the flutter of pulse throbbing beneath the pearly flesh, invited his touch.

A tremor raced through him, and he stepped back to avoid reaching out. This intimate display was not meant for him.

Still he stared, noting that her other arm was curled around a cherub he recognized as Lady Fleming's page, the lad who'd caused the row leading to Essex's challenge. He'd heard that the lad had taken the brunt of his mistress's rage, poor child. But at least he had found comfort with Titania. Based on his experience with her last night, he knew just what she had to offer. The soft lilt of her voice echoed in his memory, reawakening the ache deep within him for Joanna.

Joanna is gone. There are no substitutes, experience warned him. He backed away, raising his defenses. This visit to England must not be made any more difficult than necessary.

But as he closed the solid oak door, the wooden barrier couldn't block the tangle of emotions she created from rising within him. Horrors, he was actually hardening at the memory of her flesh beneath translucent wet linen, pressed against his after the attack.

Disconcerted, he spun on his heel and stalked down the corridor. He wanted to be in control of when and with whom he became aroused. This was unacceptable.

"Damn it, Graystock, what are you doing here? I warned you to keep away from Her Majesty's privy chambers."

Recognizing the owner of the snarl, Matthew turned to confront Robert Devereux, the Earl of Essex, who stood glaring at him, one hand fixed on his rapier hilt.

Matthew grinned, pleased to be distracted from the other business, amused at the twenty-year-old's possessive attitude toward their sovereign. Essex seemed to consider Elizabeth his exclusive property, for he challenged anyone he thought usurped his place in her favor. The earl reportedly fought several duels a year over the queen's favor if she didn't have a chance to forbid them first.

"Her Majesty asked me to look in on her parrot," he said with an affable shrug. "So I did. But rest assured, I'm a mariner, not a lady's lap dog. You're welcome to the place."

Rage sizzled from Essex in palpable waves. "Meaning I am the lap dog?"

"Meaning you're what you make of yourself."

Essex narrowed his gaze on him. "I can't see why Her Majesty made you a baron. You're nothing but a disgusting son of a merchant. You can expect to die tonight."

"I can scarcely bear the waiting." Matthew bowed, feeling the full irony of the situation. He considered the wide world his home and abhorred the stifling atmosphere of court, yet Essex accused him of wanting the queen to tie him up in leading strings. Absurd.

As Essex stormed away, Matthew reflected that he had a good ten years more experience with a rapier than the earl. He intended to let a bit of blood tonight. It might teach the young fool some manners.

As Matthew walked on, his mind returned to his morning's work. At dawn, he'd revisited the scene of last night's shooting. On his knees in the wet soil, he'd traced the clearest remaining bootprint. They would all be gone soon, washed away by summer storms. Careful measurements and a paper record were the only way to preserve the evidence.

Few clues. Fewer choices. He didn't like the circumstances. Nor had he liked the crack of a breaking branch that had brought him to his feet. Had someone followed him to the site?

He had scouted the area but found no one hiding in the dense foliage along the river. Last night's magic was gone as well. Nothing remained but the footprint tracing, concealed in his chamber. Deep in thought about how he would find the boots and their owner, Matthew turned a corner and bowled into a man carrying a large bundle. It flew from his arms and crashed to the floor.

"*Sacre bleu*! My gift to the queen!" The man scrambled for the bundle and uncovered the contents. The mass of crushed porcelain shards must have been a beautiful vase.

Matthew pulled back from the well-padded gentleman with the French accent. Despite the early hour, the man wore a brocade court costume in a glaring shade of red. Obviously he intended to impress the queen.

"I will pay for the damage," Matthew said with a stiffness he knew others took for arrogance. Damn it, he wasn't a courtier. He had no skill in making adroit apologies.

The gentleman straightened, seeming to fight for control of his temper. "Who, might I ask, are you, sir?"

Matthew managed a slight bow, as good manners required. "I am Baron Graystock. You?"

"I am Monsieur Jacques La Faye, the emissary of the rightful king of France. You have broken my gift to your queen, baron," he said.

Matthew suppressed a grimace. Just his luck to smash the special gift meant for Her Majesty. "I didn't know King Henri of Navarre had an emissary to England. I thought he was too poor."

La Faye regarded him coolly. "That is exactly why I am here. Because he has not enough funds to send a formal ambassador and many attendants. I have just returned from raising funds around the country. Would you care to contribute?"

Marvelous, Matthew thought sourly. Henri de Bourbon was the next in line for the throne, but he was Protestant, so the Catholics refused to accept him. France was torn by civil war. And now that Elizabeth had refused Henri more funds, having doled out more than she thought wise, the envoy asked for money from individuals. "You would do better to speak with Lord Essex," he said. "He is eager to support Navarre. Tell me the cost of the gift and I will pay to replace it."

"It is unique and cannot be replaced." La Faye regarded him with an assessing gaze. "Will you not be my guest this evening, instead? We can visit the city and partake of refreshments." Matthew's refusal seemed to whet La Faye's interest. "Or we could remain here, if you prefer. I wish to discuss ventures of mutual interest, from which you might profit."

Matthew couldn't imagine being interested in anything this man offered. He knew the French cause was worthy, but the only thing that interested him was repairing his ships and finding the backing he needed to sail again. Without it, there would be no next voyage. Ironic that with his success, the queen all but ordered his ventures across the sea. Yet she often left him to find the funds to do her bidding. "My thanks, but I have another engagement this evening." A duel with Essex, though he didn't say so.

He headed toward his chambers to wake up his son, determined to question him about how he knew Titania. That his motives might involve more than his son's welfare was something he preferred to ignore.

Chapter 4

Cory jerked awake a second time that morning to sunlight streaming through a crack in the window draperies. Heavens, it was well past dawn. She was supposed to be serving the queen, and Samuel should be serving his mistress.

She scrambled out of bed, built up the fire for Giordano, then knelt beside the sleeping child. "Samuel, love, time to wake up." She stroked his cheek.

Samuel smiled in his sleep, his cheeks rosy with warmth. "Mama?" he murmured.

Cory's heart ached at the love and need in his voice. Gathering Samuel in her arms, she cradled him to her, willing back her tears. " 'Tis your friend Cory," she whispered, pressing her cheek against his. "Time to wake up, sweet, and begin another day."

Samuel whimpered and clung to Cory as the pain of reality seeped into his awareness. "I know you miss her," she soothed. "You and I will put a memento on her grave later. Just now, I must take you to Lady Fleming, who will be bad tempered because you're late."

Hurriedly she donned her clothes, then helped Samuel straighten his. As they were about to leave the chamber, Giordano squawked and fluttered on his perch.

"We'd best feed him, else he'll fuss." Cory reached for the

wooden chest that held bags of seeds and meal. "Would you like to fill his little bowl, Samuel?"

By the time they arrived at Lady Fleming's chamber, Cory judged it was after seven of the clock. Jane, her ladyship's maid, opened the door, her relief at seeing Samuel obvious.

"Ah, Dorothy, you have hot water. Pray permit me to wash Samuel before he begins his work for the day." Cory bustled in, determined to take Dorothy by storm. It was the best approach, for she easily flew into tempers, as she had when she'd struck Samuel last night. Yet Dorothy wasn't purposely cruel. She was just as likely to be kind if approached properly.

Dorothy eyed Cory with a perplexed expression. "What *are* you doing with Samuel, Cordelia? Has he been plaguing you?"

"No, indeed. He's been feeding the queen's parrot." It was mostly true, she thought as she deftly washed Samuel's face. "Now wash your hands, dear. Use the soap," she admonished as he dipped his fingers in the water and reached for the towel. Grudgingly he grasped the soap. "Where do you keep his clean shirts?" Cory asked Dorothy.

Dorothy looked up from her primping before the looking glass. "His what?"

"Samuel's shirts." Cory glanced into an open coffer but saw only gewgaws and gowns.

Jane, who had been eating bread and cheese by the hearth, opened another coffer. "Here, my lady. I washed this one for Samuel to save the laundress's price."

"How thoughtful, Jane, to save your mistress the expense." Cory offered Jane an affectionate smile, and Jane's still sleepy face brightened in response. Cory knew Dorothy would avoid paying a laundress if possible. Samuel could hide the dirt under his doublet for all she cared. "Slip into this, Samuel. Now, Dorothy, Jane can attend your washing up whilst Samuel breaks his fast."

Dorothy moved languidly toward the wash basin. "The lad usually eats in the scullery. He gets crumbs everywhere."

"Ah, but here, he can learn from your exemplary manners," Cory said. He would also eat better here than if he competed for food in the busy kitchens. She tied a napkin around Samuel's neck to protect his livery. "Now dear, you must cut your boiled egg like this." The lad mimicked her dainty motions.

"That was my egg." Dorothy sounded as if she were working up to a bad temper.

"Jane will fetch you another." Cory winked at Jane, meaning she would reward her if she did.

"For certes, my lady. I would be happy to do so." Jane bobbed a curtsey and hurried off.

"Samuel will always serve you better if he has a full belly, won't you, Samuel?"

"Yes, my lady." Samuel ate a square of toast so neatly, he didn't drop a morsel.

Dorothy snorted as she dipped a cloth in fresh water. "I don't know why he's so well behaved for you. He isn't for me."

Cory tried to look sympathetic as she searched for an answer Dorothy would accept. "Lord Burghley, whom I know you admire, says we are like a looking glass for children. If they see generosity and kindness in us, they model themselves in our image. But blows do not improve their performance. His lordship doesn't recommend them."

Dorothy stared at her looking glass, as if struggling to digest this sage information but not entirely succeeding. Nor did she seem to realize she'd just been criticized for striking Samuel.

With a wink at Samuel and a smile for Jane as she returned with the egg, Cory hurried off before Dorothy could finish pondering her advice. She might even follow it for a while.

However long it lasted, Cory thought as she hurried to attend the queen, she had bought poor Samuel a small space of peace. And that was worth a good deal to her.

"Where the devil is Viscountess Wentworth? Tell her to get her impudent arse in here at once. Who does she think she is, royalty?"

Queen Elizabeth Tudor's indignant bellow was audible through the chamber door as Cory reached for the handle. Taking a deep breath, she entered and sank to the floor before the queen, who was newly attired in her costume for the day. Only her hair and face paint were not yet done.

"Here is my impudent, er, posterior, Your Grace," she said,

still in the curtsey. "I brought it as quickly as I could. I want to assure you I don't think it's a royal posterior. Only noble, and I wouldn't trade for anything higher. You handle the royal *end* of things better than anyone could."

Deadly silence reigned in the chamber at Cory's words. A terrified titter burst from one of the maids, and she clapped both hands to her mouth to contain the sound. Cory smiled up at the queen without a trace of mockery.

The queen glared at her for a long minute, but Cory saw mirth fighting for supremacy in her sovereign's stern expression. Elizabeth loved a good play on words. The question was, would she agree to be amused?

To her relief, Elizabeth flung back her head and laughed, displaying a blackened tooth. "You've an incorrigible tongue in your head, girl. Do you suggest my *end* is greater than others?"

"It's very slender, as you well know, Your Grace," Cory said, deciding honesty would serve better than another pun. But she also felt concerned for the tooth. No wonder her mistress had been bad tempered of late. "I'm glad I can amuse Your Majesty from time to time. Heaven knows you work hard enough at the country's affairs. You need an occasional jest to cheer you."

Having subsided into chuckles, Elizabeth nodded. "God's blood, you have the right of it. A pity so few recognize what I sacrifice for my country." She glanced around and noticed that her four ladies in waiting, two maids of honor, and four tirewomen were smiling.

"What are you grinning about like apes?" she roared with sudden venom. "Get out! I want a word with Cory. She will complete my coiffure, for you're all devil fisted this morn."

Ten people ran for their lives, clearing the royal tiring chamber faster than Cory would have believed possible. She must have judged aright about the tooth. It was turning Her Majesty into a bear. "Your Grace, are you in pain this morning?" she asked in a low voice.

"Of course not. Why would you think that?" Elizabeth straightened like a ramrod on her stool and glared at Cory. "You may brush my hair."

Obediently Cory reached for the brush, unpinned the queen's scant graying locks, and plied the brush with a gentle hand. "I guessed," she said, "because the Dowager Countess of Whitby has pain in her knees, which makes her roar at people. So whenever she does, I offer to apply warm compresses. I would be happy to perform such a service for you if you wish. Or perhaps oil of clove on a sore tooth would be preferred?" Cory waited, hoping Elizabeth would admit her need, though doubting it would come so easily.

"I am not your aged grandam," the queen snapped.

"Of course not, Your Majesty," she soothed, a pang of homesickness piercing her as she thought of Grandmama back at Whitby Place. "Lady Whitby is years older, but we all have pain at one time or another and could use the comfort of a friend."

Elizabeth swung around and caught Cory's hand by the wrist. "You wish to be a friend to me?" she demanded, her gaze narrowed with distrust.

"Yes, Your Grace. I expect to serve you for many years. Would it not be more enjoyable if we are friends?"

Elizabeth apparently saw her sincerity, for she sighed deeply and let go of her hand. "Cory, you're a sweet girl. You make a generous offer, and I must go and spoil it by chastising you. Two fathers have lodged complaints about you this morning. They claim you taught their children to cheat at cards last night."

Cory had brightened at the queen's compliment but groaned at this bad news. "'Tis a misunderstanding, Your Grace. I taught the children a little sleight of hand that makes it seem as if they can read another's mind about their choice of cards. But I never taught them to cheat, nor are they to wager when they conjure the cards. I've explained, and they understand." She *had* checked before she taught the trick. The youngsters present would not willingly hurt others.

Elizabeth remained unconvinced. "Card tricks are for cheating, it seems to me," she said.

"But Your Grace, they can be amusing," Cory protested. "You must permit me to show you. Some of the tricks seem like magic, and we all need a little magic in our lives at times."

The queen's expression turned wistful, but she was immediately stern again. Whatever her wish, her life clearly had little room for such things as a little enchantment. "What am I to tell Sir Harold?" she demanded. "He'll never agree that the card tricks his daughter learned are harmless."

"You need not tell him anything, Highness. I will do it." Now Cory understood the source of her problem. Sir Harold was the parent who had interrupted their game and hauled ten-year-old Isabel away. Cory should have guessed he would complain to other parents. "I will explain that I kept the children from worse trouble. Pray tell me who the other parent is."

"Baron Graystock," Elizabeth said. "He says someone won all the money entrusted to his son for new clothes. As Sir Harold's complaint dealt with cards, I am assuming 'twas you."

Cory frowned, now certain the baron *was* really as bad tempered as Carew said. "Your Majesty, Carew Cavandish insisted I take some money as a loan because I was short of funds. I assumed 'twas his to lend, but if not, I shall return it at once."

"Whitby hasn't paid your jointure, has he?" Elizabeth discerned the problem at once.

"Your Grace is very astute." Cory hoped the queen would make the next logical offer.

"I'll have one of my clerks write to him. Don't stop." Elizabeth gestured at her hair without turning around. "I like the way you handle the brush."

Cory let out her breath as she plied the brush once more. Praise the good heavens, her father-in-law would not dare disobey the queen's order. She would be paid at last.

Elizabeth closed her eyes, seeming to relax and savor the ministrations. "Hmm, when you speak to Carew's father, there is another matter in which you might aid me. You have no doubt heard what Carew did to my cousin yesterday."

Cory almost groaned again as she realized what was coming. Carew had poked holes in the Dowager Countess of Leicester's bumroll at chapel. Now there would be hell to pay.

"He must be punished, but I don't want anything too harsh. Since you'll be speaking to Graystock about the cards, pray see to this other matter as well."

Cory nodded in discouragement, knowing the queen had never liked her pretty cousin Lettice. She especially hadn't liked her when she'd secretly wed Elizabeth's favorite, the Earl of Leicester, ten years ago. Even now that Leicester was dead, Elizabeth remained miffed. Her capacity to bear a grudge was amazingly long lived.

Still, Cory knew that as queen, Elizabeth would keep up the appearance of courtesy to her cousin. Even if she was amused by what Carew had done, outwardly she must respond to Lady Leicester's complaint. "Carew only did it because Lady Leicester fussed about her back hurting," Cory said. "He thought if some bran ran out of her bumroll, it would relieve the weight."

"But she had an entire flock of crows follow her from chapel," Elizabeth pointed out, "eating up the trail of bran. She thought they were attacking her and had hysterics."

"He explained that he'd only been trying to help, did he not?"

"Aye, but Lady Leicester blames the entire affair on me. I haven't heard the end of it since." The queen's irritation melted into chuckles. "By God, she did look funny, all red in the face with those crows pecking at her bum. But I did not tell him to do it."

Cory contained her smile, knowing this was the wrong moment to share the queen's mirth. "I will see that the lad apologizes to her and offers to perform some service as recompense."

"Good. And speak to Baron Graystock. Convince him 'tis not a grave offense."

Cory sighed, knowing Elizabeth would encourage Carew to do it again if she possibly could. It was nice to be needed, but Her Majesty was doling out some nasty tasks.

"Then there's Essex," Elizabeth said as Cory fetched the queen's wig for the day. She knelt and offered the auburn concoction decked with jewels for inspection. "He has challenged Baron Graystock to a duel. I want you to stop him."

Cory looked up in surprise. "I, Your Majesty? You are the only one Lord Essex listens to."

Elizabeth rearranged the large ruby that would hang from the wig just above her forehead. "Dear boy, he imagines I favor the baron over him, which is nonsense. But he's so fond of me, he sees slights that aren't there." A fond smile curved her lips. "I don't wish him to risk a duel, but I prefer not to forbid him. He's been asking to go to France to support Henri of Navarre's bid for the throne. I've had to refuse, so he's been in a temper. And then that foolish page gave him my letter to

Graystock." Indignation tightened her expression. "That lad should be whipped."

Cory sucked in a breath, alarmed. "Oh, no, Your Grace. The child did not do it on purpose. He cannot read and misunderstood his orders. Whipping wouldn't prevent the problem in future. Not only would it be unkind, it is also impractical."

Elizabeth bristled like a hawk mantling over its prey. "Do you suggest *We* are unkind?"

Lord, she was testy this morning, Cory thought. Definitely in pain from the tooth. "Your Grace did not have the full information, and without it, you reached a natural conclusion. I am honored to provide you with the details. With them, I know you would never be unkind."

Elizabeth's ruffled feathers subsided. "Very diplomatic, madam," she said dryly. "Now are you going to speak to Essex or are you not?"

"I fear I would not be successful, Your Grace."

"I note that you are most successful at wheedling people into doing things they don't want to do. At my request, you will try, will you not?"

It was a supreme compliment to be asked rather than ordered by the country's sovereign. Cory sighed in resignation. "I will try, Your Majesty, but I cannot think he will agree."

"You can be uncommonly persuasive when you wish." Elizabeth seemed satisfied. "And 'twill save me another tiff with him. Now, one last thing."

Cory winced. How could there possibly be more?

The queen's expression became troubled. "First my tire-woman disappears. Now this new threat."

"Did you learn something more about Moll?" Cory asked, trying to display the wig with steady hands despite her concern for the absent tirewoman.

"Of course I did," Elizabeth snapped over the wig. "You don't think I would replace her without sending word to her home? Her mother says she'd heard nothing from Moll in days."

"Something terrible must be wrong, Your Grace." Cory's alarm increased. She appreciated the queen's efforts to find Moll, but the news was chilling. "That's not at all like Moll."

"I agree. I have asked Captain Wells to look into the matter. But that's not the last of our difficulties." Elizabeth indicated that Cory should put on her wig. Obediently Cory rose, moved behind the queen, and prepared to settle the auburn tresses on her mistress's head.

"A crossbowman shot at a woman from the palace last night," Elizabeth said in a gloomy tone. "The foolish chit has not come forward, so I wish you to find out who it was."

Cory lowered the wig with care. "How did you hear of it, Your Grace?" she asked, knowing the queen must be referring to her own danger last night. How could word have traveled so fast?

"Baron Graystock told me about it. He rescued her."

Cory started and almost dropped the wig.

"What *is* wrong with you this morning?" Elizabeth demanded, half turning on her stool to glare over her shoulder. "First you are late this morn. Now you're as jumpy as a squirrel."

Cory stood frozen, holding the wig in midair, too stunned to speak. Good fortune, the man who had rescued her was Carew's nasty-tempered old father? That couldn't be.

"Cordelia," Elizabeth barked. "Are you unwell?"

"No, Your Grace," she whispered, her mind spinning.

"Then kindly put on my wig and stop hanging above me like an overripe fruit." With a snort of exasperation, the queen turned back on her stool, arms crossed expectantly.

Forced out of her stupor, Cory scrambled to collect her scattered thoughts and fitted the wig to Elizabeth's head. "It's just that, er, I was the one shot at last night," she confessed.

"What?" Elizabeth twisted all the way around this time, both fists planted on her hips. "Cordelia Hailsworthy, you could have been killed. I forbid you to go out again like that alone."

Cory straightened the hairpiece. "I'm sorry, Your Grace."

"I can't think why you didn't tell the baron your name last night," Elizabeth grumbled, calming at her apology, "but you seem to have your reasons for the odd things you do. So you were the one he said was watching Giordano. Don't you have enough to do?" She clucked her tongue at Cory's tendency to take on other people's burdens. "Well, as he has charge of the investigation, you're to speak to him about it. And remember, I'll not have you endangered, do you hear?"

Cory could only nod, her head swimming. How could her

rescuer be Baron Graystock, the most unreasonable, thoroughly misguided parent in this half of the hemisphere? The
baron could be no pirate prince, either. She'd never met the
man of her dreams in the flesh, but now the chances of it happening seemed as remote as the north star. Carew's father was
an ogre. She had learned that in the two weeks she'd known
Carew.

As she fetched the oil of clove and prepared to coax Elizabeth into letting her administer it, the queen rose. "Cory," she
demanded, "why would someone shoot at you?"

Cory had asked herself the same question many times. She
could think of no one who bore her a grudge. Her friends
loved her. Those who had expressed disapproval still seemed
to tolerate her, such as the younger maids of honor who appeared jealous of her favor with the queen, or the parents who
disapproved of her card parties. None of them seemed like
murderers. Her father-in-law had been so eager to be rid of
her, he'd torn her away from her beloved foster children and
the dowager countess. She could call his unkindness many
bad names, yet he would not stoop to murder to avoid paying
her jointure.

The question followed her like a black cloud after that,
along with the original worry.

Who had shot the bolt at her? And why?

Hellfire and brimstone, the idiot had missed the mark. He
settled before the fire, as if untroubled by the news, but the
urge to shout his frustration warred within him. If not for that
Cavandish bastard hiding in the shrubbery, they would be rid
of Viscountess Wentworth.

A dozen times he had imagined the task. He'd chosen his
crossbow archer because of his skill in the hazardous art of
felling wild boar. He should have succeeded, given his ability
to stalk his prey in utter stealth. So easy to follow the woman
along the riverbank, to hide behind thick shrubs in the night
and let fly the crossbow bolt.

Except the damn baron had been there before him, sitting
silently in the rain. His archer said he hadn't even seen him
until he sprang to the viscountess's aid.

He shifted in his chair, masking his disappointment. He
prided himself on mentoring his associates. It won him faith-

ful followers who would support him when the time was right. He would advise the fellow, and they would try again.

Except the damned baron would give them problems. Having sailed and fought under the renowned Sir Francis Drake, he thought he was infallible, and now he was to investigate the shooting incident. His associate had heard it from a footman, who knew a maid of honor, who had eavesdropped on the queen as she spoke to the baron. It complicated things.

Twice before, this man had killed for him. He could do it again. But they must not underestimate Matthew Cavandish's mulish persistence. They had too much to lose.

Chapter 5

Matthew set out for London on foot that morning, determined to learn more about the man who had shot the crossbow. He'd erred to think the queen would turn it over to the sheriff or her royal guard. Yet how could he have foreseen that she would assign him to the investigation?

Now he would have to see the alluring Titania for more than a conversation about his son. The queen had sworn to ferret out who she was. All Matthew lacked at this point was her name.

He rubbed his aching neck, a mixture of frustration and anticipation clouding his mind like the shimmer of last night's mist beneath the moon. His glimpse of the fairy queen this morning, looking so fresh and innocent in slumber, had whetted his male appetite. Seeing her regularly at court would be a dangerous distraction. He was already juggling multiple responsibilities. Now, with a murderer on the loose, one missed clue could mean disaster.

He must not slip in this task. The thought of Titania coming to harm was more intolerable than seeing her, talking to her, or knowing her.

Carew tagged along, throwing pebbles at squirrels, seeming full of energy. Due to a stomach upset, Lady Russell had been unable to take charge of him, and Matthew had dared not leave him alone at court. Gossip would be flying about the murder attempt, and the last thing he wanted was Carew close to dan-

ger. He would have to arrange a distraction while he talked to
the cordwainer. Once they returned to court, he didn't know
how he would keep his son out of the affair.

At the Royal Exchange, Matthew opened the shop door of
Master Henry Howe, one of London's most prominent mem-
bers of the Honorable Company of Cordwainers, and guided
Carew in ahead of him. The strong scent of cured leather as-
sailed him as he took in the scurrying apprentices and diligent
workmen exercising their craft.

A well-dressed man in his fifties, Master Howe stepped forward to greet them. After the formalities, Matthew cleared his
throat. "Might we speak alone for a moment, Master Howe? I
have urgent business to discuss."

"Indeed, my lord. Pray step this way to my personal workroom." Master Howe bowed, and Matthew saw the subtle
change in his face as he realized his visitor had not come to
purchase boots. Howe's time was money. If Matthew monopo-
lized his work day, business suffered a loss.

"But first, perhaps I need a pair of boots," he lied, needing
Howe's cooperation, even if it cost him.

"But of course, my lord." Howe's smile brightened. "Permit
me to send for the wooden last used for your previous pair. I
will check to see that it still provides a proper fit."

As Matthew mentally rearranged his funds to cover the expensive, unneeded boots, Carew tugged at his sleeve. "Father.
Father, what about—"

"Not just now, Carew. I would like you to wait in the main
shop." By Neptune, he still had a pair of perfectly good boots
from his last visit. Why hadn't he thought to meet Howe that
evening instead of interrupting his work day?

"Father, couldn't you . . . that is, would you—"

He turned, chastening words on his lips, but bit them back as
his gaze met Carew's. His son's face was full of hope as he
eyed the high, glossy boots displayed in the shop window.

Matthew cursed his own thickheadedness. The boy was thirteen and had never owned a pair of high boots. It was the perfect gift and would keep Carew occupied while he talked to
Howe. Why hadn't he thought of it to start? He could have
avoided purchasing a pair for himself.

With a wave, he recaptured Master Howe's attention, where

he and an apprentice searched a shelf of wooden lasts. "My son requires a pair of boots as well," he said.

The bootmaker was clearly pleased, but it was Carew's smile of delight that awakened a pang in Matthew. How many times had he seen that look when he returned to visit his son? Not often. As an infant, Carew had wiggled and screamed when Matthew had held him. Perhaps he had squeezed too hard, but he'd been terrified of dropping him. No wonder Carew had always quieted when his grandmother took him. She had always been able to soothe the lad.

So he'd done the best thing and left Carew with his mother and older sister Rozalinde. Since he'd lost Joanna, another loving woman was best. Two were even better. Matthew had had nothing to offer an infant.

Not until he was six had Carew finally ventured out from behind his Aunt Rozalinde's skirts, curious about the man everyone said was his father. He'd followed Matthew during that entire visit, refusing to be separated without wailing and tears. Matthew had woken in the night to find Carew snuggled against him in the big bed. The tenderness of that moment had touched him, making his son's sobs all the more painful as Matthew left on his next voyage.

But children didn't understand the passage of time, did they? After five minutes, Carew had most certainly turned to other pursuits and forgotten him.

Sure enough, at seven, Carew hadn't remembered him. They'd had to start all over, although within a week his son had again latched on and refused to be separated from him.

Should he have stayed in England for the sake of his son? The question had plagued him at each visit. But what could he offer the boy? An empty heart? Since his son had seemed to thrive with his grandmother and aunt, Matthew had felt sure he'd given him the best. Some years later, after Matthew's younger brother Charles had married, Carew had stayed with him and his wife Frances in their Dorset home. As Carew seemed to enjoy the company of Charles and Frances's many children, both natural and adopted, he had left Carew there.

He would have sworn Carew was happy, so his son's hostility and angry accusations on his last visit baffled him. Seeing Joanna's gold blond hair and gold-flecked brown eyes in his boy hurt even more each time Carew had lashed out.

A short time later, with his wallet many pounds lighter, he was ushered into Howe's private workroom and offered refreshment. With Carew occupied, being fitted for his boots by an apprentice, Matthew swallowed some of the wine and plunged into the subject at hand. "I am looking for a man who made a footprint in a pair of your boots. Someone who frequents court, I'm guessing. You serve the court more than any other cordwainer in London town, do you not?"

Howe appeared perplexed as he refilled their wine flagons. "It is my privilege to serve many noblemen at court, my lord. Why do you think this print was from one of my boots?"

Matthew considered how to explain his odd request. "The bootprint had your mark, the H, stamped in the sole. Plus the print had the distinct high-quality heel you use on boots made for riding, not for walking. I knew the pair had to have come from your workshop."

Howe swelled with pride at the compliment. "Indeed, my lord, other cordwainers make heelless boots, but I am one of the few who caters to the wealthy owning mounts. The heel helps keep the foot in the stirrup." He laid a square of finely cut, stacked wood before Matthew for his inspection. "May I recommend this heel for your own boots? It will be cut to fit, of course."

Howe was ever the salesman, Matthew thought, examining the stacked wood that had been carefully pegged together. This was exactly the type of heel that had made the print. "Fine. Now would you be so good as to name the men at court for whom you made boots with heels like this?"

Howe raised his eyebrows, as if surprised by his insistence on the subject. "Let me think." His nimble hands caressed the stacked wood as he considered the question. "I made a pair for the Earl of Essex last year. Then there was a knight, but I cannot remember his name." He opened the door to hail a passing apprentice, then returned to his seat. "Sir William Norris bought a pair of boots some time ago."

By the end of his visit, Matthew had the names of four men who either frequented or lived at court and had had boots with heels made for them in the last few years. In addition to Norris and Essex, there were Lord Burghley and Sir Francis Knollys. Matthew could not imagine that Burghley, the Lord Treasurer, could be guilty, but a good investigator should check all leads.

Yet of the four, none would consent to wear worn boots, and from long experience at tracking, he could tell the heels had been well worn. He saw in his mind's eye the prints in firm soil, showing clear evidence of Master Howe's distinct wooden heel except for the sharp slant of the back, outer edges.

It was possible that one of these men had given his boots to a servant. Gifts of a master's or mistress's used footwear and clothing were a benefit of being in service. If they didn't fit, they could be sold in the market, where they might pass from one owner to another. Hell, the boots could have had numerous owners. He was probably off on a wild-goose chase.

He cursed the formidable task before him as he and Howe emerged from the office into the shop. His mood grew blacker as he saw Carew huddled with a group of rapt apprentices. Carew grinned and announced the name of a card. The apprentices gasped in astonishment.

Matthew's blood heated in fury. By Neptune, his son was doing a card trick. If the rascal were wagering too, he would rip his ears off.

"I must collect Carew," he said to Howe, ready to put an end to the foolery.

But Howe seemed to realize the potential importance of the information he had just shared. "My lord, is there a special reason you seek this man?"

Blast. His son was corrupting a dozen impressionable youngsters, maybe even emptying their pockets of their pay, and Howe wanted more talk. "Someone wearing a pair of your boots . . ." He stopped, realizing he was about to blurt out the truth. "Was engaged in a dangerous activity last night," he finished instead.

As the words left Matthew's mouth, Carew's head twisted around. Matthew clenched his jaw and looked away. Blast it, the boy had the sharp ears of a hound and the curiosity of a cat. "I cannot think Lords Essex or Burghley were involved," Howe said far too loudly. "The others, I do not know."

"I'm sure you're correct." Matthew said his farewells quickly and hustled his son outside.

The exact thing he'd meant to avoid had happened. Carew was now involved in the investigation of an attempted murder.

* * *

Matthew strode down the street, furious with himself. Curse his inability to hide his meaning in clever phrases. His blunt honesty had landed him in another coil.

Carew bounded beside him, brimming with interest in what must have sounded to him like exciting intrigue. "Zounds, Father, what happened last night? What was the fellow wearing Master Howe's boots doing?"

Matthew skidded to a halt and glared at Carew. "You're not to do card tricks in public ever, Carew. Thank God you weren't wagering. If I catch you at it again, you will be punished."

"If I wager or if I do card tricks?" Carew said, making an impudent face.

"Both," Matthew roared, Carew's cheeky insolence firing his temper. "And you're to forget everything you heard me say to Master Howe. Do you understand?"

"About the man in the boots?" Carew returned to his original question. "You said he was doing something dangerous? Was he running a bawdy house?"

"What do you know of bawdy houses?" How had his innocent child even heard of them?

Carew looked instantly contrite. "Nothing, Father. I just know they're a dangerous activity for the people who own them. So I thought he might be running one."

"I would rather you didn't discuss bawdy houses with anyone, Carew." Satisfied that his son hadn't actually been to a bawdy house but had merely heard the term, Matthew walked on.

"*You* heard of them." The old resentment flared in Carew's tone. "How old were you?"

Matthew winced at the images Carew's question conjured. He'd visited his first bawdy house with Drake in the Spanish Main. Matthew's first woman since Joanna's death had been a tawny-skinned beauty with skills in the bedchamber he'd never imagined existed. With her, he'd closed his eyes and first spun the fantasy that the female he bedded was his wife.

"I was eighteen." The mere memory hurt. "I'd probably heard the word before, but it didn't mean anything to me until then. May it never mean to you what it means to me now."

"What does it mean to you?" Carew asked, wide eyed with interest.

"Disappointment," he told his son, in a tone he hoped clearly indicated the end of the subject. "Loss, pain, and loneliness. Things I never wish you to know."

Wedged in a corner of the queen's green antechamber, Cory glanced up at Robert Devereux, Earl of Essex, and wondered whether she was making any progress. He was so spoiled, picking fights over nothing and refusing to apologize. When she'd broached the subject of his ridiculous duel, instead of responding, Essex had backed her into the corner.

"Please, my lord," she pleaded, trying to conceal her irritation. "Give up the duel with Baron Graystock. Someone could be hurt."

"I might be killed." The earl gazed at her, as if fully aware that his heated glances were said to smite the female heart with love. "Dare I hope, darling Cory, that you would care?"

"Of course I would care," she snapped, annoyed with his ridiculous attempt to force her into an amorous declaration. "It would be the silliest reason in the world to die."

Her terse answer only seemed to strengthen his resolve. "I'll give up the duel on one condition." His long fingers closed on the flesh of her waist as he leaned close.

Cory braced her hands against his chest to hold him at arm's length. He was so pompous, she could hardly imagine he'd been brought up in Lord Burghley's household after his father died. He was nothing like his loyal, hardworking guardian, who cared so deeply for others.

"Did you hear me, Cordelia?" Essex's sharp question recaptured her wandering attention. "I said I'll give up the duel if you'll kiss me."

Heavens, she was in trouble now. "You wouldn't want to kiss a sorry old widow," she said. She hadn't been kissed by anyone since Thomas and preferred it remain that way.

He grinned with pleasure at this obvious opportunity to flatter her. "Ah, Cordelia, sweetling, you're anything but an old widow. You have no idea how lovely you are, with your dark hair and white skin." He pressed closer until his hips molded against hers. "Let me convince you of the pleasures you will find in my arms," he pleaded in winning tones.

As he bent to find her lips, Cory averted her face so that his mouth met her hair. Undeterred, he leaned to kiss her neck. Cory's thoughts raced, searching for an escape. Although she disliked the method, there might be an easy way to accomplish her task for the queen. "If I kiss you, will you promise to send a message to Baron Graystock, apologizing?"

"I'll call off the duel," Essex murmured, tickling her neck unbearably with his moustache.

Magnificent, Cory thought. He won't apologize, but at least he won't duel. Though in Cavandish's place, she would still want to kill the idiot. "Very well," she said aloud. "If you promise. But be warned, I've no skill in this. You'll wish to make it quick." She squeezed her eyes shut and awaited his assault, expecting something like Thomas's sloppy caresses.

"Quick is not the way of the thing," Essex crooned, sliding one hand beneath her chin and tipping up her face. "I'll wager your husband never kissed you properly, as I shall."

Cory set her mouth in a firm, resistant line as Essex angled his head, searching for her lips. Certain he wouldn't give up the duel any other way, she steeled herself for the ordeal.

Matthew stopped dead in the entry to the queen's green antechamber and stared at the couple in the corner. He recognized Essex's ruddy hair and swaggering posture at once, even with his back turned. He recognized the woman Essex was kissing as well. With a grimace, he averted his gaze. So Titania was sweet on Robert Devereux.

A burn of jealousy snaked through him. He would kill the louse, trifling with every woman at court. But she was *letting* him trifle with her. He had wanted to preserve her image in his memory as pristine as the glittering spray from last night's waterfall. Now it was ruined.

Go, he ordered his feet. *You've seen enough.* But he couldn't help looking. Essex caressed her neck as the kiss continued. Disgusted, Matthew whirled on his heel and stalked out.

As he turned down a corridor, he collided with a maid of honor carrying a heavily ladened tray. He caught the tray in his arms, along with her, to save the crockery from crashing to the floor. What the devil was her name? He couldn't keep the queen's pesky women straight one from another, especially when they hung on him and chattered until his head rang. He wanted to brush them away like flies.

"My dear," he began. She beamed with such intensity, he realized she took his address as a personal endearment. "Who is the new woman at court with the dark hair and white skin?" he asked to dispel the notion. "I believe she somehow serves the queen?"

Her face fell at his interest in another female. "You mean the Viscountess Wentworth?"

"She was caring for the royal parrot last night."

"That would be her." The maid made a face. "She's been at court for a six-month and is a terrible meddler, always putting her nose in other people's business."

He could attest to that truth. "Go on."

"She keeps a private court some evenings, as if *she* were the queen. But the people she attracts are the oddest sort." He nodded for her to continue, and she launched into a recitation of the latest gossip. "Well, let me see. The children always go. That's to be expected, since she offers card games. Then there're servants and foreigners. And of course Ann Sims, though she's such a milksop, she'd like anyone. Lord Burghley even stops by at times. But no one else of importance at court likes Viscountess Wentworth, nor should you," she warned, as if suddenly aware of that possible danger. "She hated her husband and says she'll never wed again. He was a terrible rake, so I cannot think why she was not a wife to him, except their fathers forbid them to consummate the marriage until they were seventeen, and he died before that. So I guess they didn't consummate it, else why would she be a maid of honor to Her Majesty, when the post is usually for unmarried women? But she's young enough, and they say she's a virgin, and her father-in-law wanted to be rid of her." Out of breath from her recital, she leaned near and cupped one hand to her mouth, as if to share a deep secret. "And it's no wonder. They say she's also a conjurer, able to do magic, making things appear and disappear."

Matthew frowned in disbelief. "What manner of things does she conjure?"

"Playing cards, of course."

Playing cards? Matthew shook his head. People who claimed to conjure things usually chose something of value, such as gold or magical apparitions of dead relations—things people would pay to see. "Why would she want to conjure playing cards?" he asked, baffled.

The girl giggled, as if she, too, found it absurd. "She loves

card games and anything related to them. Everyone plays at her
gatherings. She was teaching her tricks to some of the children
the other night. I believe your son was one of them. Isabel Gar-
diner's father was furious."

Matthew's hopes plummeted as he absorbed the implications. Titania must be the female who had won Carew's five
pounds. "Does she play for money with the children?" he demanded.

The girl seemed hard pressed for something unfavorable to
say. "Well, no," she admitted, "I've never heard that said."

"Then who took my son's money?" he muttered mostly to
himself.

"Oh, it could have been her," she piped up, full of helpful,
negative information. "Her father-in-law hasn't sent her
widow's jointure since she arrived at court, so she's short of
funds. 'Tis clear she cannot outfit herself as required for the
coming revel. She might have played for money."

Matthew was sickened. Could she have taken Carew's
money? He could hardly believe Titania, the woman of al-
abaster beauty, capable of such a thing, but Carew had said . . .

He wracked his memory, trying to remember exactly what
his son had said. He'd muttered something about losing the
money, then something about playing cards. Then he'd been so
excited about a female who could make cards appear and disappear. He'd assumed it was someone Carew's own age.

Matthew thrust the tray back in the maid of honor's hands,
bid her good day, and left the palace, determined to forget Titania and concentrate on his ships. If they weren't repaired, he
couldn't sail again, and the queen demanded that he sail. He
also had his son to support, as well as a goodly number of men
depending on him for their livelihoods.

As he rode toward the docks at Deptford, he resolved to forget about Viscountess Wentworth, the virgin widowed meddler
and card conjurer. At least for as long as he could.

Chapter 6

Cory sank to a brocade-covered stool across from her friend and fellow maid, Ann Sims, and bit into her bread. The queen had taken noon dinner in private, and they had mere minutes to eat before they must accompany Her Majesty on her afternoon walk. "I am so worried about Moll. What do you suppose could have become of her?" Cory asked her friend.

Ann blinked her pale blue eyes in concern. "I cannot think. I've never known her to miss a single day of her duties in two years. Now, suddenly she's missing for days on end."

Cory rubbed her temples where a headache threatened. "Ann, do you know if she had a close friend? Someone she might have told where she was going?"

"I believe she had become close to the emissary from France. Once she even mentioned going to speak to him after her duties were done for the day."

Cory nodded, resolving to speak to Jacques La Faye. Ann's words confirmed what she had already guessed and Moll had recently hinted. "What can you tell me about Baron Graystock?" she asked, moving to her next subject.

Ann smiled her weak, watery smile. "Oh, the great adventurer. He's very eligible and terribly handsome. Every unwed woman at court has designs on him. He brings home amazing treasures from the four corners of the world, especially the Spanish Main, where he spends much time."

Cory pushed past the gossip to the heart of the matter. "Her Majesty wishes me to speak to him about his son. Do you know if he cares about Carew?"

Ann blinked again. "I'm not sure if anyone knows. The baron doesn't speak of personal matters. And since the lad's been turning the court into chaos with his pranks, he'll be fortunate if his father doesn't take a whip to him."

"He hasn't been so ill behaved this week as last," Cory protested.

Ann finished her bread and stood up. "Perhaps, but I wonder how long 'twill last. I admire you for agreeing to speak to the baron, but you'll have a hard time of it." She raised her pale brows. "He's a man of few words, but he comes to see his son every year like clockwork. Never misses a visit. Except for last year, when he was caught in a tropical hurricane. This year he was chased by Spanish galleons out of the Caribbean and is said to have escaped by a mere hair's breath, which accounts for his late arrival. You're fortunate to have him looking into this difficulty of yours from last night. I can't imagine who could mean you harm."

"Nor can I." Cory sighed, vowing not to walk out alone again. "But I'm sure I'll be perfectly safe if I stay in company, especially here in the palace. Now tell me, Ann. Carew says his father is very"—Cory searched for a neutral word—"strict. Is that true?"

"I suppose. He's a mariner and abides by ship's discipline, even on land. Simple food, early to rise, that sort of thing. He sailed around the world with Sir Francis Drake in fifteen seventy-eight."

That was over ten years ago, Cory thought, as she finished her meal and she and Ann changed into walking shoes. She had to respect a man who had the discipline to live the life of an explorer and be so successful, as Baron Graystock seemed to be. But she couldn't excuse his seeming lack of understanding for his needy thirteen-year-old son.

Cory stood on the deck of Baron Graystock's famous ship, *The Revenge*, later that afternoon and absorbed the hum and clatter of activity. Men were everywhere, bare chested in the heat as they mended sails, replaced rigging, and repaired the great fighting galleon.

"I am Viscountess Wentworth," she said to the stocky sailor with a false leg who introduced himself as Hugh Mannerly, the boatswain. "Can you tell me where I would find the baron? I wish to speak to him."

At her request, he stumped off to fetch his master, his peg leg pounding on the wooden deck. After the queen's walk, Cory had sought the baron but hadn't found him at the palace. A groom had directed her to the docks at Deptford, where she had ridden with a gentleman usher.

The boatswain returned and bowed before her. "The baron asks that my lady attend him in his cabin, if you would be so kind," he said with grave courtesy. "If your ladyship don't mind going below deck, 'twill be out of the sun."

She nodded agreement and followed him to a hatch leading to the deck below. A ladder disappeared into the murky depths. She stepped onto it and found it steady, though it was awkward backing down a ladder in full skirts.

Once on a firm floor again, the boatswain led her through the below-deck maze to the back of the ship and threw open a door. To Cory's astonishment, the cabin resembled a tropical paradise. A bank of open windows built into the stern flooded the chamber with light. Before them grew lush tropical palms in pots, flanked by lacy green ferns. Gleaming rows of seashells caught in fishing net hung from the ceiling, and the heady scent of cinnamon filled the air.

Most intriguing of all, a pure white ivory horn hung on the wall to her right. It wasn't elephant ivory. She had seen such a tusk before, and this horn was too thin. Nor did it resemble a walrus tusk. What creature was it from?

"The baron will speak with you momentarily, Viscountess Wentworth," the boatswain said, holding the door wide and motioning her in.

She stepped into the cabin onto brightly colored carpets and walked straight to the horn ornamenting the wall. As Hugh closed the door behind her, she touched the cool, twisted ivory with one fingertip, intrigued.

"Did you come to see me or my collection?"

Cory nearly leaped out of her slippers. The baron sat at his desk, shielded from the door by an unusual screen made of heavy paper stretched on a wood frame.

The queen had told her who he was. She shouldn't be surprised. But like his men above deck, he was naked from the waist up. All she could do was stare.

He didn't rise to greet her, as was proper. Instead, he lounged in the high-backed chair and examined her, looking every bit the pirate prince in this setting, so reminiscent of the wild Caribbean. Except for one thing. He had shaved away his magnificent pirate's beard.

Despite her disappointment, she swallowed hard as she gazed at his sleek, muscular shoulders and bronzed chest. Surely she'd seen men without shirts before. But she could not recall a single one looking like Matthew Cavandish.

He was magnificent, his potent masculinity speaking to her in a tongue both fascinating yet foreign. To her alarm, she understood his message all too well. Every nerve of her thrilled with awareness of him.

His gaze burned with mesmerizing intensity into hers. Her vision of the world shrank, excluding all but him. Something deep within her tightened, a hard knot of yearning that longed for release. Physically, he looked so like the ideal man she had invented in her mind.

But Baron Graystock had the soul of a cantankerous old man, she reminded herself. He'd just snapped at her like a nasty-tempered old bear. "I misunderstood Hugh. I thought you were to join me, baron." To her relief, she sounded cool and controlled. "I *have* come to see you, but the horn is fascinating. What is it?" Deliberately she returned her gaze to the horn and traced its descending spiral, pretending more interest in it than him.

" 'Tis from a unicorn," he announced in a bland tone as he leaned forward to scrutinize her.

She caught his motion from the corner of her eye. His bare flesh rippled with the shift of underlying muscle and sinew, making her mouth go as dry as desert sand.

He was teasing her, and not in a nice way, taking her for a gullible female with little brain. She knew unicorns were merely legends. And polite behavior strongly suggested he ought to put on a shirt, but he made no move to do so. "Did you personally take it from a unicorn?" she challenged, concentrating on the horn.

"No, I bought it from a man, who bought it from someone

else, who said it was from a unicorn. Don't you believe he spoke the truth?" Sarcasm crept into his tone.

"Do you?" she demanded, irked as well. He might go without a shirt, but he seldom went without his barriers to intimacy. Last night, when he had lowered them, the moment and the circumstances had been unique. He was letting her know that they would never come again. "You *don't* believe it, do you," she stated, crushing her interest as she faced him.

"I have learned to question everything I am told." He rose from the chair with languid grace and glided to a position opposite her. "I doubted his claim from the start. In time, I learned it is not from a unicorn. It is from an aquatic creature, a type of whale. I've seen them swimming off the coast of the Americas. The Straits of Magellan, to be precise."

Cynic, Cory thought. To want the talisman from a magical creature enough to acquire it, only to destroy his own belief in its magic. And he mentioned the Straits of Magellan to let her know he'd been around the world, yet he didn't believe in the magic that very world held. "I suppose you've seen a great deal," she said to test her theory.

"I've seen everything, Viscountess. *Everything.*"

Even her, half naked, she remembered with a shiver. He seemed to remember as well, for his gaze had a hot, steamy quality, much like last night. Much like the hot jungle nights of the Spanish Main must be. Her palms grew damp and perspiration trickled down her back. Her hand crept to her throat, the neckline of her smock seeming too tight. "And you're tired of it all?" she demanded, determined not to be daunted. "So tired, you sit in the rain for hours until a lone female in danger forces you back to civilization?"

"I sit where I wish," he said with exaggerated politeness, as if he had deliberately provoked her response and now mocked her for it. "What can I do for you, Viscountess?"

"What you can do, is stop being you for a few minutes and be who you were last night. When we shared the gingerbread," she blurted, her usual outspokenness overcoming common sense and even courtesy.

She thought something flickered in his eyes. Surprise? Interest? Or was it dislike? No, not that. He didn't dislike her or he would put on his shirt. The air leaped with sexual energy, and she felt certain he enjoyed provoking her with his maleness. It made her lightheaded, giddy. Or was it the heat of the cabin, which was overpowering, despite the open windows?

"Viscountess Wentworth, you should forget everything I said last night," he taunted.

She walked to a chair, her knees all but buckling as she sank onto its welcome support. "I don't want to forget. I liked you better then," she said with deliberate coolness.

"And now you don't." His tone was amiable, as if it was exactly the reaction he'd wanted.

"That's right, because now you're acting like Carew's father, who is a nasty-tempered old bear. I could hardly believe it when I heard you were he."

Displeasure fueled his smoldering gaze as he stared down at her. "Is that what he told you?"

"That's what I know. Carew didn't have to say a word. His concern about your coming told me enough."

"How interesting," he said, as if nothing were further from the truth. "I repeat, madam, let us come to the point of your visit. What can I do for you?"

His extreme politeness grated on her nerves. So different from last night, when she had glimpsed his soul through a tear in his elaborate mask. Yet she must accept the things that people said of him as true. He was a man of few words, brusque manner, and no heart. No wonder Carew called him a dragon. It was probably more apt than a bear, as a dragon could look splendid while still being deadly. Ah well, there was nothing for it. She dived in anyway. "You can stop being rude, for one thing." She folded her hands in her lap and adopted her most earnest air. "Then you can inquire if I am recovered from that man shooting at me. After I say, 'I am reasonably recovered, though the thought of it still makes me anxious,' you can tell me the queen assigned you to look into the affair, which she told me. Then you can ask me a few questions."

He stared back at her a full minute before a faint smile curved his lips. "You do enough talking for two people, madam."

There. She'd made him smile, and he looked almost human again. "I do what is necessary."

"*Is* it necessary? Others generally wish to speak for themselves."

"Oh, they may say a word or two," she teased. "*You* may say more, if you insist. But pray be warned." She grew serious and gazed directly into his eyes. "If you don't keep up your side of the conversation, I will keep it up for you, because I came to speak to you about your son."

The cold barrier fell back into place. "My son is my responsibility. I don't appreciate interference."

His displeasure was so thick in the chamber, she could have cut it with a knife and eaten it for dinner. Unlikable man. How had she ever imagined him a pirate prince? He was a dragon lord, always ready to breathe fire. But she knew his one soft point—he had been loved as a boy. She must gain his sympathy for Carew by touching him there. "There's always room in a young person's life for people who care," she entreated. "You had more than one parent, and probably caring friends of the family as well. As I understand it, you only see your son once a year and had the misfortune of missing last year's meeting. I've seen more of him than you in the last two weeks and have come to care deeply about him. So I believe I qualify as a caring friend of the family."

At the flush on his shaven cheeks, she wondered if he would explode at her frank intrusion into his relationship with his son. But any show of emotion seemed a good sign, so she plowed on. "I've come to explain to you that Carew did make a hole in the Dowager Countess of Leicester's bumroll at church," she said, brushing past what had to be his guilt at seeing Carew so seldom. "But I assure you it was with kind intentions. She had complained that her back hurt, so he tried to relieve her of the weight of her bumroll. That's why he made the hole. I pray you, do not punish him for his misguided actions. 'Twould be better to discuss with him the other ways he might have chosen to help." She held her breath, wondering how he would reply.

"What choices did he have?" he demanded.

"Well, if her back hurt, he could have offered his arm for her to lean on for support," she improvised, determined to brave it out for Carew's sake. "He could have offered to carry her train, to remove some of the weight. He could even have suggested that she need not wear the heavy garments, that she was attractive without them. The point is, he must learn to think before he acts. He's an intelligent boy, though I'm sure you know that, being his father." She couldn't help letting a touch of sarcasm creep into her last words.

A long silence followed, with no visible reaction on his part, and Cory's temper grew short. What did it take to reach the tender place she knew lay barricaded behind his brick wall of cynicism and reserve?

"You're sure he wasn't trying to embarrass her?" He still sounded unconvinced.

"Very sure. Though I must admit Her Majesty probably enjoyed the crows' frightening Lady Leicester half to death. But that wasn't Carew's fault, and he did try to shoo them away. Wait, I'll show you how it happened."

She jumped up, suddenly sure he would forgive Carew if he could envision the scene. "The bran was running out of Lady Leicester's bumroll, scattering on the ground as she walked into the Chapel Court. You know where that is." She pretended she was Lady Leicester, stepping with self-important grandeur into the courtyard. "She wasn't halfway across the yard before a flock of crows descended on her. She became hysterical." Thoroughly wrapped up in the story, Cory clasped both hands to her head to show Lady L's terror. "Carew saw what was happening and ran after them, waving his arms." She traded parts and dashed across the cabin, imitating Carew's actions. "But the rooks at Hampton Court are very fierce, especially when they're hungry. They refused to fly away. Lady L screeched her head off. Carew ran and shouted at the birds. The crows screeched at him until they sounded like Lady Leicester." She imitated the crows, but stopped as Lord Graystock turned away. What was wrong now?

His shoulders shook, and she realized he was struggling to contain laughter. "Oh dear, have I been a complete ass?" she ventured.

A faint grin adorned his lips as he turned back. "Lady Wentworth, do you often imitate crows?"

"Only if the story is about them." How badly she wanted him to remain human. "I would do crow imitations all day, my lord, if you would agree not to punish Carew too harshly." Her voice softened as she remembered Carew's penitent expression during their earlier discussion. "I have asked him to apologize to her ladyship and offer to perform some small service as a token of his sincerity. The queen also asks that he not be whipped or given any severe physical punishment," she added. "As do I. Carew is too fine a lad to be ruined by beatings. He needs love and understanding." She knew by his expression that she had passed far beyond the boundaries of polite interest, or even the benevolent concern allowed a family friend. But she might as well finish what she'd begun. "I assured him that you would understand once I explained."

Silence stretched after her words. Her spirits fell. She had gone too far.

"What do you know of raising children?" he said at last.

She pressed her lips together in frustration. Rude, impossible, infuriating man. "I know a good deal. I have two children, ages nine and eleven, and they're terribly mischievous, so I understand exactly what it's like, dealing with their antics, but I would never strike them. They—"

"I thought you were a childless widow." He stepped closer until he towered over her.

Cory winced. He'd struck a sore point, but that would not stop her from speaking her mind. "You thought correctly," she admitted, straining to cloak the sorrow that insisted on creeping into her voice. "Marcus and Letty are my husband's children out of wedlock. I have cared for them since they were infants, and they're very dear to me, as if they were my own. But I don't suppose you can understand that. Carew told me you wouldn't, and I'm beginning to believe him."

She took a deep breath and plunged on. "Despite that, you will hear me out. Carew loaned me five pounds because I was short of funds and had to purchase a white silk kirtle for the queen's coming masque. Because I was desperate, I agreed, but only with the understanding that I would repay him. Now Her Majesty says you believe he lost the money at cards, but that is not the case. If you will wait until my father-in-law sends my jointure, I will repay you with interest. But I pray you do not punish him for wagering, for he did not." Having run out of breath making this impassioned speech, Cory awaited his reply.

"I have one question, Viscountess." The baron's face was a blank mask, devoid of emotion.

"What is that?" Would he examine her story from every angle? Ask hard questions? Seek advice about how to handle his son? She braced herself, ready for anything.

"Why were you the royal parrot's nursemaid last night?"

"How do you know I was caring for the parrot?" Cory cried, exasperated by the irrelevance of his question. "Why should you care?"

"The queen asked me to examine the creature. I saw you asleep on the settle. Why did you take on the old lady's task?"

"Because she had a bad head rheum. I sent her home to bed," she snapped. Unable to bear any more, she rose and stalked toward the door, enraged and hurt. Such an important issue, and all he wanted to know was why she had sent Thomasine home.

People who couldn't love their children shouldn't be parents, she muttered to herself. How terrible for poor Carew, to be shackled for life to this unbending, unloving, mannerless dragon of a man. He might be a great adventurer who had sailed around the world with Sir Francis Drake, but in her opinion, he might as well have stuck his head in the sand the entire time, for he refused to explore his own heart.

"Viscountess," he called after her.

"What?" Pushed to the breaking point, she spun to face him but couldn't bear the sight of his masklike face. Squeezing her eyes closed, she clenched her fists. "If I stay one more minute, I'll badger you about Carew until you wish to toss me through those windows into the Thames. I care that much for him."

In the silence that followed, she half opened her eyes to sneak a look at him. He stood much nearer than she'd expected.

"Unfortunately, we are not done with the business at hand," he said evenly. "Do you have any idea why someone would shoot a crossbow at you?"

She'd been so impassioned about Carew, she'd forgotten about her danger last night. "No," she said wearily.

"Do you have enemies? Have you, er, disappointed someone?"

"No and no." She was aware of the acerbic tone of her reply but didn't care. "I am well liked by many, though that may come as a surprise to you, not knowing how to like people yourself."

"I see you are hysterical, madam. We will continue this discussion another time." His mask was icy with disdain. "I intend to find the culprit, whether you cooperate or not."

"I live at the palace. You may come to me any time." She backed toward the door, then turned and fled, intent on escape.

As she scrambled up the ladder to the upper deck and emerged into the late-day sun, she sought to understand his displeasure. He had resented her intrusion into the vulnerable places of his soul last night. He considered her impertinent in her attempt to reach him today.

So be it. She would not try such tactics again. It was not her affair if he failed in his relationship with his son. Yet she sensed he would care deeply if all hope of love from that quarter died.

As she and the gentleman usher rode back to Hampton Court, Cory realized something more. She burned with envy of the baron. She yearned to sail away as he did on his marvelous ship. She wanted to cast off her old ties and start life anew on the other side of the wide blue sea.

But she was being foolish, she told herself. Women couldn't be adventurers, and the exotic islands of the Spanish Main probably didn't hold the treasures she imagined. Yet the sight of the lush tropical growth in the baron's cabin had touched her imagination, just as the heat of his steamy gaze had touched her passion mere minutes ago.

Closing her eyes, she saw in her mind's eye her pirate prince. Only now, his ship was known to her, along with his face. And although it was foolish, she indulged in her fantasy that he would sweep her into his arms and bear her away to her dream paradise, a land of shimmering white sands and perpetual tropical heat.

Chapter 7

Matthew stared at the closed door of his cabin after the viscountess's departure, fighting to maintain his customary detachment and failing. He was shocked, outraged, and at a loss in the company of this female. The way she stimulated him was as amazing as her unruly tongue.

But her confessions had astounded him the most. She had cared for the royal parrot all night to relieve the old woman who was ill? No one at court was that kind. He was even more astounded that she was bringing up her dead husband's bastard children and loved them like her own. If the eldest was eleven, she'd been a child herself when she'd begun. Outside of his own family, he hadn't met anyone in years with such generous instincts. Certainly not at court.

He raked his hair with one hand, trying to sort through her story about Carew's money. If what she said were true, Carew hadn't lost the money wagering. His son had kindly lent it to her. But why had Carew let him think worse of him than he deserved?

Pained by his son's choice, doubly pained to know Carew had lied to him yet seemed to trust her, he dropped onto the window seat. Below on the quay, he saw Titania mount a horse held by a liveried escort and set off toward London. He must stop thinking of her as the fairy queen. Yet the unsettling feelings she aroused in him refused to leave at his command. He was as bad as Essex, he thought in disparagement. Unbridled lust raced through him every time she appeared.

Worse than that, in her presence, he lost control of their interactions. Never in the past ten years had he felt so vulnerable.

She's in love with Essex, he reminded himself. The length of their kiss had suggested great passion. A woman of her sincerity wouldn't indulge in such behavior without a genuine motive for doing so.

That thought was chased by another. If she loved Essex, someone should stop her. The earl was too pompous, too self-absorbed. He wouldn't hesitate to worm his way into a widow's bed, then move on to another as soon as he'd had her. She would be hurt in the end.

You've been assigned to investigate the attempt on her life, not break up her love affair, his reason warned. *She wouldn't thank you, and Essex would want to duel all the more.*

But Matthew wasn't sure he could avoid interfering. If he thought something, he usually said it, given the chance. He just hadn't had the chance today. The viscountess's sharp tongue had spared her his own blunt observations. She was nothing like his sweet, eager-to-please wife.

Yet for a few charmed moments last night, he and Titania had shared a poignant bond. He'd hoped to keep the memory sacred, much like his wife's. Except the Titania he'd imagined didn't exist in the flesh. The real Titania insulted him by trespassing on his family problems. She told him how to handle his son, then informed him that he didn't understand a thing. Come to that, she'd called him a nasty old bear. He'd almost forgotten about that.

Frustrated and furious, Matthew strode to his desk and dropped into the chair. Grabbing his quill, he scribbled two items on his supply list, hoping to take refuge in work.

The quill snapped under the pressure of his hand, and he threw it aside. Damn it, she was rude and inappropriate, yet she stimulated the most amazing level of lust in him. Why should that be? Just because he'd seen her half-naked last night? If so, he would be better off never seeing her again.

Unfortunately, he had no choice. He was assigned to find the culprit who threatened her. That meant he must tolerate her lectures and her one-sided conversations again.

Yet he *had* learned something valuable from today's lecture, fairness reminded him. Although she might conjure cards, she hadn't won the five pounds from Carew. Having heard the words from her own lips, he believed her. She was too honest, too open to lie. He paused, then forced himself to admit what else she was. She was too perceptive of his pain.

She had broken through barriers that had been unpenetrated for years, stirring up the old longings that had driven him half-mad when he'd first lost Joanna. He wouldn't go through that again for all the Spanish gold in the world.

In future, he must avoid lengthy discourse with her. But he decided she was right about one thing, despite the distasteful way she'd conveyed it. He must try to talk to his son when he returned to Hampton Court.

An hour later, Matthew finished calculating the foodstuffs he would need for his next voyage, then bid Hugh enter when he knocked.

"A message, m'lord." Hugh offered a single sheet of vellum sealed with red wax.

Matthew broke the seal, scanned the few lines, then tossed it back to the boatswain.

"What is it, m'lord?" Hugh eyed the seal, clearly wondering at the message's source.

"Read it. The Earl of Essex has canceled our duel." Matthew snorted with derision. "Her Majesty requires his presence. He excuses me this time, but I'm not to cross him again."

"Shall I alert your seconds?" Hugh's face reflected acute relief.

"Thank you, Hugh. I'd all but forgotten them." He gestured Hugh to a seat, wishing he could live aboard ship instead of at court, where he bumped into idiots like Essex.

"Begging your pardon for bringing up the subject, m'lord, but Lady Wentworth's a most caring gentlewoman," Hugh ventured, propping his wooden leg on a stool, "and she seemed mightily concerned about Master Carew."

Matthew gazed at the ceiling of the cabin pointedly, to show he knew Hugh had been listening from above and had made out some of their conversation. "You may meddle in my affairs all you wish, Hugh, but *she* may not."

"She didn't seem like the meddling sort to me. More the

motherly sort," Hugh speculated, pretending not to know what he meant. "Master Carew needs someone to care for him, m'lord."

"He has my sister-in-law, Frances. He's attached to her," Matthew grunted, Hugh's words scalding him like boiling oil. How dare he suggest the viscountess should take part in his affairs?

"Begging your pardon, m'lord," Hugh said in a tentative tone, "but Master Carew needs you, despite how good your sister-in-law and brother are with him."

"Then why the devil do you say he needs Viscountess Wentworth? And quit begging my pardon. I'm bad tempered but I don't bite. Especially not you." Matthew propped his elbows on the table and cradled his throbbing temples in both hands. It was the closest he could come to apologizing to Hugh, who had taught him everything he knew after they left England. Thanks to Hugh's persistence, they'd caught up with Drake and his crew at Panama. Thanks to the letter to Drake from Matthew's brother-in-law, the Earl of Wynford, he, his younger brother Charles, and Hugh had been accepted for the voyage.

The journey up the west coast of America, then across the Pacific and on until they reached the Far East, had been the adventure of a lifetime. For over two years, he had explored at the side of Drake. In the Japans, they had fought pirates and dined like kings on the spoils after defeating them. In the exotic East, he had seen the extremes of tropical paradises as well as hardships and battles that killed half their crew. Yet he considered it a marvelous experience, and he would never forget all he'd learned from Hugh about sailing, fighting, and living off the land.

In return, he'd cared for Hugh when he lost his leg, helping him find reasons to live. They'd been through too much together to mince words.

Hugh bent over to adjust the stool more to his liking. "I think you should wed again, sir. The Viscountess Wentworth would be an admirable mother to Carew."

"You're mad." Matthew stared at him. "Why would you even say such a thing?"

"I worry about Master Carew. I hear things at court."

Damn the gossip at court. "So I should wed for my son's sake," Matthew grumbled. He heaved a cushion at Hugh, which his friend used to prop his leg higher. "Then I can sail off and feel guilty about leaving two people behind instead of one."

Hugh cast him a crafty glance. "Or you could not sail off at all."

Matthew scowled. "You hate the winter here as much as I do. It makes your leg ache."

"So it does," Hugh allowed. "Still, if you asked her, the viscountess might agree. I understand her father-in-law keeps her on a tight lead, even denying her access to her own funds. You could help her, and she could help Carew."

Matthew couldn't believe this was coming from Hugh, who ought to understand that no one could take Joanna's place. "And what would I have? A woman who's in love with Essex and probably letting him bed her?"

"I thought she was a widow who'd never been a wife," Hugh said in surprise.

Matthew recalled the gossip repeated by the maid of honor. "Who have you been talking to?"

"I told you I hear things," Hugh said, defensive. "I may be one-legged but I'm not deaf."

"You handle yourself better than men who have both legs. Have you been to visit your lady love?" Matthew teased, wanting to change the subject.

"I called upon Susan and was well received," Hugh said with considerable dignity, referring to a serving maid he'd met at court two years past. "But my point is, Essex probably isn't bedding her ladyship. Not if she never knew her young husband."

"How could she be wed to Thomas Hailsworthy and still be a virgin?" Matthew snapped. "He had a reputation as a rakehell at a young age. Everyone who's ever been to court heard it from his father, who seemed proud of it. Besides, I saw the viscountess kissing Essex earlier today."

"Essex would kiss a post if he thought it was female," Hugh snorted derisively. "Wouldn't have nothing to do with what the post wanted, from what I hear."

But Matthew shook his head as he turned to the windows. Enough about the viscountess. He would think about the white sands of the island he had found along the coast of America.

Closing his eyes, he conjured up the image of his paradise.

When it was winter in England, the land he had discovered, so fertile and filled with game, was washed by the warmth of a golden sun. Tropical trees stretched to the skies, green and inviting, and vivid red flowers bloomed in profusion. How he longed to build a house there and establish a base for himself with a few select friends like Hugh. The devil with England, its frigid winters and political traps.

Darkness fell, and Matthew returned to court. As he and Carew sat in his tiny chamber eating their suppers, his son sulked and refused to be drawn out. Matthew didn't want things this way between them, but whenever they disagreed, Carew took it wrong.

Matthew looked out the palace window to the garden beyond. A blaze of torches lit the courtyard, and a bevy of children frisked in the starry night.

"That's Viscountess Wentworth," Carew said, following his father's gaze. "She invited me to join them for a torchlit game of blindman's buff, but I knew you would say no."

Hiding his indignation at his son's unfair accusation, Matthew picked out Titania—a lithe, dancing female with a glossy dark braid swinging down her back.

As he took in her appealing figure, his protective feelings warred with jealousy over her interest in Essex. Hard on the heels of jealousy came dismay. He ought to be disinterested if she were sweet on Essex. He ought to be pleased she was occupied elsewhere. She wouldn't trouble him, as many women did.

Except that she set his blood on fire like a dry ship put to the torch. As he watched her, painful interest flooded his body and mind. "Why does she do that?" he demanded of Carew.

"Do what? Play with us? She says it's more fun for us than getting into mischief." Resentment at missing the fun was obvious in Carew's tone. "The queen agrees. But I knew you wouldn't let me go. She's the one you forbid me to see again. The one who teaches us cards."

So Titania was also the leader of children's games, though her reason for it sounded sensible. It kept them out of mischief while wearing them out. "I know who she is now, and you didn't ask permission," he said, letting more of his resentment show than he'd intended. "I've no objection to your joining that type of game." It was the perfect opening to bring up Carew's lie about the money and how Carew had let him think the female was his age rather than an adult, but his son's pouting countenance warned him to wait. They would quarrel if he mentioned it now.

As they watched, Titania ducked to avoid being tagged by the child wearing the kerchief. Her belling skirts bobbed around her as she laughed and dodged. She looked enticing and full of vigor as she played with the children. Their happy shouts rang in the night air. The flicker of torches held by footmen lent the scene a magical air. He wished he could feel that carefree again.

"You ill, Graystock? You don't have that fever from the Caribbean again, do you?" Carew always seemed to sense his moods and comment on them. The insolent use of his title showed he wanted to be provoking.

"No, Carew, I don't have the fever. Haven't had it in years." As if to belie his words, sweat popped out on his forehead as Carew joined him at the window, eying him keenly. Matthew considered a reproof for the use of his title, but it wouldn't pass his lips.

Carew studied him a few more minutes, but soon lost interest in favor of the laughing friends outside. He gazed at the frolicking crowd, a wistful expression on his face.

Relieved to be free of Carew's scrutiny, Matthew returned to the problem at hand. He'd sworn to attempt to reach his son, even before the viscountess's insulting insinuations that he didn't care. He must try another approach. Uncertain of where to start, he grasped at the first positive thing at hand. "Lady Wentworth appears to be your friend."

"I'm sure you object to *that*." Carew's voice was heavy with sarcasm.

"She came to *The Revenge* to speak to me about you."

"She said she was going to talk to you. I told her she'd do as much good to take a long walk off a short quay."

"You're not to speak to a lady in that manner," Matthew snapped, appalled.

"Calm down, Graystock. I didn't say it that way. I told her you wouldn't understand. You don't, either," Carew finished glumly.

Matthew's gut contracted as he realized the width of the

breach between them. Was it possible he might not be able to reach his son across the gap? He must try again. "On the contrary, I agree with her proposal. You're to apologize to Lady Leicester and explain why you damaged her bumroll. Then you will offer to do her a service."

"I already apologized," Carew said in a heat. "I promised to clean her chopines tomorrow night. I can do things without you hanging over me."

Matthew's concern that Carew would refuse to apologize fell away, to be replaced by another anxiety. He must bring up the money now. "I'm glad to hear it, but I have another question. Why didn't you tell me you loaned the viscountess the five pounds? You let me think the worst of you."

Carew turned away. "You wouldn't have approved of a loan either. You disapprove no matter what I do."

Matthew saw pain in Carew's every movement, yet he was at a loss as to how to relieve it. "I don't always disapprove," he protested, groping for words to ease the strain between them. "But you loaned five pounds to a person you've known a scant two weeks. It isn't wise."

"She'll repay me. You'll see," Carew shouted, leaping up, his hands balled into fists. "You just don't trust her. You don't trust anyone."

"It's not that I don't trust her. But it isn't wise to loan large amounts of money to people on short acquaintance. Besides, that five pounds was for your new clothes. I trusted you with it. I had hoped you would take good care of it and enjoy paying the court tailor yourself."

"I can get along without his services."

"Your sleeves don't cover your wrists. I won't have it said that I don't clothe my son."

"So whip me, as Grandsire Cavandish used to whip you."

Matthew grimaced as he remembered when he'd turned thirteen, the age his father had deemed old enough to be switched for severe crimes. He'd been switched only once before he'd vowed never to commit a switchable sin again. But he'd slipped a number of times after that and had his due. According to his upbringing, he should switch his son for ruining Lady Leicester's bumroll, except that Carew hadn't meant it as a prank. "Not for this," he began, "but Carew—"

"Not for this?" Carew lashed out, resentment contorting his

face. "But next time, if you're in the mood? You'll flog me and then go sailing off on your ship, as you always do."

"I'll not flog you. Not ever. Why the devil would you say such a thing? I've never laid a finger on you, though many times you deserved it." Anger boiled over in Matthew as he leaped to his feet. "Why do you fight me all the time? I want what's best for you."

"Then let me go back to Uncle Charles and Aunt Frances. I was happy until you came back. I would be happier still if I never saw you again." Carew raced from the room, slamming the door behind him.

Matthew slumped in a chair, fighting the sudden tightness in his throat. Why was it like this between them? His son was changing. As a small boy, Carew had adored him, hanging on him the entire time he was home, weeping when he left on his journeys, tearing his heart apart. But two years ago, for the first time, Carew was angry and defiant at his departure. Now on his return, it was even worse, and he didn't know what to do.

Chapter 8

"Ohhh, baked apples. My favorite!" Bess Hawly, assistant to the queen's starch woman, clapped her hands with glee as she joined the assembly in Giordano's chamber that evening.

Cory looked up from her place before the fire, which warded off the evening's damp chill, and patted the bright carpet beside her. "Come sit, Bess. Jane made the apples, and they'll be ready soon, thanks to Giordano's sharing his fire."

As if he understood his name, the parrot squawked and sidled back and forth on his perch. Old Thomasine, his keeper, scolded him, and he subsided as she offered him some seeds.

"Time for music." Cory took her viol from its case, and everyone came to attention, clearly eager for the treat. Cory surveyed her little company. The group changed slightly each time they gathered, depending on duties, but many of her friends were present tonight. After a long day in service, they were all ready for recreation. With her bow, she touched the viol's A string.

"Music will be splendid." Meeks, a gentleman pensioner, spoke from a nest of cushions.

Cory tested the next string on her viol as Carew opened a pouch hanging from his belt and produced a reed flute. She smiled at him, then at Thomasine, who sat with Samuel. The lad was sound asleep, his head in her lap. "Carew, what task did Lady Leicester give you?" she asked as she adjusted the string's peg.

"Clean her chopines after she wears 'em to the playhouse on the morrow," he grumbled. "She still thinks I wished her to look foolish, but I didn't. I didn't want those lousy birds to follow her."

"We know you didn't." She gestured to his flute. "What have you been working on?"

Solemnly he put the instrument to his lips. The spritely tune of "The Gypsy Round" filled the chamber. Cory joined in on her viol as the others sang.

Despite the cheerful music, Cory's heart swelled with pain. Why couldn't she be happy? She had many things to be thankful for tonight. For friendship and music. For the sugared apples baking on the hearth. For the queen's praise because she had prevented the duel. "How did you do it?" Elizabeth had asked after learning that Essex and Graystock would not fight.

Cory's pleasure at the queen's approval dimmed a little as she remembered Essex's greedy kiss. "I was, er, persuasive, as you suggested, but I didn't like doing it. He's too hot tempered, Your Grace." But she knew Elizabeth liked his pretty compliments too well to send him away.

It was those very compliments, both to the queen and to her, that made Cory uneasy. They flowed much too freely, especially since the kiss. His lustful gaze followed her everywhere if they were in the same room. And since the shooting, she saw a threat in every move of those she could not like, especially knowing that whoever wished her harm would try again.

Moving her bow over the strings, she tried to shake off her worry. The music swirled around her, along with her friend's voices. These people loved her. She should be happy, raising their spirits. Yet she missed Letty, Marcus, and Grandmama so much.

As the round ended, a page pulled out a pack of cards. "Please, a card trick, Cory."

"Very well, Ralph." She placed her viol and bow in the case and knelt before Ralph on the carpet. "Shall I do the one where I guess the name of the card you choose?"

"Yes, indeed! You'll never guess the one I pick." He handed her the colorful stack of cards.

Cory shuffled them with practiced ease. Everyone's eyes

gleamed with excitement as she handled the cards, and she loved to astound them, to give them hope that magic really did exist in the world.

She fanned the cards and bid Ralph choose. He selected one from the middle and shared it with the others, not letting her see. As she distracted her audience with words and movement, she rearranged the pack, then had him slip his choice into the middle. Rising, she twirled in a circle, chanting the words she and Letty had composed years ago.

Mystery of mysteries, magical voice, reveal to me my friend's secret choice.
Show me the answer, show me the way, to amuse my friends when we're at play.

As she twirled, she sorted through the stack, easily seeing the card Ralph had chosen, face down among the others she had secretly turned face up. She plucked it from the deck and stopped spinning. "You chose the queen of hearts."

"She really is magic," Ralph insisted to the others, pointing at the card.

"She's also the queen of our hearts," Sarah Vasavour said from her place beside Carew.

"No, no, Elizabeth Tudor is the queen of our hearts. I will settle for princess of hearts if you like," Cory laughed, returning Ralph's cards and tousling his hair affectionately. Catching up her big spoon, she poked the apples in the pan. "They're ready," she announced.

"Hurrah," the chorus of voices chimed. As they all dug into the savory fruit stuffed with cinnamon and dripping with melted sugar and butter, another tirewoman slipped in.

"Gert, welcome." Cory put down her spoon as the woman bent over for a swift embrace. "I wasn't sure you would be able to join us. Is Her Majesty asleep?"

"She's abed but complainin' she cannot sleep." Gert sat down and accepted an apple. "But I'm done a-toiling for the night so here I be." She pulled off her shoes and flexed her tired feet.

"Have you any news from Captain Wells about Moll?" Cory asked. As a special friend of the captain's, Gert would be the first to hear.

"That I have not. And I'm right worried about her, my lady," Gert said between bites.

Cory frowned. "Why would she simply leave, without a word to us or her family?"

The company shook their heads in puzzlement as they savored the hot apples.

"I saw her days ago in the green antechamber when I went to fetch milady's fan," Samuel piped up around a mouthful of apple. "The Earl of Essex was trying to kiss her and she was saying nay. They didn't see me, but I saw them. She had to hit him to make him stop."

"The earl is as bold as brass with us maids," Bess agreed, putting down her empty bowl. "And him sweet on Lady Sidney. I say he has his nerve, taking what he wants from poor girls without a by-your-leave but wantin' to wed the noble widow, though he hides it from Her Majesty."

Worried by this, Cory wondered if Essex might be connected to Moll's absence. The earl was known to take his pleasure with comely maids, though she hoped he had not done so with Moll.

A tap sounded at the door and Lord Burghley peered in. "It smells like the Azores in here." Cory reached for a bowl to give him an apple, but he stopped her. "I would love to stay, but 'tis late and I must return to my lady wife in London. I stopped only to say that Her Majesty cannot seem to fall asleep. I believe the French envoy, Monsieur La Faye, has annoyed her now that he's back. He continually begs for funds. I realize 'tis not your night to attend her, but you are so adept at soothing her . . ." He trailed off, his bushy white eyebrows raised in hope. Everyone at court rested more peacefully when the queen was in good humor.

"What a loyal friend you are to Her Majesty, my lord. I am ever amazed to know you have served her faithfully for over thirty years. You are a treasure in her life."

His answering smile was accompanied by a flush of embarrassment, making her wonder if she'd done right to compliment him in company. But heartfelt praise was a scarce commodity at court, where people clawed for advancement and favors, and she decided her praise had not been amiss. Rising, she moved to where she and Burghley could speak in private. "I would happily go to her, but does she not have Essex with her? They were playing cards when I left."

"Nay, they quarreled and Her Majesty sent him away," Burghley said, disapproval of the earl clear on his face. "At times I cannot believe I raised him, Cory. He demands things of the queen, and when she refuses, he grows uncontrollably angry and insults her."

Cory sent him a sympathetic look. "He still wishes to go to France?"

"So he can play soldier in Navarre's bid for the throne," Burghley said. "That was why they quarreled, I suppose. Navarre has Paris under siege, and we cannot help but be affected here."

"I shall attend Her Majesty," Cory hastened to reassure him. "And I shall do what I can to see that La Faye does not annoy her. He is undoubtedly troubled by events at home." She didn't mention that he might also be missing Moll. Though Cory didn't know La Faye well, Moll had hinted that the Frenchman had been especially kind to her. Cory guessed that they were in love.

Burghley saluted her with a grateful expression, and she rushed into her concern about her friend. "My lord, I am worried about Moll Dakins. You probably heard she has disappeared. Now Her Majesty says her family has not heard from her in days. Is there any way we can help Captain Wells look into the matter?"

Burghley looked thoughtful. "The best thing is to let him handle it. He's very capable. But your concern is well taken, Cory. We are all glad you've come to court."

Cory bowed her head in appreciation as the baron left, closing the door behind him. She was glad to help the queen, but she couldn't be glad about being at court as long as it separated her from her family. She missed them so.

But she must shrug off dismal thoughts if she were to survive. Rejoining the group, she held out her hands to her friends. "Come, 'tis time for prayers." They scooted into a circle and followed her through the worship, though smiles hovered on their lips. This was a moment they all liked.

"Thank you, Lord, for your bounty," Cory began, starting them off in their circle of thanks. "I'm thankful for Jane, who made us the special apples, even after she worked hard all day." Pleasure wreathed Jane's face at the compliment. "Carew, what are you grateful for?" Cory asked.

Carew smiled at Sarah, but he knew better than to be grateful for her friendship again. Cory had insisted he extend his thanks in another direction tonight, even as she made certain he had no chance to put his hand up the girl's skirts. "I'm grateful to Cory for talking to my father today. He didn't switch me for ruining Lady Leicester's bumroll." He gave Cory a brief, fierce hug.

"I'm grateful to Samuel for finding my purse," Sarah said. "My father would never have given me another shilling if he'd known I lost it." She leaned over to kiss the lad, who had finished his apple and was nodding sleepily against Cory's knee.

Meeks was next. "I'm grateful for—"

The door swung wide, revealing the white-clad figure of the queen, fists akimbo, her face pale without paint. "What are you doing, Cordelia," she demanded in icy tones, "holding court behind my back. They said you did it as if *you* were queen. I didn't believe them, but here's proof."

"Your Grace, I'm glad you've come." Cory hopped up, hoping her sincerity showed as strongly in her face and voice as she felt it in her heart. This solitary woman must be as lonely as she, for she had no family or close friends. "We have such pleasant times, I wondered if you would consent to join us," she indicated the assembly with a sweep of her hand, "but our company is so modest, I was embarrassed to ask."

Instead of roaring at her, as Cory half expected, the queen seemed shocked speechless. Full of hope, Cory led the queen to the place of honor before the fire.

Silence settled over the company as they waited for the queen's majesty to speak. Elizabeth sank onto the cushion offered, seeming at a loss for words.

"Cory says something special to God 'bout you every night," Samuel piped up drowsily. "Says you're the greatest ruler of England as ever lived."

Elizabeth's expression softened as she fixed her gaze on the sleepy child cuddled against Cory, then surveyed the circle of faces. "Is this true?" she demanded of Carew.

"Absolutely, Your Majesty!" he swore, thumping one hand to his heart.

" 'Tis true," chimed the others.

"Won't you have a delicious baked apple?" Sarah Vasavour handed the queen a bowl. "And you could tell us about the time you made the water clock in Whitehall garden spray the Spanish ambassador. 'Tis ever so funny," she told the others. "Just wait 'til you hear."

The queen's anger vanished. With a grin, she launched into the story. At her imitation of the Spaniard's ire as he was drenched by the surprise spray, Carew rolled on the floor with laughter. The others chuckled with pleasure. The palace clock tower chimed as she ended the tale.

"Half past eleven," Cory announced, rising. "Time for bed, sweet imps." She guided the pages to the queen for a blessing, then shooed them from the room.

Jane gathered the sleeping Samuel in her arms and departed. Cory kissed each of them, then waited as the queen blessed them, which she did with a good will.

She'll sleep better knowing she has friends, Cory thought as the queen preceded her down the corridor to her chambers. As she allowed Cory to tuck her into her great bed, she pronounced Cory's little gathering a rare success.

"We would be honored to have you any time you choose," Cory assured her. But as she sought her bed in the maid's dormitory, she worried about Moll. First her friend disappeared. Then the crossbow was fired on the Thames. It gave her the frightening sense that something serious was wrong at court, and she had little idea what it could be.

The boots must go. His associate would hate to give them up. They were his best, worn as they were. But the baron had gone back to the river to study the prints. His associate had reported seeing him leave the palace and had followed at a healthy distance, relying on the thick trees and shrubbery to hide him. His error had been stepping on a branch, but his agility at climbing trees had saved him. His green doublet had blended with the leaves.

But the boots must go. No question remained in his mind after hearing that the baron had measured the footprints and traced their shape on paper. Cavandish knew enough about footprints to find the person who had worn them.

One trouble after another was making a simple matter complicated. It was a nuisance after things had gone so well. If he succeeded with his plans, he could rise to heights beyond his wildest dreams. But he must not let an error by an associate expose him.

He would insist that the boots disappear forever. Tonight.

Chapter 9

"My lord baron, the queen is with the Earl of Essex. She asks that you wait." The maid of honor on door duty with the palace guard that evening made eyes at Matthew, inviting him to flirt.

In no mood to be badgered by another husband hunter, he crossed to the window and turned his back to her. He hated waiting for the queen's pleasure.

Sir Walter Raleigh swaggered up, wearing a magnificent pearl-studded doublet. "Heard the news, Graystock?" he asked. "The queen will give the French envoy a magnificent gift for King Henri of Navarre at her coming reception."

"The devil she will." Essex pushed through the door from the privy chamber. "I will personally present any gift to Navarre when I go to France. How did this rumor start?"

Raleigh raked Essex with an arrogant gaze. "I thought you started it."

"Not I," Essex snapped. "Cease spreading nonsense at once." He glared at his chief competition for the queen's favor. "I cannot fathom how Her Majesty tolerates riffraff at court." With a sniff in Raleigh's direction that included Matthew in the insult, he stalked away.

Raleigh smirked and swept off in the opposite direction. Matthew plodded into the privy chamber to answer the queen's latest summons. Elizabeth sat in a pool of candlelight, dressed in a glittering costume of silver and white. He bowed over her hand.

"I have scant time before my revel begins, Graystock. Let us dispatch our business with speed." Elizabeth waved her white plumed fan languidly. "Have you a vizard for tonight's entertainment?" She pointed to her own jeweled mask on a table.

Matthew scowled. He already wore a black velvet doublet that was so tight it reminded him of the doublets he'd hated wearing to his father's revels as a child. "I have not the time to play games, Your Grace. I spent the day working on my ships."

Elizabeth rolled her eyes heavenward. "Very well, Graystock, I'll come to the point. I wish you to wed again. I've chosen a well-born, wealthy girl for you. You will have no complaints."

He tensed. First Hugh, now the queen brought up the abhorrent subject of marriage, and her interest in the subject would be far harder to ignore than Hugh's. "Your Grace, I do not wish to wed again," he said firmly. "Since Joanna—"

"Since your first wife died, you've been charging around the world like an old fool. And you're not that old."

"I don't charge around—"

"Don't argue with me, Graystock. Do you ever look at a woman these days?"

"None save Your Grace." He congratulated himself on giving the right response for once.

"You're a poor liar, Graystock," she harrumphed, seeming to see through his flattery. "Never mind. Marry this girl. She'll bring you enough gold to finance your next voyage."

Her statement drew him up short. "What of the funds you promised?"

"I cannot give you the four thousand pounds we discussed," she said succinctly.

Dismay settled on him. He couldn't sail without the queen's backing. His share of the recent voyage's profits covered only part of the expenses of the next voyage. Without ready gold, he had only his income from Graystock Manor, but that was Carew's inheritance, and just now, those funds were reserved for repairing the house and reclaiming the land.

Without ready gold, he would be trapped in England, and soon winter would come. He would be locked in the jaws of cold weather and even colder memories. "Your Majesty, if I were to—"

"If you were to wed this girl, your problems would be solved."

Matthew deliberately relaxed his jaw to avoid grinding his teeth. He'd come here expecting to be grilled about his investigation of the murder attempt. Instead, the queen withdrew her pledge and offered him some woman's money instead. He refused to stoop to such tactics.

He groped for other financing possibilities. He had several sponsors, but they were putting up small amounts. Nothing like four thousand pounds. Jonathan would loan him part of the money, but his brother was in France, and Matthew wouldn't dream of troubling his sister-in-law, who was with child again. He could ask his eldest sister, Rozalinde, to advance his annual payment from the family business, but she wouldn't give him a shilling if she knew it was for a voyage. She would favor the queen's proposal, say he should marry and stay home, as she always did. Devil take it, what was he to do?

"My lord, are you chasing phantasms?" Elizabeth called him sharply back to attention. "I said the girl I have chosen is highly beddable."

"I wouldn't wed her for that reason," he snarled, annoyed that she should think he would. And he didn't want to get married. Since Elizabeth knew it, and since she was generally pleased if her male courtiers remained unwed, he smelled an ulterior motive.

"*Almost* everyone at court likes her," the queen continued. "I've told her to meet me in the green antechamber immediately after the masque. You will be there instead. Ask her to wed."

Almost everyone liked her? That didn't sound promising. "Haven't you told her your plan?"

The queen looked marginally uncomfortable. "You must woo her until she says yes."

What the devil? Why should he? "Your Majesty, even if I agreed to wed her, which I haven't, why should I woo her? I don't even know the girl."

"If you don't sweep her off her feet, she'll talk her way around it," Elizabeth stated. "As she does everything. I can't afford that."

Suspicion wiggled in his mind like a worm. If the girl could talk the queen out of things, she would be headstrong like his sisters, an unpleasant prospect. "You cannot afford it? Why not?"

Elizabeth looked him in the eye as she fanned herself with a calm, steady hand. "Her father-in-law requested my assistance in finding her a husband. I agreed."

"He paid you to marry her off," he said flatly, disgusted that the man would do such a thing, though he knew it happened all the time.

Elizabeth lifted her chin with a regal air. "I needed the gold to pay Sir Roger Williams, whose troops aid Navarre, so I . . . Bah, I'll not explain to you. Do as I say. Wed the wench. Then I want her to remove the annoying Monsieur La Faye to your estate at Graystock. He drives me mad with his incessant demands for men and funds. I've done all I can to put Navarre on the throne and still he makes no progress. He's had Paris under siege since May, but the city shows no sign of relenting. Come to that, mayhap you should go to France to help your brother."

He stiffened as Elizabeth cast a new issue into the confusing medley. With Jonathan serving as the queen's chief spymaster on the continent, his safety was always a source of family concern. "Are things going wrong in France?" he demanded. "Have you heard from Jonathan?"

"I fear your brother is taking undue risks. I have heard nothing from him for some while, but his last dispatch suggested he meant to enter the besieged city itself."

Damnation. Why would Jonathan enter a besieged city? Matthew resolved to send a message to his brother as soon as the annoying masque was over. His sister-in-law must be half-mad with worry, expecting another child and her husband on dangerous intelligence missions.

"She has an excellent widow's jointure." The queen's words intruded on his thoughts. "You could sell some of her land to raise the money you want."

Matthew forced his mind back to the subject at hand. "She has what?"

"I said she is a widow." Elizabeth raised her voice. "For a number of years, though she's younger than you. Are you not attending, sir? We are speaking of your marriage."

Unfortunately, he'd heard far more than he wished. "Is this marriage an order or a suggestion, Your Grace?"

The queen frowned, her lips pursed. "I suppose 'tis a suggestion," she barked at last.

Matthew wanted to roar at her. "I'll not wed some woman solely for her money," he snapped.

"Very well, my lord. But don't you want to know whom I had in mind for you?" Elizabeth cast him a coy glance.

He sighed. She could not tempt him. She ought to know it, but he supposed he must play her game. "Whom did you have in mind, Majesty?"

"Cordelia Hailsworthy, Viscountess Wentworth."

Titania? She wanted him to wed the queen of the fairies?

A torrent of desire struck his loins like lightning, and he flinched, despite his attempt to suppress it. By Neptune, the queen would put him in bed with the woman who aroused him, worried him, and made him furious all at once. He would be mad to agree. Added to that, the Earl of Whitby kept her widow's jointure for his own purposes, parted her from her children, and paid the queen to marry her off. To wed her solely for her money, then sink it into his ships, would put him in the same league with the abusive earl.

And what of Essex? The earl would be out for his blood, not that the idea frightened him, but it could become awkward if he were challenged to duels all the time.

"Your Grace, it is impossible." He groped for a reason and found one that sounded fairly rational. "Marriage is supposed to be a loving state, and we are not in love."

"You are the last man I expected to hear say that, Graystock." The queen regarded him in perplexity. "You've never mentioned the word before. I didn't think you knew what it meant."

"I had love in my marriage, as did my father and mother."

Elizabeth looked unsympathetic. "Very well, Baron. I'll find someone else to wed her. He can ensure she isn't shot at again."

The threat against the viscountess's life returned to trouble him. "You might have difficulty finding a man to meet the qualification, Your Grace. Someone who agrees to marry her might not be adept at keeping her safe. We still don't know why she was shot at." And she might object to being sold off, he thought. "How much did the Earl of Whitby give you to see her wed?"

"If you're thinking to pay him back on her behalf, you will have some difficulty. He gave the treasury five thousand pounds in gold."

He couldn't possibly raise such a sum quickly. Even Rozalinde, as head of the family business, didn't have that much ready gold. "I cannot manage it," he agreed, wondering why he'd even thought to try.

"Very well." She clapped her hands.

The guard opened the chamber door and bowed deeply from the waist. "Your Grace?"

"Baron Graystock is departing. Pray send in Sir Christopher Hatton."

Matthew backed toward the door as Elizabeth tapped her chin with one finger. "I must see who else I can tempt with the viscountess," she said, as if thinking aloud. "Perhaps Sir Francis Knollys. I'll have *him* meet her in the green antechamber tonight."

Matthew halted. "Not Sir Francis," he interrupted. The idea of Viscountess Wentworth in the arms of the balding, rotund Sir Francis made him ill. And the man was one of his suspects.

"Oh, you're still here, Baron?" Elizabeth pretended to have thought him gone. "Why should I not wed her to Sir Francis? Since you've declined the honor, 'tis not your affair."

"No!" he barked, aware that he sounded irrational and not caring. "It's not safe. Not yet."

Elizabeth narrowed her eyes. "Don't tell me you suspect . . ."

"I don't know, Majesty, but I ask you to wait." He had already inspected Lord Burghley's boots by Howe and found them in perfect order, as he had thought they would be. But three pairs remained to inspect before he would know anything for certain. And as long as he had to attend the queen's time-wasting revel, the important task must be postponed.

She seemed content with his answer. "I shall have her meet someone else in the green antechamber. And I expect to hear your report as soon as possible. Enjoy the revel, Baron."

"Little chance of that," he muttered, backing away again.

"Well, give it your best effort," Elizabeth called after him, her sarcasm biting. "Your reputation as a dashing adventurer will surely sweep all the ladies present off their feet. Don't think I haven't noticed how my maids of honor swoon when you appear."

He stopped in the doorway. "I don't enjoy their attentions, madam," he said with complete sincerity. "I would rather sit quietly by your side than be troubled by their nonsense."

Elizabeth nodded with approval. "Very good, Graystock. For your gallantry, I shall save you a dance tonight. 'Twill make Essex furious, but you have earned my favor."

She stuck out one hand and waved it at him to kiss, and he had to trudge all the way back into the chamber to kneel before her. She really did go too far, he thought as he honored her slim fingers, setting him up in a senseless competition with the young earl. She was playing with the Viscountess Wentworth's future as well. "You don't care if the viscountess is happy, do you?" he demanded, then realized he'd been too blunt, as usual.

"Why should anyone have better than I?" Her approving gaze changed swiftly to displeasure.

Her pain spoke to him, and he suddenly understood her as never before. Despite her sparkling finery that marked her as a queen, despite over thirty years as a powerful sovereign, she had never enjoyed an open, loving relationship with a single family member, let alone a man.

Little wonder she hated her maids or gentlemen to wed unless she had a specific reason of her own for forcing a marriage. If she couldn't have love, why should anyone else? In his loveless state, he understood her loneliness, but not her desire to take it out on others.

He supposed that was because he'd been more fortunate than she. He'd enjoyed a mutual love with a woman once in his life. That memory would sustain him in the years to come. It had to. He bowed stiffly. "God'den, Your Grace."

"God'den, sir." Elizabeth clapped her hands, and the guard, who had retreated as their discourse continued, reappeared.

Matthew backed out of the chamber, a black mood settling on him. The queen's needs would be met if she found the viscountess a husband, but what of the viscountess?

He would have to warn her. It would give her time to make plans, to flee court, if necessary. Hadn't the maid of honor said the viscountess had sworn never to wed again?

But what would he tell her? If he explained that the queen

wanted her to marry, he would have to hide the reason, that her father-in-law had paid the queen to find her a husband, and he was a terrible liar, as Elizabeth had pointed out. Confound it, why must the viscountess's difficulties be his affair?

But the image of her hugging Carew that night on the Thames reminded him why. Her kindness and caring for others must not go unrewarded.

That image led to another—of Titania, rising half naked from the water. It would take a supreme act of will not to touch her again. He'd had a hard time restraining himself when they first met, as well as on board his ship.

He frowned as he thought of a particular courtesan he usually sought when he gave his men shore leave in the Caribbean. He needed to visit that woman now, but she was half a world away.

Too bad, he mocked himself as he approached the great chamber where throngs of people gathered for the queen's entertainment. He would have to wait until his next voyage. He would warn the viscountess of the queen's plans for her, discuss with her the shooting incident as he investigated the attempted murder, but otherwise leave her alone.

He strode into the great chamber, feeling grimmer than he'd felt in years.

Chapter 10

In the great presence chamber of Hampton Court, Cordelia dipped a curtsy to another maid of honor and glided in time to the music, her white silk gown rustling with satisfying richness. She held her brass lamp high so its light glittered on the spangles of her gown. Carew's money had been spent on this lavish creation. As it was too late to unspend it, she would enjoy herself.

She had never seen a court masque, let alone performed in one. Its music, poetry, and dances directed by the master of the revels entranced her. As she drew back with her partner, the queen appeared and moved to the center of her maids, a vision of white and silver like the dazzling moon. Applause burst from the audience gathered for the entertainment.

As the crowd expressed its appreciation, Cory spied five young imps, Carew among them, watching her from the gallery. They were supposed to be abed, the rascals. Carew's father hadn't given him permission, nor would the pages' masters and mistresses approve.

She curtsied to her partner, Ann, whose headdress of silver stars teetered as she moved. Cory's own headdress felt as if it were crushing her forehead, but she danced on. The queen had personally rehearsed them for this event. She didn't want to make an error.

The queen appeared girlishly slender in her sparkling gown.

Gauzy veils floated from her headdress, and her lace ruff gleamed, as if studded with stars. The dim light softened her features, so that she appeared young and lovely. As Cory advanced and performed the required figure with the queen, a male performer sang of Diana, Queen of the Hunt, whose symbol was the moon.

"I wish to see you in the green antechamber after the masque," Elizabeth instructed under cover of the singing. She moved on to the next lady in the dance without another word.

Wanted to see her? What about? Cory wondered as the masque ended. The queen accepted the applause as Cory and the others hovered in the background. Male courtiers outnumbered female, she noted as she quit the floor. Elizabeth liked court entertainments to focus on her. The men would vie for the right to partner her in a dance, to bring her dainties from the refreshment table. Essex bowed over her hand as Sir Walter Raleigh glared, waiting his chance to approach.

If Elizabeth was being courted by her nobles, how would she join Cory in the green antechamber? Why did she even want to at a time like this?

As Cory entered the darkened corridor, holding her heavy headdress before her, she bumped into a masked man. "Oh, Sir William, your pardon."

"How do you know 'tis Sir William?" the knight asked in a flirtatious tone, catching her around the waist and delivering a caress.

She wiggled away, pretending the awkward headdress prevented her from remaining in his arms. She would know him anywhere, with his Adam's apple jutting out between his ruff and his sharp little beard. "You have such a distinctive voice," she said.

"But I hadn't said a word," he protested.

"You're so distinctive, you didn't have to," she assured him. And so annoying, grabbing her whenever he had a chance. Thrice he had invited her to bed, unwilling to accept her firm refusals.

"How good to know you think so," Sir William Norris crooned, entirely missing the veiled dislike in her voice. He removed his mask and grinned at her. "And so timely, as we have an important matter to discuss." He reached for her again, and

Cory backed away, moving down the corridor toward the green antechamber.

As she glanced over her shoulder, hoping the queen would arrive to save her, she saw a lad approach from the opposite direction. Could it be Carew?

Aware that Sir William had drawn closer, she turned back and was unnerved by the amorous glint in his eyes. "I-I don't know what you mean by something important," she stammered, still retreating. "Carew, is that you?" she called, raising her voice. But another glance over her shoulder showed an empty corridor. As she retreated, her foot caught in her voluminous skirts. She tripped and staggered against the wall.

Sir William seized her and plastered her to his chest, headdress and all. "Of course you do. Weren't you to meet someone in the green antechamber, my sweet?"

"I was to meet Her Majesty." Cory struggled to escape, but his hands tightened on her. Impeded by the awkward headdress, she couldn't push him away. By fortune, his breath stank of wine. He must be tipsy.

He grinned at her with what she guessed was intoxication. "I know a good many things, Cordelia," he drawled. "I know you are the most beautiful lady I have ever seen."

His lips descended toward hers, and she strained backward, desperate to escape. He had never called her by her first name, and she took it as a bad sign. Something had happened she didn't know about. "Sir William, stop at once," she cried in as commanding a tone as she could.

He straightened, displeasure clouding his face, though he did not loosen his hold. " 'Tis a mere kiss, Cordelia. A prelude to sweeter things to come between us."

"You are mistaken, sir. There is nothing between us. Just now, I do not even find your company enjoyable."

"But did the queen not speak to you?" He refused to relinquish his grasp. "She said that if I met you in the green antechamber after the masque, you might agree to wed."

Wed? In her dismay, she forgot to strain away from his embrace.

He took advantage of her lowered guard, angling her in his arms for another attack on her lips. "You need a husband, Cordelia, to keep you out of trouble."

"I'm not in trouble," she protested, leaning backward as far as she could, "unless you refer to the man who shot at me the other night."

"Yes." Sir William beamed, as if delighted to be reminded. "You require a man to protect you *and* to keep you out of trouble. Come, do not pretend," he continued as she shook her head in perplexity. "I heard that the queen reprimanded you for teaching the palace children to cheat at cards. How many games with adults have you won with your tricks?" His loose-lipped smile widened as he chucked her under the chin. "I shall have to keep my mouth shut, my pretty one, else we'll have people beating down our door, wanting their money back. But have no fear. Once we're wed, I shall be as silent about it as the grave." He bent to claim a kiss.

Outraged, Cory shoved at him with all her strength. How dare the worm accuse her of cheating, then suggest she marry him in exchange for his silence. It was blackmail. She shoved even harder, and he stumbled back, releasing his grip. "I did not teach them to cheat," she insisted, vexed nearly to tears. "Nor do I cheat when I play."

With a huff, she prepared to stalk away, but he recovered and lunged for her, capturing her around the waist again.

"Release the lady, Sir William," a deep male voice interrupted.

Sir William froze as he gazed at someone behind her. An icy expression formed on his plump face. "Baron Graystock, this is none of your affair."

Cory froze, embarrassed to be found in Sir William's arms. The black-clad baron strolled into view, hands tucked behind his back, an insolent look on his face. "I believe the viscountess does not relish your embrace, sir," he said, all sardonic humor. "Has she refused your offer to wed?"

Sir William turned as red as the queen's cochineal-dyed petticoat. "Be gone, sir," he spluttered. "This is a matter between Cordelia and me." His hold on her loosened.

Cory broke away and retreated to a safe distance where she could stare at the baron. How did he know what had just transpired?

But the baron was not done. He glanced up and down the corridor, as if perplexed. "Good Sir William, you order me to be gone, but this does not seem to be your private chamber. Do you have the royal authority to clear this public place? If so, the viscountess will be the first to oblige. My dear," he swept her a mocking bow, "how is it I am compelled to rescue you again? Does trouble know you by your first name?"

Not waiting for a second invitation, Cory picked up her skirts and dashed for the green antechamber, more than glad to escape. By fortune, Sir William was offensive, but Baron Graystock was insultingly sarcastic. Glad as she was to see the knight's dignity chopped into small pieces, she hadn't expected the baron to turn on her. She felt as if she had just been accused of robbery on the great highway.

Appalled by the entire encounter, she flounced into the darkened chamber and dropped into a deep chair, wanting to hide. Horrors, what a night. If only the queen would come, as she'd said she would, Cory could explain she didn't want to wed anyone. Certainly not the repellent Sir William. But apparently Elizabeth had sent him to meet her. Or had he made that up?

A soft footfall warned her that she had company. Twisting in her seat, she saw the baron had joined her. He stood before the partially draped oriel window, his silhouette washed by moonlight. It illuminated the way his wide-muscled shoulders and broad back narrowed to a trim waist. His lithe, long legs were defined by tight stocks and canons molded to hard thighs. She wanted to sigh with the pleasure of gazing at him, but she knew her enjoyment wouldn't last. Her pirate would disappear the minute he spoke, leaving only crotchety, sarcastic Baron Graystock.

It wasn't fair. How could a man look so right but be so wrong? Her heart contracted with longing as she set down her headdress and glided toward him, filled with an impossible desire. She owed him her thanks for driving away Sir William. She *would* thank him.

Swept away by impulse, she slid both arms around his waist and hugged him to her, her cheek against his velvet doublet, so soft and warm. He felt like the stuff of her dreams, a man worthy of her trust, with whom she could create a golden circle of love.

Of course he wasn't. But she would touch him anyway, feel his strength, if only for a moment, before words changed him back to who he really was.

He turned slowly to take her in his arms, and she met his molasses-dark gaze. Stretching on tiptoe, she touched her lips to his. His strength enveloped her as he met her kiss with a sudden surge of eagerness. She gasped in surprise as he gripped her the same way Sir William had, but harder. And with a more masterful touch. A thrill spun through her as he explored her mouth with expert attention, his tongue slipping between her lips.

By sweet fortune, was this what a kiss should be? A dizzying sensation swept away reason, and her knees grew wobbly as her breasts tingled, crushed against his chest. She felt a sudden joy and power, as if she had just drawn a winning card in a high-stakes game.

Sinful. How could she feel this way with a man who was all wrong for her? A man whose only interest in her was lust? Carew's father had no warmth in him. Yet this was more than mere warmth. It was something she'd only heard tales of . . . it was sin. For some foolish reason, Baron Graystock made her want to sin.

Dangerous. She had never been kissed like this before. A hot sensation coiled in the pit of her belly, spreading lower as the baron kissed her harder, his hands like searing brands on her back. His tongue taught hers a dance that sent sparks of delight coursing through her blood.

Who would have thought it? The man least likely to be of interest made her want to sin.

As Cordelia's lips meshed with his, Matthew's senses reeled. He'd followed the viscountess into the green antechamber to do an unpleasant duty, to tell her the queen's wish that she wed. He'd been welcomed with unexpected kisses. How could he turn away the warmth of her lithe body clad in white and silver gossamer? Titania's ardor seemed to shimmer like the glittering water drops from their night on the Thames. No doubt it would flow away, just as water did, when he told her the bad news, but for now, he would enjoy his lust.

For it *was* lust. He recognized the devil run rampant in him. He'd avoided decent women because of the temptation they represented, but when Cordelia had brushed her lips against his, he found he couldn't stop. The feel of her, soft and willing in his arms, was like a dark gift. Ignited by the shudder betraying her excitement, he ground his hips to hers, letting her feel his need.

She didn't flinch or draw away. Instead, to his satisfaction, her lips softened beneath his. Her body melded to him, as if she were compelled by needs of her own.

A creak sounded from the corridor.

She shrank against him. "The queen is coming! She told me to meet her here."

"She isn't coming." He knew full well Elizabeth had sent Sir William to woo her. Now he had to tell her why, though he would rather push up her skirts and forget all his problems by driving into her lush, feminine warmth.

That was nonsense. He couldn't make love to this woman. She was being ill treated by her father-in-law and the queen. He wouldn't add to it.

Have her anyway, his body clamored, demanding release. Brushing the tender nape of her neck with one hand, he bent to explore its softness with his lips.

"I wish you hadn't shaved your beard," she murmured as he worked around her throat, trailing kisses up the line of her jaw.

"The queen doesn't like it." He kissed her ear.

She giggled and slipped her small hands around his neck, drawing him about to face her. "I loved your beard." She ran her fingertips lightly down his clean-shaven cheek.

He shuddered, his physical reaction to her touch extreme and unexpected. "Why?" he managed to ask, restraining the urge to kiss her again. "Court fashion is for neatly trimmed beards or no beard at all."

"But you're an adventurer." Her lips, which he now knew were silky smooth, curved in a hint of a smile as she said the word *adventurer* with the reverence reserved for gods. "I see you on your ship, sailing wild and free with the wind. It must be wonderful. I would love to sail away like that."

"You would?" She astonished him. Women didn't like such things, except for his sister Rozalinde, who was ambitious and impossible when she got an idea into her head. She could also be loving and tender, but she was stubborn and uncooperative if things didn't suit her. Her husband bowed to her wishes so often, it shocked him. He had loved how Joanna had been the exact opposite of Rozalinde.

"I sailed to France once with my father." Cordelia seemed unaware of his surprise and disapproval, her eyes dreamy with her vision of adventure. "It was wonderful! I wasn't ill from the ship's motion for an instant. I know I could sail to the wonderful places you've been. Is it true, there is never snow or winter in the Caribbean? That they have fruit all year round and palm trees grow wild?" At his nod, she sighed deeply. "Is there one place you especially love?"

"There's a deserted island off the shore of America," he admitted. "It's a tropical paradise."

"I should love to see such a place at least once in my life."

The heat of her zeal captured his interest. He had a sudden image of the two of them, naked on crisp white bed linens, making love in the tropical warmth. Would she reach fulfillment as quickly and freely as she contradicted him, with unchecked passion flashing in her eyes?

What a dangerous thought. "Do you know why Sir William came to meet you, Viscountess?" It was time to break off this foolishness and get to business.

He felt her breathy scoff close to his neck. "No, why? For a jest? And please call me Cordelia. Viscountess seems too formal now, don't you think?"

He ought to remain formal with her. He needed a barrier to check his desire. "No jest," he said briskly, knowing the hated moment had come. "The queen wants you to wed and feels he will do."

A shiver ran through her body, and she sagged against him in seeming defeat. "Oh, no," she moaned. "Not that."

He tightened his grip on her silk-covered waist, meaning to support her. Yet the yield of her warm flesh beneath the fabric made him want something more. "You didn't know?" he asked quietly, groping for his self-control like a sword.

"No." She straightened, moving her hands to his shoulders as she searched his face. "Why would she do that? I thought the queen hated her attendants to wed. I would be content to remain single forever in order to serve her."

Words failed him. What could he tell her? "It seems that your situation is different. It seems . . ." He halted, at a loss.

"Yes? It seems . . ." she prompted.

He stared into her wide, limpid eyes, their green so poignant, reminding him of spring and new beginnings. But there was no new beginning for her. Once again, she was being used by people who had no concern for her needs or feelings. "It seems that your father-in-law paid her to . . ."

She jerked back, her eyes wide with horror. "Lord Whitby?

He paid the queen to marry me off? No!" she gasped. "How could he? That's horrible."

"I'm sorry, but I thought I should warn you." He berated himself as her eyes clouded with tears. He'd blurted it out like a brute, and she was devastated, just as he'd feared.

She groped her way to the chair, as if blinded by the horrible news. Dropping into the seat, she buried her face in both hands. Her slim back and graceful shoulders shook as she wept. Suddenly he remembered how, when he'd been ten, his little sister Lucina had stubbed her bare toe on a rock and come crying to him. It had been years ago, but he knew what he'd done. The question was, should he do it now? He didn't trust himself to touch Cordelia.

Her devastation decided him. Her father-in-law's betrayal must be a terrible blow. Personally, he would like to skewer the bastard. Kneeling by her chair, he cradled her in his arms. She buried her face in his doublet and wept.

"There, there," he soothed, wondering how he'd come so far since the night by the Thames. The hardened warrior who hadn't comforted anyone for years wasn't doing too badly. He felt awkward and at a loss for words, but he knew, if he let himself think about it, that physical closeness could comfort. He just hadn't for years.

Drawing her to her feet, he sat on the chair and settled her into his lap. As docile as a child, she sobbed against his shoulder while he rocked her and murmured soothing nonsense.

"I still can't believe it." She hiccuped, then excused herself, one hand to her mouth in an endearing gesture. "I thought I was safe from his attempts to marry me off when I came here. Being wed to Thomas was so terrible, I hoped I should never have to marry again."

"I'm so sorry." He wished he knew some way to help her.

"I was only thirteen when Thomas tried to bed me," she choked through a new rush of tears. "Everyone knows that's too young to bear a child. His father ordered him to wait until we were seventeen, but he wouldn't. Whenever the earl wasn't looking, Thomas badgered me. Soon, he was trying to force me. He behaved more like a spoiled child than a viscount, never caring what was best for me. He wanted what he wanted."

"It must have been horrible for you."

"It was. We lived in the same household from the time . . ." She broke off and made a valiant effort to choke back her tears. "From the time my mother died. My father died a year later. I couldn't escape Thomas, so I did a hundred things to make him leave me alone. I kicked him in the shins when he tried to kiss me. I ran away into the woods and climbed the highest tree where he couldn't follow. I even put an icicle down his doublet once when he wouldn't let me go."

"You are to be congratulated on your inventiveness. He sounds quite persistent." She rewarded his comment with a lopsided half-smile, and he realized he was somehow finding the right words. They even seemed to be helping.

She straightened on his lap and took the handkerchief he offered. "I held firm, and he eventually gave up. Except if he couldn't have what he wanted of me, he would have it with other females. Anyone would do."

She blew her nose as he rubbed her back.

"You're terribly patient to listen to this nonsense, er . . ." She removed the handkerchief from her face and gazed at him. "I just realized I don't know your Christian name. What is it?"

"Matthew." He stilled in anticipation, waiting to hear his name on her lips for the first time.

"Thank you, Matthew." Her heartfelt tone touched him to the core. "I've never spoken to anyone of Thomas save Grandmama." She laughed wryly. "You've been so kind, I forgot that Carew says you're an old dragon who breathes fire. Although you *are* nasty tempered at times. But other times, I find it hard to believe you are his father. You kiss well, too. It doesn't fit."

He winced at her candor and odd logic. Other females swooned over his romantic reputation as a brave adventurer who had journeyed to exotic lands and brought home wondrous treasures. But she thought of him first as Carew's father, an area where his achievements were naught to brag of. It was the damnest relationship he'd ever been in. One minute he was lusting for her, the next he was comforting her as if she were Lucina at age four. And the hell of it was, he never stopped wanting to kiss her.

As if reading his thoughts, she lifted her head. "You know, I've never been kissed like that. I didn't know it could feel so lovely. You are very expert."

He snorted, hardly able to endure the strange compliment. Nor could he bear to bring up the fact that he'd seen her kissing Essex. Did her comment on his expertise mean she didn't love the earl? Or did Essex not kiss as well? "Let me know if you would like lessons," he said, seeking shelter in sarcasm rather than confront the issue. Hell, he didn't want to know where Essex fit in this uncomfortable equation.

She laughed a bit shakily. "Yes, well, now I understand why Thomas used sex to salve his wounds. His father wasn't exactly loving. His mother was dead. His grandmother would have loved him, but he was a bully at an early age and wouldn't let her. So he had sex instead. Oh, dear, what am I saying." She covered her mouth with her hand and offered an apologetic glance. "I don't mean that you're like Thomas."

So she thought of his kiss as sex to salve her wounds? He disliked the idea, but wasn't that what he was doing? If *he* did, why shouldn't she as well? "Be sure to let me know when you want some of my special salve, my lady. I'll be glad to oblige." He deepened his sarcasm since she'd missed it the first time.

"You see, there you go." She wrinkled her nose at him. "You can be quite horrid at times, Matthew. Just like Thomas."

"Only in words, not in deeds, like him." He was irked she should even consider comparing him to her husband. "Shall I say that I'm at your disposal? My lady's slave, willing to console her as required?"

"That sounds lascivious." She gazed at him reproachfully.

"It is. You inspire lascivious impulses in me."

"You're jesting again." She laughed nervously and glanced away.

"I am not jesting. It makes no sense, but there it is. Of course I will not give in to the impulse again, but I thought I should explain." He meant it too. He must not take advantage of her. It was bad enough that Essex and Norris appeared willing to do so.

"If you're not jesting, I thank you," she said primly, straightening her back. "But I agree we'd best not act on it. A simple pat on the shoulder must suffice after this."

If it was going to suffice, he needed to get her off his lap fast. It was all he could do to hold himself in check. Tonight, he had no illusions that she was a fairy queen. Touch told him she was flesh and blood. "Let me make a suggestion," he said, determined to be diplomatic. "As the queen insists you marry, tell her you are willing to entertain her recommendations while you look around. That would be better than having to accept whoever she thrusts at you. I'll send some prospects your way," he added, remembering that someone must guide her away from Essex.

"Truly?" She narrowed her eyes at him as if a new thought had occurred to her. "How is it that you are the queen's confidante on the subject of my marriage?"

"We were discussing the need to find the person who shot at you. This came up. You were in danger the other night. Danger may follow you even now."

She raised her eyebrows in surprise. "I didn't think I was in danger inside the palace. Only if I walked out alone."

He breathed with relief as she seemed to accept his explanation and let him change the subject. She would never guess the queen had first proposed him as her husband. "That may be the case. We cannot know for sure."

"Do you think I could find an acceptable husband?" she asked, brightening as she returned to the subject. But she immediately became gloomy again. "If you help me, what can I do for you in return? All I know how to do is perform card tricks and darn netherstocks."

You can kiss me again, he wanted to shout. His loins were on fire with need for her. "You can help me with Carew," he said instead, though he wanted to bite his tongue the instant the words were out. He resented the way his son trusted her more than him, yet he was going to need help soon. "Lady Russell wishes to return home to Dorset, and whenever I leave him, he gets into mischief. Even with her present, today he stole and ate a whole lamb pie meant for the queen's dinner. Just after he'd had his own dinner, too."

"He is a handful," she agreed.

It was hard to admit he needed assistance, especially to her. Yet he could think of no one else at the palace his son would obey. From Lady Russell's accounts, he had been a terror their first week at court until the viscountess took him in hand. Since the widow didn't have her own children to look after, and since Carew liked her so well, it seemed logical to ask for her help. Plus he needed to keep both her and Carew out of his investigations. "Yes," he admitted with reluctance. "I cannot be with him all the time."

"In truth? You'll let me help with Carew?" Her face lit up as if a dozen candles glowed beneath her creamy skin. "Oh, thank you." She clasped him to her in an exuberant embrace.

The self-control he'd worked so hard to build crumbled. By heaven, he couldn't take this. Seizing her chin, he crushed her lips beneath his. She yielded, seeming overcome with surprise that quickly changed to ardor.

Inflamed from having her on his lap so long, he savored her kiss as he loosened her bodice. Her flesh was silky smooth as his fingers burrowed beneath layers of brocade and linen to find her breast. The soft nipple hardened as he touched it, and he dropped down to nuzzle her throat. Her pulse fluttered beneath her white flesh, setting his blood humming in response.

"We aren't supposed to do this," she murmured between kisses, sounding awed that they were.

"Mmm." His animal instincts drove him to plunder her mouth, his tongue flicking into her depths to taste her sweetness. She was as rich and welcoming as frothy cream. His blood heated.

She leaned away, breaking the kiss. "Then why are we?" she panted, clearly as aroused as he.

"Can you stop now?" he growled, bending to taste her throat. "I can't."

"Nor I," she breathed, tilting back her head, gasping as he nuzzled the loosened fabric at her breast. "Not yet. In a few minutes, perhaps."

A crash of breaking pottery shattered the silence of the room.

Cordelia vaulted from his arms, clutching her drooping bodice, as a writhing figure wrapped in a window drapery hurtled to the floor.

Shocked out of his lust, Matthew leaped to his feet, his dagger drawn, prepared for foul play. But as he studied the size of the figure fighting its way from beneath the drapery, he had a sudden, unpleasant notion of who it was. "Carew," he barked, infuriated. "Is that you? Are you hurt?"

A head poked out from the burgundy drapery. "I meant no

harm, Father. I wanted to know if Cory would be my new mama."

Footsteps sounded in the corridor. The master of the revels peered around the door, holding a lamp in one hand. "Is anyone hurt? That was quite a crash."

"No one is hurt," Matthew said stonily, mortified by the destruction Carew had wrought. "My son broke something. Pray tell Her Majesty I shall see it replaced."

The master examined the scattered fragments. "I believe 'twas a gift from the Spanish ambassador. Her Majesty said it was so ugly, it gave her nightmares. She won't mind." He said good night and left, a twinkle in his eye, as if he understood all that had transpired in the chamber.

Carew had crawled out from under the drapery during the exchange and inched away. Cordelia stood, stunned, her back to the door.

"Carew, don't think you will escape punishment for this prank," Matthew warned, incensed that his son had watched him fondle Cordelia. Good Lord, he'd almost undressed her. His thirteen-year-old son had heard him say he wanted to do lascivious things with her, had seen him kissing her breast. He wanted to shout with rage.

"Don't be cross." Cordelia suddenly came to life. "He only wants to know your intentions. I'm sorry, Carew. I'm not going to be your mama. But I am your friend."

"No?" The disappointment in Carew's voice was palpable. "But you were kissing and doing things Father says *I* mustn't do. Don't people who do them have to get married?"

"Not necessarily," Cordelia began.

"Stop this at once!" Matthew shouted, mortified that she was answering Carew's impertinent questions so patiently. "You are encouraging him to pry, madam. He'll learn nothing of good behavior or obedience if you do that."

Her smooth brow creased with displeasure. "You *are* a nasty old dragon after all, Matthew Cavandish. Why? You needn't be."

"Eavesdropping is wrong, and he *must* learn right from wrong," he snarled, barely able to contain his anger at her lack of understanding.

"Uncle Jonathan eavesdrops all the time," Carew protested, still inching toward the door.

"Your uncle works for the queen obtaining secret intelligence. He does not pry into the privacy of his family or friends," he exploded. "Go to your chamber at once."

"It's *your* chamber." Carew set his mouth in a stubborn line.

"Then go to my chamber at once," Matthew bellowed. "You did not have permission to leave it in the first place. You're supposed to be in bed, asleep."

"I have to clean Lady Leicester's chopines first."

"Then clean them and come to bed immediately. I'll be waiting, and if you don't come promptly, I'll thrash you within an inch of your life."

"Stop it, both of you!" Cory cried, stamping her foot. "Can you not calm yourselves and discuss this matter rationally? Matthew, you said I might help you with Carew, but when I try to do so, you fly into a temper. You're just embarrassed because Carew saw you kiss me."

He rounded on her, enraged. She had no idea what she was talking about, trying to explain his mad lust for her to a child. "Silence, madam. I've heard enough from you tonight."

"I won't be silent. I have a right to speak."

"If you are foolish enough to explain everything you do to a child, then you shouldn't have any rights at all," he roared, at his wit's end.

Her eyes glazed with tears. "What a horrid thing to say." Whirling, she raced from the room.

It was then he realized that Carew was long gone.

There. He'd managed to kill his lust for tonight. Better for both of them. And he *had* been embarrassed. The first time he'd made love to a lady in years, and his son had been watching. It was all too much.

"I told you he was a monster, Cory. One wrong word or deed and he turns into a fire-belching dragon, complete with a tough hide that no one can get through. Though I doubt there's a heart underneath, so why bother." Carew bent over Lady Leicester's chopines in the small Fish Court off the kitchens and scrubbed at the shoes with a stiff brush.

"Yes, you warned me." As Cory worked the pump, she tried to hide her disappointment in Matthew, along with her dislike for the odor issuing from the high-soled shoes meant to protect the wearer from street refuse. She stood back to avoid being splashed as she pumped. Although she had changed out of her white silk, she still didn't want to get wet.

"I swear, the great countess stepped in a dung heap on purpose," Carew complained, sticking a chopine under the pump. "She can be nice, but if she's angry, there's hell to pay."

Everything was hell of late, Cory thought glumly. "Carew, you will remember not to say inappropriate things to your father, won't you? It just makes him angrier."

"What difference does it make? He still finds reasons to explode."

Cory's heart ached at the violence of Matthew's outburst, but she couldn't let the matter rest. "How do you feel about him when he does that?" she asked cautiously.

"Excellent. I rarely get a response out of him. He's usually as cold as an icicle," Carew said with nonchalance as he plied his brush with vigor.

Cory refused to accept his explanation. "Is that what you want from him, a response? Any kind at all? Or would you rather he ruffled your hair and said he loved you?"

"My father, say that?" Carew looked aghast at the idea. "He doesn't love anyone."

"I hear that people who have been hurt often avoid love because they're afraid."

"My father isn't afraid of anything. Why do you think he sails around the world all the time? And why do you take his part? He roared at you." With a resigned expression, he began on the other chopine. "He was doing so well, too, until I lost my balance and fell."

She didn't know why she was taking Matthew's part. He'd hurt her dignity, but she was so fond of Carew, she couldn't bear to think there was no hope for the boy and his father. "Carew, will you try something for me? The next time he roars at you, will you say, 'I didn't do it on purpose, Father. I'm sorry.' Then when he calms down, say, 'Father, I love you.' "

Carew wrinkled his nose in distaste. "He's not going to say he loves me in return."

"No, he won't. Not at first," Cory said decidedly. "He'll probably look uncomfortable and change the subject. But say it anyway, will you? You do love him, don't you?"

Carew dropped the chopine, which was now fairly clean, and sat back to consider the question. "No, I don't. I loved him when I was little, but I don't think he cares much about me. So why should I give a fig about him?"

"He always comes home to you."

Carew rolled his eyes. "Once a year. Uncle Charles and Aunt Frances are always there for me, but him? Never. When I broke my arm falling out of the cherry tree, Aunt Frances took care of me. Uncle Charles taught me to ride. I studied with my cousins, but when they went to Oxford, I had to stay behind because Father hadn't decided about my education. What does he want for me? Does he tell me? Does he ask me what I want? No."

"He hasn't said anything about your education since he returned?" Cory asked, leaning on the pump handle.

Carew shrugged. "Uncle Charles tried to talk to him two years ago, but he just got mad and shouted, which is his specialty. I don't think he knows what he wants, but why should I suffer because of him?"

So much pain to sort through. Cory couldn't tell where hers stopped and Matthew's and Carew's began. She was still reeling from yesterday's shock of learning that the pirate of her fantasy was Carew's evil dragon of a father.

"I can't get the mud out of these crevices." Carew squinted at the cork soles of the chopines.

"Where? Let me see."

Carew held out a shoe, pointing to the narrow space between the cork sole and the fabric upper that covered the foot.

"I see. We need a knife or tool to scrape it out. Let's check in here for one." Cory picked up the lantern and led the way into a seldom-used scullery. "Whew, it smells like spoiled meat in here. No wonder no one uses this room." She checked a cupboard. "Nothing in here." She pulled at the door of the next cupboard, which refused to budge. "Drat this thing." She put down the lantern and tugged with both hands. "It's stuck."

"Here, let me open it with this." Carew stepped up with a rusty poker from the hearth. Inserting the tool into the crack between the door and its casing, he pried.

Cory pulled hard at the same time, and suddenly the door flew open. A foul stench many times stronger than the unpleasant odor in the chamber poured forth.

Cory stared in horror at the interior of the cupboard. The

form of Moll Dakins hung inside, a macabre, gruesome form
with a purple face and a protruding, blackened tongue, clearly
several days dead.

PART 2

~⌒~

Chapter 11

Cory gagged and backed away from the cupboard. "Carew," she choked, "run for help." Her knees buckled, and she sank to the floor, trying to control the nausea and horror that threatened her.

"What is it?" Carew pushed past her and looked into the cupboard, despite her feeble tugs on his shirttail to hold him back. "God almighty." He turned away, his face contorted with revulsion. "Don't touch her. I'll fetch my father. He's good with emergencies."

"Yes, do." As Carew raced away, Cory groped for a stool and pulled it toward her, incapable of doing more than gripping its spindle legs. She must not look at poor Moll's grotesque face or contorted body, nor think of the pain her friend must have suffered as she died.

Placing her cheek against the stool's smooth wooden seat, she closed her eyes and prayed for deliverance. Soon Matthew would arrive to deal with this tragedy. A man who was terrible with his son but good with emergencies. A man who dealt well with murder. After their recent encounters, she wasn't sure what she thought of him. All she knew was that she longed to lay this terrible new burden in his capable hands.

Matthew bent over his chart books in his chamber, plotting the route of his next voyage, but the work failed to hold his attention. The tempest of his quarrel with his son and Cordelia still raged in his mind.

It was hopeless to think he could assist Cordelia in any way, or that she could help him with Carew. He disapproved of the way she talked to his son. Her frank opinions about their kiss exasperated him. After he'd found his son had been watching, he'd roared at them both like a wounded beast.

Carew had fled rather than face his anger, as had Cordelia. Blinded by desire for her soft body pressed against his longing flesh, he'd been relieved not to have to face them.

For that very reason, he had driven her away. Now that he realized what he'd done, he wondered—had he shut out Carew all these years because he was afraid of what would happen if he didn't? Did he fear the responsibilities and the vulnerability that came with touching the emotions of another and feeling theirs in return? Was he afraid of hurting others as well as being hurt?

Matthew peered out the window at the tower clock. One hour, and still Carew hadn't come to bed. Far from wanting to thrash him, an idle threat he would never carry out, he was worried. Where was he? He should have finished cleaning the chopines long ago.

The clock struck one in the morning. Then half past. Every time he thought of Carew embracing the fairy queen, the image was followed by the poignant memory of standing by the misty Thames, eyes closed, as Titania reopened the portals to his youth. Her voice had soothed him like a soft spring breeze, her hand had touched his arm. For the briefest of instants, he had felt loved and able to love. He had been a boy once more . . .

Carew burst into the chamber.

Startled, Matthew bolted from his seat. "Carew, where have you been? It's late."

Carew leaned against a chair, gasping for breath. "You must . . . come quickly," he forced out.

Relieved to see Carew in one piece, yet alarmed at his words, Matthew stuffed his shirttails into his trunkhose and hustled Carew out the door. "Lead the way. Is someone hurt?"

"Yes, hurt." Carew wasted no words but sprinted down the corridor.

Matthew raced after him through the maze of passages,

stairways, and courtyards to a seldom-used scullery, haunted by the fear that someone had been more than hurt.

A shadow seemed to fall over Hampton Court as Matthew closed the cupboard door on the body and tied it shut with a complicated knot of rope. He wanted no one else to find the poor girl by accident.

"I'll rouse the captain of the guard," he said to Carew. "The queen must change residences as soon as possible. Her life may be in danger. But first we must tend to the viscountess."

He studied Cordelia, who sat gripping a stool, her face the color of gray chalk.

"It's that missing tirewoman, Moll Dakins," Carew said in a low voice, pointing to the cupboard. "She disappeared before you arrived without a word to anyone. Not even to Cory, who was her closest friend. Cory had been worried about her for days."

"That explains why she's in shock." Matthew took one of Cordelia's hands. Her flesh felt cold to his touch. "We must get her warm again."

As he lifted her in his arms, her devastation cut him like a knife plunged through the ribs. He knew the signs of shock. The open, glassy eyes staring at nothing. The lack of tears.

At sea, he'd watched a wounded man slip without warning from shock into death. Though the viscountess had no bodily hurt, a wound to the spirit could be just as bad.

He must put her to bed, but it couldn't be in the maids' dormitory. The girls would scream if he entered as they lay in their night smocks, which would hardly comfort Cordelia. His chamber must be her refuge.

He carried her back through the dark palace, Carew close behind, until they reached his room. He pushed open his door, and settled her on his bed. He must see her revived before he went to alert the captain of the guard. "Carew, can you remove her slippers? I'll loosen her corset so she can breath more easily." He ran one hand down her back, searching for her laces. To his surprise, he felt only her soft, unrestrained flesh beneath her kirtle bodice and smock.

Aching awareness of her fragile-boned, uncorseted body filled him, and he had to suppress the idiotic wish to take her in his arms. Instead, he captured her wrist between thumb and forefinger. A hint of pulse whispered beneath her smooth flesh. Her daffodil scent engulfed his senses, poignant with new meaning since she had praised his kisses.

"Her shoes are off," Carew announced, standing before him. "I left her stockings on, though, for her feet are cold. That's not good, is it, Father? Shall I build up the fire?"

He nodded at Carew, pleased by his mature concern. "Yes, and put on the warming pan," he said. "You'll need to warm the sheets if her natural body heat doesn't return." With care he lowered Cordelia into a reclining position, then arranged the quilts over her. As he bent over her, she stared blankly at the overhead canopy, giving no sign that she saw him.

Keeping one eye on her, he put a kettle on to heat. Then he rummaged in a coffer for a packet of herbs from his voyage. They released a soothing aroma as he poured boiling water over them.

Returning to the bed, Matthew covered Cory's forehead with his palm. She was much too cold. "Cory, can you hear me?" He held the steaming cup near her face. "Can you drink this?"

She did not reply, so he sat on the bed and eased her into an upright position. She sagged, forcing him to brace her against his chest as he offered the cup. "Just a sip," he urged, anxious that she show signs of recovery before he left. " 'Twill be soothing. Come, Cory." He used the nickname his son called her, hoping she would respond.

Cory stared at the fire, too numb with shock to understand what she was being asked to do. Moll had been murdered. *Murdered.* The word rang in her head.

In the depths of her despair, she became aware of gentle hands supporting her—big hands, rough and calloused—and a gentle voice urging her to do something. What was it? Warm pottery touched her lips, and she understood she was to drink.

She swallowed a mouthful of the hot liquid. The taste of chamomile and other herbs warmed her throat and stomach as their scent seeped into her mind, reminiscent of Grandmama's comforting brews. She gulped more, eager for relief from the pain. Death had taken her friend.

"Good. Very good."

The soothing voice rewarded her, the tone so like her mother's when she'd been ill as a child. Only this voice wasn't female. It had deep masculine vibrations. With it came a strong arm that held her against a warm expanse of chest, wrapping her in the protection she craved. Groping for the hand with the cup, she clung to it in desperation, needing something solid in the treacherous, frightening world where death walked.

"M-Matthew?" she managed to stammer.

"You are in no danger," he soothed. "A little more of this good brew and you'll find you can sleep. You'll be much stronger when you wake."

"Moll," she half whimpered, cringing at the memories. "Someone hurt her . . ."

"She's at peace now." He cupped her hands in his capable, warm grip.

She drank more of the hot tea, and he rose, passing the cup to Carew, who took his place. Sudden cold settled over her, attacking her with painful shivers.

"Here, drink more," Carew urged, holding up the cup. "My father says 'twill help."

"That's right, Carew. You're doing well. Stay with her until she sleeps. I'll return as soon as I've notified the captain of the guard of Moll's death." Matthew's voice receded. The door thudded shut, leaving her alone.

The old terror of being left surged within her. *Don't go*, she wanted to cry.

"He'll be back," Carew reassured her, apparently understanding the words in her whimpers. "He said he would be."

Cory fastened on the promise and tried to force down her fear as Carew helped her sip from the cup. Whatever hurt or anger Carew felt at his father's leaving each year, at least he trusted his word that he would return. How she wanted him back now, in this time of disaster.

Disaster. The horror of Moll's contorted face returned, with a wave of fear that threatened to drag her into its depths. She squeezed her eyes closed and tried to pray, but all she could do was wonder why it had happened. Was some lunatic killer on the loose?

Whatever the reason, if Moll knew it, she had taken the secret with her. Cory's hopes for a peaceful life serving the queen dissolved like salt in water, leaving bitter brine. She had not been unduly afraid as long as she stayed in the safety of

company and the palace, but now murder had occurred within
the palace itself. She feared she might be next.

An hour later Matthew returned to his chamber and found
Cory sound asleep. His herbs had done their work. Carew had
also succumbed to exhaustion. He lay on the other side of the
bed, fully clothed, wheezing softly in his sleep.

The poignancy of the scene held Matthew captive. When
was the last time he had experienced tenderness, or closeness
for that matter? Yet he had cared for Cory most carefully earlier. He, who had been out of touch with tenderness, had given
it to another in need.

He settled on a stool beside the bed. Despite the late hour,
he felt wide awake after his talk with the captain. Seeing Cory
and his son sleeping so peacefully brought bittersweet memories. Of watching Joanna deep in slumber, growing large with
their child. Friend and lover. Bride and wife. Later, motherless
Carew had clung to his wet nurse, a fretful infant who wanted
her milk and nothing else. He had squalled with anger whenever Matthew tried to hold him.

Bittersweet memories. Most bitter, not sweet.

More pain had followed the loss of his wife. His father had
died within several weeks. They'd all known his weak heart
left him little time. But after his father's funeral, Matthew
couldn't bear Dorset anymore. His widowed mother took
charge of Carew, shutting Matthew out as she used his son to
ease her own loss. Overwhelmed, he'd turned to Hugh, an old
friend and accomplished boatswain. He, Hugh, and Charles
had set off to join Drake, despite his mother's protest. Surely
the hardships of the voyage and the thrill of danger would dis-
place the pain in his heart.

He'd cannibalized what was left of his soul as if it were an
old hulk of a ship, to be torn apart and used. He'd taken to the
sea with a natural aptitude, but it was no use. He couldn't out-
sail a broken heart.

Matthew stood up, needing to shake off the memories. An
ivory comb on his bedside table caught his eye. Carew must
have fetched some of Cordelia's things at her request. A single silky hair, black against ivory, lay twined in the comb's
teeth.

He didn't touch it. Instead, he examined a letter lying be-

side it, addressed to Cordelia. It might offer some clue as to
why someone was trying to kill her. Spurred by that hope, he
slid it from the table and moved to the window where a candle burned.

Beloved daughter, the letter began in a crabbed, shaky
hand. *How can you think we do not miss you? I have written
to you oft. If you never received my letters, the blame lies with
my son, the earl, who insists he cannot spare a man to carry
them. As if I did not know he sends his own letters to London
weekly. I have sent you this letter by a peddler and pray it
reaches you. Know that for every one letter you receive, I have
written a dozen others, telling you of our love.*

Matthew drew an unsteady breath, overcome by the love
couched in the words, as well as the baseness of the earl who
stood between the two women. The rest of the letter was full
of amusing tales of children's and servants' deeds that would
have been humdrum except that each was told with such caring wit, they became charmed events. Turning to the end, he
found it was signed, *Yours with abounding love, Henrietta
Hailsworthy, Dowager Countess of Whitby*. This would be the
woman Cory called Grandmama.

He stared at the letter, a sea of confusing emotions rolling
through him. He should be glad that Cory shared such a loving bond with the dowager countess. Yet he felt disgruntled, as
if their intimacy shut him out. He had nothing even slightly
akin to their closeness in his life.

Unsettled by the emptiness that followed the realization, he
refolded the letter. A scrap of cloth fluttered to the floor as he did
so, and he picked it up. Would the smaller letter enclosed explain
it? It was written in a childish hand, much blotted with ink.

Dearest, favoritest, bestest Mama in the entire world,
*Grandmama says that I am far too extravagant with
my salutation to my honored mother and should begin
this letter again, but I positively, absolutely will not do
so, as every word I write is heartfelt to the best of my
poor ability to set it forth. Hence, I send you my original letter, as writ by my hand, and hope you will excuse
the blots, but the quill did drip so, and Marcus shouted
suddenly so that the ink and I both jumped, and it truly
could not be helped.*

Matthew sighed in sympathy for the painstaking effort the
child had spent on the letter. Its grubby appearance testified to
the labor it had cost her, just as her effusive expressions testified to her love. Wishing his tie to Carew could be as strong
as what Cory had with this girl, he read on.

> *Marcus has been hounding me to tell you of your New
> Year's gift. I swear upon my oath of honor I meant to
> keep it secret, but I wearied of waiting, so here 'tis. I am
> stitching a kirtle for you from the enclosed cloth, though
> I am no brave needlewoman and am better at getting
> into mischief, or so says Grandmama, but she also says
> my work will please you, so do be pleased, dearest
> Mama, and come home to us as swiftly as ever you may.*
>   *Your forever loving daughter, Lettice Henrietta
> Hailsworthy*

Matthew refolded the letter, along with the enclosures, and
slid it back with the comb. So this was Letty, Cory's foster
daughter. The child sounded like a terror, though her letter ex-
uded love like a charm. He would give anything to have someone express their love to him in such a way.

His brothers and sisters loved him, but he was morose and
behaved in so unlovable a fashion, they never exchanged en-
dearments like the ones Letty wrote. His mother loved him,
but she had grown forgetful as she aged and couldn't seem to
remember which son he was. And with Carew, he feared it was
too late for them to share such affection.

Hurt. The word Cory had said in her grief echoed within
him. She had loved Moll and now suffered for it. Yet she continued to give away her heart to one person after another. She
was a tender mother, a caring daughter, so loving and easy to
love. How did she do it despite the pain?

His mind clouded with anger as he thought of the injustice
done her by the Earl of Whitby. How dare he sell her like a
piece of chattel? And what was the queen thinking to foist Sir
William Norris on her? What would Elizabeth say when she
learned Cordelia had refused him? Worse yet, that Matthew
had helped her? The royal temper would flare.

Yet he resolved to face her anger, convinced he must protect Cordelia from further misery.

More than that, her life was in danger. An undercurrent of evil prowled the court. First a crossbow archer. Then a strangler. With the motive unknown, everyone and anyone was suspect, yet few men at court appeared to have the skill or the inclination to investigate.

It fell to him to work with the captain of the guard in search of the culprit. He had no reason to think the incidents were related, but as they'd come so close together, and as the two women had been friends, they could be. It was too sinister a possibility for him to ignore.

Chapter 12

They had found the body. He'd heard it from his favorite informant, Benjamin Carter, a palace porter who managed to be everywhere and overhear a treasure trove of things.

"Dead as a log," Ben had confided to him, clearly feeling privileged to be heard by someone of his status. And although he already knew, he pretended he didn't. How easy to act shocked and outraged.

He'd been genuinely shocked by Baron Graystock's demands to see Lord Burghley's boots. Damn him for being so efficient. Ben brought him that news as well. The baron had examined Lord Burghley's boots and told Sir Francis Knollys he wished to see his later, though why theirs, no one knew.

"Mark my word, the baron suspects 'em," Ben had said as they sat in his private withdrawing chamber. "Men close to the queen, too."

He had rewarded Ben for his information, as he always did, no matter the subject. Best not to single out any part of what Ben offered. Take it all, pretending he simply enjoyed palace news.

Let Graystock inspect all the boots he wished. He would never find the pair worn at the crossbow shooting. Nor would Moll Dakins spill any more secrets to Viscountess Wentworth or to anyone. Moll was dead. In that, his favored associate had not failed him. But his plans were not yet fully safe. They must dispose of the viscountess before she told what she knew.

Cory opened her eyes to daylight and an unfamiliar set of bed hangings fashioned in deep blue. Where was she?

As she propped herself on one elbow, she spied Carew lying at her side, covered with a blanket, sound asleep. Ah, that explained it. She was in Carew's chamber.

Great heavens! It was also his father's chamber.

A partial memory of last night returned. She had embraced and kissed the pirate of her dreams, only to see him turn into a dragon breathing fire. And now she was lying in his bed.

She jerked to a sitting position and nervously scanned the small chamber.

Matthew wasn't there.

Relieved, she threw back the covers and sprang to her feet. If he did arrive, she didn't want him to find her lolling in his bed. It was improper, embarrassing, and . . .

Heat crept to her face as she recalled the thrill of his kisses last night. She had returned his caresses with an enthusiasm that could only be described as unseemly, as were her candid comments afterward. But he had been so kind, so comforting about her past with Thomas, she hadn't been able to help it. She was so lonely at court, and it had been so long since anyone besides Grandmama had cared for her. How easy it was to accept his kisses.

Disquiet shot through her as she remembered their later disagreement. Matthew had the most rigid ideas about child rearing. Honesty was best, in her opinion. If she'd lied to Carew about why she'd been kissing his father, the boy would eventually learn the truth and feel betrayed.

Kissing Matthew *had* been reckless. Probably for the best that he'd turned into a dragon and brought her to her senses. He was not the stuff of her dreams and she knew it.

Grief struck Cory as she remembered what had come after leaving Matthew. She sagged against the bedpost as sorrow at her friend's death returned in full force. In life, Moll had asked for nothing. She had worked tirelessly at her post, mending torn seams, sewing on jewels, and dressing the queen. She had made time for her friends as well, helping Cory with her

French since she'd had little practice. Most unusual that Moll knew the language, a girl in her position, but her father had been French, so she shared her gift freely. Only in death would she receive the ministrations of others.

It seem so unfair.

Cory vowed to perform the tasks required for her friend with loving care. She must consult the examining physician to learn the cause of death. She must notify Moll's family and provide funds for a suitable funeral. She must also comfort Monsieur La Faye. If she had interpreted Moll's hints correctly, he would be grieving. Most important of all, the murderer must be found.

Cory turned to awaken Carew. She had no time to lie abed, feeling helpless. She must discover who had done this terrible thing. And whatever her problems or desires, service to her sovereign was still her primary task. If she changed clothes quickly and hurried to the workroom where state affairs were conducted, she might avoid Elizabeth's displeasure at her tardiness.

Back at the maids' dormitory, Cory washed and changed clothes. With her hair newly braided, she felt better and sailed through the corridors greeting gentlemen pensioners, chamberers, and ushers. To her relief, she did not encounter Matthew. She would prefer not to see him today.

But as she turned into the chamber leading to the queen's cabinet, she caught her breath. Matthew stood before the queen's door, talking to the gentleman pensioner on duty. As she entered, he looked up, without a doubt hearing her silly gulp across the room.

She couldn't run away. Not since he'd seen her. Mustering her composure, she moved across the chamber, head high, expression serene, as if she hadn't kissed him with flagrant abandon last night. As if he hadn't done the same to her.

"Good morrow, Baron. Master Simon." She nodded to each of them, praying her voice betrayed no hint of her inner turmoil. "How is Her Majesty this morn?"

"Well enough, Viscountess, considering the tragedy of last night." Master Simon bent over her hand. "You are recovered, I trust, from your ordeal?"

"I am greatly saddened by Moll's passing." She pressed his hand at his genuine concern.

"I cannot think who would have done such a thing." His blue eyes gleamed with sympathy.

"Viscountess Wentworth, I require a word," Matthew cut in. "If you would be so kind as to walk with me." He offered his arm, making it awkward for her to refuse. Full of trepidation, she placed three fingertips on his black linen sleeve and let him lead her away from Master Simon.

"What is it, my lord?" She inclined her head in his direction but avoided his gaze.

He guided her to the far end of the chamber and paused by the window.

"You might hold my arm more securely," he said. "I'm not poison, you know."

His tone was mild, but she read irritation in his insistent stare. "I know you're not."

"You don't act it."

A ray of sun burnished his brown hair with gold, rendering him even more handsome than last night. Nervous and self-conscious, Cory clasped both hands before her, her heart thundering in her chest. She was going mad. One look into his eloquent brown eyes had her trembling with the anticipation of more kisses. Why had he moved her so last night? Why did he move her now?

Of course she had discerned the reason. The emptiness of his life spoke to her. By fortune, he needed a circle of love as much as she did.

The difference between them was that he didn't know it. Nor would he know how to gather loved ones around him if he did, as was evident by his troubles with Carew. Yes, that was it. She had responded to him last night because she recognized his loneliness, so similar to her own. But it didn't make them kindred souls. On the contrary, they seemed destined to disagree.

"I have a prospective husband in mind for you," he said, launching into the subject she least expected. "He is the youngest son of the Earl of Derby and lives in the country on his father's estate. If you will permit, I can arrange an introduction."

Cory blinked in surprise. "I thought after last night's disagreement, you would want nothing further to do with me. You quite clearly said I was in the wrong."

"I was . . . remiss in directing my anger at you last night."

He looked as uncomfortable as if he'd swallowed a whole carp. Yet in admitting his error, he had swallowed something more difficult to contend with than a fish. "Thank you for your courtesy in saying so," she managed in neutral tones, smoothing her skirts to hide any hint of a smile.

She had been sure last night that he would never understand his son, but he had been kind to her after she found Moll. With his apology as added incentive, she would not give up on him yet. "I also thank you for your kindness last night. As to meeting your friend, you are generous to think of me, but could we delay the matter? Just now I must discover who killed my friend."

"You're to keep out of the investigation," he barked, seeming horrified that she wanted to be involved. "Captain Wells and I will find the killer."

"You will?" She stared at him in gratified amazement. He had many duties, yet he took on another without hesitation. "That is most generous. I don't know how I could ever repay you."

"I am the most qualified person available to look into the matter," he said, suddenly stiff again.

"Surely I can do something for you in return," she offered, imagining the time and effort he would spend investigating a murder, not to mention the possible danger.

A long pause stretched between them, during which he appeared to grow even more uncomfortable. "If you are still willing . . ." he began, then stopped.

"Yes?" She smiled encouragingly. "Pray go on."

"Lady Russell is leaving court on the morrow. I have many affairs to conduct in the coming days, and I cannot leave Carew without adequate supervision."

Her relief to have his help in finding the murderer ebbed as he returned to the root of their disagreement. Though he clearly needed assistance and she longed to give it for Carew's sake, they would quarrel. As she considered how to remind him of that fact, she came to another realization. He was panicked by Lady Russell's looming departure. How hard to be a sole parent, with no partner to turn to for help. She and Grandmama had always managed Letty and Marcus together. "I would be honored to assist with Carew." She summoned her

courage to continue. "If you promise not to object to the way
I talk to him."

"I can't promise if you say outrageous things as you did last
night," he snapped. "I'll not raise my voice, but I reserve the
right to object."

She narrowed her gaze at him. "That's hardly good enough,
sir. I won't be told I've spoken improperly, especially in front
of Carew. There was nothing wrong with what I said last
night. Nor with what we did. We are two unwed adults. We
hurt no one."

At her veiled reference to their kisses, his expression
changed. The passion of last night flickered in his eyes like a
dangerous flame. Thank fortune her skirts hid her knees, because they trembled as if they were no more substantial than
marmalade. "Then how did you intend to explain to Carew
what we were doing?" he demanded.

The question was unsettling, she admitted. Yet she would
reply honestly. With a nervous swallow, she took a stab at
what she thought had happened. "It was a mistake in judgment. A man and woman can find each other attractive in the
physical sense, yet in no other way. Sometimes they act on it
before being sure, but if it doesn't go too far, no harm is
done."

"You find me attractive in the physical sense?"

The provocative innuendo in his tone sent her blood racing,
but she lifted her chin, determined not to be intimidated. "Aye,
my lord," she said. "I do."

"But not in any other way?" He smiled sardonically.

"I do not mean that the way it sounds," she said hastily, realizing she might have offended him. "You have many admirable qualities. You are an honest man, a bold adventurer, a
splendid fighter. I simply mean we are not inclined to, er, fall
in love." There. She'd said what she meant and was glad. She
preferred to put all her cards on the table during her turn.

He wore a bemused expression. "I've never known a lady
to admit to physical interest without giving love as an excuse.
You are unique, madam."

"Heavens, how could I be otherwise? I told you about my
husband. He taught me very clearly that physical passion has
nothing to do with love."

"I see your point." He grinned ruefully, as if he understood but was also sorry for it. "Let us return to the question of my son. You are willing to assist, and if we disagree, we will resolve our difference in private, not in front of him. Will that satisfy you?"

"We *will* disagree, sir, but I agree to those terms." She hurried on, wanting no misunderstandings between them. "You are also most kind in offering to find the murderer. I thank you, but I insist on helping. This person must not remain free to kill again."

"Don't you trust me?" His gaze still burned into hers. "I am known for succeeding at the things I undertake."

The attraction leaped between them, and she fought the ever-present desire to nestle in his arms. His reputation for accomplishing what he set out to do *was* alluring. "I am reassured, of course." She wished his scrutiny did not make her flush like an untried girl.

"Then we have an agreement," he stated without acknowledging her discomfort. "You will assist me with Carew; I will find Moll's killer. And Viscountess," he paused, eyebrows raised, "I still insist you not explain to Carew why we did what we did last night."

"What if he asks again?" she demanded. "Leaving him ignorant of the ways of the world is as bad as encouraging him to find out for himself."

"All you need say is that we do not intend to wed."

"But he'll want to know why it was permissible for *us* to kiss but he may not kiss Sarah—"

"Madam," he interrupted with some force. "He understands a good deal without your explanations. I insist you stop there."

She frowned, thoroughly annoyed with him. Honestly, the man seemed to have forgotten what it was to be young and newly aware of the opposite sex. "You could at least call me Cory, Matthew Cavandish," she said, piqued that they had reached an impasse. Yet if she argued now, he might revoke their agreement.

The door to the queen's cabinet opened, saving her from further temptation to dispute. Lord Burghley emerged. "Viscountess, I'm glad you're here. Could you attend Her Majesty?"

Excusing herself to Matthew, Cory crossed the room, keeping her expression inscrutable. But inside, she was shouting hallelujah. She was going to mother Carew, this time with his father's approval. He'd even agreed to disagree with her in private rather than shouting his rage in front of half the court, though in her opinion, their disputes were just beginning.

As for the killer, despite Matthew's wanting to find the culprit alone, their combined efforts would be needed. And she sensed that they must hurry. If the queen changed palaces soon, the clues would remain behind. If that happened, they might never learn who had taken Moll's life.

"Great gods, I have too much work to do to change palaces now, my lord. We keep court here for another month," Elizabeth shouted at Burghley as Cory entered the workroom behind him. As usual, he accepted the abuse, waiting for her anger to wear out.

"I understand, Your Grace," he said in his mild, reasonable manner when she ran out of breath, "but the change is recommended for your safety."

Elizabeth glared at a thick stack of dispatches Cory recognized as French, then rose from her chair and paced, her firm step full of restless energy. "Ah, Cordelia, you are here at last."

"Yes, Your Majesty, I—"

"No excuses required," the queen interrupted. "I am fully aware of the reason behind your absence. I have been badgered about it ever since the alarm was given." She gestured at Burghley, as if he were to blame.

"With your permission, Majesty, I shall retire to work with the clerks on the letters we just discussed." Burghley took a sheaf of the papers and backed away.

Elizabeth flung out one hand in dismissal. "Yes, yes, go. Cory shall send for refreshment. I am weary to death of bad news from the continent."

The pain of her toothache seemed to have left her, Cory thought as she opened the door and signaled for Master Simon to send for a light repast.

"I hate changing residences," Elizabeth complained to one of her ladies, who had risen to her feet when the queen stood up. "I have too much to do. I sent four thousand men and more pounds to Navarre last autumn after Henri III was assassinated, but instead of taking Paris and getting himself crowned,

Navarre runs off to visit some trollop. Philip of Spain sends money to oppose him, and Navarre's worse off now than if I'd sent nothing."

"I believe he was not adequately served by one of his commanders in an earlier battle for Paris, else the city would have been his," Cory ventured as Master Simon entered with a tray. She motioned for him to set it on the table. "Navarre may like the ladies, but he's a fine battle strategist, 'tis said." She poured wine into a silver cup.

"He thinks with his ballocks, as *I've* said." Elizabeth vented her ill humor as she diluted the wine with water and downed the mixture. "Isabella of Spain couldn't rule a cabbage patch, but her father would marry her to a Frenchman and put her on the French throne. He threatens to send the Duke of Parma's army from the Netherlands to put her there. And what does Henri do? He personally leads the men I sent him into battle and nearly gets shot. Then instead of pressing his advantage when he wins, he indulges his baser instincts. Now he has Paris under siege again and people are dropping like flies, but it serves no purpose. France's civil wars will never end."

"I thought the dispatches said he stood a good chance of taking Paris and being crowned," Cory said, unable to remain still.

Elizabeth flung back her head and addressed the heavens in exasperation. "Even the sensible Cordelia contradicts me today. Is the world turned upside down?"

Cory sighed and apologized. The queen was certainly in a temper today. One could only nod in agreement and try to keep the peace.

"To finish it off, why would someone murder one of my tirewomen?" the queen went on. "The poor wretch never hurt a fly."

Cory jolted to attention. "Oh, Your Grace, it is much on my mind. We must find the killer, and will you not change palaces to ensure your safety?"

The queen narrowed her eyes and stared at Cory without answering. "Leave us," she suddenly ordered Lady Carey. "I wish to speak to Cordelia alone."

Cory groaned inwardly. She hadn't said anything so terribly wrong.

Elizabeth took a plum and bit into it. "Well, Cory," she said when they were alone. "Have you agreed to wed?"

Surprised by the transition to the new subject, Cory shook her head. "I don't understand, Your Grace."

Elizabeth finished the plum and reached for another. "Come, come, you're no blushing girl. Sir William Norris asked you to wed. When shall I order the ceremony?"

"How do you know he asked me, Your Grace?" Cory stalled for time, but the unpalatable truth tasted bitter on her tongue. Matthew had spoken truly. Though she had hoped he might be mistaken, Elizabeth Tudor had indeed taken money from Lord Whitby to marry her off.

Elizabeth raised her eyebrows and cast her a sidelong gaze. "*We* are the queen. *We* know many things, so don't put *Us* off," she said, adopting the royal *We*, as she did when playing the great sovereign. "Don't put him off, either. Be quick with your answer and make it affirmative."

Cory felt a sinking in her stomach, despite her hopeful talk with Matthew. Choosing a man she found tolerable seemed even more imposing by light of day. "If I may be so bold, Your Grace," she ventured, "Sir William does not suit. Might I choose someone else?"

The queen glanced at her sharply. "Do you have someone in mind? Speak up. Don't stand there with your mouth hanging open like a foolish sheep."

"I, er, don't have anyone specific in mind," Cory floundered, caught off guard. She hadn't expected to name someone today. "But I will. I promise I'll find someone suitable."

The queen snorted as she bit into another plum. "You will set impossible standards so that no one can reach them, Cordelia."

"Rather like you, Your Grace?" Cory countered, hoping to gain Elizabeth's sympathy. The queen had turned down suitors for years, finding one reason or another to reject them. Cory suspected the queen feared marriage and all it entailed.

In a different mood, Elizabeth might have enjoyed the reference to the many men who had wooed her, but not today. "A queen has different requirements in comparison to other women. Only a man of outstanding integrity could share her throne. You need not be so rigorous, Cordelia. I can name a dozen suitable men. Baron Graystock, for one."

Cory stiffened, wondering if the queen were serious. Matthew Cavandish aroused her senses, but the last thing she wanted was to be tied to a man who would abandon her. "No, thank you, Your Grace."

"You would be a free woman once he left for the Spanish Main." The queen winked conspiratorially. "And you could aid me in the bargain. You could take that annoying Monsieur La Faye, who is constantly at me for aid, on your wedding sojourn to Graystock Manor."

"I could not marry Baron Graystock." Cory was determined to stand her ground. "Nor does he want a wife, so I cannot help you with Monsieur La Faye."

Elizabeth snorted. "If a man likes a woman in bed, he'll do any manner of things. Graystock wants you. He'll agree."

"Why do you think that?" Cory burst out, so astonished she forgot etiquette entirely.

"I've seen how he looks at you." A crafty light glinted in Elizabeth's eye.

Had Matthew really brought up the subject? Or had the queen? Cory had a strong suspicion Elizabeth was not being entirely honest with her. "Why don't you order Graystock to take La Faye away? You don't need a wedding for that," Cory asked bluntly.

"Silly chit. He'd resent me and be less useful if I did. Not that half my courtiers don't resent me, a woman, telling them what to do. But you'll pacify him. He'll forget to be resentful when he's burrowing between your legs." The queen strolled to the window, munching another plum.

Cory felt uncomfortably like a prize breeding cow being readied to meet the bull.

"Once you're wed, you can also remove that annoying Carew," Elizabeth continued. "Do you know he ate the meat pie meant for my dinner yesterday? I wanted to box his ears." She sounded far angrier with Carew's latest antic than she'd been when he ruined her cousin's bumroll.

Cory retreated a step, wishing the queen would dismiss her. This was growing worse by the moment. Her Majesty would marry her off to Matthew, then make them take a state visitor on their wedding journey. Did Matthew know of this scheme? Judging from the activity on his ship, he was outfitting for his next voyage. He hardly had the aspect of a man considering marriage. "Your Majesty, I thought perhaps to consider the youngest son of the Earl of Derby," she hedged.

"In truth?" Elizabeth had turned to gaze out the window, but she swung back at Cory's statement. "I wasn't aware you were acquainted. He's not been to court since you arrived."

Cory fidgeted miserably from foot to foot. How could she possibly find a suitable husband before the queen thrust one on her? "He comes well recommended, Your Grace. I thought—"

"There! You don't know him," Elizabeth crowed in triumph. "And you do know Graystock, though he's a bit of a bore at times. I'm none too pleased with that son of his, either. Carew should stay at Graystock Manor; his father could visit him there instead of at court. It would be a more sensible arrangement. Wed him, Cordelia." She turned back to the window, an exasperated expression on her face. "I certainly took on more than I expected when I agreed to this affair."

The sinking feeling grew in Cory's stomach. Elizabeth wasn't the only one who had taken on more than she'd expected. She had hoped that by coming to court, her father-in-law's attempts to force her remarriage were over. Instead, the pressure intensified. And the queen clearly intended to suit her own purposes by attaching unpleasant duties to the decree.

A tap at the door interrupted Cory's troubled thoughts.

"Baron Graystock, Captain Wells, and Dr. Rowley, Your Majesty," Master Simon announced.

"Ah, the report on Moll Dakins." Elizabeth gestured the three men in.

Cory noted the uneasy glance Matthew cast her as he and the others greeted the queen.

"Your Majesty, perhaps you would wish to hear in privacy what the good doctor has discovered," he suggested as soon as Elizabeth was seated.

The queen turned to her. Cory pressed her lips together and shook her head. She refused to be ejected from the chamber. Not when they were about to discuss Moll.

"Cordelia was fond of the girl," Elizabeth said. "She'll badger me 'til I tell her what you've learned, so she remains. Proceed."

Dr. Rowley launched into a long review of where Moll had

been found, how she'd been tied in the cupboard, and on and on. Cory thought she would explode before he got to the point.

"She appears to have been strangled by something wrapped around her throat," he finally said with an apologetic air, as if afraid of offending their delicate female sensibilities. "Probably something like a stocking, as there were few bruises. She wouldn't have suffered long."

"She wasn't hung until after, to hold her in the cupboard," the captain added.

"But she would have cried out," Cory interrupted, unable to believe Moll could have been strangled without putting up a rousing fight. "Someone would have heard."

"Without a doubt," Dr. Rowley said with a reproachful look suggesting she shouldn't ask, "but cries can be smothered in a feather cushion."

"Come, come, you keep us on tenterhooks, Dr. Rowley," Elizabeth interrupted. "Tell us your theory at once."

"Yes, she must have been restrained somehow." Cory was determined to hear the worst.

Dr. Rowley replaced his apologetic look with a suffering expression. "Someone stronger must have sat on her to hold her down. Her wrists were bruised, showing she put up a fight."

"But why would anyone want to kill her?" Cory insisted, wondering why he was holding back information. "She had no money. She had nothing anyone wanted."

"There is one possible reason," the captain said helpfully.

The doctor glared at him, as if resenting the interruption.

Matthew stepped forward, also appearing uncomfortable. "Your Majesty, won't you please hear this news in private?" He sent Cory a sidelong glance.

It must be something terrible, Cory thought, her throat tightening with fear. "Please, Your Majesty, don't send me away," she pleaded. "I must know."

To her relief, Elizabeth took her part. She nodded for the doctor to continue.

"Well, er, she was, uh." He hesitated. "She was . . . begging your pardon . . ."

"She was some months gone with child," the captain blurted.

Cory felt the blood drain from her face. Matthew was

watching her intently, and she struggled to hide her distress. She could bear this terrible news.

Her stomach disagreed. It rebelled in a violent contraction. Overcome by nausea, she bolted from the chamber.

She raced past the gentleman usher at the door, four gentlemen pensioners, and a group of ladies in waiting, skidded down one corridor and raced up another. Jerking open the first available door, she staggered outside and was ill in a bed of pansies.

As she straightened, despair gripped her, and she let the sobs come. Now she understood the pallid tinge to Moll's cheeks, the sad expression she had glimpsed when Moll thought no one was watching. Her unwed friend had carried a child, and she, who prided herself on her nurturing abilities, hadn't noticed a thing. She had been of no help to Moll in her time of need.

Except what of her attachment to Jacques La Faye? This was a confusing factor. If Moll had loved the Frenchman, surely the child she bore had been his.

Except what if Moll had become with child before she knew the depth of her feelings for La Faye? Or his for her? What if she had hidden her condition from him for fear of rejection?

Cory groped for her handkerchief as bile burned her throat. Little wonder Matthew had attempted to keep her from the truth. It hurt to know what little she did.

Yet she must know the truth, and his wish to keep her in the dark was a sign of more trouble ahead between them. She was glad to escape him, though he might have intended to follow, for he'd been saying farewell to the queen. But he would not know where she was.

How she wanted to be with Grandmama, to put her head in her lap and cry her heart out. But with her friend far away, letters must serve instead. When life became too difficult, she would take them out and reread the loving words. It was the best she had just now.

Cory started toward the dormitory, then remembered she had left Grandmama's most recent letter in Matthew's chamber last night. Keeping a careful watch so she didn't encounter him by accident, she fetched the letter. Then she fled to the chapel, wanting to pray and collect her thoughts. She should speak to Jacques La Faye, who was no doubt suffering from his loss. But just now she was more worried about her coming visit to the Dakins family. How would she ever tell them that Moll had died in disgrace, murdered, and several months with child?

Chapter 13

Matthew opened his chamber door and studied the room. Empty. He'd looked everywhere for Cory, but no one had seen her. Neither Carew nor her friends knew where she was.

He sat on the bed and smoothed the indentation her head had made in the pillow last night. She had looked ill when she'd rushed from the queen's chamber. He'd tried to prevent her from hearing the bad news about her friend, but she had refused to let him shield her.

How like her to insist on knowing the worst about someone she loved. She was fiercely loyal, and he admired her for it, but it was wrenching to see her pain. She refused to let him protect her, and he felt the sorrow she endured as acutely as if it were his own.

One thing was certain. He must not let her investigate the murder. It was too dangerous, especially now that his worst fears were confirmed. The muddy footprint found on Moll's dark kirtle skirt as Wells and Rowley had examined the body matched those made by the crossbow archer's boots. He'd even compared it to the tracings he'd made. They were identical, down to where the outer edges of the heels failed to show. Without question, Cory was targeted by the same malicious maniac who had killed Moll.

And despite the danger, Cory was probably even now asking questions, trying to solve the mystery. Given her loyalty to her dead friend, he didn't doubt it. How would he ever keep her safe from harm?

He needed to find Cory, but he ought to be here when Carew returned from a supervised visit with Sarah, a suggestion of Cory's that Matthew approved. As he sat down to wait, he spotted a pair of lady's chopines. Carew had been cleaning Lady Leicester's chopines when Cory found Moll. His son must have brought them along last night so they wouldn't be lost. Lady Leicester would be irate if they weren't returned.

Picking up the footwear, he headed for the door. He would return the shoes quickly and still be here when Carew returned. He might yet find Cory as he sought Lady Leicester's lodgings. He would also pass the Earl of Essex's lodgings to reach his mother's, but chances of encountering the earl were slight. If they did meet, it might be an opportunity to examine the man's boots. Matthew burned with the need to find their owner, and he intended to set about the task without delay.

As for his son, upon his return from Sarah's, Matthew vowed to take him and Cory to the queen, where the extra guards were. They must be kept as far as possible from his murder inquiry.

After some time in the chapel, Cory felt able to bear her sorrow and resolved to call on Monsieur La Faye. He might know something that would shed light on Moll's death.

Outside the chapel, she bumped into Dorothy Fleming. "Cordelia," the older woman greeted her. "Have you seen that imp, Samuel? He was to accompany me on my walk in the gardens whilst Jane saw to my laundry. Now I have no servant to attend me."

"I'm sorry, I haven't seen him," Cory said as they crossed the chapel entry hall. As she opened the door to the Chapel Court and Dorothy stepped outside, Carew leaped from behind a pillar and raced across the entry hall. He flung both arms around Cory in an exuberant embrace. She staggered under his affectionate assault, thinking it odd. Carew hugged her in private but never in front of others. He said it was too embarrassing at his age.

"I have something to tell you," he whispered in her ear under the pretext of the hug. "I didn't think I needed to before, but since we found Moll, I must."

She returned his hug, understanding its purpose now. "What is it, dear?"

"My father took me to the cordwainer's the other day."

At the mention of a bootmaker, Cory excused herself to Dorothy, asked her to wait in the courtyard, and closed the door. "How lovely," she said, trying to hide her anxiety. Surely Matthew wouldn't tell Carew about his investigation. "Did he buy you your first pair of boots?"

"He did, but that isn't why we went." Carew spoke in a rush of excitement. "He said someone wearing a pair of Master Howe's boots did something dangerous the other night, and I know you were shot at. I heard it from Sarah, who heard it from her maid, who heard it from—"

"You must not listen to gossip, Carew," Cory admonished, appalled at how the servants spread talk at the palace. Yet it was usually the fault of their masters and mistresses, who thought nothing of speaking before them as if they didn't exist. "I was shot at, but I don't want you involved in any way. It's too dangerous for you even to know about it."

He nodded, his features pinched with concern. "I know, but I couldn't help overhearing Father. Master Howe said he didn't think it was Lord Burghley or Lord Essex, but it might be one of the others. I'm worried for you. Tell me what I can do."

A knot of anxiety tightened in her stomach as she realized one thing she and Matthew hadn't discussed. If she were the target, everyone around her was in danger. "You've learned something you were never meant to know, Carew," she said solemnly. "You must not discuss it with anyone save me. You say Master Howe mentioned the Earl of Essex?"

"Yes, and Father went to Lord Burghley's this morning and came back looking almost cheerful. I'm sure it wasn't Burghley who shot at you."

"How do you know your father went to Lord Burghley's?" she asked, baffled as to how he'd gotten so much information.

"Lord Burghley's usher told me. I'll wager Essex was the one who shot at you. He can be a bastard at times." He embraced her again, a ferocious bear hug so full of boyish concern that she did not correct his language. "Let me take care of you, Cory," he begged. "I cannot think why someone would try to hurt you. Everyone else loves you."

Someone didn't love her, she thought, although she couldn't think the Earl of Essex would try to kill her. "Carew, one last question before we forget all this and enjoy the pleasant day. What does it have to do with Moll? You said you needed to tell me since we found her."

"I'm not sure, but bad things are happening." Carew pushed back the hair hanging in his eyes. "First to you, then to Moll. I keep wondering who's next."

Terrified that Carew might be targeted for asking suspicious questions of the wrong people, Cory realized she must take firm charge of him. Opening the chapel door, she waved to Dorothy.

"Dorothy, I have promised Carew's father to take care of him," she said as the woman rejoined them. "But just now I must run an important errand. If he is very obedient, would you let him attend you on your walk? I will collect him as soon as I am done." She turned to Carew. "You will be as good as gold for Lady Fleming, will you not?"

Dorothy smiled brightly at the prospect of so mature a page to accompany her, and Carew nodded meekly. Cory breathed in relief. Given her customary self-interest, Dorothy would demand Carew's full attention during the walk. He would have no chance to get into trouble while he carried her train, fanned her when she got hot, and served her in a hundred other ways.

As Cory watched them set out, she resolved to visit the Earl of Essex immediately. Though she didn't know exactly what she was looking for, she could ask to see his boots by Master Howe. If nothing more, she should be able to tell if they had been worn in the mud.

Another thought was foremost in her mind as she hurried down the corridor. Samuel had seen Essex and Moll together just before she died. He'd been trying to kiss her, and she had fought him. Now that she knew Moll had been with child, she would ask him about that as well.

After returning Lady Leicester's chopines, Matthew approached the Earl of Essex's lodgings. The outer door stood open, and a slender female with dark hair stood on the threshold. The earl loomed over her, a distinctly amorous expression on his long narrow face.

Recognizing Cory's hair and figure, Matthew glided backward, sure Essex hadn't seen him.

"I wish to see your boots by Master Howe," he heard her demand in an authoritative tone.

Matthew advanced on them, outraged at what she was doing even as he was perplexed. How had she known to question Essex about his boots?

"I would rather show you something else," the earl crooned, reaching for Cory. "Come into my chambers, sweet, and I will—"

Matthew could barely contain his rage as Cory struggled in the earl's arms. "Do you make a habit of mauling unwilling females?" he demanded.

"I do not discourse with river scum," Essex scoffed as he saw who confronted him. "Be off." But he released Cory, who retreated behind Matthew to straighten her disarrayed bodice.

Matthew's gaze bored into Essex. "I am questioning suspects about the recent attack by the crossbow archer," he stated, all too willing to use a blunt attack.

Essex stepped back a pace, frowning. "What has that to do with me?"

"A good deal, since I understand you own a pair of Master Howe's boots, and the culprit wore a pair made by him." Matthew smiled congenially as Essex turned pale as a parsnip. "If you would fetch the boots, I will examine them."

Essex appeared even more ruffled. "The queen expects me to take noon dinner with her."

"This will take only a minute," Matthew said firmly. "You may go, Viscountess," he said without turning around. "I will handle this matter." Despite his relief that she would be removed from the situation, he was glad to have seen her with Essex. Her angry, pointed gaze at him hardly suggested she loved him. Although memory of the couple's passionate kiss in the green antechamber still burned in his mind, she had struggled against his embrace just now.

Essex grew more agitated as they entered his chamber and he sent his servant, a dark-haired man who sounded French, for his boots.

"So," Matthew continued as the earl fidgeted with his ruff. "Someone shot at the viscountess, as you have no doubt heard.

I wonder why? Could it be because she rejected your efforts to bed her?"

His head-on attack seemed to scatter Essex's self-possession in a dozen directions. "I should challenge you to a duel for suggesting such vile nonsense. Women of all stations beg for the privilege of sharing my bed. I have no need to invite unwilling females."

Matthew grinned, pleased with how his bluntness had unnerved Essex.

"Was Moll Dakins one of the women you so graciously permitted to share your bed?" Cory asked as she followed them inside.

With effort, Matthew contained a rebuke at her outrageous question. "Madam, I thought you were gone."

Cory stood her ground, a defiant gleam in her eyes. As the earl's servant brought his boots and Matthew took them, Cory crowded in close to look.

"I believe I told you to go." Matthew gritted the words from between clenched teeth. Turning the boots over, he noted Howe's characteristic H pressed into the soles, as well as the stacked wooden heels. Their edges were well defined, not in the least worn from walking.

"What do you see?" she demanded, glancing from the boots to his face.

"Nothing." He handed the boots back to Essex.

Cordelia pushed past him to confront the earl. "I heard you were recently trying to kiss Moll Dakins in the green antechamber. She was struggling against you and saying nay."

"Viscountess, it would be improper to discuss such a subject with you," Essex spluttered.

"Ah, so you don't deny it," she countered. "Remember, the woman has been murdered. If you don't want to be considered a suspect, I suggest you tell us everything you know."

"I had nothing to do with her demise." Essex held his ground, his tone icy.

"Perhaps. But you might have had something to do with her being with child." Cory smiled coolly as she shot her cannonball into the fray.

Essex looked horrified. "Did she say I was the father? Others had her before me. The slut's morals were as loose as her tongue."

Matthew wondered how Cory could bear to hear such things said of her friend, but she merely shot him a triumphant glance. "So you did have her in bed," she said to Essex.

"She was more than willing," the earl yelped, realizing she'd tricked him into the admission. "With me as well as others who paid her. You could have had her too, Graystock," he finished.

"He wouldn't," Cory contradicted. "He's not that sort of man, to take advantage of a poor girl who was so desperate for funds, she would let men use her."

Matthew flinched at the direction the exchange was taking. How had she put herself in the thick of this affair? With apparent ease, she had Essex blabbing of how he'd bedded Moll. Her bluntness bested his. "You paid Moll?" he asked. Facing Essex, he put Cory behind him.

"I gave her gifts for being so accommodating," Essex admitted, smoothing his hair with an unsteady hand.

"Who else bedded her?"

"For an upstart merchant's son, you ask the most impertinent questions, Graystock. In a lady's presence, too." He looked pointedly at Cory in an attempt to reestablish superiority.

Matthew imagined Cory's wide-eyed interest in the proceedings. Devil take it, why didn't she go away. This wasn't safe, especially if Essex were guilty. "Viscountess, I pray you would leave us," he ordered.

"He said that to distract you," she insisted, moving closer behind him. "Answer the question, Lord Essex, or you know the consequences. Whom else did she bed with?"

"Many had her," Essex blabbed, clearly eager to turn suspicion away from himself.

"Who, specifically?" Matthew repeated, holding hard to his temper at the earl's insensitivity.

"Yes, answer the question," Cory pressed. "Or do you prefer to remain the only suspect?"

Essex again blanched. "I know Sir William Norris had her. And I didn't kill her. You're proving to be a true troublemaker, Graystock, to suggest such a thing." Essex seemed to gather himself for a new show of bravado. "I should have killed *you* when I had the chance."

Matthew's control snapped. "Care to try now?" He reached for his rapier.

Cory pushed past him and planted herself between him and the earl. "My lords, you cannot fight here. There is not room."

Essex sent her a seductive smile that sickened Matthew. "Ah, sweet," he said dramatically, "would you sigh for me, were I to face the danger of a duel?"

"No!" Matthew spat without thinking, surprised to hear Cory say the same thing. "You wouldn't?" He turned to her, baffled. "Why not?"

Her green eyes blazed with indignation. "I wouldn't sigh for him for all the gold in Byzantium."

Matthew wanted to shout with relief.

The earl's face turned red, then purple. "Cordelia, you led me to believe—"

"That I am your supportive friend," she finished smoothly, all mollifying attention now. "And I am. As I know your wish to wed the widowed Lady Sidney, I can help you convince the queen you must get an heir. She will soon agree that Lady Sidney is an appropriate match for that purpose." Her smile softened until it was like an after-dinner sweet, dripping with syrup.

Matthew recognized her ploy as she turned to the one topic Essex couldn't resist. Himself.

"Lady Sidney worships the ground you walk on and would be loyal and loving to the death," Cory said. "You're a fortunate man, and she is fortunate to have your regard."

Ever egotistical, Essex basked in the praise. "She does worship me. Before her husband died in battle, he bid me care for her if he failed to return. Of late, I grow increasingly fond of her."

"How admirable, Lord Essex," Cory said. "Why don't you seek her out now? Imagine how her face would light up upon seeing you. And if you requested her hand—"

"The queen would be furious," Essex interjected.

Matthew wanted to snort. The queen's fury, nothing. The selfish young earl cared only for his own interests.

"Her Majesty would forget in time," Cory said in a most convincing manner, "especially if Lady Sidney leaves court once you're wed. She would be happier at your estate anyway, with her daughter and the son she will no doubt bear you. You would be her hero and ensure her future."

"I could rescue her from her widowhood, couldn't I?" Essex took her suggestions to heart all too readily, Matthew thought, as the earl sauntered off to find Lady Sidney, seeming lost in the heroic dream Cory had created for him.

As he disappeared, Matthew found Cory smiling with grim satisfaction. "We handled that rather well."

"*You* reduced him to a doddering idiot." The exchange had left Matthew feeling vastly uneasy. Although Essex's boots hadn't been involved in the crossbow shooting, he still believed the hot-tempered earl capable of violence in a fit of rage. He couldn't eliminate him yet as a suspect, and if he were guilty, Cory was in great danger.

Cory shook her head. "I merely suggested his favorite subject to him."

"You will have to explain something, madam. I saw you kissing him the other day." He held up a hand to halt her protest. "Yet you think nothing of practically accusing him of murder, asking him deeply personal questions, then sending him off to propose to another woman. Why?"

Her green eyes danced with sudden amusement. "You saw us kissing? I only did it as payment for calling off the duel with you."

Matthew could barely contain a string of mariner's curses. "You kissed that bastard so I would lose the chance of cutting him to ribbons? I would rather you had not."

"The queen assigned me the task of stopping him. I did my duty."

She smiled in her sweetest manner, which he knew was trouble. "You think you're a clever puss. But Her Majesty would be outraged to know *how* you accomplished your objective."

"But she won't hear. We women take great pains to keep her happy, else everyone's life is miserable. If she knew of all the women Essex has kissed, she would have apoplexy, for there have been many, I assure you. But tell me, my lord, if I had wanted to wed Essex, why would you object?"

He cleared his throat, trying to decide how to reply. "For one thing, since he was involved with Moll, he's still a suspect in her murder. But even if he isn't guilty, he's hardly the sort to be considerate of his wife. He said ugly things about Moll in your presence, which surely hurt to hear as she was your friend. And you see how he bedded Moll even as he was wooing Lady Sidney to be his wife. You would have been unhappy with him."

Chapter 14

Cordelia stared at Matthew in astonishment. She had expected him to warn her away from the queen's favorite to avoid Her Majesty's wrath. Instead, his first concern was for how Essex's talk about Moll might have hurt her, then, for her happiness.

Blinded by the sudden moisture that gathered in her eyes, she turned away, her throat tightening. No one but Grandmama had cared about her happiness in so long. How ironic that it should be a man wedded to the sea who chose to champion her cause, instead of someone who could love her as she wished. All the great Baron Graystock did was lust for her, by his own admission, although she hadn't found him so cold or detached when she'd been in his arms. Nor was there anything but kindness in the words he had just uttered.

Struggling to master her emotions, she turned back to him. "I thank you for your concern." She paused, troubled both by what she had learned of Moll and by the difficulty she still faced. "My poor friend. She must have let Essex bed her for the money to feed her family. If only she had told me. I would have found funds for her some other way."

"Of course you would have." His voice was low and gentle. "But you must not blame yourself."

"We must speak to Sir William Norris." She refused to wipe

her watering eyes for fear he would remark on them. Valiantly she blinked, hoping the tears would dry.

"*You* must take care of Carew for me," he said firmly as he tucked her hand in the crook of his arm and led her away from Essex's lodgings. "You can keep him with you whilst you wait on the queen, who has agreed to double her guards. At least I'll know the three of you are safe."

"Despite how well I handled Essex?" She couldn't resist casting him a pert glance.

His expression darkened. "It might not have gone so well if I hadn't been present. You must be careful of whom you speak to alone. The lunatic may try again to harm you."

She allowed he was right, though she thought she was right as well. "I cannot stay with the queen every moment," she reminded him. "And I refuse to be ruled by fear. If I suspect everyone, I'll go mad."

"I understand, but do not go anywhere alone, and let me handle the questioning."

His patience seemed strained, and she thought it wise not to press him further about the questioning. Still, she felt shut out by his refusal to discuss the matter, and her loneliness returned. Whenever she thought she might grow close to this man, he found a way to put distance between them. "Her Majesty is displeased with me for refusing Sir William," she confided, hoping he would open up again. "But I'm glad I did, especially if he bedded Moll." She paused, then added, "She's not terribly pleased with you, either."

"She discussed me with you?"

"Now you know how I felt." She felt instantly penitent for her desire to discomfit him. "She only said Carew ought to stay in Dorset and you should visit him there." Blood rushed to her face as she remembered how the queen had also suggested they wed.

He seemed to sense she had left something unsaid, for he stopped in a courtyard and scrutinized her. "What else did she say?"

"About Carew? That is all." She would rather die than discuss marriage with Matthew, especially since he lusted for her, and she supposed she felt the same thing for him. How else could she explain the heat that rose within her when he was near?

He didn't appear to believe her. "Did she press you about your marriage?"

Cory decided a half-truth was better than an outright lie. "She expects me to make a decision soon."

"I thought as much. Did she mention whom she thought you should wed?"

She shifted uneasily. "We discussed the Earl of Derby's son."

"Who is not at court just now. Did she agree to send for him, so you could meet?"

"No," she admitted miserably.

"Then who else did she name since you refused Sir William?"

His relentless questions backed her into a corner, and Cory swallowed convulsively, sure he could read her mind. "You," she whispered, unable to meet his gaze. "She said it could be a reasonable arrangement, though of course she's mistaken."

Matthew struggled against the onslaught of desire that attacked him at Cordelia's words. A reasonable arrangement wasn't the term he would apply. Wildly arousing or madly enticing was more likely. "I can't just wed you, sell your land, spend your money on my ships, and sail away. It would be wrong," he stated with conviction.

Her stricken expression cut him to the core. Blast. The queen must not have told her everything. She'd most likely left out mention of the money. He should have known, but as usual he told the truth and hurt her in the process. "The queen had promised to back my next voyage," he explained, wanting her to know he'd refused out of consideration. "She changed her mind, instead offering you in marriage. She wanted me to use your inheritance in place of her funds."

The desolation in Cory's face increased, and he felt worse than ever. "I'm sorry. I would gladly do whatever is required to ensure your happiness, but I'm sure that's not it. Far better that I should inspect the background of any man you choose to consider."

"Of course." She lifted her head proudly, and he saw the supreme effort it took to mask her hurt. "With you gone most of the time, we would not suit in the least." Grasping a fist full of skirts, she moved toward the door leading to the queen's privy chambers. "I'll go to the queen now. You can be about your affairs."

Matthew cursed his bluntness as she walked away, the stiff line of her back unyielding. Yet she seemed more vulnerable to him than ever in that moment. Damn it, why couldn't he have been more diplomatic? But in the world of a seafarer, dexterity with words was not valued, and he was out of practice.

The idea that he had once more put distance between them pained him, but then he would be leaving England soon. She would do better to seek a husband, not spend time with him. She deserved a man who would stay with her always and return her passionate emotions in equal measure.

Still, it was a bleak knowledge that Titania's quicksilver beauty, her wry humor, and her valiant heart could never be his. But what could he give her in return?

Turning in the other direction, he willed himself to work, his balm to all pain. He had sent a message to his brother Jonathan's wife that morning to see if she had heard from him. He expected her reply by return messenger. In the meantime, he would call on Sir Francis Knollys and Sir William Norris. With two suspects cleared, one of them might be their man.

After that, he must speak to Captain Wells, who was to question some linen weavers about the unusually large handkerchief used to tie Moll Dakins's body in the scullery cupboard. He found it odd that something so distinctive should have been left behind. A clever criminal wouldn't make that mistake. But perhaps he'd had nothing else on hand to do the job. Perhaps he'd meant to remove it later but never had the chance. Perhaps the handkerchief didn't even belong to the person who'd killed Moll. The murderer might have taken it from another, either because his need was urgent or because he wanted to deflect blame from himself.

A thousand explanations were possible. It remained Matthew's task to discover the truth.

Cory rushed up the stairs, misery chasing her like hounds after the hart. Why should she mind if the queen had suggested Matthew wed her and he'd refused. Hadn't she done the same?

Wasn't it clear to her that they didn't suit?

Certainly it was. But that didn't stop her from wanting what she couldn't have. She still wanted her mother after all these years. She wanted to be with Letty, Marcus, and Grandmama, but she couldn't. The peddler woman should have said she was made for loneliness, not love.

Reminded of her painful losses, she turned in the direction of Monsieur La Faye's lodgings. She must collect Carew from Lady Fleming, then help serve noon dinner to the queen. But she would take half a minute to express her sympathies to La Faye and appoint a later time when they could meet. And tonight, she must pay her last respects to Moll before her burial.

Matthew paused at Norris's door and knocked. "Good afternoon, Sir William," he said, after a servant admitted him. "I wish to examine your boots by Master Howe." He had a suspicion that this might be the culprit, as he had just seen Sir Francis Knollys's boots and absolved him of guilt. They had been worn a great deal for riding, but the heels were as good as new. They could never have made the footprints he'd seen in the mud. And he already disliked Norris for forcing himself on Cory.

Seated before the fire, his shirt mounded over his rotund belly, his netherstocks ungartered, Norris squinted at Matthew with displeasure. "You want to see my boots, Graystock? Whatever for? Always thought you were a lunatic. This proves it."

"I'm not susceptible to flattery." Matthew let sarcasm lace his response, sure Norris knew why he asked. "Send your servant for the boots."

Norris remained unrattled. "I gave them to one of my servants months ago. They were old. Look here, sir, does this have something to do with whoever shot at Lady Wentworth? If so, you're following the wrong trail. I assure you I had nothing to do with it."

"Are you sure the boots are not here? Perhaps I should look."

"Look all you like, but you won't find them. Robert will show you where I keep my footwear." He waved to his servant, who hovered in the background.

Furious at his denial and increasingly suspicious, Matthew

followed Robert into the next chamber, where he was invited to search a coffer full of boots and shoes.

Norris lumbered in to stand at the door, glaring at Matthew as he searched. It took a good quarter of an hour to determine that no boots by Master Howe lurked in the coffer. Irritated that Norris had stood by, never offering his servant's help, Matthew straightened.

"To whom did you give these boots?" he asked, conceding that they weren't here.

"Geoffrey Hall. But he left my employ shortly after of his own accord." A defiant expression marred Norris's face as he tucked in his shirttails. "Took the boots with him."

He appeared sincere to Matthew, or was he simply a good liar? "Where did he go?"

Norris raised his hefty shoulders in a shrug. "Said he'd taken a position serving a gentleman in the city. I didn't ask the man's name." He named a city parish where Hall had said he would live. "I spoke to the queen this morning," he continued, his face changing into a smirk. "She still applauds the idea of my wedding Viscountess Wentworth. I'm to try again."

Matthew tensed. "She'll turn you down as she did last time."

"Do you hope to have her for yourself? Is that what you're up to?" Norris challenged.

"I merely wish her to make a free choice in her best interest."

"Ha." Norris snorted with derision. "That leaves you out, then, doesn't it."

Matthew ignored the jab. "You say you had no part in the shooting incident with Viscountess Wentworth, but what of the death of her friend, Moll Dakins. I understand you bedded her."

"What if I did bed her? That doesn't mean I killed her. Quite the opposite, for I was sorry to lose her. She was a most enjoyable little thing."

Matthew was repulsed. Norris apparently felt no remorse for bedding an unwed girl yet he refused to marry her or even serve as her protector. "Did you know she was with child when she died? Was the babe perhaps yours?"

"Who knows whose child it was," Norris sneered. "She

bedded many men for the money. It could have been any one of us."

"Do you know who else she slept with?" Matthew asked.

"Sir Francis Knollys had her regularly, but she charged him more than me because he's old and ugly," Norris laughed.

Matthew found the man's openness disarming, but he still didn't trust him. What had seemed a straightforward issue of guilt was becoming muddled, and Norris was giving nothing away. "And you're certain you've not spoken to this servant, Geoffrey Hall, of late?"

"I have neither seen nor spoken to him."

That didn't mean he hadn't sent a message, Matthew thought. Planning to visit Geoffrey Hall on the morrow, Matthew strode off. He still did not absolve Norris of a connection to the crossbow incident, but why would he kill Cory if he wanted to marry her? It made no sense.

But then perhaps he'd had nothing to do with it. Hall might have acted on his own, or been paid by someone else. If they just knew why someone wanted Cordelia dead, it might be easier to determine who was threatening her life and why it was connected to the murder of Moll.

As he set off for the stables, Matthew ran into the messenger he had sent to his sister-in-law earlier in the day.

"The lady is most upset," the man said, handing him a sealed letter.

"I thank you." Matthew paid him and scanned the message from Margaret. "Damn." He stuffed the letter in his pocket and turned toward the stables again, lengthening his stride. Margaret had heard nothing from Jonathan and was greatly distressed. He would visit her on the way to the shipyard and assure her that if his reckless brother was in danger, Matthew would go to France himself. He just hoped his brother would send word soon that he was safe.

He imagined Margaret's anxiety and renewed his vow never to wed. Why make some poor woman miserable with his yearlong voyages. It was his livelihood and hardly something he could simply discard like a worn pair of boots.

Still, he couldn't help wishing he could fulfill Cordelia's needs, both by marrying her and loving her the way she deserved. It was impossible, of course, but her selfless desire to reach out to others touched him. He was learning to appreciate her for her own special qualities, instead of comparing her to Joanna all the time. His dead wife had been the sole measure against which he judged women for so long, but Cory was broadening his view. She was a woman to admire, and she had already suffered more than her share of sorrow.

Chapter 15

Cory went through the ritual with the other maids of honor of serving the queen her noon dinner. She and La Faye had set a time to talk, but it could not be until the morrow. The poor man had seemed bent down with anguish at the mention of Moll's name. Her heart ached for him. If only she could have stayed to comfort him, but her duty to the queen could not wait.

It was public day, and the great hall was thronged with people who had come to admire their sovereign while she dined on elaborate dishes. Many of them wished to ask favors and would offer petitions as she walked among them upon leaving the hall. Extra guards had been set due to the recent incidents. All the maids of honor and ladies in waiting were present, wearing their best gowns to increase the pomp and ceremony surrounding England's queen.

When it was her turn to serve, Cory fetched a silver platter of roast capon from the table. Carew was leaning against a chair nearby. "I'm bored," he mouthed as she removed the silver cover and offer the sliced meat and peas to the guard who was the queen's official taster that day.

She raised her eyebrows at Carew in warning. The rascal wasn't bored. He'd been making eyes at Sarah Vasavour, who was standing at the other end of the table. The pair were just waiting for an opportunity to slip away together when no one was looking.

"Be good or else," she mouthed back at him, rolling her eyes toward Sarah as the guard took his eating knife, stabbed a piece of capon, and put it in his mouth.

Carew smirked at Cory, suggesting he was in the mood to be anything but.

"My God!" The guard suddenly expelled the mouthful of food and bent double, seized by a fit of coughing. "Water!" he screeched, his hands clasped to his mouth. "Poison."

Everyone in the great chamber froze except Cory. She slammed the platter on the table and leaped for the water ewer, filled a goblet, and thrust it at the guard. "Rinse your mouth." She held an empty dish cover for him to spit in. "Quickly! Again," she ordered as he obeyed.

"Hot," he panted, guzzling the water and spitting, then repeating the process. "Hot." He sank to his knees, clutching his throat. "Majesty, I die."

Elizabeth rose from the table. "Who has done this terrible thing!" she thundered, full of righteous fury in her red spangled gown ladened with jewels. She whirled and pointed at a maid of honor. "Fetch Dr. Rowley. Hurry, girl!" The maid raced off.

Dr. Rowley arrived within minutes, his black robes flying as he cut a swathe through the crowd. People parted in silence to let him through. The guard was on the floor by that time, groaning piteously. Elizabeth bent over him on one side, Cory on the other, both chaffing his wrists with cool water and urging him to lie quietly until help came.

Lord in heaven protect us, Cory thought. *The killer had struck again. Would the poor man die a slow, painful death as the poison ate away his mouth and throat?*

"Let me look." Rowley knelt by the guard, who sobbed as he opened his mouth.

It was then that Cory noticed Carew's amused expression, and an unpleasant suspicion occurred to her.

"Sir," she said to Dr. Rowley from her place at the guard's feet. "Is his mouth burned?"

"Not at all," Rowley said. "What the devil are you complaining about, man? Your mouth looks fine. A little pink, but no burns."

"Hot," the guard moaned again.

"Would you be so good as to fetch that platter?" Cory waved to the maid who had followed the physician back to the hall.

Cory cast a stern glance at Carew as she took the platter and
studied the capon. In disgust, she held it for Dr. Rowley to see.

"A great quantity of red pepper was added to this dish."
Rowley surveyed the silent crowd, his expression radiating
disapproval. "How did it happen?"

Carew snorted with suppressed laughter.

Infuriated and mortified to know that Carew had so violated
her trust, Cory stalked over to him, grasped him by the ear, and
dragged him from the great hall.

Cory knelt in the darkened chapel before Moll's closed coffin, Carew at her side. He wasn't going to escape his father's
wrath this time. Nor the queen's. Nor hers. Not after frightening the entire court. She had managed to protect him from a
beating by the queen's guard. But she wouldn't protect him
from a reasonable consequence. Thank fortune that Matthew
had been away at the docks all day. It had given her time to
speak sternly to Carew and make him understand why his
prank was so terrible. She thought it would also sober him to
see Moll's burial preparations. He needed a reminder of the serious side of life.

Her tactic seemed to have worked. He knelt beside her,
seeming subdued. "Carew, you frightened everyone half to
death." She couldn't help but bring up the subject again.

"No one was hurt." He still seemed determined to defend his
behavior.

"Not physically. But there's been a murder in the palace.
Poisoning is not a jest."

"The taster looked funny, howling and fussing that he was
going to die when he wasn't," Carew insisted, fidgeting on the
kneeling bench before the altar.

"I understand, but that doesn't excuse what you did." Cory
paused, wondering what she could say to impress upon him the
seriousness of his error. "You must not seek enjoyment in the
pain of others. I expect you to apologize to the guard and offer
to run all the errands he requires around the palace for one full
day. We will let him choose the day."

"Oh, very well." Carew sighed. "You talk to him. He'll be
angry when he sees me again."

"I won't talk to him for you," Cory said sternly. "You will
face him yourself. If he's angry, it's no more than you deserve.

And of course your father will also punish you. I hope you see that a jest can be out of place. Think first before you do such a thing. Better yet, discuss it with a friend and attend to his reaction. You're old enough to make an intelligent judgment."

Carew looked penitent as he gazed at the closed coffin. Decay had taken too strong a hold on Moll's body to show it at her funeral. It must be put below ground as soon as Cory visited Moll's family on the morrow. "Why did you do it?" she asked, realizing with sorrow that more lay beneath Carew's prank than the desire for a laugh.

"Why shouldn't I. No one cares what I do."

Cory heard the mixture of defiance and hurt in his voice. "Your father cares."

"No, he doesn't. He doesn't give one damn about me."

"Carew, even if you believe that, do as I suggested. Tell him you didn't mean to hurt anyone. Tell him you love him."

Carew leaped to his feet. "Why do you keep saying that? He'll just say I have a foolish way of showing it. I hate him. I do. I'm going to bed and I don't want to see him tonight. Tell him I died. Tell him he doesn't need to bother with me ever again." He stood in the light of the single candle, his breath quickened with anger, his fists clenched.

"I care about you, Carew," Cory said quietly. "I love you."

He stared at her with haunted eyes full of pain, and although he held back for the space of a heartbeat, he finally lunged into her embrace. "It's all right," she whispered as his sobs awoke her own despair. " 'Twill take time for your father to admit he loves you."

He pulled back, his face twisted with misery and tears. "My father and I don't have time. We never have." He poised to race away, but something held him back. "I'll go straight to my chamber," he said, suddenly calm beyond her expectations and his years. "Don't worry about me, Cory. I'll be all right."

His slender figure melted into the darkness. Cory let him go, immobilized by his unfulfilled needs that were so like her own at his age. She wished she could wipe away his suffering, but instead, he had wanted to reassure her, proving he could be mature and considerate.

Yet he would be inconsiderate and uncommunicative with his father the next time he saw him. All because he and his father had no time to heal their wounds. If they did, there might be hope, but Matthew's life was at sea.

The idea filled her with jealousy when she thought of the lands he visited, of the tropical weather in the new world. How she would like the freedom to travel and begin life anew.

A creak sounded in the chapel, and Cory jumped. "Who's there?" She twisted in all directions to see. Dead silence met her question. The high ceiling of the chamber soared into darkness above her. Shadows seemed to leap with menace, and she started at another creak. For the first time in six months at Hampton Court, she was afraid.

A light appeared at the far door, diminishing to a tip of flame as the bearer approached. Jane materialized out of the darkness, clutching a bundle under one arm. "I've brought Moll's things, Cory." Her voice was subdued in the silent chapel. As she stopped and set down her candle, the flame grew. "How did she look?"

"Terrible." Cory reached for her friend and the two embraced. "So bad, they put her in the coffin and nailed it shut. They'll let her family look at the funeral if they wish, but I could not do so again. It was too horrible for words."

Jane nodded and passed her the bundle. "The queen thought you would want to decide how to dispose of her things."

"Yes, of course. Perhaps there's something here to tell us who killed her." Eagerly Cory lay the bundle on the bench and opened the large square of linen that served as a covering. There was little within. She fingered a length of pale blue satin and a roll of pretty ribbons Moll had received from the queen. A comb and a brush. Some smocks and an extra apron. That was all. "How odd. She had more things than this, I'm sure." Cory smoothed a smock, wishing desperately for answers. "I gave her a pretty wooden box painted with flowers for her natal day. She kept trinkets in it. Hairpins and the like. Was it not there?"

"I saw no such box in her cupboard." Jane appeared perplexed.

"She kept letters in it, too. I know because she told me. What could have happened to it? Do you suppose one of the other tirewomen took it?"

Jane shook her head. "I doubt it. They would have thought it unlucky. Because of what happened to Moll, you know."

Upset by the loss, Cory unfolded the linen smocks, searching each one. "Surely the letters haven't just disappeared," she said with some heat. Had someone taken them? Had a clue to the murderer's identity been among them?

As if in ominous portent, the candle beside Cory flickered. A chill touched her back, as if someone had opened the chapel door to listen and watch, disturbing the air currents of the vast chamber. The hair on the back of her neck prickled, and she stole a hasty glance over her shoulder. Nothing but yawning dark met her gaze.

"What kind of letters did she receive?" Jane asked, all curiosity.

"Her father was the son of a well-to-do merchant back in France. After he came here for religious reasons and started a family, they didn't prosper," Cory explained as she refolded the smocks, disappointed at finding nothing. "But he still taught the entire family to read and write. She had some notes from Monsieur La Faye. She also wrote to me several times, so I wrote her back." As Cory checked the apron, she felt the crackle of paper within the pocket. "Ah, here's something." She drew out a square of vellum, revealing her own handwriting. "I remember writing this. She had just written to me of how much she cared for Monsieur La Faye, so I promised to help her arrange their marriage if he asked."

"Ugh," Jane said, shuddering. "Don't know how she could care for him. Twenty years her elder with a big gut besides. He's not at all nice to most of us servants. Acts as if we don't exist, so I can't think he fancied her enough to wed her. Not that I thought her unworthy," she added at Cory's reproachful glance. "But I think he was more likely just bedding her and she got the wrong idea."

"We must not question what Dame Fortune saw fit to bless her with," Cory said firmly, determined to believe in La Faye's affection for her friend. "People see things in each other that outsiders often cannot understand. Perhaps he cared for her in his own way." Saddened by the lack of answers to her many questions about Moll, Cory returned the letter to the apron pocket and prepared to reassemble the bundle. The cloth holding the items caught her attention. "Where did this come from?"

"It was with her things," Jane said. "It seemed a handy way to keep everything together."

Cory held up the large rectangle of cloth. "It's rather large for a handkerchief, but too small for a table napkin. What do you suppose it is? It's very good linen."

Jane shrugged. "Probably an extra scrap from the seamstress. Shall I put the whole thing in the maids' dormitory for you?"

"Yes, pray do. I will visit her family on the morrow and give everything to them, all but my letter to her, which will be my keepsake." The cloth wasn't a scrap, for it was perfectly hemmed on all sides, but Cory let it go. It didn't signify where the cloth had come from. "I know. I'll put everything in a wicker basket instead of using the cloth," she said, brightening. "That way I can make her mother a gift of a market basket without her feeling beholden. She'll think it was Moll's."

"An excellent idea." Jane yawned, and Cory bid her go to her bed.

As the maid drifted away, the darkness swallowing her up, Cory knelt, wishing to recapture her earlier serenity. But after several minutes, she knew it was hopeless. Her former calm had fled.

A floor board creaked behind her. Cory whirled to search the darkness, her heart racing with alarm. Matthew's tall figure glided out of the shadows. "Great fortune," she breathed, laying a hand on his sleeve to be sure he was real. "You gave me a start."

"Fortune, as you so frequently call on her, is with you tonight. 'Tis a friend, not a foe." He shifted her hand, gripping it with his own, and she felt grateful tonight for his strength. In his presence, she felt safe.

Yet she sensed an added depth of melancholy in him. "Have you seen Carew?" she asked.

"No." His expression was as grim as a storm at sea. "But half a dozen people told me what happened the instant I arrived back at court. Why people are so eager to bear bad news, I'll never know. I decided to wait until morning before Carew and I talk. Otherwise I might do something rash. I'll go to bed when I'm sure he's asleep."

She nodded, relieved at his decision to speak to Carew after his anger had cooled. Once he might have acted in the heat of his initial rage. The change gave her heart.

"You are going to visit Moll's family on the morrow?" he asked.

"Yes." She turned to the coffin where it stood on trestles and ran one hand along its rough wooden top. "I didn't want some messenger to drop the news on them without kindness to cushion it. We'll have the burial the next day."

"Can they afford a funeral? Who paid for her coffin?"

Cory was too embarrassed to admit she'd had no ready coin to pay the carpenter. She'd had to give him a pearl necklace instead.

He frowned at her over the flame of the candle as she failed to answer. "I will attend to everything, and you will not gainsay me." He moved closer to the coffin, his expression so grim that the words to thank him died in her throat. "I hate funerals," he muttered very low.

"They remind you of your wife?" Cory asked, then wondered why, in this moment of new loss, she should dredge up past pain.

He stared at the dark wood, his gaze seeming fixed on something beyond the present time and space. "It was years ago. I've accepted it."

She knew he hadn't. He had deprived himself of human intimacy after he lost the two most important people in his life. She would have done the same if she hadn't had Grandmama. The old woman had enveloped her with so fierce a love, Cory had been unable to resist. "It's natural to need closeness with others," she observed. "We all do."

He didn't answer. In the eerie, darkened chapel, the bleakness of his life spoke to her. At too young an age, he had been forced to drain the goblet of human pain to the dregs and never recovered from it. As had she. But unlike him, Grandmama had taught her that loving others brought comfort. She had showed Cory how to nurture Letty when her mother died, and Marcus when his mother deserted him. Since then, Cory had never hesitated to offer love or friendship to others. Until now, with Matthew. Still, she needed to communicate with him. "Tell me about Joanna," she said.

"Why?"

Why did she ask? In the hope that if he talked about his past, she would understand him better? In the hope that he would open up to her, and she could open her heart to him? "Just tell me anything," she coaxed, using the tones few people refused. "What was her favorite food?"

"She liked crisp apples freshly picked from the tree. When she was expecting Carew, I brought her dozens and teased her, saying she would become apple cheeked from eating so many. She would laugh and bite into one. She had perfect teeth and bowed lips, perfect for kissing."

Why did she want to know that? Cory wondered. It hurt to hear the love in his voice as he described the beauty of his wife. Yet it also made him more human, to know he had recorded each detail of his beloved in his memory. "Let's play cards," she proposed, suddenly wanting her favorite pastime to soothe her own pain.

"In chapel?"

"Why not? We won't wager. I'll deal five cards, then we'll each put out one card at a time, and whoever has the highest will take the trick. It's soothing. Play and you'll see." She fished a pack from the satin pouch at her waist and, bunching up her skirts so she could straddle the end of a bench, began to shuffle, the movement of the cards like a magician's wand, wiping away troubling thoughts.

"Will you allow me to see Carew sometimes after you leave?" she asked as she dealt the cards.

"If you like. Mayhap you can do something with him. I can't."

"What do you want for his future?" she asked. "Oxford, perhaps?" Finished with the deal, she picked up her hand and studied it.

"He told you about that, didn't he? His idiot father couldn't decide what to do with him, so he did nothing," he scoffed at himself. "I know I have trouble admitting he isn't an infant anymore. My son is becoming a man, but I'm still living ten years in the past."

"It seems too much to bear," she offered sympathetically. "You know it, but doing something about it makes it more real. I understand."

He bared his teeth in a macabre semblance of a smile. "I suppose you think I should find a replacement wife, like everyone else. But you can't substitute one person for another. The love I had for Joanna will last the rest of my life."

"Of course you can't substitute," she agreed. "Your loyalty is admirable."

"Admirable but stupid," he said bitterly.

"No," she contradicted. "I said admirable and I meant it. I understand how you feel because I lost someone I adored. Do you think I substituted Grandmama for my mother?" She paused and pressed her fingertips to her forehead, feeling bent down by the grief that haunted him as well as her. "I needed her desperately when we met, and in time I grew to love her, but it was never the same as the love I bore my mother."

"It was never as strong," he said with quiet conviction.

She folded her cards and straightened to face him, seeking his dark brown eyes. "On the contrary, it is just as strong, only different. My blood bond with my mother gave us an intuitive understanding of each other. It heightened our love for one another, but still, I love Grandmama with all my heart. No one else can make me laugh the way she does. No one else's hugs feel like hers. I was devastated to lose my mother, but that didn't stop me from learning to adore the dowager countess. And only good has come from it."

She picked up his untouched cards, fanned them, and put them in his hands. "Play."

He put down a card. She matched it with one of hers. "Aces are high. I win the trick." She took the cards and began a stack at her end of the bench. "Draw a replacement card."

"You have a penchant for pronouncements," he said dryly, obeying her command. "Where did you learn that skill?"

Once he had said she talked enough for two people. This, at least, was an improvement. "From my father, I think," she answered. "He was considered a great orator and often spoke in the House of Lords when it convened. Sometimes I questioned him when we supped because I loved to hear him speak of weighty subjects. He made everything sound so noble, so intelligent." She warmed to the subject, remembering her tall, handsome father. "He died too young, as did my mother. Small pox for her. A fever for him." She paused. "You loved two people in two different ways. Your father and your wife. Do you think it was wrong?"

"Of course not. I'm not suggesting that taking a second wife is wrong. Many men do it. But expecting to love her like the first is impossible."

She forced her voice to lightness. "Were you thinking of taking a second wife?"

"No." He turned away, shaking his head.

"Play," she ordered, slapping down a knave of diamonds.

He swung back and, without looking at her card, put down a ten of spades.

"You're not trying." She scowled at him as she took the trick.

He shrugged, taking her challenge another way. "So you've caught me in a lie. I think about taking another wife every time I come home. I ought to for Carew's sake, so he would have a mother while I'm gone. But I've never been able to do it."

She drew a replacement card for herself, then one for him. He played a king. She slapped it with an ace and took the trick. "No women who attract you?" she asked playfully.

Without meeting her gaze, he played the king of diamonds. She lost an eight of hearts to him. As he took the trick, he cast her a heated glance that kindled fire in her depths. Blood rushed to her cheeks, and she hid behind her cards as the famous adventurer wove his seductive web. But his teasing innuendo vanished abruptly. "I'll not wed for physical pleasure alone," he stated, playing a king of spades.

Her highest card left was a knave, and she lost it to him with ill grace. "Men don't have to wed for physical pleasure. They can take it where they will," she said with some heat. As he frowned, she rushed on, knowing she shouldn't blame him for the world's inequities. "You won't wed for love either, because you won't let yourself feel it again."

"With good reason," he countered. "You loved again after you lost your mother. Look what happened."

"Grandmama, Letty, and Marcus are not dead," she retorted. "Someone stands between us. One of these days, he'll move, and we'll be together again." Sometimes, when she missed them too dreadfully, she wondered if her love was worth the pain, but she must not doubt it. Not even in private. "Even if I never see them again, I can't regret loving them," she said staunchly.

He tossed down his cards and rose, moving around the bench until he loomed behind her. Cory shivered as chilly air

wafted on the chapel air currents. Her candle flickered and a
hot rivulet of wax burst forth to pour down the side of the taper.
Matthew straddled the bench behind her, his arms drawing her
close.

Cory pressed her hands over his and held on, leaning into his
warmth. They sat in silence for some time, sharing the comfort
of each other's arms. "I'm sorry for the loss of your grandmother and children. Perhaps things will change for you," he
said.

The husky concern in his voice soothed her. "I appreciate the
thought, but I'll make the best of things." She rubbed her cheek
against the velvet covering his arm.

"What will you do?"

"What I'm already doing. I love Samuel. I'll love Carew if
you'll let me, but not if you'd rather I didn't," she added as his
body tensed. A silence grew between them, not as comfortable
as before, and she replaced her cheek against his velvet-
covered arm. "You loved once as well. What were you like
then?" she whispered. "That's what I really want to know."

"I was a dreamer. I imagined myself a great poet and lover,
and all things seemed possible. To me, wherever Joanna went,
the sun seemed to follow, as if she basked in its light."

"That's very romantic."

"My head was stuffed with romantic thoughts as a boy. I had
no idea what I wanted to do with my life. My father urged me
to join him in the family business, but I preferred to write
reams of ridiculous verse in Joanna's honor, all of it terrible.
But she loved every word of it."

"Do you still have it?"

"I burned it after she died. Look, I came to see if you needed
anything, not to talk about my morbid past."

"It comforts me to comfort you." Yet she knew she had not
pierced his self-imposed reserve.

"Thank you, but what I need are answers, and we have too
few."

"Did you learn anything from Sir Francis or Sir William?"
she ventured.

"Sir Francis is not our man. Nor does Sir William seem
likely, though he still intends to demand your hand."

She wrinkled her nose in distaste. "I shall still refuse him."

"The queen may force you to accept him if you don't choose someone else."

She didn't like the sound of that. "What of his boots?" she asked to dodge the subject.

"He says he gave them away to a servant, who left his employ. Seems to be true, as I found no boots in his chamber. I intend to seek the new owner of the boots as soon as I can."

"I'll be anxious to hear what you learn." It cost her a great deal to remain quietly at the palace while he asked questions. But she needed to keep Carew safe from harm and would play her part as necessity required. With a last hug, she drew away.

He rose and bowed formally to her. "If there's nothing more, I shall bid you god'den. Oh, and there's this." He extracted a soft green fabric from inside his doublet. "I've forgotten to give it to you each time we met. It seems we always had other matters to discuss."

It was her green silk scarf. She accepted it mutely, wondering if he'd been wearing it against his heart. No, of course he hadn't. Tucking it in his doublet was merely a convenient way to carry it. She must let neither nostalgia over their first meeting nor the needs of her demanding heart mislead her. "Matthew, I hope you will . . . " She hesitated, seeking a way to give advice about Carew without being rejected. "That is, I pray you don't—"

"Beat Carew?"

"You won't, will you?"

"No, though the queen wanted me to. She was frothing at the mouth to take a switch to him, but I wouldn't let her. I said I would find a suitable punishment." He frowned, as if knowing what she wanted to say next. "I'm not in the mood for one of your sermons, Cordelia, no matter how lofty. I'll think of something reasonable and you will accept it."

She didn't much like that, though she was grateful he'd decided on an alternative to a beating. "If I can be of assistance," she offered, "pray let me know."

"I've promised not to beat him. Are you still not satisfied?" he demanded.

She would rather he discussed options with her, but she held her tongue.

He questioned her no further, but moved up the aisle, leaving her alone with the silk scarf. To her, it symbolized the essence of their relationship. He would eventually sail away; she would be left behind, holding nothing but memories.

She watched him melt into the darkness, then closed her eyes, understanding all too well Carew's trouble. The lad would take his father's leaving even harder than she. No wonder he was angry and defied the rules his father set for him.

If only Matthew could throw aside the barrier that kept him from telling his son how much he loved him. She sensed the caring beneath the surface, but he wouldn't let it out. It was too painful for him, and she had been hurt too much herself to think such a wound could be forgotten easily. She must leave them alone to find their way. And she must seek her own.

As she slipped into her bed in the dormitory, she remembered Moll's things and felt renewed disappointment over the lost flowered box. She wanted to question the women who had shared a chamber with Moll.

But it was late and she was tired. Deciding to seek answers later, she settled in her bed. As she drifted into sleep, the green scarf pillowed beneath her cheek, she remembered how the strength of Matthew's arms had felt around her. The caring and compassion in his face had moved her to tears. If only he could express those feelings to his son. And if only his caring and compassion could be hers for all time.

"She noticed the flowered box was missing, *and* she said that Moll kept letters in it. I tell you, she knows."

He had been enjoying a late-night glass of wine in his chamber and disliked being interrupted. Narrowing his eyes, he glared at his agitated associate, who shifted from foot to foot before him. "If she knows, why hasn't she done anything?" Keeping his calm, he applied logic to the problem. "She's had ample opportunity. It seems to me she doesn't know after all."

"No? What did you find in the box?"

"I told you. A letter with many blots and words crossed out. A draft."

"I knew it. Moll gave her the final letter," his associate exploded. "Viscountess Wentworth knows everything. We must dispose of her. You said yourself 'twas best to be on the side of safety. She's going to London on the morrow to visit Moll's family. We must do the deed then."

The fellow may not have the nerves for this work after all,

he reflected, noting the tense jaw and neck muscles. Still, there was no reason in the world to take chances. "Very well, make the arrangements." He felt in his pocket for coins.

His associate slammed one fist against the flat of his palm. "How will we get her alone? In London, people will bear witness to what befalls her. She may even have an escort with her."

He almost smiled at his associate's simple-minded view of their task. "She need not be alone. In fact, if she's not, all the better. 'Twill be a more convincing accident if an escort is involved as well." He held out two coins. "Purchase the necessary assistance. The other is for you."

He smiled at the cold hearth heaped with ashes as his associate quit the chamber. It had been a relief to find the incriminating letter Moll had written and consign it to the flames, even if it had been only a draft.

Had the viscountess received the final copy of that letter?

Although it seemed unlikely, he must assume she had and take no chances. It was the wisest policy.

Chapter 16

Cory grieved for Carew and Matthew the next day as she prepared to visit Moll's family in London. The two had apparently exchanged painful words last night. Matthew had punished Carew by confining him to his chamber all day, paying an usher to check on him once an hour.

It was not the penance she would have recommended. Better to have Carew apologize formally before the entire court, in addition to doing personal service to the guard whom he'd frightened half to death. But at least his confinement left her free to visit Moll's family while the queen was busy with state affairs.

Happily, when she'd called on Monsieur La Faye earlier, as arranged yesterday, he had offered to escort her to the city. Over cards, he had told her the story of how he and Moll had met, how pretty he had thought her, and Cory had warmed to him further. Indeed, he must have felt deeply for Moll, to speak so kindly of her despite their difference in status. If she had lived, he might have asked her to wed. No matter that he was years older, paunchy, and slightly arrogant. If he had been kind to her friend, it was enough for Cory.

Now, as she walked to their appointed meeting place in the palace Base Court, Cory felt in her purse to be sure she had the queen's letter of condolence, written by one of her clerks. Sympathetically worded, the letter also contained the balance of Moll's wages, but it was no substitute for a personal visit. Such news must be carried by one who had loved Moll, not by an impersonal messenger who would drop the cannonball on the family and depart.

" 'Tis the wettest summer I've ever seen," La Faye remarked as they walked among the other travelers going on foot and in carts toward the city.

"For certes," she agreed. She was grateful for his escort, sure he'd offered out of respect for Moll, though he had declined to visit Moll's family. Cory understood. He probably felt uncomfortable consoling her family since his relationship with Moll had not been sanctified by the church. Yet he had put aside his red court costume and wore only somber colors. Cory knew he was mourning. His grief, as she had consoled him in the privacy of his lodgings, had been all too apparent.

Still, he seemed intent on cheering her as they walked to London, entertaining her with talk of various and sundry subjects. Cory was grateful for his kindness in the midst of her difficult mission to Moll's family.

They found the Dakins household easily—a shabby, half-timbered dwelling squeezed between similar structures in one of the poorer sections of London.

"Madam." La Faye bowed over her hand. "I shall leave you for one hour to comfort the family. Then I shall return to escort you back to Hampton Court."

"Thank you." Cory inclined her head, then watched him disappear. With a heavy heart, she knocked at the door of the Dakins residence.

An hour later, her eyes scratchy from the tears shed as she had comforted the Dakins family, Cory emerged from the house to meet La Faye.

"Your visit was distressing?" He offered his arm with a solicitous air.

"It was very sad," Cory agreed, grateful for someone to lean on after the sorrowful hour. The Widow Dakins, a laundress by trade, had wept without ceasing, as had Moll's eight siblings. Some had babbled in French, reminding her of how she missed Moll.

As she walked in silence with La Faye, she noticed a blond

head bobbing in the crowd behind them. It reminded her of Carew. Could it be Carew?

She rose on tiptoe, trying to see. He couldn't have left Hampton Court. It would be very bad of him, sneaking away when he was supposed to be confined to his chamber.

"Is ought amiss, madam?" La Faye asked.

"I think I see someone I know." Even as she spoke, she lost sight of him among the people crowding the street. "No, I guess not." She sincerely hoped she had been mistaken.

"In France, we pick pears at this time of year," La Faye said, making polite conversation, though she was scarcely listening.

A shout rose in the street ahead of them. "Look out! 'eads up!"

People scrambled to clear the way. Cory froze as she spotted a runaway coach headed straight for them. The coachman stood on the box, straining to control the frightened horses.

"Flee!" La Faye shoved her toward what would have been safety, but his effort fell short. As he stumbled and sank to one knee, she reeled in the path of the coach.

With a strength born of terror, Cory lunged for the safety of his position and barrelled straight into him. Only half risen, La Faye plummeted backward, Cory falling on top of him.

As the horses thundered by, the deadly hooves narrowly missing them, La Faye landed hard. His head cracked against a cobblestone as the huge coach crashed past.

"Dear heaven, someone help!" Cory bent over his still body as the coach clattered away. "Monsieur, speak to me." She searched for a pulse in his neck and found it, fast and distinct, but he was terribly pale.

La Faye stirred and groaned piteously. "*Sacre bleu*, my head."

"How can we assist, madam?" A bailiff at Cory's elbow touched his cap.

"I pray you, fetch a physician," she entreated. "We must know how badly monsieur is injured. Then we will require a coach to take him home."

"At once, madam." The man departed, leaving a trio of underlings to hold back the crowd.

La Faye moaned, and Cory bent back over him. Beads of sweat stood on his forehead, a visible sign of his severe pain.

A blow to the head could be dangerous, and he would be badly bruised from the fall.

She must get him back to court and under the care of the court physicians. He had been hurt trying to save her. It was only fair she should nurse him back to health.

"What is this about an accident in London?" Matthew found Cory as she closed the door to La Faye's chamber. She was heavy-eyed with fatigue, her gown mud stained and the hem torn. He'd come searching for her as soon as he'd returned to court and heard the news.

"Monsieur La Faye has been injured, but he's resting in reasonable comfort at last." She turned and tottered down the corridor so unsteadily, he took her arm.

Matthew's concern increased. "I told you not to go anywhere alone."

She sent him a weary smile as several servants rushed past. "I wasn't alone. Monsieur La Faye was with me." She moved as if each step were a struggle. "The streets were full of people both ways. Here, the servants are about."

"He couldn't have protected you in case of danger."

"But he did. Or rather, he tried. He was injured in his effort to aid me. I should at least—"

"What do you mean?" Realizing his worst fears had come true, Matthew guided Cory into a curtained alcove and pressed her down on the cushioned windowseat. "You *were* in danger. What happened? What kind of an accident was it?"

"A runaway coach almost struck me. He tried to save me but fell. When I leaped to safety, I knocked him over and he hit his head." She closed her eyes a moment, then asked tonelessly, "You don't think someone tried again to kill me, do you?"

Her question unnerved him. He didn't know what had happened, except that his heart raced with fear at the image of Cory's being crushed by horses' pounding hooves. "You must listen to me and do as I say in future," he ordered. He took her by the shoulders, shocked by the intensity of his inner turmoil. Spasms shook her body as she buried her face against his chest and sobbed. "Don't cry," he whispered into her hair, holding her close. "It's over now." The warmth of her flesh through the light fabric of her bodice was a seductive temptation. He wanted the right to hold her forever like this. He wanted the

right to do more than hold her. But he snapped out of his lustful longings as he realized she was giggling. Or was she hysterical? "Cory, are you unwell?" He held her at arm's length.

Her smile was crooked, and a tear like a pearl slipped down
her cheek, reminding him of Titania, the fairy queen. "Forgive
me," she whispered. "I was so busy caring for La Faye, I forgot my fear. But just now . . ."

"Just now you realized what a close brush with serious injury you've had," he finished for her. "Sit for a moment, then
I'll take you to your chamber so you can rest."

"The maids' dormitory? I don't want to go there. They'll
want to gossip." She wrinkled her nose and burrowed into his
arms.

He understood perfectly. So many times in his youth he'd
wanted privacy onboard ship and couldn't have it. Not until he
became captain with a cabin of his own had he found it, though
often enough he gave it up to those who were ill. Privacy was
a precious commodity on a ship and at court. "Come to my
chamber," he said, rubbing her back. "I'll make you some of
that special tea, then leave you to sleep. I'll watch Carew this
afternoon."

"Please hold me. I feel safe with you."

Her plea melted his resistance. Gathering her close, he held
her to his heart. How tempting it was to enjoy this woman's
softness. Yet he must not take advantage of her.

"Have you seen Carew since you returned?" she asked.

"Yes, but I haven't seen the usher to know if he behaved."

She made no comment, leaving him to wonder if Carew had
been up to something. His mind was still on his son as she
asked about the investigation. "I must see Captain Wells next.
He hasn't learned a thing about that dratted handkerchief," he
said without thinking.

"What handkerchief?"

Matthew brought himself up short. Blast and damn. He
hadn't meant to mention the handkerchief.

"Tell me, Matthew. If you don't, I'll ask around."

At her threat to gather facts from unreliable gossip rather
than an accurate source, he decided to tell her. "The cloth that
tied Moll in the cupboard was an especially large handkerchief.
The last I spoke to Wells, he hadn't had a minute to check into
it. Trust him to take on a task but not do it." Damn it, he prob-

ably shouldn't have told her so much. Her continual questions, mixed with her feminine vulnerability, had him spilling the contents of the pot when he should be keeping the lid on. "Just keep away from Norris until I can talk to Geoffrey Hall. I'm going to send for Hugh Mannerly from *The Revenge*. He'll serve as your bodyguard when I can't. Until he arrives, I'll have someone watch the door to see that you're not disturbed." He guided her through the palace to his chamber.

"Thank you. I am so weary." She entered the chamber, which was cool even on the hottest day, and stared around, as if not knowing what to do next.

Suppressing his desire to take her in his arms, he closed the door, built up the fire, and put on the kettle. She had slipped off her shoes and sat on the edge of the bed, staring dully into space. "Sleep is the best thing for you," he said. "Would you like help removing your bodice and skirts?"

She nodded, and he loosened the laces up her back, then helped her out of the embroidered garment. As she rose, untying the laces that held her skirts, he glimpsed the tantalizing areolas of her full breasts pressed against her smock. It was pure hell, forcing himself to assist her with an impersonal touch.

Moments later, stripped to her smock, she graced him with a gentle smile as she nestled among the cushions. How he wanted to join her. Sensation knifed through him, and he backed away, realizing he'd best exit while he still had the will.

A new attempt had been made on her life, and instead of protecting her, he'd told her too much. She would probably wake up plotting ways to gather more information. He should never have mentioned the handkerchief.

As he closed the door behind him, concern sat on his shoulder like a black raven, predicting trouble. At least he hadn't mentioned that he suspected the crossbow incident and Moll's death were connected. He had no proof yet, but Cory had been Moll's friend, and twice now, attempts had been made on her life.

Whether she liked it or not, he was going to protect her. Except that he couldn't watch her every moment. Court etiquette forced them apart. He just hoped the added protection of Hugh, plus his own vigilance when he was present, would be enough.

Cory awoke feeling more clearheaded and calm, yet she was melancholy as well. Stretching beneath the blankets, she thought of Matthew. The panic in his eyes when he'd thought she was in danger and the protective grip of his embrace were what she craved. Other ladies might swoon over clever compliments or poems praising their beauty, but Matthew proved that he considered action more important than words. He had pressed her to his heart, seeming even more protective than on the night they had met. She sensed that he felt something more than the urge to bed her. How comforting to know she had won a friend, not just a man who wanted to teach her about sin.

Except she couldn't keep her feelings for him merely friendly. Having seen him half-naked, she wanted to feel the solid muscles of his bare arms holding her, the strength of his hard chest pressed against hers without the barrier of clothing. Her body cried out for the bliss she knew she would find in his bed. Surely it would lessen her loneliness.

Yet the idea of bedding with Matthew was pure foolishness. Passion was addictive, as Thomas had shown her. As soon as she came to crave it, Matthew would leave. She would not fall into the trap of needing a man who would desert her. He could be gone for years with no word. He could die and she might never hear what happened to him. She could . . .

She shook herself, realizing her imagination was running away with her. Better that she write to Grandmama, Letty, and Marcus to remind both them and herself of her love. And then she must help serve the queen's supper.

She must be practical and search for answers about the attacks on her and Moll's death. Not panic and frighten everyone, including herself.

As she quit Matthew's chamber, she found that a gentleman usher guarded the door. He stepped back and bowed respectfully. "You've rested well, my lady?"

"Indeed. Thank you for seeing I wasn't disturbed." She hurried off to check on Monsieur La Faye before waiting on the queen. He was still in bed but awake when she was shown in.

"*Madame la vicomtess*, you are kindness itself to look after me." He attempted to sit up but stopped, grimacing in pain.

"Please stay where you are," she insisted, pulling up a stool, saddened by his obvious suffering. "You are the one who has been kind, trying to help me in the accident. I am so sorry you were injured."

He smiled wanly. "I will mend, madam. But since you have been so generous, I feel compelled to share some information with you. It has troubled me greatly since I learned it, but I could not think whom to tell. But in light of your friendship, and since you are close to Her Majesty, I believe you are the best choice." He gestured for her to draw nearer, though his sole servant had retreated to the chamber entry. " 'Tis about the Earl of Essex. He tells everyone openly that he would fight in France, but your queen refuses him. They quarrel."

"That is true." Cory sighed. Even outsiders knew of the unpleasantness between Elizabeth and Essex, they were so obvious about it.

"One day he will go too far. Moll told me she bedded with him. They were intimate for a time." La Faye scowled at a distant point, his angry expression suddenly frightening, despite his being prone in bed. "I was displeased to hear it, but I could not object since it happened before she knew me. She told me the earl would talk in his cups. He would become enraged with your queen and call her an ugly old woman, say wild things— that he could set her aside and take her place on the throne because he had royal blood in his veins too and the people loved him better."

Cory flinched at the idea of Essex on the throne. He was a distant cousin to the queen, but he was too self-centered to rule wisely, as Elizabeth did. Could Essex be planning a rebellion and Moll had known of it? Had he killed her to keep her quiet? "I cannot tell the queen that Essex plans a rebellion if I have no proof, but I will do what I can."

He rose on one elbow and grasped her hand. His expression darkened, and she quelled, unnerved for a moment by his intense stare and the strength of his big fist, in spite of his injury. "You should have a care as well, *madame la vicomtess*. Essex is not all that he seems. I am concerned for you since what happened to Moll."

Cory tried to pull away, but he held her in an iron grip.

"Do you understand me?" he demanded. "He is capable of things that people don't realize. He gathers men about him in his personal service. He has weapons that an earl would ordinarily not have."

"I-I understand," Cory faltered, thinking he could be frightening when he wished, even in his weakened state.

"Of course you do." La Faye released her and slumped back on the bolster, as if the effort had exhausted him. "Go now, and I will rest. But I had to tell you. It has weighed on my soul."

"I thank you," she whispered, realizing he was sharing with her as much for the queen's sake as Moll's. He clearly believed Essex had done away with his lover and wanted him to be punished for the deed. "I'll do what I can."

Carew was safely under Jane's supervision when Cory arrived at the queen's dining parlor, and she breathed a sigh of relief. Though Matthew had promised to watch him, she guessed he had been called away to consult with various officials and was grateful that Jane had stepped in.

Though the supper was not a public affair, she was kept busy as Elizabeth dined with several of her nobles. Once they were served, Carew sidled up to where she stood at attention by the wine ewer. "Cory, that coach was headed straight for you," he said out of one side of his mouth. "Those horses couldn't have been out of control, because when you moved, they turned. The coach missed you only because you jumped on top of La Faye."

So it had been Carew's blond head she'd seen in the crowd. It was very bad of him to slip out, but she was glad someone she trusted had seen the accident. And he was too perceptive to be completely wrong. "You're sure?"

He nodded, his features pinched with concern. "Don't scold me for following you. I was worried."

"Your father will be furious. Did the usher know you were gone?"

"I don't think so." Carew grinned like a mad imp, appearing vastly pleased with himself, which reminded her of Marcus. "The first time he looked in on me, I pretended to be asleep in the bed. He didn't even come close enough to look at me. Sloppy work, don't you think?"

The usher had been careless in his duty, but she must not agree with him and encourage him further. "How did you disguise your absence after that?" she asked.

"A bolster in the bed wearing my nightcap."

"Carew, you must not disobey your father, especially by deceit." She felt honor bound to reprimand him, though he'd followed her out of concern. But worry gnawed at her as she considered what he'd said. "Are you sure the horses didn't seem out of control?"

"They were running fast, but I think the driver had control. And I think you would be safer walking without Monsieur Fancy Hose from now on. He's like a boiled lobster in his red. He'll end in the pot, sure."

"That's not charitable. He was injured trying to assist me. And he didn't wear red today."

"If you ask me, he almost got you killed, pushing you the way he did before he fell," Carew insisted. "I love you, Cory. How could anyone want to hurt you?"

His statement lit a light in Cory's brain as she moved forward at the queen's signal to pour her more wine mixed with water. Someone didn't love her. Someone had shot a crossbow at her and tried to run her down with a carriage. Someone wanted her out of the way.

Cory tried to mask her disquiet about the accident as she later entered the maids' dormitory to prepare for the evening's musical entertainment, though she had no heart for it.

Ann Sims noticed at once that something was amiss. "What news of Moll?" she asked in her quiet way as they changed clothes for the gathering.

"Yes, did you learn how many men she invited to bed?" Mary Islington asked in a snide tone as she fastened her prettiest kirtle skirt, clearly preparing for an evening of flirtation.

"Did you see her spend time with a particular man?" Cory pounced on the lead.

"I saw nothing." Islington turned unexpectedly surly.

"Did *you* see her spend special time with anyone?" Cory asked the other girls.

"She was a tirewoman," one said, as if having the position equaled having the plague. "Naturally she was free with her favors."

"But you saw her with someone. I pray you, tell me who." Cory planted herself in front of Islington, but the younger girl remained stubbornly silent.

"You're jealous, Mary Islington," Ann Sims spoke up suddenly. "You're enamored of the Earl of Essex but he preferred to bed Moll Dakins."

Mary Islington whirled on Ann, clearly shocked at such a forward statement from the quiet mouse. "If *I* had been the one he bedded, he would have married me."

"He wouldn't," Ann insisted. "He's like that rake, the Earl of Oxford. He'd have bedded you and walked away after, for he's wooing Lady Sidney. If he weds anyone, 'twill be her." She walked deliberately to Islington's bed and pulled a white cloth from beneath the pillow. "Even if the earl gave you his handkerchief, 'tis not a wedding ring." She shook the cloth, and it unfolded.

"What do you know?" Islington flounced over and snatched the handkerchief from Ann. "You've never been wooed by a man in your life."

"I know a good deal as I don't spend my time chattering like a magpie," Ann retorted. "I've seen you were sweet on Essex and knew he would have none of you when you foolishly offered yourself. Count yourself fortunate. The man talks rebellion against the queen. High treason. Cast your lot with him, and in a short time, your life wouldn't be worth tuppence."

Cory stared at Ann in surprise. She had underestimated her friend, assuming that because she was quiet and timid, she could be of no help in her troubles. Yet Ann confirmed the rumor of Essex's rebellion that she'd heard from La Faye.

Cory shifted to watch Islington tuck the oversized handkerchief back beneath her pillow. It looked larger than most handkerchiefs, as if it had been made to special specifications. It reminded her of the large piece of linen that had tied up Moll's things. Could it also be one of Essex's handkerchiefs, given to Moll as a keepsake from when their relationship first began?

Slipping to her friend's side, she linked one arm around Ann's waist, murmuring her thanks for the support. "I asked you whom Moll was bedding," Cory said firmly to Islington. "Essex was one. Were there others?"

Islington sniffed as she took up a looking glass and inspected her hair. "She went with Sir William Norris one night. I saw them slip off together."

Cory questioned the other maids of honor, but it seemed they had told all they knew. Thanking them, she braided her hair, her heart aching for Moll. She had been so desperate for money

to care for her brothers and sisters, she had bedded with anyone who asked her.

And Cory, who prided herself on offering her friendship, had
been unobservant, failing to see her friend's troubles. Nor had
she noticed the sharp intelligence behind Ann's self-effacing
demeanor. She had not seen the most important things about
the people she loved.

She must do better in future. And later when the other maids
were absent from the dormitory, she must compare the handkerchief Mary Islington kept beneath her pillow to the cloth
used to tie up Moll's things. Cory wasn't certain what it would
tell her if they matched, but she wanted to know for sure.

Chapter 17

Matthew backed away from the dormitory door that stood open a crack, appalled at what he'd just heard. He had come to escort Cory to the entertainment but learned that Essex was planning a rebellion. If Moll had known, she might have threatened to tell. Essex could have killed her to keep her quiet.

Suddenly the idea of Essex planning to put himself on the throne explained everything. It explained the many male followers he cultivated, as well as their frequent hunting parties where they practiced their skills with dagger and spear. It fit with the way Essex contradicted the queen on affairs of state, as well as his impulsive, often violent behavior toward others, including his sovereign. And now that Matthew had seen the handkerchief given to the maid of honor by Essex, one more clue fell into place. It was like the cloth used to tie Moll in the cupboard.

But to be certain, he would compare the two handkerchiefs closely. Which meant he must send Cory to the entertainment with Hugh.

As Cory emerged from the dormitory, smelling of wind-blown daffodils in spring, he guided her to a window and bid her sit, then lounged in the opposite corner, taking a primitive delight in her obvious response to his closeness. Sensation spiked through him in wholehearted appreciation of her charms displayed by her low-cut bodice. His blood was up tonight. He felt savage with impatience. The sooner the earl tried something in the open, the sooner Matthew could act.

"Are we going to the entertainment?" Cory eyed him, seeming baffled by the delay.

"*You* are in a moment." He shifted, feeling the pouch strapped at his waist. It contained the handkerchief found with Moll, obtained from Captain Wells only an hour ago. He had intended to trace it to its source and question the maker, but comparing it to Essex's handkerchief under the maid's pillow would be just as sure proof.

"I'm going alone?" Cory asked. "Why?"

He couldn't think of any plausible reason not to go with her. "I've sent for Hugh. Go without me." He grasped her hand and pulled her to her feet. Her soft lips parted to protest, and the overpowering need to kiss her seized him. Desire had the most annoying way of interfering with business. Releasing her, he gave her a little push. "Hurry or you'll miss the start of the music. Here's Hugh." He pointed down the corridor at the approaching boatswain.

Half turning, she glanced at him over her shoulder, still puzzled.

"Go," he urged her. "I'm not in the mood." Surely he need make no pretense with her.

She rolled her eyes in exasperation at his crass dismissal and walked off, her head held high.

Not too subtle, but it had done the trick. Matthew checked the dormitory, whose door had been left ajar by the last maid to leave. Several rush lights burned in niches along the wall, illuminating the deserted chamber with a dull glow. He moved between the beds to the one he sought. The white linen lay where the maid of honor had placed it beneath her pillow.

Spreading it on the coverlet, he examined its weave and hemming by rush light. Then he drew the other from his pouch and laid them side by side.

Except for the flecks of dried blood on the one found with Moll, the handkerchiefs were identical. Both were oversized, clearly made to special order. Both were woven of heavy linen, serviceable enough to meet a man's needs, yet of the highest quality.

Matthew fingered the maid of honor's handkerchief, then Moll's. Moll had been tied in the cupboard with what was clearly the Earl of Essex's handkerchief. It was firm evidence that Essex was involved, unless someone had used his handkerchief to make him look guilty. Still, if he were plotting treason against his queen, a truly heinous crime that would require him to dispose of her, he would think nothing of murdering a serving maid. It was a minor deed in comparison.

Matthew clenched his fists, his rage rising. Never had he been so impatient as with this slow process of unmasking the murderer. With Cordelia in danger, he wanted to storm to the queen's presence chamber, challenge the earl to a duel, extract his confession, and annihilate him without interference.

He swept the two handkerchiefs into his pouch, but as he turned toward the door, it creaked open. A woman's figure appeared in the entry. He slipped out of sight between two tall armoires.

Unable to see who had entered, he listened to the light footsteps advance into the chamber. Cory stepped into his range of view, her back to him.

"Matthew?" she called softly. "Where are you? I know you're here."

"Cory." He stepped from between the armoires.

She gasped and whirled to confront him, poised on her toes to flee.

Too incensed with the earl to care what he was doing, driven by the need to protect her, he closed the space between them and pulled her into his arms. The heady essence of daffodil on her flesh washed over him as she gazed up at him, blinking her long lashes in confused fear.

"You looked under Mary's pillow," she whispered. "She has one of Essex's handkerchiefs."

"Yes. And look at this." He released her and yanked open the pouch at his waist.

"Not here." She reached to close his pouch with both hands. "Show me in your chamber. I have something to compare it to as well. No one else must see." She opened one of the armoires and drew out a white cloth, then motioned him toward the door.

The corridors and courtyards were deserted as they crossed Hampton Court, hurrying toward his chamber. The swish of her silken petticoats was a potent reminder of her feminine vulnerability, driving him mad with the need to keep her safe.

Once inside his chamber, he bolted the door, lit a candle, and spread the two handkerchiefs on his bed. He stood back to let her study them. "This one was used to tie Moll in the cupboard." He pointed to the linen flecked with blood. "This second one was given to Mary Islington by the Earl of Essex. His personal handkerchief. Tell me they're not by the same seamstress."

"They are." Her face was hauntingly beautiful in the candlelight, despite the fear lurking in her eyes. "And Matthew, look at this." She unfolded the white cloth she had brought and spread it beside the two handkerchiefs. "This was with Moll's things when Jane brought them to me last night. It's identical to these two. I believe Essex gave Moll one of his handkerchiefs when they were involved."

"That means this one," Matthew pointed to the blood-flecked linen, "belonged to Essex as well."

She nodded. "I didn't tell you, but 'tis said Essex is plotting a rebellion against the queen."

"I heard what Ann said."

"If Moll wasn't the only person to have heard rumors, she must have done something to provoke him, such as threaten to tell the queen. Or he believed she told someone close to the queen . . ." She trailed off, as if realizing that someone was probably her.

He caught her hand and found it deathly cold.

"There's more." She looked ill, as if hardly able to bear the thoughts racing through her mind. "Monsieur La Faye was Moll's lover before she died. I believe Moll loved him."

This was news to Matthew. "How could she love that pompous barrel of lard?"

"Matthew, please. It's unkind to question her choice of men. If he cared for her, as he clearly did, it's enough. She certainly cared enough for him to confide in him. She told him that Essex would take too much wine when they were together and disparage the queen. He would rant and rave about his wish to depose her. I don't think it was an idle threat."

"Nor I." He chaffed her cold hand between his palms, trying to warm her. "Did Moll ever mention this to you?"

"In a way." Cory frowned, as if straining to remember. "On several occasions she was angry with him and whispered to me when he burst in on the queen in her privy chambers. She described some unsavory things he'd done, but not that."

"He might have thought she did. It could be the reason a hired crossbow archer shot at you. And why a runaway coach almost crushed you. But we must have solid proof it was him. More than three handkerchiefs." He paused, uncertain whether to share his further knowledge with her, then decided he must, for safety's sake. "We must have solid proof because the crossbow archer is the same person who murdered Moll. There was a boot print on her kirtle skirt when she was found. I compared it to a tracing I took of the crossbow archer's print. They matched exactly."

Cory stared at Matthew with stricken eyes. "The crossbow archer also murdered Moll? That means he really intended to . . ."

He nodded, and she appeared stunned by the implications of all they'd learned. She was living within easy reach of a madman who wanted her dead. Her slender body began to quake.

Dark need pulsed within him, spurred by the golden light of her goodness. He would not let her gifts of love and kindness to others be blotted out by evil. Before God, he would not. Driven by his fury with the unknown assailant, he captured her in his embrace.

"What am I do to?" She clung to him as if he were her sole support in a stormy sea. "I'll never know when he intends to strike next."

A fever of desire clouded his brain, mixing with his rage. "Marry me, Cordelia. I'll take you to Graystock Manor, away from this madness." Without awaiting her reply, he crushed her lips to his. She responded with anxious fervor, softening beneath his onslaught, driving him wild with need.

This was what he wanted. To protect her with his body. To let flesh speak where words could not. Without breaking the kiss, he unfastened the ties to her overgown and pushed it off her shoulders. It slithered to the floor in a silken rustle, releasing the flower scent of her flesh. Feeling for the hooks that closed her bodice, he unclasped them. She sighed as the tight garment fell away.

"Matthew," she whispered as he brushed her ear with his lips. "I'm frightened, but I'm not sure this is the answer. You don't want to be tied to me—"

"I want you, Cordelia." He clasped her hand and held it to his heart so she could feel its mad pounding. He intended to be convincing. "Let me keep you safe."

She sighed and leaned against him, seeming to accept his proposal. It was the only solution he could see. She was courageous and a fighter, but she was no match for a man who hired an assassin and could strike without warning. She shivered, her body pressed to his. "I feel safe with you, but when I think of the earl, lying in wait for me . . ."

"I won't let him or anyone else harm you. I swear it. Trust me."

Her breath came in gasps, and her heart pounded beneath his hands. "I . . . trust you, Matthew. Thomas never . . . that is, he . . ."

"He wasn't trustworthy. I'll wager he never aroused you either."

"Never. No one has the way you do."

Her admission filled him with relief. He wanted to compare favorably to her first husband. No, that was a lie. He wanted to be better. He wanted to hold her like this forever. He wanted to show her ecstasy like she'd never known before.

Fueled by her agreement, he slipped aside her circular ruff and eased the bodice from her shoulders. By the light from the candle, he gazed at her magnificent breasts, pressed up by her corset and straining against her smock. "Cory, let me help you forget everything else tonight."

At his suggestion, a tremor swept through her. She gripped his shoulders for support, which he took for consent. With one arm around her waist, he lowered her smock. He wanted to guide her to fulfillment as surely as he guided his ships to port. But with Cory, he needed more than a sure hand and perfect timing.

He needed every measure of tenderness he'd ever possessed.

"*Oh.*" She expelled a quick breath as he cupped her firm flesh, then slid his hand higher.

Realizing she liked his touch, he flattened his hand. With his palm, he circled her breast.

She buried her face against his chest, shuddering in delight. The daffodil scent shimmered from her flesh, making him throb. "I'll protect you, Cory," he rasped in her ear. "Say yes."

"Yes," she sighed, sending needles of desire darting through him. "I never felt like this with Thomas. Or with any of those fools who wanted my money and land."

Fools indeed if they didn't recognize that she was the greatest prize of all. "Did you do this with them?"

"Never. I couldn't even bear their kisses. They were," she shrugged her bare shoulders, "either lifeless or sloppy. I always stopped them." She raised both arms and cupped his face in her hands. "But you, my pirate prince, make me feel like a queen of the realm." She rose on tiptoe, a hand on each of his shoulders, gripping him with intensity. "When I was on board *The Revenge*, I wanted to escape. I wanted to weigh anchor and go skimming over the water to the south, away from all this. I still do. I don't want intrigue and insanity. I want to see cinnamon growing in the hot sun. I want to pick orchids and smell freshly grated nutmeg. I want to shed my heavy clothes and go barefooted in a land of perpetual heat."

He would willingly show her heat of a different kind. "Then let me take you there, at least for tonight."

She clasped his hands in hers, her smile blinding with its beauty. "I agree it's time you did."

Her fervent appreciation for the lands of his travels, her thrilling vow that she wanted him as much as he wanted her, sent stabs of urgency through him. Lifting her in his arms, he took the few steps to the bed and lowered her to the coverlet, remembering the last time he'd laid her there. The knowledge that he would have the right to protect her overwhelmed him as he joined her.

She reached for the buttons on his doublet. "Unfasten my laces, pray, then take off your clothes. I need to see all of you." Anxiety tinged her voice, as though she were afraid of being murdered before she experienced everything with him.

Quickly he loosened her corset, and she stripped it off, along with layers of petticoats. As he removed his own clothes, she emerged from her smock, a slim, beautiful fairy with creamy flesh. They hurried to burrow beneath the blankets and find each other in the cocoonlike bed.

He savored her eager body, twined against his. She explored him with a feverish intensity that was contagious, and he bent to kiss every plane and curve of her soft skin.

"Now?" She expelled a quick breath as her hand closed on his desire.

"Not quite yet." The excitement of her touch pushed him to the edge, but he was uncertain about the rumors. Was she a virgin or no? With gentle fingers, he explored the soft petals of her womanhood, then delved inside.

She was hot with eagerness, her tiny muscles tightening around his fingers. He didn't want to wait, but as he reached deeper, he found the barrier.

With a small moan, her body contracted. Great Neptune, she really was a virgin. She'd never known Thomas. The thought confounded him. Worse yet, he would have to hurt her to change it. He removed his hand.

"No! Wait." She tightened her arms around him. "It is my first time, but I want you, Matthew. I want to feel everything a woman can feel. Before it's too late."

The rich heat of her femininity, coupled with her fervent plea, pushed him past denying her, much less himself. Chaos drove them together, and now he would be her steadying force in a world gone mad. With relish, he set about the welcome task.

She was as beautiful as the springtime her green eyes suggested. He stroked and suckled her soft breasts until she writhed and called his name. His hands skimmed her stomach, his mouth anointing, moving lower to the realm of desire. The triangle of soft hair hiding her womanhood was alive with texture that spoke to his need. He felt as if the heat radiating from his body was reflected in her. She glowed with an aura of promise, until he could wait no more.

Braced above her, he entered her tentatively. Lulled by the bounty of her moisture, he pressed against her maidenhead.

To his astonishment, she thrust her hips upward, driving him into her depths.

Sensation shot through him. His mind reeled with pleasure, but he forced himself to pause. "Are you all right?" he panted, bracing against the bed. "Why did you do that?"

She gazed at him with starstruck eyes. "Shouldn't I have?"

"I know I hurt you."

"Other things have hurt me more. But this," she rotated her hips in a sensual motion that clasped him deeper inside her. "I had no idea how much I wanted you this way."

Need raced through him at her motions until he could scarcely think in the white-hot heat of his arousal. "I can make it even more pleasurable for you," he rasped. At her excited nod, he forced himself to withdraw and propped on one arm. Feeling between her legs, he sought the bright ruby of her desire. He imagined its hot, rich color, suffused with blood as he caressed her.

Cory moaned in response, then laughed suddenly as he stroked her. "Oh, Matthew . . . what are you doing?"

He grinned through the need assaulting him and repeated the motion. "I'm showing you the land of perpetual heat."

"It's perfect. I love it. Oh . . . heavens!"

He continued to stroke her in rhythmic movements, bending over her, occasionally tasting her sweet mouth and breasts.

"Are there mountains on your hot continent?" she gasped.

"Magnificent mountains of great size."

"I think I'm going to fly from the top of one." She gripped his shoulders, an expression of awe on her face.

"Good. I'll help you." He renewed his sensual assault, and she responded eagerly, pressing against him, panting in small, ladylike gasps.

Her cry of pleasure as he brought her to fulfillment was a moment to be relished. In triumph, he cradled her against him and gazed into her passion-flushed face as she experienced the throes of ecstasy. He continued to stroke, until at last, she sighed deeply and unclenched his shoulders. "I love the tropics, Matthew. Take me there often, will you?"

"Without question, if you'll respond like this every time."

Her smile was sated and languorous as she nodded agreement and reached for him, guiding him back into her moist depths. As he descended carefully, then rose toward the heavens, she urged him on with hands, lips, and voice, pushing him toward his own pinnacle. For the first time in years, he was making love to a woman with eyes open, his gaze locked with hers.

He hadn't expected to be touched by her. He'd expected to be physically pleased but emotionally detached. But as he hovered at the brink of culmination, the eloquence in her gaze moved him to the edge of tears, forcing him to close his eyes against her sweetness.

As he rocked to completion, he recognized her strength. She who had never sailed uncharted seas had a will as powerful as that of the ancient mariners who had braved the unknown to discover the New World. She was every bit as intriguing and mysterious as the unmapped lands he visited on his voyages. He wanted to possess her more than he'd wanted anything in years.

But could he prevent her from becoming with child? She must not be sacrificed on the altar of womanhood as Joanna had been.

Yet in his blind eagerness, he had taken no precautions to protect her from pregnancy, and he cursed himself for a fool.

Chapter 18

Cory wandered in confusion the next day, buffeted by opposing emotions so strong, her mind reeled. One moment, arousal heightened her senses as she recalled the scintillating magic of Matthew's touch, pleasuring her with feelings she had never known before. Reaching fruition in his arms had been the crowning moment of a journey to an exotic new world she never wanted to leave. She had gone with him willingly to a foreign shore. She could not return to the mundane, ordinary world.

Leaning against a mahogany chest in the queen's presence chamber, Cory shut out the droning voices of Elizabeth Tudor and the Italian ambassador as they discussed prices of goods. She knew the blood had risen in her face and the other maids were watching, suspicious because she and Matthew had failed to attend the entertainment last night. She couldn't help it. The glory of being one with him was too heavenly to forget.

But in the next moment, her emotions swung the other direction with alarming intensity, prompted by the mere mention of a name.

"I wonder if the Earl of Essex will join us," Mary Islington whispered to another maid with a petulant sniff. "I'm tired of listening to boring old men. I want to have some fun."

Terror clutched Cory by the throat at hearing Essex's name.

Her heart beat against her ribs, and a cold sweat bathed her body. By fortune, how easily she could die, as Moll had.

To escape the earl, she had chosen marriage, a state she hated. Yet she wanted it with Matthew. He had sought an audience with the queen that morning, and Elizabeth had named a date for their wedding, though she had insisted they tell no one until she made the announcement.

But soon Matthew would take her in his arms each night, and together they would flee the horror. They would bask on the sunlit shores of their mutual desire. During the light of day, he would stalk Moll's murderer and expose the devil's wicked plans . . .

Yet once the man was found, Cory realized Matthew's reason for marrying her would be gone. He would set off on another voyage, and she would be left alone amid the shredded memories of intimacy.

She couldn't bear to think of it. Her worst nightmare had come true. Her pirate prince had sailed out of the mist and snatched her from the jaws of death. Thrills ran up and down her spine as she remembered the night they had met. Yet her dream was nothing more than that—a fantasy. Ultimately, Matthew would behave the way he always did. He would leave.

What had she been thinking, to conjure up such a dream? An adventurer didn't stay home and live a comfortable family life. He sailed away to secret coves of silver sand and lush tropical growth, places where she could never go.

Desolation spread through her like dark water. She and Carew would be abandoned again.

She gazed with affection at the lad where he sat by a window, clearly as bored as Islington with the forced idleness. But at least he was safe, as was she. Matthew was even now preparing to go to London and find Geoffrey Hall, but he'd left Hugh behind to act as bodyguard. The sailor was in prime condition, having demonstrated his fighting skill to reassure her.

"I can do things others can't with this wooden leg," he'd told her proudly. "Once kicked a log back into the grate after it rolled out and set a fire. Man with two legs o' flesh couldn't do that."

She felt secure in his keeping. Secure enough that she might have him take her to call on Monsieur La Faye later for cards.

But first, when this interminable audience was over, she must question the other tirewomen about Moll's flowered box. At Moll's funeral earlier that morning, Mistress Dakins had accepted her daughter's few humble belongings in the sturdy basket Cory had provided. Cory was able to keep the Earl of Essex's handkerchief, as well as avoid explaining it to Moll's mother, but she still wondered about Moll's box.

In the meantime, she must stand in the queen's presence chamber, looking ornamental while Elizabeth haggled with the Italians. So she would think of Matthew, how his hands worked magic on her flesh, making her agree to anything as long as he touched her again and again.

Essex might be brewing a rebellion, but he wasn't ready to launch it yet, Matthew realized as he prepared to go to London after Moll's funeral. The earl must still have work to do, else he wouldn't need to silence people like the poor tirewoman, if he were indeed the one who had done so. And now that they were certain the person who had murdered Moll had also attempted to kill Cory, Matthew must find Geoffrey Hall. The man might tell him a thing or two, as well as show him the boots.

"Message for you, my lord." Hugh thumped into Matthew's chamber, his peg leg tapping briskly on the wooden floor. Carew trailed behind him, dragging his feet and looking sullen.

Matthew took the folded paper. "You're not with Lady Wentworth?" he asked Hugh.

"Nay, she's with Her Grace and the other maids. They've finished with the Italians for the day and are now entertaining the French emissary, Monsieur La Faye, who's up and about again. Her ladyship has everyone a-playing at cards, and the loser has to give the winner a sincere compliment. Can't be about looks, neither." He chuckled. "Has to be about character or deeds or suchlike. A good exercise in noticing things about others, I'd say. She's quite safe," he hastened to assure Matthew. "Her Majesty has a dozen guards about. I just came to deliver this message to you. I'll go right back."

"Good. I checked on Essex. He's gone hunting for the day," Matthew said. "All the better."

Hugh nodded, and Matthew turned to Carew. "I want you to

stay with Cordelia and Her Majesty while I'm gone. Hugh will be on guard."

"Why can't I go to the city with you?" Carew complained, an uncooperative belligerence lurking in his eyes. "Something's happened. I can tell because you and Cory are acting odd."

"Nothing's happened."

"Then why were you here together last night when I came to bed? *With* the door locked. I had to wait ages to be let in." His angry gaze accused as he emphasized the last few words.

Guilt stabbed Matthew as he remembered his son's snide teasing after Cory had left for her dormitory. He felt even more guilty for failing to protect Cory from pregnancy last night. It must never happen again. "Hugh, would you excuse us for a moment?" At least he could tell Carew about their marriage, which would undoubtedly please him.

"Something *has* happened." He sat down and motioned for Carew to do the same. "Cordelia and I intend to wed, but I ask you not to tell anyone yet. Her Majesty wishes to announce it."

Carew's mouth curved into the first genuinely happy smile Matthew had seen since he'd come home. "Hurrah!" He plucked off his cap and sent it spinning out the window. "I'll have her all to myself after you leave."

Carew's words were like losing the wind in the middle of a sailing race. He *would* have to leave Cory behind. Yet the present situation was far too dangerous to consider other options to marriage. He had personally sat outside the maids' dormitory half of last night, guarding Cory while she slept. The disturbing knowledge that Essex was fomenting a rebellion beneath the queen's very nose, coupled with Cory's arousing influence on his male appetite, added to the concern that a murderer was on the loose, had kept him wide awake.

He and Hugh had traded places at dawn, and Matthew had caught a few hours of sleep. A wonder he had slept at all. Everything had changed with the act of taking Cory to his bed. Her virgin sweetness, coupled with her urgent need for protection, consumed him like a fire. He had thought of neither his voyages nor his future. Only the need to fit his body to hers and find fulfillment in that brief space of time.

Deciding to ignore Carew's snide comment, Matthew gestured Hugh back into the chamber, then ripped open the note.

Most worshipful baron,
    A fellow came by my shop yesterday to see if I would
purchase a pair of cast off boots I had made. Their heels
looked like those you described during your recent visit,
so I thought to report the matter for your consideration.
In addition, the boots you commissioned for yourself and
your son are complete. I am, in all appreciation, your
servant,
    Henry Howe, London Cordwainer

Matthew refolded the note and tucked it in the pouch at his waist, mentally adjusting his plans. He would visit Geoffrey Hall, then Master Howe. He wanted to see that pair of boots.

"No, sir, I don't know him. Good morrow to you." The old woman householder closed her door in Matthew's face as he stood on her stoop in Aldgate Ward. That made the fifth person he'd questioned. What the devil was wrong with people in this ward?

Matthew regarded the oak door, baffled, then stepped into the street and resumed his walk. A London ward was not that large. Someone would know Geoffrey Hall if he lived here.

But the people he'd spoken to thus far had denied knowing him. In fact, the instant he said Geoffrey's name, doors slammed in his face.

As he strolled down the principal street, he studied the neighborhood with its many churches. Thinking he might receive a straight answer from a religious man, he selected St. Andrew's Church and passed beneath the carved stone arch over the entrance. The dim interior was a stark contrast to the light outside, despite the overcast day. He stood for a time, waiting for his eyes to adjust, then approached the altar.

"May I be of assistance, my son?" An older man stepped from behind the altar, his black robes fluttering around his short, lithe frame.

Matthew plunged in, hoping he would not be rebuffed again. At least there was no door to slam in his face. "Are you the curate here?"

"That I am, my lord. And you are not of this parish, for I do not recognize you." The man had alert gray eyes that reflected interest but not suspicion.

Matthew liked that about him at once. "I am Baron Graystock. Perhaps you can help me. Do you know everyone in the parish?"

The man nodded. "I know everyone who attends church faithfully, my lord. I am John Cox, doctor of divinity."

He would be intelligent if he'd taken his doctorate, Matthew thought, studying the man. He also looked honest, and he felt sure he could trust his word. "I'm looking for one Geoffrey Hall. I understand he lives in this ward."

"He did live here." The curate gathered his robe close. "Are you connected to him, my lord?"

Matthew hesitated, then decided he would lose nothing by being candid. "No, I am acquainted with his former master, Sir William Norris. I wish to speak to Hall."

"That would be impossible, I'm afraid," the curate said. "Geoffrey Hall died some days ago."

"Died? How?"

"I don't know all the details, but it appears he was accosted late at night. He was found stabbed to death, lying in the street near his lodgings."

Of all the things Matthew had expected to find in the search for Hall, it wasn't this. He'd expected to find the owner of the boots and the boots themselves. "Did he leave any belongings behind?"

"You might ask his landlord," the curate said. "But I suspect he kept whatever it was in lieu of rent, as I heard Hall could not pay."

"He told Sir William he was employed by a gentleman."

The curate gave him a sympathetic look. "I'm sorry. All I know is that he came to our ward a six-month ago and appeared to be well off. But within a short time, he had difficulty paying his rent. He had no work that I heard. I cannot think why he left a good post with a knight, but I suspect he was involved in something unsavory, to be killed when he had nothing to steal."

A sense of foreboding seized Matthew. Could Hall have been hired by their murderer to assist with certain deeds, then killed because he knew too much? "What size of man was he?"

"Oh, very large." With both hands, the curate outlined a tall man of considerable breadth.

"Would you say his foot was larger than mine?" Matthew asked.

"Indeed, much larger," the curate asserted. "His feet were tremendous."

That ruled out Hall as the one who had worn the boots. "Thank you, sir." Matthew dropped a coin in the man's hand. Confident that he had learned the truth, he left the church.

Hall was not the one who had shot at Cordelia and killed Moll, Matthew concluded, after calling on the dead man's landlord and confirming the description of him. His feet would have been far too large to fit Norris's boots. Not that he had found them. The landlord didn't remember Hall's owning an expensive pair of boots, even worn ones. Hall had probably sold or traded the boots. Norris hadn't thought to mention that his gift hadn't fit his servant.

Anxious to return to court to ensure Cordelia's safety, Matthew hastened to Master Howe's.

"I don't have the boots," Howe explained after greeting Matthew cordially and presenting him with the boots he'd commissioned. "I had no need to buy an old pair of my own boots made to order for a customer. The heels, as you said, were worn to steep angles around the outer edges."

"You should have bought them. I would have repaid you." Matthew chaffed at Howe's shortsighted frugality. "Who brought them to you? Might he still have them?"

Howe tugged his ear, clearly embarrassed by his oversight. "A fellow named Toby Green brought them to me. He does odd jobs for me if I'm short handed. Shall I send one of my lads to look for him?" he offered, seeming anxious to compensate for his error.

Matthew shook his head. "Don't trouble. How do I find him?"

Howe grinned. "That's easy enough. Stroll down the street looking reasonably prosperous, and he'll be there in a trice, offering his services, looking for a way to earn a copper. Toby's as honest as the day is long but with few resources, though he'd give you the shirt off his back if you were wanting. Once saw him give his only bit of bread to a beggar child. I bought him dinner for a sennight for his kindness."

Matthew thanked Howe, paid for his and Carew's boots, and

followed the cordwainer's advice. Within a few minutes' walk, a scabby old man approached, his gray locks trailing on his shoulders. The top of his head, when he whipped off his cap and bowed, was bald, and he had almost no eyebrows.

"Carry your parcel for ye, m'lord?" he offered, his gaze humbly cast down.

Matthew stopped to assess Toby. The man reminded him of a seaman he'd once rescued from a sinking French ship. He'd been nearly broken by service under a vicious captain, but once healed of his wounds and back to work, he'd proved a loyal crew member. All it had taken were adequate food and decent treatment for a time.

"Are you Master Green?" he asked. Toby nodded eagerly. "I understand you offered Master Howe a pair of boots yesterday. If they are still available, I would like to buy them."

The heavy folds around Toby's eyes lifted as he gaped in surprise. "Ye would? Ye're sure?" At Matthew's nod, he bowed, ever polite. " 'Twould be my pleasure to sell them to ye. Would you care to follow me to my lodging so's I can fetch 'em, or would you prefer to wait here?"

Matthew wanted to see where he lived, so he motioned for Toby to lead the way. The dirt-floored shed behind a house hardly qualified as a lodging, but it appeared to be Toby's abode. Toby pulled the boots from a shelf, polished them on his ragged shirt, and tendered them to Matthew. "Sure ye want 'em, yer lordship?" he asked. "Ye needn't buy 'em if ye'd prefer new."

Matthew stepped outside into the light and examined the boots. Their brown leather was soft and supple, showing they had been cared for despite their age. Howe's mark adorned the sole, and the heels were worn to steep inclines around the outer edges. Although he would have to compare them to his tracing of the crossbow archer's prints, he felt certain these were the same boots. "Where did you get them?" he asked, glancing up at Toby.

Toby looked flustered. "I didn't steal 'em, m'lord. Honest I didn't. Values my skin too much."

"Oh, I believe that. Howe vouched for you." Given Toby's derelict appearance, Matthew didn't think him able to steal a peascod, let alone a pair of boots. "Just tell me one thing. Did these boots belong to Geoffrey Hall?"

"Don't know a Geoffrey Hall. Don't know who they belonged to," Toby said earnestly. "They was tossed out, ye see. The gentleman clearly didn't want 'em, so I felt 'twas my right to claim 'em." He lifted his gaze to Matthew's, as if wondering whether to say more.

Matthew thought his long answer boded well. "I am Baron Graystock," he said. "I am interested in knowing where you found these boots. If you tell me, I'll reward you amply."

Toby remained silent, although something flickered deep in his eyes. Unsure of what it meant, Matthew tried another question. "What I want to know is, who threw out the boots?"

"If I tell ye, ye won't get old Toby in trouble, will ye?" he asked, looking anxious.

"I will not. In fact, if you tell me everything to the best of your knowledge, I might know of a position for you."

Toby's gaze reflected hope mixed with equal parts of doubt.

Matthew silently urged him to say more. Despite his lousy hair and rags, his eyes were honest and kind. Instinct suggested that reasonable treatment would win his loyalty. It seemed cruel for a man to languish in the streets if he had a will to work.

Scratching his head, Toby seemed to come to a decision. " 'Twas late at night," he said, lowering his voice, though no one was nearby to overhear. "Saw 'em tossed out of a coach onto a rubbish heap."

So the crossbow archer had realized that Matthew was searching for his boots and disposed of them. "Did you notice anything specific about the coach?"

"Pulled by four horses. Near new, I'd say. Paint shone in the lantern light. Coat of arms on the side." Toby described the coat of arms in detail.

Having heard what he wanted to know, Matthew produced a coin. "Would you like to work for me, Toby? A pound a year, lodgings, and all you can eat."

The offer did its work. Minutes later, Matthew was hiring an extra horse for the ride back to Hampton Court, while the roguish-looking Toby lounged against a stone wall, his expression suggesting he hadn't a care in the world. Hell, he was glad he'd done it, but what was he supposed to do with the rascal? He was too dirty to take back to court.

*   *   *

Matthew took Toby back to court anyway, dirt and all. What else was he to do? In one of the sculleries, he ordered a tub and hot water. Carew popped in, apparently having heard the news. Gossip ran in the court like his crew for fresh water when they found dry land.

Eyes widened in interest, Carew lounged against a table and listened as Matthew argued with Toby, who refused to get into the tub.

"You can't stay here unless you bathe first, and you do want to stay, don't you, Toby?" Matthew cajoled, wanting to order the fellow but afraid he would bolt. "Stephen, here, will scrub you." He tossed Toby's shirt to a scullion, who looked none too thrilled at the prospect.

"Water's poison. I got delicate skin," Toby argued. He'd given up his shirt, apparently thinking he was to have a new one. Now he clutched his ragged trunkhose for dear life.

"Your skin is flea bitten, not delicate. You've scratched it raw. If we kill the fleas, the itching will stop and your sores can heal," Matthew reasoned.

Toby set his mouth stubbornly. "You can't get me in no tub o' water. 'Twould be my death."

Matthew cursed under his breath, careful that Carew couldn't hear the foul expletives.

"Matthew, where are you? 'Tis Cory," a cheery female voice called. "Do you need help?" Footsteps sounded at the scullery door.

"Lord o' mighty! Don't let no gentlewoman in here." Toby blanched and covered his scrawny chest with both hands.

Matthew hid a grin as he recognized an effective strategy. "Sorry, Toby, but when Viscountess Wentworth decides to do something, there's no stopping her." He raised his voice. "In here, my lady. We are getting on in our own fashion, but you do have a knack for these things."

"I'll be in straight away," Cory called out.

"Lord 'ave mercy." With a yelp, Toby kicked off his shoes and leaped into the tub, rags and all, ducking as far down in the water as he could.

Cory swished in, with blue embroidered skirts rustling and gold earrings swinging. "Oh, the poor man," she cried, catching sight of Toby cowering in the tub. "Carew told me about him and I came as soon as I could. I have soothing herbal ointment for your sores after the bath," she assured Toby in her kindest voice, which Matthew would rather she reserved for him. She knelt beside the tub, taking up a cloth. "Let me wash your back," she offered.

"Thank you, m'lady." Toby spoke without moving anything save his mouth. After being so belligerent and combative, he submitted meekly and with obvious embarrassment as she plied soap and cloth. Stephen pitched in, and Matthew retreated to watch, wanting to chuckle at the old fellow's predicament. Caught half naked before a gentlewoman, the fight ran out of him faster than a family with ten children ran out of food.

Shortly after, Cory departed to find Toby clean clothes, though Matthew guessed her true purpose was to allow Toby privacy to wash his more personal parts. With a chuckle, Matthew drew up a stool and propped one boot on its seat. "Care to give me the rest of your clothes?" he drawled. "I would say they're clean by now."

Scowling, Toby dredged trunkhose and netherstocks from the water. He dumped them on the stone floor with a slap. "Gets her own way all the time, don't she?" he grumbled.

"That she does. And makes you like it whilst she does it, too," Matthew grinned.

"She'd charm a false leper outta 'is sores. Where'd you find 'er?"

"Dame Fortune brought us together." And Dame Fortune could bring some people terribly ill luck at times, Matthew reflected as he watched Toby bathe. He couldn't make Cory happy. It was her ill luck that she must marry him to avoid being murdered. And Matthew was going to enlist Toby's help in keeping her safe. He might be old, but he noticed details that other people tended to ignore. Such as the coat of arms on the coach from which the boots had been thrown.

Cory returned in a whirlwind of activity. She insisted on cutting Toby's hair, snipping it short, then combing out the fleas and cracking their shells as if she did it all the time.

As she worked, she wheedled more information from Toby than Matthew had managed to glean in over an hour. He'd been a soldier in his youth, then a traveling field hand and laborer, but as he'd aged and become less productive, the work had dropped off.

"You look splendid, Toby," Cory assured him back in Matthew's chamber where they had attired him in some of Matthew's clothes. "I'm sure you feel better as well. Here are bread, ale, cheese, and fruit." She pressed his hand. "And Matthew," she flung her arms around his neck and kissed his cheek, "you did a splendid thing to bring him here. I'm so pleased." With that, she bustled away to attend the queen, her face radiant.

Matthew watched her until she was out of sight. If he'd tried for weeks on end, he couldn't have pleased her this much in anything but bed. And she attributed her joy to his rescuing someone from death's door.

If that were the case, he would do it again. In fact, he might arrange for it weekly, especially if she kissed him like that every time.

"What did ye 'ire me fer, m'lord?" Toby asked, attacking the food with relish.

"Her ladyship's life is in danger, Toby. I have one other person to help me protect her. Hugh, the fellow with the wooden leg. It's not enough, especially since there's my son as well. I need someone on guard all the time, including through the night, which means taking turns."

"You want me to protect her ladyship?" Toby said in awe around a mouthful of bread.

Matthew nodded tersely. "She believes in you. I trust her judgment."

"She said that *after* you brought me here." Toby lifted his almost nonexistent eyebrows.

He was right, and Matthew was at a loss to explain his decision. He supposed he sensed a kindred soul in Toby, his heart withered but his courage of iron.

"Well, whyever ye done it, I owe ye a grand debt," Toby continued, "and I always pays me debts. Anything ye need, m'lord, any service, ye've only to ask."

"Then I'm asking," Matthew said promptly, more than ready to make use of a new partner. "I have several threads to unravel in this coil. I want to find out who threw those boots away. "

Toby squeezed his forehead into a field of thoughtful furrows as he washed down his bread with ale. "As the coach pulled away, I heard the fellow inside call to the driver in frog talk."

"French?" Matthew asked. "He spoke French to the driver and he understood?"

"Seemed to. The driver said somethin' back in frog talk."

"But was the man French or was he English and spoke in French?"

Toby shrugged. "Couldn't say."

Matthew's hope of learning more from Toby diminished. Someone who spoke French told him little. Half the court and part of London spoke the language, as did the Earl of Essex. Though if the coachman had spoken French, it was more likely he was a Frenchmen. Few servants knew another language unless they were from that country.

It was only a little help, except they did have the coat of arms. Matthew didn't recognize them from the description, and Cory was too new to court to know them. He preferred not to ask around at court to avoid stirring up talk. Instead, he and Toby would ask coachwrights in London if they had made a coach with the arms in question.

Matthew guessed that Geoffrey Hall had sold his boots to someone who had then worn them to murder Moll and shoot at Cory. Whoever it was had probably also been involved with the runaway coach that had almost struck Cory, which might be the same coach from which the boots had been tossed. He *would* find out who owned that coach.

Carew was of no help the next morning, refusing to let Matthew's dilemmas rest.

"Are we leaving court after you marry Cory, Graystock?" his son nagged as they went to chapel for a special worship service called by the queen. "If we don't, there's no bedchamber for you and her. I have to have some place to sleep."

Matthew sighed. Carew might want to know, but he also wanted to be annoying, for he was calling him Graystock again and asking rude questions. "Son, I don't want to talk about it."

"But I want to know when we'll leave."

Carew's eloquent eyes begged, filling Matthew with guilt. He stopped in the entry hall outside the chapel. "I haven't received the queen's consent to leave yet. We'll have to wait and see."

"I'll convince the queen if you think she'll say no," Carew offered. "I'll tell her you're longing for Cory and need your own bedchamber—"

"Don't you dare say a word," Matthew ordered. The last thing he needed was his son talking to the queen about his desire to bed Cory. "Her Majesty will consent when she's ready."

"But you're ready now. Least you were the other night." Carew's grin was far too cheeky. "Besides, we need to leave 'cause Cory's in danger since she was almost run down."

Matthew's anger erupted. "What are you talking about, Carew?" he demanded. "What do you know about someone being run down? Have you been listening to gossip again?"

Carew flipped the hair out of his eyes. "Ever since I saw Cory almost struck by that coach—"

"You saw it happen?" Matthew clutched his son's arm in alarm. "That was the day you were confined to your chamber. What were you doing there? You could have been run down as well."

"No, I couldn't. They didn't even see me." Carew tossed his head carelessly.

"But I saw plenty. I don't think the horses were out of control. I think the driver guided them straight for Cory." He shuddered at the memory. "I'm glad I saw it so I could convince her it wasn't an accident. Aren't you?"

Matthew's anxiety for his son's safety exploded within him. "No, I'm not glad. You could have been killed. You still could be. I'm most displeased that you eluded the usher and left the palace unattended. You're not to do it again."

"But Father, just let me tell you—"

"Baron Graystock, are you coming to worship?" the gentleman of the chapel interrupted, gesturing to indicate he was about to close the door.

"I think you've said and done quite enough, Carew," Matthew said as he guided his son toward the entrance. The possibility that Carew could be murdered for what he'd seen overwhelmed Matthew, along with the fact that he'd confided his suspicions to Cory but not to his father. "Not another word."

"But I think you—"

"This is a serious affair that's already gotten one person killed. I don't want you hurt," he whispered as they found seats among the other courtiers. "You're not to mention it to anyone, do you understand? For your own safety, put the entire affair from your mind."

Carew's expression turned sullen and Matthew wanted to groan. He didn't know what to expect of his son these days. He ought to punish Carew for sneaking out during a punishment and putting himself in danger, but it seemed like a vicious cycle. And the damage was done. His son knew too much. Now Matthew must ensure that no one learned of Carew's suspicions.

To unsettle him further, Carew shot him an angry glance. "Why can't you be more like Cory? She doesn't talk to me the way you do."

"No, she spoils you rotten."

"She does not. She feeds me well, too. Better than you ever did."

It was true, unfortunately. His son was growing at an astounding rate, and Cory saw he ate plenty of healthy foods. It was something Matthew had always found difficult to arrange at court. "Well and good, as long as you don't eat too many sweets," he said, picking up a prayer book.

Carew glared at him. "Why did the queen wish you to marry Cory, anyway?" he whispered as the worship began.

"Her Majesty wants me to take her money for my ships. She's using it as an excuse not to provide it herself," he said, wishing to end the subject. "But I won't take anything from Cory. I'll find another way to finance my voyage."

His statement widened the gap between them once more. His leaving was always a sore point between him and Carew, as well as with Cory. Because of it, she would be better off without him in the future, but unfortunately for her, they must wed to ensure that she lived to see that future. In fact, they had best wed quickly so he could protect her more easily. He was getting little sleep at night.

But he wasn't the culprit pushing them into marriage. The murderer was the guilty party, driving them together in the face of danger. Marriage was a last-ditch effort to hold the castle against the assault, and he must be successful. In truth, he was possessed by a raging desire to succeed. For the first time in the painful years since his wife's death, he felt a passion for something besides his voyages. His blood churned with a driving need to preserve Cordelia Hailsworthy's life.

Chapter 19

Matthew talked to four coachwrights the next day, but none of them had made a coach with the coat of arms he described. He then had to confront the queen and insist she make the public announcement of their marriage. In response, Elizabeth sat down and penned a letter to the Earl of Whitby, saying she had concluded their business as required. But she brushed off Matthew's demand that she announce their betrothal, claiming too many state affairs required her attention.

The woman was a royal champion at procrastination, Matthew thought. She whetted his appetite for Cordelia, then made him wait. She probably wanted to keep Cordelia for herself.

Blast, he thought wearily as he returned to his chamber, where Cory was writing a letter to her grandmother. The sooner they were wed, the sooner he could take full control of her safety without maddening, sleepless nights spent outside the maids' dormitory.

He gazed at her, bent over her paper, a tender smile tugging at her lips. Today, her obvious love for the old woman and children touched a raw nerve in him. Pain and guilt crashed against the floodgates, pounding to get in.

"You would give your life for them, wouldn't you," he said from his place by the hearth.

She appeared startled to find him watching her, but he had

demanded she not be out of his sight. She'd wanted a quiet place to write her letter, so he'd sent her here. Her dark hair glowed in the sunlight. He imagined how the strands of raven silk would feel beneath his fingers. Everything about her invited his touch, but that meant unleashing painful emotions. Desire warred with reluctance, and reluctance won. With a supreme effort, he kept his hands to himself.

"Of course I would," she said with exaggerated meekness. "They are my family. I would do the same for you if necessary once we are wed, like a dutiful wife."

"What is your point?"

"Must I have a point?" she asked in an oddly mechanical voice. "I promise to be dutiful. Isn't that what you want?"

It wasn't like her to be so lifeless, especially about something as important as her marriage. She must be irritated with him about something. "That's rather extreme," he probed. "Duty doesn't require wives to die."

She raised her chin sharply and glared at him. "I don't think you're in a position to criticize someone else's extremes."

So she thought him too extreme at times. "You're extreme as well. Your idea of duty is absurd," he snapped, annoyed by her criticism, no matter how subtle.

"So is yours," she shot back. "You're dutifully hiding something from me even now. 'Tis the husband's duty to protect the wife and tell her nothing, because she's too stupid to understand."

He didn't like her implication. "You're not stupid, but it *is* my duty to protect you."

"Then tell me what you're doing about the murder. And about the boots." She banged a fist on the table in frustration. "I know you found them, for Carew showed them to me."

"Carew?" Matthew's rage returned in full measure. "Must he have a crossbow bolt through the head or a coach and four run him down before he'll listen to me and keep out of this?"

"They are in full sight in the chamber where he sleeps," Cory countered in accusing tones. She pointed at the leather satchel sitting in the corner.

Matthew cursed his assumption that his son would leave the satchel alone. Snatching it up, he threw it in a coffer and locked the lid. "There. Does that satisfy you?"

"No." Cory folded both her arms. "What happens now? How do we prove it's Essex?"

She was so certain Essex was their culprit. Well, they would see. "I will pressure him. We'll see if he gives himself away."

"How will you do that?"

Matthew had been formulating his strategy. He should probably share certain details with her so she didn't accidentally interfere. " 'Tis time to show him the boots. He didn't wear them personally, but someone he hired did. He'll recognize them."

Cory didn't seem to understand. "If you show him the boots, he'll say he never saw them before. We'll learn nothing from that."

"We'll show them to him when he's least expecting it. In an unguarded moment." Matthew unlocked the coffer and removed the boots again. "I'll ask Toby to wear them."

Cory rose to examine the footwear. "Tell me why you're sure this is the pair." She turned one over and traced the H on the sole. "Did this mark show in the prints?"

"Yes. It stands for Howe, the cordwainer. The wear of the heels also showed in the prints." Matthew described the boot prints in the mud as well as the single print on Moll's dark stuff skirt. "The numbers I wrote down and my tracing of the print match these boots exactly. I also showed the boots to Norris yesterday and he recognized them as his old pair, given to Geoffrey Hall." He finished with how Toby had found the boots and his own conclusions about how the crossbow archer, who was also Moll's murderer, must have thrown them away to keep from being implicated. "Hall's feet were too large for the boots, so we know he didn't wear them. But he was doing something to assist the culprit, for he was disposed of, just like Moll. The thing that interests me is why the person in the coach and his driver spoke French."

Respect glowed in Cory's eyes as he finished his explanation, confirming that he'd done the right thing to share details with her, though he decided to keep quiet about his efforts to trace the coach. "We must see if Essex has any intimates who are French," she said. "He makes no secret of wanting to go to France. Perhaps he has some French allies who would benefit if he took the throne. There are a good number of them, either living in England or visiting."

"I noticed he had a French servant the day we were at his chamber. That fellow who fetched the boots."

Cory returned to her chair, now relaxed and smiling. "I know the one you mean. Thank you for speaking openly. I wish us to be this way all the time. I was never able to speak frankly with Thomas or my father-in-law."

He wanted to tell her that he wasn't the least like her first husband or father-in-law. That any oaf could do better than they had by her. But her only experience seemed to have been with oafs until now. And perhaps he was oafish in his own way, wanting her so much in bed. "I trust that running my household will be an improvement over running Whitby Place," he said quietly.

Cory winced, and he wondered what he'd said, but in the next breath, she made it clear. "That's why he sent me away. The dowager countess and I had taken over the running of the household. We tried to stop when we realized how much he hated it, but all the servants, even his stewart, came to us for advice or just the pleasure of our company. We wanted affection and companionship. He preferred to wield power like a king. So he sent me to a half dozen noble houses, trying to marry me off. When he finally sent me here, I thought he'd given up."

Her sorrow cut him to the quick, and he wanted to comfort her the way he had the night of the masque. The ivory brocade she wore made it difficult not to touch her. Its graceful neckline framed her creamy bare throat like a masterpiece of art. If Cordelia wanted him to talk instead of making love to her, she would be better off in coarse sacking with no shape. "I'm sorry he hurt you," he said.

"He could be ruthless when he wanted something," she responded. "Most men are."

He flinched as her arrow struck. It was an unintended target, but painful just the same. He didn't want to fall into the same category as her father-in-law—ruthless when pursuing his desires. Yet perhaps he was being ruthless in taking her to his bed, which he wanted to do again as soon as possible. "He's out of your life now. You can forget him," he said.

"He's not until I'm married, which hasn't happened *yet*," she reminded him tartly, glancing up.

How well he knew it. If they were, he would be coaxing her

into bed even now. Stepping to her side, he touched her dark hair, the curls sliding through his fingers as he searched for a way to introduce another necessary subject. "Once we are wed, I wish you to benefit fully from our union, especially in my absence. There are many details to see to. Where shall we begin?"

"Once we're wed, I can assist *you* with certain needs."

He felt a moment's misgiving. They couldn't be thinking of the same needs, for her to mention them so calmly. "Which ones?" he asked cautiously.

"Your need to form a circle of friends to crew on your ship," she said primly, folding her hands in her lap and avoiding his eyes. "I will help you identify men who are loyal and caring. Men like Hugh. He's charming, you know."

His needs wilted as he stared at her in disbelief. "Charming? Mariners?"

"You needn't worry. I'll help you," she said with a superior air. "You will be glad of their company during your voyage. True friends are invaluable in a difficulty."

True friends indeed. The type of friendship she meant was the last thing he required or wanted of the majority of his crew. He imagined Cory's gatherings for evening games and prayers, then substituted his dirty, poorly mannered men gathered around him, waiting with rapt expressions for his praise, and almost laughed. Mariners didn't want kind words or prayers. They formed loyalties over time based on mutual needs. She didn't know what she was talking about.

Rising, he stalked across the chamber, hoping she wouldn't say anything else absurd. Imagine, trying to convince him of such a thing.

She raised her chin in a gesture he now recognized. "I merely wish to assure myself of your safety on your voyages," she said. "But if you won't discuss it, we can discuss how I will nurture a family for you—people to love you when you are home. I wish to adopt Samuel as soon as I can find Lady Fleming a replacement. She should have an adult to fetch and carry for her, not a child. I'll arrange it, and I'll make him and Carew happy, for I'm rather good at that sort of thing."

Hell, she was better than good. She was superb, except for this foolishness of turning his crew into a circle of friends. But she had strayed far from the subject on his mind. "I'm referring

to property and income," he said. "I will insist Whitby pay you
your jointure, but I wish to provide more."

She grinned at him unexpectedly. "You can learn not to turn
into a dragon. That would be an excellent provision. I'll help
you," she added as he frowned. "You've done a marvelous
thing in bringing Toby into our circle. He's just the sort I had
in mind to build your crew. Tough but caring. Loyal to a fault.
You have a keen sense of people that's invaluable, Matthew."

He wanted to kiss her generous, provocative mouth when
she talked to him like that. To avoid doing so, he reached past
her for the bottle of ink and corked it. "Cordelia, could we
please stay with the topic? I wish to know you're provided for
while I'm gone."

She shrugged with exaggerated nonchalance, avoiding his
gaze. "Arrange what you wish. When you're gone, I'll
unarrange anything that displeases me."

She returned to her writing with a serene air, and Matthew
realized why she had avoided the subject. She wanted to bury
her head in the sand like an ostrich, to pretend he would never
leave. The same trouble he had with Carew was going to haunt
him with Cory.

How could he obey the queen's wish that he rove the seas for
his livelihood, yet maintain closeness with a wife in England?
He hadn't thought to face the dilemma, yet here it was. And
having lost her mother at an early age, Cory would take his
leaving far harder than her calm response suggested. He sensed
her hurt from her very choice of words.

Carew stuck his head in the door, Hugh looming behind him.
"Cory, it's time," Carew said. "Everyone's ready, but we can't
use Giordano's chamber. It's turned upside down, being
cleaned."

"Oh, dear." Cory's mobile expression slipping from excited
anticipation to dismay.

"What's wrong?" Matthew growled, irked by the timing of
the interruption.

"It's time for cards and prayers, but we have no place to
gather," she explained.

"Prayers? At this time of day?"

"Prayers are appropriate at any time of day." Cory was un-
ruffled by the skepticism in his tone. "We cannot manage them
later tonight. Everyone has duties."

"Bring them here," he said without thinking. Anything to make her smile again.

Her face lit up, as did Carew's. "I'll fetch 'em." He disappeared, leaving the door ajar.

As Cory folded her letter into a packet, Matthew inwardly cursed their lack of closure on the subject of her future. She had insisted they be open about everything. Eventually they must discuss arrangements for when he was gone. She could not avoid it forever.

"May I use your sealing wax and seal?" she interrupted, searching his worktable.

He found the wax, resigned to broaching the subject again later. She would never wish to discuss his leaving. He knew that. Tugging the signet ring from his finger, he placed it on the table as she lit the taper. When the seal was ready, she pressed his ring into the liquid wax.

The sweet, hot odor rose, reminding him of the intimate warmth he and Cory created together. He stole a longing glance at the bed. Cory and her incessant card playing. He would far rather that they were alone together so he could . . .

The door banged open and Toby entered, followed by Carew, Samuel, and a dozen other people whose names he couldn't remember. Pages, ladies' maids, gentlemen pensioners, and tirewomen saluted him, then settled on the chairs and cushions.

Packs of cards popped out of pouches and pockets. Cory moved among them as games began. People counted scores aloud, laughing. By Neptune, he hadn't realized he would feel invaded. To him, its scale rivaled that of Attila the Hun when he'd occupied France with his hordes. His only privacy at the crowded court was in his bedchamber.

"Awfully good of you to have us, my lord," a gentleman pensioner said.

"Er, of course, Meeks." Matthew would die rather than admit his discomfort.

"Aye, my lord, you and her ladyship are jewels." His female gaming partner offered a toothy smile.

He couldn't remember her name for the life of him, but Cory came to his rescue. "His lordship *is* most generous, Gert. Thank you for your kind words." She paused with a hand on his shoulder, serene and in control of her little kingdom and her adoring subjects.

She was the jewel, Matthew thought, knowing he was going to hate sharing her with these affectionate hordes.

Chapter 20

Matthew's concern about keeping Cory safe escalated the next day as he answered the queen's summons to an emergency council meeting. To him, emergencies meant danger.

To cause further problems, he had to bring Carew. Cory, under Hugh's guard, was directing the starching of the queen's neck ruffs. Carew despised the smell and refused to stay with her. As he had sent Toby to talk to coachwrights, Matthew had little choice but to bring Carew along.

"The Spanish ambassador called on me yesterday, my lords." Elizabeth angrily paced the council chamber. She had included a dozen available councilors and courtiers, including Lord Burghley, Sir Christopher Hatton, the Earl of Essex, and Matthew. They stood by their chairs, unable to sit as long as Her Majesty was on her feet. He glanced at Carew, hoping his rascal son would stay out of mischief, especially since the queen seemed to be brewing a storm.

"The ambassador has heard that at the coming reception for the foreign ambassadors, I will give the French emissary a generous gift of gold for his master, Henri of Navarre," Elizabeth continued brusquely. "It is not true. Who started this rumor?" Her cheeks were ruddy with temper, which seemed augmented by the tightness of her cream-colored kirtle embroidered with green plants from the New World.

The assembled men coughed, scraped their chairs, and looked everywhere but at the queen. "No one here has spread such gossip, Your Majesty," Lord Burghley finally spoke for them.

"You know I have no more gold for him," Elizabeth roared, unleashing the tempest. "Yet everyone whispers that I do. One of my ladies told me the story only this morning. I refuse to tax my people, so I repeat, there is no more gold for France. I hate the reports of siege and famine in Paris, as you do, but we cannot afford more unless you personally wish to contribute to Navarre."

She glared around the chamber at them, and they hastily lowered their gazes. No one wanted to delve into their pockets once more, except for Essex, who alternately pleaded with the queen to play soldier and threatened to go without her permission. "Your Majesty, my troops are—"

"You're not to have troops. Disburse them at once," the queen snapped, turning away. "My lords, I want this gossip stopped," she insisted, waving dismissal. "Keep your eyes and ears open for the culprit who started it, and in the meantime, put about word that 'tis false."

"How the devil are we supposed to stop gossip?" Lord Burghley complained to Matthew as they took the air in the flower garden. "It's like the plague here. Rampant and out of control. Short of telling La Faye outright that the gossip is a lie, I don't see how we're to disillusion him."

"He probably started it himself," Matthew said, relieved that the emergency had been no more serious than a false rumor. "I must speak to him on another matter. If you will take Carew to Hugh for me, I will convey the bad news to La Faye."

"Of course I will. I like your son." The old gentleman smiled and set off toward Carew, who sat beneath an arbor looking cross and bored.

Matthew waved to Carew, then headed back to the palace. He was pleased that his son had heard nothing dangerous, but he wasn't pleased with Elizabeth. She hadn't hesitated to give him a new duty as he'd prepared to leave the council chamber.

"If that Jacques La Faye asks me one more time for money, I'll murder him where he stands," she had ranted. "By fair means or foul, you will take him from court once you're wed."

"Your Grace," he'd protested in rational tones, "I must first learn who killed Moll Dakins and who wishes Cordelia dead. I have reason to believe the Earl of Essex might be involved." He had felt honor bound to mention the possibility of Essex's being a danger.

"My Robin?" The queen had flown into a royal rage. "My sweet Robin loves me and would never harm anyone I hold dear. I won't hear a word of it."

Matthew had scowled, hating her insistence that she was right all the time. Nor did he appreciate her expecting him to take La Faye on his wedding journey. "Your refusal to believe does not make it false. Your Robin could be involved, and I intend to find out."

Elizabeth had stood nose to nose with him, radiating fury akin to her royal sire's, despite the fragility of her slender, aging frame. "I could still wed Cordelia to Sir William," she had growled.

She would too, Matthew thought, feeling bad tempered and on edge as he was admitted into La Faye's apartments only to collide with a dark-haired man. The fellow grunted an apology, bid farewell to the servant with whom he'd been talking, and slipped out the door. Matthew studied him as he retreated down the corridor, realizing he was Essex's French servant. He'd also been one of Essex's party yesterday as they returned from hunting. The French were everywhere, he thought as La Faye's other servant went to announce him in the inner chamber.

The ring of female laughter floated to him from within. La Faye had an admirer?

"I have nine and sixty points, *madame*," he heard La Faye say in triumph. "Twenty-nine points in my largest suit and forty for my four knaves. Can you best that?"

They were playing cards, and the game was Cent, from the sound of it.

"La, monsieur, I regret to say that I can," the female laughed, a delightful trill in her voice. "I have forty-eight points in my largest suit as well as a foursome of queens."

The female's voice sounded suspiciously familiar.

"All four queens! *Mon Dieu*," La Faye groaned in mock despair. "And I lacked but the queen of hearts to complete my royal sequence. Vanquished by the queen of hearts."

"Poor monsieur."

It was Cory, with Hugh nowhere in sight. Great Neptune, just because she was visiting in a private chamber didn't mean she should dismiss her bodyguard. Matthew was led into the chamber where they sat at play with glasses of wine nearby, entirely too cozy for his taste.

Cory looked up. "My lord, what a surprise."

She looked more guilty than surprised as he towered over her. "I thought you were directing the starching of the queen's ruffs," he said.

"I completed the task."

He scowled before exchanging bows with La Faye, who still had a bandaged head from his recent accident. "I can stay but a minute," Matthew said as the servant brought him a chair. He didn't much like La Faye, with his love of crimson clothing and his ready smirk. The man was physically repellant and personally annoying, but that wasn't enough reason to snub him, and Cory seemed to think he had saving graces. "The viscountess and I intend to wed," he said, wasting no time in preliminaries. "We invite you to visit Graystock Manor with us after the ceremony."

Displeasure flickered in La Faye's eyes before it was masked by a magnanimous smile. What did it mean? Matthew tried to guess as La Faye offered congratulations and teased Cory in well-bred phrases until she blushed. Did he want Cory himself? And why hadn't he responded to the invitation? Undoubtedly Matthew had been too blunt, his most famous fault.

"Where is your estate, my lord?" La Faye swung his gaze to Matthew unexpectedly.

"It's only three hours away by coach." Cory leaned forward, her enthusiasm saving Matthew the need to reply. "And very beautiful, I hear. Court is so crowded. We'll be much more comfortable there. You'll have a whole suite of rooms rather than these two cramped ones. Come, monsieur, do you agree?"

To Matthew's surprise, La Faye accepted the invitation with alacrity and fell to discussing various country pastimes with Cory. He'd anticipated a refusal, almost hoped for one to escape the envoy's fatuous company. But an order from the queen was an order, he admitted wearily. If this plan had failed, he would have had to find another. His duty was to remove La Faye from the queen's vicinity, and remove him he would.

"Who was that fellow talking to your servant when I arrived?" His abrupt question drew Cory's and La Faye's surprised stares. But he wanted to know more about the man.

"I do not know. Let me ask Antoine." As La Faye called for his servant, a spasm of pain crossed his face. With shaking hands, he reached for the bandage on his head.

"Let me do that for you." Cory jumped up and repositioned the bandage with gentle fingers.

"Thank you, my dear." La Faye smiled wanly and patted her hand.

Matthew noticed with distaste how the Frenchman's heavy jowls gave him a piggish look. "Who is that man you were speaking to when I arrived?" he demanded of Antoine as he entered the room. He had no intention of letting La Faye distract him from the subject. "Does he work for the Earl of Essex? What business did you have with him?"

"That is François, my lord." Antoine inclined his head with deference. "He is a fellow countryman, so we exchange pleasantries from time to time."

"What's he doing in the palace if he works in the stables?" Matthew demanded brusquely. "I saw him return from hunting with the earl the other day. His duties would lie with either the horses or dogs."

"Many men take their personal servants hunting," La Faye intervened, clearly annoyed by Matthew's probing. He made a visible effort to gather himself, as if Matthew depleted his patience as well as his strength. "Really, my lord, I do not like your tone. You sound as if you suspect Antoine of something. He is an honest and upright servant, I assure you."

Matthew didn't care about Antoine. He sensed something odd about François's relationship with Essex, but he couldn't put his finger on it. Nor was there any reason why Antoine or La Faye should know about it, except they *were* all French. "I don't see why a man like the earl would bother to take a house servant hunting," he said to Antoine, ignoring La Faye's muttered protests and Cory's reproachful stare that silently begged him to stop. "He has yeomen of the stable and the kennels aplenty to accompany him. Why take this François?"

"Ah, I see the confusion." Antoine smiled with sudden understanding. "You do not know that François is a great hunter of the wild boar. He is most skilled with the spear. It is a dangerous but exhilarating sport for those who excel."

Matthew mulled this over. "By the by, did you know that Moll Dakins was with child when she died?" he said to La Faye, then shot Cory a look of warning not to interfere.

La Faye's face twisted in distress. "*Diable,* no. Are you sure?"

"The royal physician was definite about it," Matthew said without a shred of mercy. "Did she tell you where she was going the night she died?"

La Faye bent forward in his chair, as if the news made him sick to his stomach. "I was not at court at the time," he choked. "Viscountess, if you will excuse me, I am horrified by this news."

"I'm so sorry that you had to learn it in this way, monsieur." Cory patted La Faye's shoulder. With a glare for Matthew, she gestured to Antoine and moved toward the ewer stand, apparently intending to fetch La Faye some water.

"I'm sorry too, but someone murdered Moll, and all suspects must be considered," Matthew said conversationally. For reasons he couldn't explain, he didn't believe La Faye's grief had much depth.

"My lord, do you suggest you suspect me?" La Faye asked, his tone appalled.

"I didn't say that." He wasn't sure what he suspected, but he was saved from further argument as Cory and Antoine returned, the servant with a basin of water, Cory with a damp cloth that she offered to La Faye.

"We must go, Cordelia." Matthew moved toward the door, not bothering to bow to La Faye, who was holding the cloth to his face and couldn't see him anyway. "Oh, I meant to tell you, La Faye, there will be no special gift of gold for France at the queen's coming reception. The rumors you might have heard are false. Come, Cordelia."

So, he thought as he guided Cory down the corridor, Essex and François both have a taste for danger. An interesting bit of information.

"Matthew, how could you bring up Moll's child?" Cory was adamant in her disapproval. "He could have been the father. If he hadn't heard from gossip, he was better off not knowing at all."

"If he didn't know, he wasn't that close to her." Matthew tightened his jaw, disliking the Frenchman. "If she loved him, she would have told him. If he had cared for her, he would have sensed her condition. A man notices such things about a woman if he is intimate with her regularly." He shot her a steamy glance.

Cory blushed to the roots of her hair. "Men aren't supposed to notice such things."

"I do." He would never forget the changes in Joanna's body within days of her conceiving Carew, and Cory showed none of those signs. What a relief to know she wasn't with child.

"I'm still unhappy with you," she insisted, squirming under the intimacy of his gaze. "He couldn't possibly have killed Moll. He was away from court, as he said."

"What if he was displeased about Moll's being with child? What if he killed her because of it?"

Cory bristled at the idea, as he'd suspected she would. "That's impossible. He cared for Moll, as I told you. You saw how distressed he was when you mentioned the child. Besides, a man in his position would have no need to kill a woman for a reason such as that."

Matthew acknowledged she was correct. If a man wanted to be rid of a lower-status woman he'd gotten with child, he could pay her to leave him alone. Or if he wasn't susceptible to the condemnation of the church court ruling his parish, he could simply ignore her. "I wonder about this François, though. He's French, and Toby heard the man in the coach and his driver speak French when they threw away the boots," he said, reminding her of the crucial detail.

"Yes, and he is Essex's servant," Cory agreed. "Essex seems more likely to have someone murdered to protect his rebellion. La Faye, on the other hand, would hardly kill Moll, then have me shot at, all to help Essex."

"I agree with you there," he said. "La Faye strikes me as too selfish to help anyone if it required much effort on his part. And François is in Essex's company all the time. He's clearly prized for his special skill. I've also noticed he has small feet. *He* might have worn those boots."

Cory stilled. "Oh, dear," she said in a nervous voice. "Do you mean—"

"Essex might have paid him to shoot the crossbow at you," Matthew pressed on. "And François might have driven the coach when the boots were thrown away. He would have wanted to be rid of the boots, and he speaks French. Cory, from now on, you must avoid François."

She nodded, looking anxious. He was sorry to upset her, but he had to be sure she understood the danger. They had no definite proof of who was threatening her. It was best to keep an open mind.

To reassure her, he kissed her, then found her lips so delicious, he sampled her sweet depths. "Let us retire to my chamber, Cory." He caught her hand and kissed her fingertips.

She turned a becoming pink. "Do you think we should? Before our wedding?"

They shouldn't, but fulfillment of their desires lifted them both to another plane, and he burned for her all the time, like a volatile torch, steeped in pitch and plunged into the core of the flame.

But he must not get her with child. The first time, he'd been beside himself with need and forgotten his vow to be cautious. He must not repeat the error.

As for La Faye, his sixth sense told him the man might be dangerous, but if not that, he was certainly worthless. He wasn't going to enjoy having him visit Graystock Manor with them.

Chapter 21

Cory sat with the maids of honor, Lady Fleming, Jane, and the queen in the green antechamber the next morning, feeling tense and wretched from lack of sleep. All night, Matthew had stood guard outside her door, but the sense of impending danger had tormented her dreams.

Once more, deadly crossbow bolts had whizzed past her head, so real she had started up in bed, gasping and drenched in sweat. With the fear came memory of the thrill, of her rescuer's body pressed to hers as they hugged the ground. How she longed to lie in the security of his arms by night. Instead, they were both cross and tired by day, wondering if the killer would strike again.

The queen was in a foul mood as well, reprimanding all who displeased her. Samuel had been clouted once for clumsiness. Even Cory hadn't escaped her displeasure when she reminded Elizabeth of the need to announce her nuptials. The queen had barked that she was in no mood.

Cory had shut her mouth and kept her impatience to herself.

Yet Carew managed to amuse the queen, which was a major feat.

"Giordano, you are an unprincipled rascal. Stop that." Elizabeth burst into chuckles as the parrot fluttered from Carew's hand to the arm of her chair and dipped his beak into the embroidered pocket of her ornamental apron. "What does he want?" she asked.

"Something to eat. See?" Carew pointed as the bird emerged from her pocket, dribbling a trail of tiny seeds.

"And how did those seeds get into my pocket, Master Cavandish?" the queen asked with mock indignation.

Carew rolled his eyes toward the ceiling, all innocence. "I cannot guess, Your Grace."

Elizabeth laughed aloud, and Cory took a seat on a cushioned stool away from the others. With Her Majesty occupied, she wished to sit quietly. The need to chat wore on her nerves.

"Your Grace, the Italian ambassador wishes to meet with you," Lady Carey said as she entered the chamber. "He brought you this gift." Balanced on her arm was a delightful little creature with soft brown fur, bright black eyes, and a long curling tail.

"A monkey. Isn't he dear?" Elizabeth's face was wreathed in smiles as she bade Carew take the parrot and crossed to Lady Carey. "Tell him I'll see him in the Paradise Chamber." As Carey left the chamber, the monkey hopped willingly onto the queen's arm, and she fed him a dried fig. Elizabeth chuckled. "The greedy thing. He reminds me of you, Carew, at table."

The queen was still smiling at the little creature's antics when Essex entered, attended by his French servant. At the sight of the pair, Cory gripped her stool in panic. She had meant to avoid them both, yet here they were, all in the same chamber. As Essex flirted with the queen and admired her monkey, the Frenchman sent Cory a malevolent stare.

Frozen in place, Cory searched the chamber, realizing she was without either Toby or Hugh.

"I conducted the ambassador to the Paradise Chamber, Your Majesty," Lady Carey said, returning. "He awaits you there."

"Come, come, all of you," Elizabeth ordered. "You, too, Essex. Attend me."

As the queen turned to quit the chamber, Essex postured for the maids. Seeing the girls simper, Elizabeth whirled to scowl at her favorite, who donned an innocent expression.

As Elizabeth swung back to scold the maids, Essex leered at Cory over the queen's shoulder.

Shaken by a wave of dizziness, Cory clutched Samuel for

support. The child gazed up at her in confusion, unable to understand her odd behavior, but she dared not explain her fear.

As she struggled to think what to do, Matthew entered the chamber, followed by Toby. She started up, relieved to see him, but stopped in consternation. Toby was wearing the crossbow archer's boots.

An attack of shivers shook Cory. By fortune, she wanted Matthew at her side. But instead of coming to her, he bowed over the queen's hand, then stationed himself by the hearth, arms folded, surveying the room. A wave of cold swept over Cory, followed by burning heat. She checked to see if Essex had noticed the boots, but he was still flirting with the maids. Her terrified heart banged like a hammer, threatening to break her ribs.

Exasperated by Essex's behavior with her women, Elizabeth beckoned to Lady Carey and, with the monkey on her arm, marched off to meet the ambassador. Essex continued to flirt with the maids.

Toby crossed the chamber, bowed to Essex, and bid him good morning. Essex ignored him, instead snapping his fingers at François, who had been trying to flirt with an uneasy-looking Jane. At the earl's summons, he left her with reluctance. Toby stepped forward, flaunting the boots.

François halted midway to the door and stared at Toby's feet. Then he turned and fixed his dark, glittering eyes on Matthew. The venomous intention Cory read in his gaze was terrifying.

She could bear to see no more. Gripping her skirts, she darted from the chamber. Great heaven above, Essex hadn't recognized the boots, but François had. It was a sure sign that François had once owned them.

Wanting to hide, she ran all the way to Matthew's chamber. As she burst into the room, pain lanced her side, and she grasped the bedpost for support. For what felt like hours, she stood that way, laboring for breath, but gradually her racing heart slowed. Cory found a chair and sat down, too stunned to think what to do next. She started as Matthew came quietly into the room.

"I'm certain the boots belonged to François." He closed the door and, moving to her side, slid a protective arm around her shoulders and drew her close. "Can you bear to talk about it?"

"Why didn't you warn me?" she burst out, rising from her chair to face him.

"I didn't want any gossip about it beforehand." Matthew seemed unalarmed.

Cory wanted to throw something at him. As if she would gossip. Blast his careful control as danger built to a crescendo. "You confronted him, didn't you?"

"Of course, but Essex refused to let Captain Wells arrest François. He wouldn't even consider that the man might be guilty. I told him he was harboring a murderer; he told me to mind my own business or suffer the consequences." Matthew snorted in disgust.

Cory swallowed back a cry of frustration. "The queen will insist he is arrested, will she not?"

"I spoke to her about it. She called Essex to account for his servant in my presence, but you know how he is. He talked sweet to her and insisted I was merely doing this to spite him. She said just because François had once owned the boots didn't mean he had killed Moll. Someone else had worn them. Since François is not English, Elizabeth took the easy way out. She ordered Essex to send François back to France. He has two days."

Cory was not consoled. "François is a murderer. I know he is." Frustrated by Matthew's apparent lack of fear, she grasped his shoulders. "I almost died on the spot, standing in the same room with him, knowing he was the one."

"You were in no danger. If you had been, Toby and I would have protected you. I bought him a new dagger, and he's quite good with it."

She hadn't noticed Toby's weapon, nor did she feel secure around François, regardless of who was there to protect her. Still shaken, she wrapped her arms around Matthew's broad chest and cradled her cheek against his shoulder. "Essex must have hired François to do these terrible things," she quavered, a tightness squeezing her throat.

"We have no proof that Essex is the one behind François's actions. But I intend to find out."

Cory fought to control her alarm as she realized what he meant. He had shifted the focus of danger from her to himself. "What are you going to do?" she all but shrieked, gripping

Matthew harder. "François will try to kill you before he leaves the country. I know he will."

"I intend to catch him at it and unmask the man behind him in the process." Matthew's tone was like ice, and his gaze was fixed on a faraway place that excluded her.

"How can you be so calm?"

"I'm tightening the noose."

How could she forget that he lived in a place of deep shadow, where his intimate dialogue with danger served as his focal point? He had no fear, having lost everything he valued. The habit of shutting out others remained as he performed the intricate dance with the devil. The ultimate outcome could be his death. If not this time, then another. And he didn't care.

The idea made her desperate. He was deliberately distancing himself from her as he prepared to offer himself as bait to their enemy. She was better off leaving him be, yet she hated that cold barrier, keeping them apart. "By fortune, make love to me. Please, Matthew. Help me forget whoever is doing this." She pressed the length of her body against his, luxuriating in the feel of his hard muscles. She came closest to reaching him when they made love. If she coaxed him into the land of perpetual heat, it could work again.

He emerged from his mental shadows to stare at her, as if seeing her for the first time since he'd arrived. Lifting one of her bodice laces, he held it away from her body, following it with his gaze to her waist. With sensual slowness, he pulled until the bow untied. Thrills raced through her as her bodice gaped in back. "I will make love to you, Cordelia," he whispered, slipping his fingers between the laces to loosen them. "But not by fortune. I control my own destiny."

Unwilling to argue, she captured his hand and pressed it to her breast. "Kiss me, Matthew. When you do, I know we're still alive and no one can touch us."

He obliged her with willing fervor. The flame within her ignited, building swiftly to fever pitch. But as his mouth moved hungrily against hers, she recognized his reserve. Had it been present the other times he'd made love to her? Had she been too full of her own passion to notice? She didn't think so. He had left the shadows behind those nights.

She shouldn't demand he forsake them. She risked wounding them both.

But when his eyes darkened, when he seemed beyond reach, she could not do otherwise. She had learned that human touch could fan the flame of the spirit. If Matthew was to be her husband, she wanted him alive with feeling. Not a wounded spirit that roamed the seas, cloaked in endless night.

Their third joining was all she had hoped for and more. It cleansed Essex from her mind, and she basked in Matthew's passion like an exotic orchid opening to the light. He was tender with her, yet his kisses were fierce and demanding as their lovemaking progressed. She welcomed him into her depths with a frenzy of urgency.

Together, they soared to heights she had never known were possible. Her cries of fulfillment seemed to set him glowing with a light of his own. It told Cory that this much was right. It might be only a temporary effect, but by offering her body, she drew him out of the shadows.

It would have to be enough. It might even be best this way, for soon he would be gone on another voyage.

She would be alone once more.

Matthew cursed his mind-drugging passion for Cory as he stood with her in the great hall that evening. He'd been insanely careless, indulging his lust and soaring on their mutual fulfillment without protecting her from becoming with child.

They were sailing straight for destruction in more ways than one, and Cory was totally oblivious to her effect on him. She distracted him from the business at hand by dressing in her finest garments. Her peacock blue bodice fit her like a second skin, molding to her breasts and waist, transforming her into an exotic, magical creature with gleaming flesh. The men in the chamber reacted like predatory beasts, casting her covert, hungry glances. He was the worst of them, and he cursed his arousal at the very sight of her.

From the depths of his memory came a vision of Joanna, a gaunt shadow of the laughing girl she'd been. Relentless, it reminded him of how Carew's birth had sucked away her life's blood.

He shook his head to destroy the image, but it would return to mock his weakness with Cory. She had no idea what she risked.

The chamber was crowded with courtiers, ready for the

queen's reception to honor the foreign ambassadors. But to Matthew, the hammer-beam ceiling cast menacing shadows that even blazing candles couldn't dispel. His earlier confrontation with Essex and his servant had set gossip flying. In two days, François would be banished from England, and Matthew felt certain the Frenchman would attempt to murder him as a farewell gift. He would watch Essex and François carefully once they arrived tonight, but he wouldn't mention them to Cory. Tension in the hall already ran high enough.

As the musicians began, a man in dress armor bumped into him, turned, and captured his hand with a delighted cry. "Matthew Cavandish! Well met. You're back from sea."

"Sir Roger." Recognizing the captain of the queen's troops in France, Matthew pumped the officer's hand with enthusiasm. "How go the French wars?"

"Terrible, as usual." Sir Roger Williams grimaced. "Your brother has done nothing but worry us, doing all manner of dangerous things. Did you hear he was captured when intercepting a message from the Duke of Mayenne to the Bishop of Paris? The two were planning a raid to smuggle food into the besieged city. Jonathan escaped and there was no raid, but it was close."

Matthew nodded, glad to know Jonathan was well but wishing his brother were home. "His wife hasn't heard from him of late. She's terribly worried."

Sir Roger pushed back his thinning hair. "I called on her earlier to say I'd seen him well and in good spirits just four days past. If Jonathan *El Mágico* Cavandish turns up once a sennight, we know he's still in one piece. But something does trouble me." He cupped a hand to his mouth and spoke very low. "We've heard reports that George Trenchard was seen again."

Matthew raised his eyebrows at the mention of the powerful Englishman who was once betrothed to his sister Rozalinde, then betrayed her and England to work for Spain. "I thought he died in the sea battle at Enckhuysen years ago."

"Your sister *hoped* he went down with his ship, but no one knew for sure." Sir Roger dropped his hand and smiled at Cory. "Won't you introduce me to your pretty companion, Cavandish? How is it you always have the most beautiful of women at your side?"

"This is my wife to be, although the betrothal is not yet public, so pray do not mention it." Matthew realized his manners were sorely lacking, as always. More than that, Cory must have heard most of what they'd said, for she was frowning, her brow knit in ridges. He quickly conducted the introductions.

The queen interrupted with her entrance. She swept up to them in a billow of black velvet enriched by a stomacher encrusted with winking diamonds. Frowns were apparently the fashion tonight, Matthew noted, for an exquisite one marred Elizabeth's high, white forehead.

"Why hasn't this rumor died?" she snarled to Matthew. "Everyone's talking of the lavish gift England will present to La Faye. We cannot promise money the treasury doesn't have."

"You could give this, Your Majesty." Carew appeared out of nowhere, holding a gilded box. Matthew started. Confound it, what was his son doing here? He was supposed to be in bed.

Carew pressed the box into the queen's hands.

She looked skeptical as she examined it from different angles. "What's in it?" she asked.

Matthew held his breath. Knowing Carew, it was a large, hairy rat.

"Look and see, Your Grace," Carew urged her, tracing a proper bow.

The queen opened the lid and peeped inside. Her eyes widened with surprise. "Master Carew, are you sure I can give this away?"

"As if it were your own," he assured her proudly.

The queen turned the box so everyone could see a gleaming mass of gold coins.

Matthew almost choked. Carew had obviously taken the queen's concern about a gift for Navarre to heart, yet he couldn't have obtained so much money by honest means. "Where did you get that, Carew?" he demanded. "You know I don't approve of—"

Trumpets drowned out the rest of his words. People rushed to take their places for the entry of the visiting envoys and their attendants. Elizabeth snapped the box shut and strode to her great chair on the raised dais. Carew dodged away, disappearing into the crowd.

"I'm sure it's all right," Cory whispered, squeezing Matthew's arm as courtiers jostled them in their haste. "I must go to my place now, but I will bring Carew to your chamber after the ceremonies to talk."

A last waft of her daffodil essence lingered as she joined the other maids flanking the queen. Matthew resigned himself to trouble. Carew had no honest means of amassing so much money.

By the time the gifts had been presented by each country to the other, the chamber buzzed with excitement over the queen's gift to France. The coins had been counted and found to equal two hundred pounds. Certainly not a fortune, but a far finer gift than the trinkets the English councilors had presented.

"How clever the queen is," Matthew heard someone say, "to pretend there was no special gift to help place Navarre on the throne, then to produce one."

Essex, who stood nearby, snapped at the person, saying it should never have happened as he was supposed to go to France and make any such gifts. Great Neptune, Matthew had been so preoccupied by his son, he'd forgotten the earl. As he pressed his way through the crowd, intending to see what new information he could glean from him, Sir Roger caught his arm. "Don't believe I know La Faye. Will you introduce me?"

"Of course." It was the last thing Matthew wanted to do, given his dislike of La Faye, but he would do his duty. "Don't you see Navarre often?" he asked. "I thought you would know his envoy."

Sir Roger laughed ruefully. "I see Navarre's captains, yes. But him? Rarely. He's always fighting. The few minutes he isn't, he's chasing women. Catches them, too."

Matthew left La Faye and Sir Roger deep in conversation and sought out Essex. The earl stood with François several paces from the queen, looking disgruntled as the Swedish and Italian envoys vied for her attention. Probably hadn't gotten enough attention himself, Matthew thought. He was finding it increasingly difficult to picture the young, overdressed fop capable of plotting murder, let alone treason. Yet if he weren't the one, who was?

"I understand you're not pleased with how Her Majesty conducts the nation's business," he said in low tones as he moved to the earl's side.

Essex's head snapped around. "What do you know about it?"

Matthew summoned a lazy smile, purposely taunting the earl. "I just wanted you to know that *I* know."

"Know what, you bastard?"

Matthew noticed that François's expression had darkened. "I know all about your plans," he said with studied care.

Essex drew himself up to his full height and glared at Matthew. "I have no obligation to let you harass me." He turned away and favored Mary Islington with a smile.

Determined to use the moment for discovery, Matthew stepped close to the earl and slipped his hand into Essex's trunkhose pocket. His fingers closed on fabric.

With a snarl, Essex whirled away, leaving a large piece of linen in Matthew's hand.

Matthew shook out the handkerchief and examined it with interest. The hemming, the size, the quality of the fabric, everything about it was identical to the other three handkerchiefs—the one found with Moll's body, the one found with her personal effects, and the one given by Essex to Mary Islington.

"Did his lordship give you a handkerchief like this, Mistress Mary?" he asked, just to be sure.

The maid blushed, her gaze shifting to Essex. "Aye, he did. I kept it beneath my pillow, so I would dream sweet dreams about him, but someone took it."

"Did you also give a handkerchief like this to Moll Dakins?" Matthew asked the earl. "They're so unusual. Are they specially made?"

"What if they are? Damn it, Graystock, I'll make you sorry you ever met me," Essex snarled.

"I already am." Matthew saluted the earl, stuffed the handkerchief in his own pocket, and strode from the chamber. It confirmed the link between Essex and Moll's death, yet he didn't trust it fully. Someone else could have placed Essex's handkerchief with Moll's body.

He recalled the smoldering hatred in François's eyes and wondered if the man might have strangled Moll with Essex's handkerchief. He believed that possible, but why would he leave the cloth with Moll? If he worked for Essex, it didn't make sense.

The only thing he knew for certain was that François would try to put him off the trail of his secrets forever, and Matthew intended to catch him in the act.

On his way back to his chamber, Matthew's mind leaped ahead to the coming confrontation with Carew. Not only must he wait for the murderer to strike again and protect Cory and Carew from harm, but he must also settle domestic matters. Constable, guard, and parent. He didn't know which he was from one minute to the next.

He didn't want to think badly of Carew, but where could he have gotten so much gold without stealing it? Or borrowing it against some collateral that would be forfeit if it couldn't be repaid?

Cory's face was drawn and tired as she opened the door, but Carew strutted in his new boots from Master Howe, showing a bravado that was annoying, under the circumstances.

"Carew, you listened well in council meeting yesterday," he began reasonably. "I'm pleased you wanted to help the queen, but I'm also worried. Where did you get all that gold?"

"Does it matter where I got it?" Carew said cheerfully. He lounged against the table and picked his teeth with a wooden toothpick.

"It matters very much," Matthew said gravely, "especially if someone has been injured in your acquiring it. Or if you have made promises you cannot keep."

"What if no one was injured?" Carew asked with irritatingly good humor, refusing to look him in the eye. "In fact, what if they never even know?"

"Look at me and try to understand." Matthew crossed the chamber and rested both hands on Carew's shoulders, but the boy averted his gaze. "Even if they never know, if you did something wrong to acquire the money, it's still wrong."

Carew pulled away from him, his expression turning sullen. "There's no pleasing you. I do something good and you hate me anyway."

"I don't hate you. But you must not—"

"You do hate me. You only think of what you want. What about what I want?" Carew hurled at him. "You didn't even let me tell what I knew of the coach that almost hit Cory."

"You know something? What?" Matthew demanded.

Carew described the coat of arms on the side of the coach. "I tried to tell you, but you just told me to mind my own affairs. Now you'll probably want to shout at me because I saw it."

He wasn't shouting, Matthew thought in despair. "I only want to keep you safe."

"That's what you always say. I'm nothing but a-a toy to you, to keep safe on the shelf when you're done playing with it." Carew burst into sobs and raced from the chamber.

Cory started to follow him, then stopped, her arms dropping to her sides as if in defeat. "Oh dear. Why does this happen?" she choked.

At the sign of tears glittering in her eyes, Matthew's anger dissipated. "You see how it is." He shrugged, feeling hopeless. "I try my best, but he hates me."

"He doesn't hate you." Cory held out pleading hands. "He needs you. But every year, you leave him again, as if you didn't care."

"Of course I care, but he's been happy with his aunt and uncle. I can't take a child on raids, and the queen wants me to go." This had always been the difficulty, impossible to resolve.

Her expression softened as she absorbed his pain. "It is a problem, I'll grant you. I can see that if you showed how much you cared for him, he might be even more unhappy each time you left. But I think you must take the risk." She wiped her eyes with her handkerchief. "I'm going to find him, but I wish you would try to tell him you love him, both with words and deeds."

Matthew's conscience writhed with guilt. He thought he'd shown his love for his son by doing the right things for him, by placing him with nurturing relations and providing well for him. Yet for the first time, he saw himself through Cory's eyes. She thought because he went away each year, he felt nothing for his son. In truth, he felt too much. He'd left in the first place because he thought Carew better off with his widowed mother than with him. He'd meant to spare Carew contact with the ugly ache in his soul. But had he instead denied comfort to them both?

The idea had never occurred to him. Now that it did, he knew that despite the possibility of Carew's rejection, he would have to try and find out.

And he must complete the work Toby had started of tracing

the coat of arms. Without question, the arms Carew had described were the same ones Toby had seen the night he'd found the boots.

His son was right. He should have probed for every detail Carew had observed, for clearly the coach that had almost struck Cory was the same one from which the boots had been thrown away.

Chapter 22

On François's second to final day in England, Matthew sent Toby to interview more coachwrights. After seeing him off to London, he went to work on his ships. If the culprit thought Matthew was engaged elsewhere, Toby might learn more. He left Carew and Cory with Hugh and the queen, knowing they were well guarded that morning.

At close to the noon dinner hour, he returned to court. He was just about to seek Cory and Carew so they could dine together when Toby returned.

The old man didn't look so old today. His cheeks were ruddy from activity, and he'd gained weight in recent days, looking almost stalwart in linen leggings and a brown tunic. He nipped into the chamber and closed the door. "Got somethin' ta wet the whistle? I'm bone dry."

Matthew poured Toby a cup of small beer from a jug. "Learn anything?"

"Called on the last two coachwrights in London but 'ad no luck. Since I'd 'eard of a tavern that François favors, I went there. Played at dice with some of the regulars and learned he sometimes comes in a coach with a nobleman's coat of arms. One fellow even sketched the arms for me. Same as I saw that night. Fellow said François seems to know the fellow what drives the coach as well. The old man sometimes joins him in the tavern for ale."

"You did well, Toby. How many coachwrights are left in the city?"

"None, though there are still two in Southwark and one in Smithfield."

"I'll talk to them this afternoon. You've done enough." Matthew was uncomfortable with the amount of information he'd shared. He'd had to, so Toby would know the danger as he helped him, yet too many people were learning the secrets, and gossip seemed to spread like magic at court.

As Toby beamed at the praise, the door latch rattled, as if someone had accidentally bumped against it. Toby got up and opened the door.

No one was there.

"Someone was there. 'eard 'em." Toby leaned out the door and searched the corridor.

"It was probably someone passing by."

"Or someone listening at the keyhole." Toby closed the door and rejoined Matthew at the table. "I don't like it."

Matthew agreed. The scent of murder seemed to hang in the air.

After taking noon dinner with Cory and Carew, Matthew put them under the watch of both Toby and Hugh and set off to talk to the last coachwrights. As he headed for the first on the list, he fervently hoped the coach hadn't been made in another town.

At the second of the three remaining establishments, Matthew spoke with the barrel-chested, bowlegged Master John Piggott, who nodded vigorously when Matthew showed him the coat of arms sketched by Toby's tavern acquaintance. "Aye, m'lord, I know those arms. That coach is one of my best works," he said with pride.

"Who commissioned it?" Matthew asked, relieved to have found the correct source at last.

"Why, it belongs to the Earl of Essex." Piggott seemed surprised he didn't know.

Matthew squinted at the man. "But those are not his arms."

"No, they belong to his sister's husband, Lord Richard Rich." The craftsman preened as he divulged the information. "They don't get on, Lord and Lady Rich. Lord Essex commissioned the coach for her so she could go about as she pleases. He often uses it himself."

At Matthew's request, Piggott gave him the location of Lady Rich's town house. He had no desire to pay a social call on the wife of Lord Richard Rich. She would be likely to tell her brother that a baron had come asking questions. Instead, for a few shillings, he bought clothing appropriate to a servant, changed into them in an alley, and stowed his good clothes in his satchel.

At Lord Rich's rambling brick house, he encountered a stableman who conducted him to his superior, the household coachman, where he cleaned the coach. Matthew recognized the coat of arms on the side panel at once.

"We don't need 'elp," the coachman snapped as he brushed the coach's velvet upholstery.

"I thought her ladyship might like a well-mannered coachman to assist her," Matthew said.

The coachman sat back on his haunches and scowled at Matthew. "I'm the only coachman 'ere and 'twill stay that way. Besides, 'er ladyship's up north with 'er family."

It was just what Matthew had wanted to know. "So mayhap her ladyship's coach goes out from time to time in her absence?" he suggested. "Just for a bit of air."

The coachman frowned until his eyebrows met. " 'Er ladyship trusts me with 'er coach. No one takes it out when she ain't 'ere save 'er brother."

Matthew nodded, pleased with what he had learned. He took his leave and strode down the drive and out the back gate. The coach belonged to Essex's sister, and someone had used it when disposing of the boots, as well as in the attempt to kill Cory. François, being in league with Essex, had made friends with the coachman and the pair used the coach when they pleased. More links to François and perhaps to Essex. But none of them were solid proof of Essex's guilt.

On François's last day in England, Cory was so tense, she could hardly breathe properly. Her anxiety grew worse as she approached the queen's privy chambers. The queen was to receive a delegation of tradesmen from Sussex, but by the grim expressions on her ladies' faces, Her Majesty was in a temper that day.

"Where is my gown?" Elizabeth shouted as Cory entered the inner sanctum. "The one with the silver tissue and blue velvet given me last New Year's Day by the Earl and Countess of Sussex? 'Tis not in its place."

"Your Grace, I do not know." Despite her forewarning of the queen's bad mood, Cory was taken aback. "I will consult the mistress of the robes. She will know."

But the mistress of the robes didn't know. Worse still, two other gowns were discovered missing. Cory questioned the servants and all the queen's ladies. No one had seen the gowns, nor had they seen anyone who didn't belong in the queen's chambers and might have taken them.

The queen chose another gown and went to receive the delegation. Cory waited on her with the other women, but she was uneasy. For she suspected who had taken the queen's gown.

"Carew, did you sell one of the queen's gowns?" she demanded, cornering him in his father's chamber that afternoon.

"Aye, I sold it, and two others," he admitted. "She has more gowns than any woman under the sun has a right to. I thought she wouldn't miss a few."

"Oh, Carew, how could you?" Cory sighed. "Her Majesty's mistress of the robes inventories all her gowns. A number is assigned to each one, and its description is written in a big book. She may not wear all the gowns, but she *knows* them all. She has them paraded before her from time to time, to remind herself that she is a great queen with riches at her command."

"That's pompous of her, don't you think?" Carew appeared entirely serious. "She should sell them and give the money to the poor if she can't wear them all. That's what I was taught."

Cory struggled against the urge to laugh at his reasonable logic applied in such an unreasonable way to the spinster queen who had nothing but gowns to comfort her. She lost the battle and giggles overcame her. "You naughty boy. How did you manage to take something as voluminous as three gowns without being seen?"

"I slipped in when the mistress of the robes was snoring on the settle. Don't you think it's a better use of the money to support the King of Navarre than to keep a gown she seldom wore?"

"You should not have done it," Cory admonished. "Who bought them from you?"

"The Countess of Leicester bought all three."

"Carew," she said as reproachfully as she could. "You know how Her Majesty feels about the countess. And what you did is almost the same as stealing."

"It would be stealing if I'd kept the money, but I didn't. I gave the money to Her Majesty. She's the one who chose to give it to Monsieur La Faye."

He appeared to consider his logic flawless, and despite her worry over what François might do before his departure, despite her fears for Matthew, Cory had to stifle another urge to laugh. It was too funny, selling the queen's own gowns to raise the funds she required. "The countess will flaunt the dresses in the queen's presence," she pointed out, "and Her Majesty will be furious. Carew, we must get them back."

"Lady Leicester will want her money."

"And Monsieur La Faye has it," Cory finished. "Oh, dear. Do you suppose he would return it if he knew what you'd done?"

Carew pulled a face. "I'm not keen on asking him."

"You'll have to, Carew." Cory could think of no other solution. "And we'll have to tell your father, for he'll eventually find out." Cory couldn't see any way around the difficulty that didn't involve Matthew. As if he read her thoughts from a distance, the man in question opened the door.

"The queen is hysterical. What's happened?" Matthew asked.

"It seems that Carew, er . . ." Cory wavered, unable to proceed as Matthew's expression darkened with suspicion.

But Carew didn't hesitate. "I sold three of the queen's gowns to the Countess of Leicester to raise the money Her Majesty needed for France," he stated, daring his father to object.

Matthew's expression shifted to shocked disbelief. "You did *what*?"

"I know it's upsetting, Matthew, but I pray you, don't be cross," Cory rushed to say. "Carew will right the wrong by returning the gowns to the queen, won't you, dear?"

"That hardly solves the problem." Matthew shook off her hand as she reached for it, his rage clearly building. "How will you repay Lady Leicester? Don't you know what it takes to earn that much money? You gave it away without a thought."

"I'll soon have my money from my father-in-law," Cory protested. "I will repay you the sum."

He radiated displeasure as he stared at her. "I will not take your money, Cory."

"She's trying to be generous, and you can't even thank her." Carew stepped forward, looking shockingly mature as he cast a withering gaze on his father.

Matthew faced him. "I don't expect you to understand, but it's wrong for me to take her money. Besides, it's your behavior at issue here. You've stolen from the queen."

"So I'm a thief, now," Carew sneered. "And you can't wait to sail away to escape my odious company. I'm trash beneath your feet."

"I didn't say that. You're my son—"

"Which equals trash." Carew's pretense at calm disintegrated. "I hate you. I wish I never had to see you again." Unable to hold back his tears, he flung open the door and crashed into a gentleman usher who stood just outside, fist raised to knock.

Carew and the man struggled for balance, then Carew raced away as the usher collected himself. "The queen wishes to see you, my lord," he announced and closed the door.

Matthew swore.

"I'll explain to Her Grace." Cory's heart ached from the painful exchange she'd been unable to prevent.

Matthew moved for the door as stiffly as a man twenty years older. "*I'll* explain to her why Carew did what he did. I know he was trying to help, but he goes about it wrong."

"At least let me come with you." Cory hurried to the door ahead of him. "Carew can return the gowns when Lady Leicester brings them. Come now, it's really not so bad."

"I disagree. It's as bad as it can be."

She flinched at his cold tone. The rift between father and son gaped wider than ever.

She tried to take some consolation in the news later that day that François had been taken to the docks by the Earl of Essex and would depart the country that night. She had difficulties to deal with, but at least Matthew wouldn't be murdered before her very eyes.

Cory sensed Matthew's concern over the quarrel as she entered his chamber after the supper hour. She had known from the start that he needed an adult equal to talk to, and she needed his confidence and trust, if nothing else. "Come," she held out one hand. "Sit with me."

"I cannot. I haven't seen Carew since we quarreled. He's probably hiding somewhere, waiting for me to find him and make peace with him. He's done it before."

"We'd best look for him," Cory agreed. "I'll check the chapel and the great hall."

Matthew rose. "Hugh will be here any moment. He'll go with you. I'll check the corridors of the Base Court, the Clock Court, and the kitchens. We'll meet back here."

Some time later, Matthew returned to his chamber without Carew, hoping Cory and Hugh had had more success. His son was sulking tonight, that was sure. He hadn't seen him anywhere.

"We didn't find him, nor has anyone seen him," Cory said as she and Hugh entered. "We didn't see Toby either, but I left word with everyone I saw."

"I suppose we'd better check the same places again." Matthew was resigned to another search. "We probably went to one part of the palace while he was in another."

As he reached for the door, it opened and Toby dashed in, panting with haste. "M'lord, I 'eard Carew was missin'. 'E told me earlier today you was a-sendin' him back to Dorset to 'is aunt and uncle. Said 'e was leaving at once with Hugh."

"Clearly not." Hugh's leathery face creased with concern.

"By fortune, he's run away." Cory's stomach turned over as she imagined Carew alone on the road in the dark.

"We must ride immediately," Matthew said. "Toby, please order horses for yourself, her ladyship, and me."

"At once!" Toby ran out the door as Matthew pulled on his riding boots.

"Thank you for assuming I would want to come with you. I won't bother to change." Cory followed Matthew to the door. "When we find him, you're to tell him you love him, Matthew Cavandish, or I swear, I'll—"

"I do love him. He should know that!"

"*How* does he know? How do you show him your love?"

The agony etched in his face told Cory he struggled with the question often. He knew quite well he had long ago stopped showing anyone, including his son, what he felt.

"I'm to say, 'Carew, I love you,' and that will change every-thing?" He raised his head and gazed at her with stark eyes. "You know he won't believe me."

"It would be a start. You've never told him before," she per-sisted. "You might also say you're not angry he ran away. That you were worried about him, and that often people who are worried act angry, but they aren't."

"Aren't they?"

Cory knew he probably *was* angry at Carew for his past sneers and disrespect, but she wanted desperately to help Matthew get past that.

But with the way things were, the possibility of accomplish-ing such a feat seemed about as likely as flying to the moon. Words wouldn't matter, she thought bleakly as they rode to-ward London, if Matthew left his son again soon.

A fire blazed in the hearth when they returned to Matthew's chamber two hours later. They had caught up with Carew, walking on the southern road from London. Praise fortune he was safe. Cory dropped to her knees before the welcome warmth of the fire. Her hands were chilled, but her heart was colder still at the silent anger between father and son.

When they overtook Carew, Matthew had ordered him to mount behind Toby, using an angry tone that brooked no argu-ment, then said nothing more. They had ridden swiftly during the return journey, making discussion impossible. Cory sensed Matthew had donned a mask of rigid silence on purpose, wait-ing until he trusted himself to speak. But now, his anger burst forth.

"I don't know what's gotten into you, Carew." He whipped off his cloak and flung it on a chair. "What did you think to ac-complish by running away? You couldn't go all the way to Dorset by yourself."

"What do you care? I could drop dead on the road and you wouldn't mind." Carew sank down with Cory before the fire.

"That's untrue," Matthew snapped. "If I didn't care, I wouldn't have gone to fetch you."

"Was it your idea or Cory's?"

"Mine, damn it," Matthew roared. "I was worried about you."

"If you're so worried, why don't you let me go back to

Uncle Charles? Anywhere's better than with you." Carew's mouth quivered as he held back tears.

"Can you not spare me two weeks when I come home? Damn it, you're my son. I love you."

Cory closed her eyes and gritted her teeth at the pain in Matthew's voice. Yet shouting his love in enraged tones wouldn't endear him to his son.

Carew said nothing, but his disbelief was obvious on his face. Ignoring his father's declaration, he kicked off his shoes and stretched out to warm his feet and hands.

Matthew turned away and picked up a goblet from the table.

"You'd best not drink that," Cory said. "I don't remember putting it out. It must be old."

Matthew pointed to the bottle of wine on the table. "I had this bottle saved. Hugh probably opened it, knowing I would need a drink when I returned." He raised it to his lips.

"Hugh wouldn't open the bottle unless you requested it—" Cory began.

"Don't you ever listen to what people say?" Carew shouted at his father. He leaped up and, with a sweep of his arm, dashed the goblet from Matthew's hand.

Wine flew everywhere, splashing on Carew's arm and over the nearby bed hangings. Carew clutched his arm and shrieked in pain.

"My God, it must be acid!" Matthew leaped for the water ewer. Cory took one look at the holes eaten in Carew's sleeves and grabbed the basin.

As Matthew poured water directly on Carew's burns, she caught the water in the basin. Her heart thudded so hard it shook her entire body. Bad burns could be fatal.

Carew cried out in pain again and again as the water welled over his skin. Cory struggled to focus on making sure the burn was washed clean of acid.

Please, God, she prayed in silence, *don't let it be that bad. Don't let Carew die.*

PART 3

Chapter 23

"It hurts. God, it hurts." Carew bent over his injured arm, sobbing.

His agony throbbed through Cory as if she were the one wounded, but she must remain calm and assess how badly he was hurt. Peeling away the burned fabric of his sleeve, she inspected his arm. "A blister is already forming to protect the skin. That's good." She smiled at him encouragingly, relieved that his injury wasn't life threatening. But he was pale, and she felt for his pulse, which was racing. He was drenched in sweat, suggesting he could go into shock. Fetching a blanket from the bed, she wrapped him in it.

"This is all my fault." Matthew cradled his son's arm in his hands, his face a mask of anguish.

Carew jerked away and buried his face against Cory's shoulder, weeping harder. "You're not sorry. You hate me."

"I don't hate you." Matthew's words were a moan. "I love you, son."

"You'll go away and leave me again, like you always do," Carew bit out.

"No, I won't. I'm staying. I won't sail again until you're old enough to go with me." Matthew reached out and touched Carew's arm.

The passion in his vow sent shivers shooting up Cory's spine. He thrilled yet terrified her. Could he keep such a promise? Although Carew desperately needed his father in his life, the queen expected Matthew to sail. Yet she believed Matthew could do anything he set his mind to. He could surely find a way.

As if comforted by his father's promise, Carew's tears gradually subsided. He didn't look as if he believed Matthew fully, but the desperate wish to believe shone in his eyes.

Matthew must have seen it, for he held out his arms, and Carew lunged into them. They sat on the floor, Matthew cradling his son, brown hair mingled with gold.

Cory turned toward the windows, pooled tears spilling from her eyes. *Be glad for them,* she told herself as she wiped them away. Carew had suffered, yet his pain had brought them together. Never had she thought to see the boy cling to his father as if he would never let go. And for the first time, Matthew's face was relaxed and unguarded, his soul bared. The top layers of his defense had peeled away, revealing a hint of the tenderness beneath.

Yet even as she thanked heaven that the tragedy had turned to a miracle, she knew that the testing of this pledge hovered on the horizon. God, help them all.

She turned back, thinking she should attend to Carew's arm, but then realized she couldn't interrupt. The healing of two hearts was too important just now.

"Hurts." Carew gripped his father's hands to keep them in place around his middle.

"I know it does. I'm sorry. More than I can say." Matthew rhythmically rocked Carew.

Carew sobbed again, and Cory moved closer, hoping to cheer him. "Carew, you saved your father's life. You should be proud." Sure enough, he turned up a hopeful face to hers. "Come now, what you need is sleep," she urged. Bed was the best place for all of them, given the late hour. "I'll fetch some healing ointment and bandages. By the morrow, you'll feel more yourself."

But as she unbuttoned Carew's doublet, helped him remove his clothes, and pulled a clean nightshirt over his head, she had another horrifying vision of Matthew lifting the goblet to his lips.

If he had taken the contents into his mouth . . .

She turned off the fear before it could paralyze her. She must rely on anger to preserve her strength. Aggression must be her weapon. Because without question, Essex had struck again.

Matthew slumped by Carew's side on the bed, drained by the crisis and the guilt that crushed him. He'd deliberately provoked François, expecting the Frenchman to attack him. Instead, he'd unleashed the lunatic's wrath on his innocent son. What a fool he was.

His agony was compounded by the new understanding of how his annual departures had hurt Carew. His son did need him. By promising to stay, he'd broken through the barrier between them. And although Carew hadn't said he loved him in return, they had a chance now. He would sacrifice anything to give his son the security he needed, even if it meant he couldn't sail for years.

How would he resist the queen? What would he do instead for a living? He pushed away the worries, knowing he could deal with them later, and gestured for Cory to go. "I will stay with Carew until you return."

"I'd best clean up the acid first." She refused to let him help her. Instead, she found some wool rags and began gingerly mopping up the corrosive, oily substance.

"Be careful. We don't need you burned as well," he cautioned as she worked. "And leave the rags for me. I'll need them to trace the acid."

She agreed and departed, but as she left, he felt guilty. He ought to send word to Captain Wells to detain François on suspicion of murder. He ought to . . .

He shifted on the bed, preparing to rise, but Carew stopped him. The pleading in his son's eyes tore at his heart. "I'm not going to leave you," he soothed, noticing the lad's slender fingers were so like those of Joanna, who had given him the precious gift of their son. He'd not taken enough care of that gift. Thanks to Cory, he'd learned his error in time.

He smoothed the rebellious hank of hair from Carew's forehead. The boy's eyelids drooped with exhaustion, and the familiar ache of loss tightened within Matthew. If losing Joanna had hurt him, how must Carew have felt, losing him every year? Why hadn't he seen how Carew must have needed him, how much he still needed him? He couldn't walk away when his child was hurting. He must never go back on his word.

A worm of panic hatched as he considered what staying implied. The promise didn't make him a better parent. What if they continued to quarrel? He couldn't bear that.

He searched for ways to crush the worm. Fastening his gaze on Carew's angelic face, he remembered that Cory would help him. After all, he had followed her advice and, for the first time, told Carew he loved him enough to stay.

It was the first positive thing that had happened between them in years. His leaving had created the barrier between them in the past. Determined to put his son first, he kicked off his shoes and settled down to concentrate on Carew.

At the definite sign that he was staying, Carew smiled wanly, gripped Matthew's hand more tightly, and closed his eyes.

Carew was fast asleep by the time Cory returned. Matthew waved her over to the bedside and watched as she dotted ointment on Carew's blisters and wrapped his arm loosely in fine linen.

"May I see you in the corridor a moment before I retire?" she whispered as she finished.

Matthew led the way, wanting to say a few things himself. The night's happenings strongly suggested a need to change their plans.

"I spoke to Captain Wells about what happened," Cory said as the chamber door closed. "I asked if it was too late to have François detained, but the ship has already departed for France. Wells said he'd seen it off with his own eyes."

"That does it. I've had all I can take of court," Matthew seethed. "First thing in the morning, I tell the queen we leave the day after the wedding."

To his relief, she agreed with everything he said. "Your father-in-law has sent word for me to meet with his man of business to sign the marriage papers," he added. "You'll have your money soon."

"You can use it to repair your ships." Her earnest offer told him how much she'd come to trust him.

"I promised not to sail," he snapped, missing the sea already. But he would never go back on his promise. Truth be told, Carew's need for him pulled stronger than the sea's lure. "I refuse to live off my wife's money. People will say I'm a fortune hunter." He frowned. The queen had set the winds of change blowing in his life, but now, a veritable storm of feelings whirled through him—renewed love for Carew mixed with the fear of letting him down, appreciation for Cory mixed with a blinding lust for her body.

He'd been meant to die tonight. Only by his son's angry gesture had he survived. Carew had paid a terrible price by taking the pain meant for him.

Danger seemed to lurk in every corner of the palace. The wisest choice was to leave.

Matthew learned two things about the acid in the next days. First, it was oil of vitriol, made by heating sulfur until it changed to a caustic semiliquid that burned flesh, cotton, and other like materials. With no apothecary at or near Hampton Court, it must have come from London.

He walked the streets of London, asking at each shop if someone had purchased oil of vitriol, and if so, was it a Frenchman, but no one had. None of the apothecaries had been visited by a dark-haired, dark-complected Frenchman, either, and Matthew was growing discouraged until, after stopping at Master Howe's, he noticed an apothecary's shop at the end of the street.

The apothecary's clerk replied in the affirmative when asked. Yes, a dark-haired, dark-complected man in garments befitting a court servant had purchased oil of vitriol a few days ago. Although he'd spoken English, he'd had an accent that could have been French.

"François must have purchased the acid," Matthew told Cory upon his return. "There are many dark-haired serving men at court, but none of them have an accent save François."

"We know that it was François, and we know he worked for Essex. But how do we prove it?" Cory worried her apron with nervous fingers. "I asked everyone along your corridor if they'd seen who entered your chamber that night. No one had. If a woman had sneaked in for an affair, they would all have noticed. But since it was only someone trying to murder you, no one heard or saw a thing."

Matthew was surprised to hear her voice such a sentiment. "It's not like you to be cynical. The hour was late. People were asleep, which was François's plan." But he, too, was discouraged. He had never failed at something he set out to do, yet despite the clues they'd found, he was no closer to proof of who had set François to murder. Escape from court still seemed the best way to protect Cordelia and Carew.

François was gone. Thrown out of the country like a sack of refuse.

He sat in his big chair, studying the five young men who lounged about his chamber, drinking wine and vying for his favor because he reportedly paid his associates well. Which one of them would best replace the man he'd lost?

In many ways, François had been forced out at the right moment. Cavandish had been too close to discovering the truth, and the queen, in her generous idiocy, had robbed the baron of a servant to torture for information. Not that Elizabeth realized there was information to be had. She believed him innocent, the foolish old woman. How he loved to make her think he was one thing when he was really the opposite. She believed herself so superior, she never imagined someone could live in such close proximity and still dupe her.

The thought gave great satisfaction, as always. His secret was safe, and he would find the necessary assistance from one of these men. He would need that assistance, too, if Cavandish kept poking his nose in places it didn't belong, which seemed likely.

He rose to pour more wine into each of the men's flagons, assessing them. He knew the fires of greed, ambition, or sex drove most men. He would choose one of these five, learn his weaknesses, then use him to his fullest capacity. Yet he must choose with care, for he had no wish to be discovered. Eventually it would make no difference, but just now, it was too soon.

Chapter 24

Tension grew at the palace in the next few days. People saw Carew's bandaged arm and asked questions until the story of the acid leaked out. Several courtiers begged Her Majesty for permission to retire from court and received it. Everyone was on edge.

Toby slammed through the door as Matthew sat in his chamber one afternoon, trying to enjoy a quiet moment by the window. "M'lord, 'er ladyship's family's a-comin'. I sent her to the courtyard on a pretext, as you told me to do when the coach were spied."

Matthew leaped to his feet, anticipating Cory's pleasure when she saw her family, but worried as well. Back when he'd received the queen's approval to send for them, on the night of the masque, the danger hadn't been nearly as acute. Nor had they known Moll was dead. By the time the commotion had subsided and Matthew remembered they were coming, it was too late to bid the dowager countess stay away. A letter couldn't have reached her once she was on the road. He would have to ask Her Majesty to take extra precautions to protect Cory's family.

What would he say to them, he wondered as he headed for the courtyard. He couldn't tell them of the danger immediately, and he wasn't used to making small talk with women and chil-

dren. But then Cory would do all the talking. He knew her well
enough to know that.

Cory was already halfway to meeting the lumbering old
coach as he entered the Base Court. The vehicle listed to one
side and its paint peeled. Had the Earl of Whitby no better
coach to spare? The coachman, too, looked old for the job. He
halted the horses and climbed down from the box with
painstaking slowness. The footman looked as if he possessed
less than the full complement of intelligence, and his aged
counterpart seemed to be blind if his prolonged fumbling at the
door handle was any indication. Indignant at Whitby's obvious
lack of regard for his own mother, to send her in such a con-
veyance, Matthew stepped forward to greet his new family. He
would do better by them.

The coach steps were lowered, and a young boy tumbled
out, landing in a heap. He wore a plain brown jerkin, but his
carrot red hair stood out. It had to be nine-year-old Marcus.

He leaped up, a bundle of energy clearly ready for activity.
"Mama!" he shrieked and barreled across the courtyard into
Cory's arms.

An older girl stepped out in a more subdued manner, but her
composure didn't last. Catching sight of Cory, she hiked up her
skirts and, with garter ribbons flapping, charged after her
brother.

Cory withstood the second loving assault with a rapt expression on her face. "Marcus, Letty, I am so happy to see you.
I love you. I adore you. A thousand kisses." She acted out her
last words, peppering the pair with kisses.

Matthew had seen Cory in such throes of ecstasy only three
other times. He didn't like comparing those events to this. It
touched one of his raw nerves. He seemed to have more than
his share of the cursed things. They were like beached jellyfish
when the tide was out, exposed and sensitive, waiting to be
scorched by a blast of emotional heat from Cory or Carew.

Carew materialized beside him, looking just as uncomfortable with the display of affection as he was. Like father, like
son.

Marcus fastened his arms around Cory's waist and refused
to let go. Letty latched on to her mother's side so that Cory appeared to have sprouted an extra head.

"You're never going away again, Mama," Marcus said as the

trio moved clumsily toward Matthew and Carew. "Never, ever, ever, ever, again. Promise?"

"I promise," Cory laughed and turned a radiant face to Matthew. "Matthew, did you send for them? Why didn't you tell me, you wonderful man? Thank you! Thank you, a thousand times."

"It was a surprise." Matthew regarded her pleasure with resignation. For days he'd imagined her joy at seeing her family, but he knew she recognized the danger as well.

A stately woman who must be the dowager countess approached with a dignified step. Small and thin but perfectly mobile, clad in an old-fashioned black gown, Henrietta Hailsworthy, Dowager Countess of Whitby, stopped before him. She, at least, was going to show some restraint so he could greet her properly.

He bowed over her hand. "Lady Whitby, you are welcome to court. Allow me to introduce my son Carew."

She surveyed first Carew, who sketched a bow, then Matthew with sharp eyes of celestial blue set in a face of wrinkled silk. "You've reunited my family, granting our dearest wish," she said. "Don't you think a kiss would be more the thing?" She presented her cheek.

Ordinarily Matthew would decline such an aggressive invitation, but he wanted her to like him. Drawing a breath, he leaned over and kissed her whisper-dry cheek.

She snatched him into a ferocious hug that nearly crushed the air from his lungs. Despite her diminutive stature, she was far stronger than he'd imagined possible. Not content to stop there, she bussed him loudly on the cheek.

He willed himself to find something good about her. She smelled pleasantly of cloves. Her hand was cool, dry, and not unpleasant as she patted his face. Perhaps he could survive the onslaught of emotions this family heaped on him.

"My girl trusts you, Matthew Cavandish," she announced in a voice loud enough to reach the rooftops. "See that you don't break her heart like my varlet of a grandson did."

Matthew stared at the dowager countess, not sure how to respond to her incredible greeting. He was uncomfortably aware of Carew watching with great interest, probably wondering if he would remain civil or snap at her for assuming he and Cory were involved.

"I understand what your grandson did to Cory, Lady Whitby," he said evenly. "If he were alive today, it would be my pleasure to beat him black and blue. Since he is not, I intend to wed Cory and take good care of her."

"Is this true, Cory? Do you wish to wed him?" Lady Whitby looked to her granddaughter-in-law, who nodded with misty eyes.

Lady Whitby smiled. "I believe I like your young man, Cory. Do call me Madam Henrietta," she insisted to Matthew. "Everyone does."

"The earl calls her Hellacious Henrietta," someone giggled.

"Letty," Cory warned, her tone severe.

"But he does, doesn't he, Grandmama?" Letty grinned at her grandam, who grinned back.

"He does, but you needn't shock the poor man," Lady Whitby rebuked her without rancor.

"I'm hungry," Marcus whined, tugging at Cory. "When do we eat?"

"Marcus Hailsworthy, if you'd eaten your dinner as I bid you, instead of sneaking sweet suckets, you wouldn't be so hungry," Madam Henrietta scolded.

"I did eat it," Marcus vowed, not the least daunted by her reprimand. "The only part I left was the turnips, and they're the offal of the devil. The earl said so." He looked from Matthew to Carew, as if seeking confirmation that his behavior was justified.

"He said turnips were awful, not offal," Letty corrected her half brother with superior disdain. "Offal means manure. You're always getting things mixed up."

"Turnips *are* manure of the devil," Marcus retorted heatedly. "You're not so fond of 'em yourself."

"That's spawn of the devil, not offal of the devil." Letty planted both hands on her hips. "A devil doesn't defecate turnips. You are such an imbecile at times."

Matthew winced. Despite Cory's disapproving expression, she did nothing to stop them. He, on the other hand, was not willing to accept a family that was as unruly as a hurricane.

"Enough!" he roared. Five sets of eyes snapped to him, looking as if they feared for their lives. "Your grandam is tired from the long journey and you're keeping her standing here while you argue about manure," he said to the children. "If you've such an interest in it, I'd be more than happy to introduce you to the queen's collection. The shovel always stands at the ready for disobedient or badly mannered youth."

Letty looked with perplexity at Cory. "Mama, what does he mean?"

"I mean," Matthew said sternly, "that once I marry your mother, I intend to adopt you and your brother, and as your father, I expect proper behavior. You will shovel until the stable is clean if you and your mouth can't behave."

At his promise to adopt the children, Cory clasped her hands together and sent him a heartfelt smile of joy that was better than any words of thanks.

Letty regarded him, slack jawed. "You wouldn't make a girl shovel manure. 'Twould be improper."

"Yes, he would," Carew chimed in, sounding eager to contribute. "I've shoveled plenty, and my grandsire made all my aunts do it when they were girls. Aunt Lucina had to clean the entire stable when she was five, for stealing a horse."

"Well, I haven't stolen anything," Letty said with righteous indignation.

Matthew rewarded her statement with a winning smile. "No? What of the time you're stealing from us even now? I'll show her the shovel," he said to Cory. "Come, Lettice." He held out his hand.

"I don't have to go, do I?" Letty glanced at her mother for support.

Cory withdrew her protective arm. "You must obey your adopted father in everything, Letty. That goes for you too, Marcus. Run along, dear, and have a few fun hours. We'll save you a bite from supper. That is, if you aren't too exhausted from shoveling to eat."

Letty blanched as she saw her mother was serious. "Your pardon, my lord baron," she said. "I didn't mean to be rude, but *he* started it." She glared at Marcus, who stuck out his tongue.

"You can't foist the responsibility for your behavior on other people," Matthew said to both children. "As I see it, the pair of you have two choices. You can do as you're told and exercise good manners, or you can spend your time moving manure. Choose one."

"I'll take the first." Letty hastily lowered her gaze.

"I'm glad to hear it," Cory cut in. "I know Marcus will too.

Let us begin again, please, and do it properly this time. Children, this is Baron Graystock and his son Carew. Baron Graystock is going to adopt you as soon as we're wed." She sent Matthew another heart-stopping smile. "Lettice, greet your adopted father."

The girl stepped forward and dropped into a graceful curtsey before Matthew, her curly head bowed. "Greetings, my lord. I am honored to make your acquaintance."

He bowed in return. "And I, yours, Mistress Lettice." For a moment she seemed almost civilized, and as she raised her face to his, he even admired her unusual eyes. They were like brilliant bits of stolen blue sky gleaming against her pale skin. He nodded his approval of her new behavior and raised her from her curtsy. "We will come to understand one another," he said, wondering why this was easier with someone else's child than his own.

"Yes, my lord," she said demurely, but mischief twinkled in her eyes as she retired and her brother made his bow. Matthew didn't want to consider what it meant. He asked Madam Henrietta which trunk she wanted and supervised its handling as the children became acquainted.

"You got shuttlecock and quoits?" he heard Marcus demand of Carew. "Bow and arrows? I've got things to trade. Wait'll you see my collection of dead spiders. One's as big as your hand."

"It isn't that big, Marcus. Don't tell lies," Letty scolded her half brother. "But we would like to play a game," she said more politely to Carew. "What have you got?"

Carew shuffled his feet, seeming embarrassed. "None of my games are here."

"Where are they, then?" Letty demanded, smoothing her flyaway mop of curls.

"At my aunt and uncle's in Dorset."

"We'll send for your things, Carew," Matthew called as Letty and Marcus exchanged glances, telling him how odd they thought this arrangement. Why had he never realized how painful it was for Carew to lack his own home?

"That's all right. I'd much rather see this place." Letty eyed the grandeur of Hampton Court with interest. "Do you really get to see the queen?"

"I do. And speak to her, too." Carew straightened with pride at her interest. "Come on. I'll show you the chapel. It has the most fantastical carved ceiling you've ever seen, and it's painted blue, same color as your eyes," he said to Letty, which seemed to please her.

"Supper is in fifteen minutes in my chambers, Carew," Matthew warned.

"Yes, Father," Carew said, on his best behavior.

The trio disappeared into the next courtyard.

"You handled that well," Henrietta said as he led her and Cory to his chamber, wondering how he was going to keep them safe. He couldn't be everywhere at once.

"Yes, thank you, Matthew." Cory leaned against him and pressed his arm. "They can be unruly at times, but I thank you for bringing them here. I can't tell you how happy it makes me."

"Unruly puts it mildly," Matthew agreed, wishing that they could be alone together. It was bad enough to realize that living with the children was going to be like sitting amid lit fireworks. Every time he turned around, they would be shooting off in new directions, undoubtedly singeing bystanders. "Mistress Lettice has a mouth on her as busy as the Thames River traffic on market day."

"Why Matthew Cavandish, you're doing it again. You have a sense of humor." Cory appeared astonished.

"As a lad, I was known for jests and humorous pranks," he admitted, glad to rediscover vestiges of that youth. "But you know, ladies, Letty and Marcus get their bluntness from the two of you." Cory's shocked gaze warned him she'd never considered such a thing. "Perhaps they learned their worst behavior from the earl, if he calls his mother Hellacious Henrietta," he amended, "but you are also models for their manners and speech."

"I try to be discreet," Cory protested, looking miffed.

Madam Henrietta chuckled as she gazed at Matthew. "You've found a good man, child. He sees what's what straight away. I thought I deserved the freedom of bluntness due to my advanced years, but he's right."

As Cory argued with the dowager countess about the origin of her bad habits, Matthew reflected that he had much work before him, adjusting to his new family. Madam Henrietta wouldn't be difficult, but the children would be an uphill trek.

The potential danger at the palace also concerned him. He had warned the queen of it, and she had finally agreed to change residences, but that was all. Essex sneered at him whenever they met, as if challenging him to prove him guilty. Matthew wished he could, but as he'd had no success to date, he would settle for wedding Cordelia and taking them all away from court.

The rest of the day was spent in frenzied preparation for their wedding. Cory wanted everything just so. Matthew wanted her in bed.

Instead he had to put Carew and Marcus with him in the big four-poster when he wasn't guarding Cory. Madam Henrietta, Letty, and their coach and carts of possessions were squeezed into a chamber at the opposite end of the palace. Yet he must be grateful the lord steward had found them something. Despite recent departures, space was still short at court. The queen had assigned two guards to the dowager countess at night, one at the door and one at the window.

"Do you think anything will happen now that François is gone?" Cory asked during a private moment. "Is my family safe?"

Matthew saw she craved reassurance and decided not to frighten her with dismal predictions. "I wanted them here for your sake, especially since we're to wed, so let's not dwell on it. All will be well, and in a few days, we'll leave court."

The next day Elizabeth announced their impending marriage, and Cory went about her wedding arrangements, smiling as if she couldn't have been happier. But Matthew noticed she checked all food before serving it and sniffed every beverage before offering it. She was afraid of another attack, as was he.

He also noticed that despite the demands on her, Cory found time to play cards. She played Cent with the pages and with Carew, Letty, and Marcus, insisting it was good for them to practice their addition. She played with the other maids of honor, claiming it kept the girls from flirtations with the married men who attended the queen. She played with Madam Henrietta, though the old lady quickly settled in and formed her own crowd of followers eager to be entertained. Cory even played with Monsieur La Faye in his private lodgings.

"I don't like your going off alone," Matthew chastised her

the day before the wedding, during a rare moment of privacy in his chamber.

"I wasn't alone. I was with Monsieur La Faye," she said as she rearranged clothes in a coffer for their wedding journey. "Besides, Monsieur will accompany us on our journey. I'll have to be with him all the time then."

Matthew slumped in a chair, the prospect of continual company with the fatuous La Faye far from pleasant. François might be gone, but he had a feeling that their troubles were still far from over. Or was he just in a bad mood from Marcus's keeping him awake last night, thrashing in his sleep? "I don't trust that man. Promise me you won't go to his chamber again."

"Oh, very well." Cory packed the last of the clothes and closed the coffer lid, at the same time closing the discussion of possible danger. "If you object to my playing cards in La Faye's lodgings, I'll bring him here. Will that suit?"

"No. He'll whine at me for money to support Navarre. I'll wager he's collected over two thousand pounds. It's time he took it to his king. I would enjoy seeing the back of him."

Amusement lit up Cory's face. "I cannot think you're jealous of him."

Matthew scowled at the coffer. "I'm not jealous. He's as slimy as a rock in a stagnant pond."

"He's always well mannered," Cory pointed out.

"It's no use taking chances. He's French, and the people who threw away the boots were French. That's enough for me to distrust him."

"You don't mean you still suspect him of hurting Moll?"

As she gazed at him in disappointment, Matthew realized he did consider La Faye a valid suspect. "Just promise me," he pressed rather than admit his thoughts.

"I promised before, though I don't agree," she said with a pout.

Matthew didn't care if she agreed with him. He cared about keeping her and the others safe and about making the most of this private moment with her. But before he could manage to kiss her, the subject of Marcus arose.

"He battered me black and blue last night," he said in response to her question about how he'd slept. "He's the most restless sleeper I've ever known. He even swears in his sleep. You should wash out his mouth with soap."

"His grandsire talks that way, and Marcus imitates him. It's for the best that we're quit of him. You'll be a far better influence."

How was it she turned every negative into a positive? He captured her around the waist and sought her lips with his own. "Cory, I want a proper night with you after we wed."

"Where? We've no private chamber." A smile of pure delight spread across her face as he slipped one hand down her bodice and teased her flesh.

"Hell, I'll find one." He would, too. He would arrange for them to make love in private on their wedding night if it was the last thing he did . . . if they weren't all murdered first.

Letty and Marcus settled in at Hampton Court quickly. By their first full day at court, they were into mischief. As Matthew entered the Paradise Chamber to check for assassins before the queen and her maids arrived, he saw that the demon children, as he had nicknamed them, had decorated the two stately lions crouched on either side of the queen's throne. Who else had access to his old clothes? The lion on the right wore his old pork-pie hat, tipped at a rakish angle. The other on the left was regal in a gardener's floppy straw affair. And they both sported full beards and mustaches of brown crewel wool.

The queen was so proud of the lions, a gift from the Prince of Orange some years ago. She considered them symbolic guardians protecting her throne. If she knew who had desecrated her pride and joy, she would have them thrashed on the spot.

Despite his lack of sleep, his denied need for Cory, and a killer waiting to attack at any moment, the dressed-up lions struck a comical note in Matthew's upside-down world. He leaned against the door frame and laughed until his sides hurt.

"My lord, pray what is so amusing that you block this entry, making a spectacle of yourself?" La Faye poked his head into the chamber, his nose as crimson as his doublet from a head rheum.

Matthew pointed at the lions before bursting into another round of hilarity. La Faye's expression reminded him of the lions', head held high, manner stuffy, full of his own self-importance. He imagined the clean-shaven La Faye wearing one of the woollen beards, the pork-pie hat perched above his large ears, and exploded with mirth.

La Faye sniffed. "Those ruffian children have been at work, I see. I cannot fathom why her ladyship wants them about." He groped for his handkerchief and sneezed. "If you'll take my advice, you'll box their ears."

Matthew purposely scorned La Faye's advice, if for no other reason than he detested the man. By the end of the day, he realized his error. He should have issued some reprimand, for Letty and Marcus could not behave for more than five minutes at a time. Worse still, they enlisted Carew, as well as Samuel, whom Matthew had agreed to adopt too, in their "experiments," as the demon children called them.

They tussled at the noonday table and upset Matthew's goblet of strong spirits into the meat platter. When no one was looking, Marcus touched a lit candle to the mix. The sudden burst of flame singed the hair and clothing of everyone seated nearby.

The demon children next entered the kitchen and dropped missiles into the rising bread to hear it hiss as it deflated. The cook caught them and drove them away, brandishing a roasting spit and shouting with rage. Matthew had his hands full, placating the enraged cook, keeping the misdeeds from the queen, and disciplining the children.

He tried to be patient, but no matter what Cory or Madam Henrietta did to punish them, they seemed unfazed. Cory confined Marcus to Matthew's chamber. She sentenced Letty to hard labor with her sampler. As the resulting tangle of thread grew dirtier and uglier, Matthew felt sure it would be more fit for a cow wipe than a wall decoration. Cory and Henrietta even insisted they all play acrostics with pen and paper, making up verses with hidden messages.

But no one could watch the children all the time. And when the demon children learned that Monsieur La Faye would accompany them to Matthew's estate, they took to teasing him. They began by sneaking things from his chamber. When he complained that things were missing, they put them back when he wasn't there. La Faye was baffled at first, then angry, then convinced his chamber was haunted. Matthew knew it was the children because he caught Marcus coaching Carew in how it was done. He was so incensed, he spanked Marcus until he shrieked. Cory rushed to intervene, convinced her precious child was being killed, and they had their first real quarrel.

"Please don't strike him," she pleaded with Matthew in his bedchamber. "He'll hate us."

"Great Neptune, I didn't hit him hard. He made all that noise to get your attention," Matthew growled. "We cannot allow such behavior. He'll grow up with no sense of right and wrong."

"Then we must speak to Marcus, not punish him physically," Cory said, visibly struggling to swallow back her tears. "May we not try that first? Please?"

Matthew gave in, especially since she insisted on sitting in his lap and kissing him to mend their quarrel.

"Children, you must not tease Monsieur La Faye." Matthew looked on that evening as Cory spoke to the children at table.

At Cory's order, Samuel looked guilty and squirmed on the bench, scattering crumbs down his jerkin front. Letty continued to eat her soup, as if Cory couldn't be speaking to her.

"I won't do it anymore. I promise." Carew appeared eager for their approval since Marcus had arrived. The younger lad apparently annoyed Carew as much as he did the adults.

Matthew nodded. Although he sensed Carew didn't entirely trust his promise or his love, they had forged a truce. At times, they even enjoyed a game of chess or read a book together without a spate, and their progress gave him considerable pleasure. Carew had also improved in his behavior toward Sarah Vasavour, though that was in part due to strict supervision.

"Well, I don't like the old frog," Marcus announced loudly. "He's nasty."

"I don't like him either." Letty put down her spoon with a disdainful air. "He is not nice."

"Monsieur La Faye is the queen's guest." Cory's tone was the sternest he'd heard her use yet with her children. "It doesn't matter how you feel about him. Avoid him if that suits you, but when you do encounter him, you must be on your best behavior."

"But he's odd," Marcus objected. "He walks around at night after everyone has gone to bed."

Matthew's hackles rose. "How do you know? And what was he doing?"

Marcus shrugged. "I couldn't sleep so I followed him. He just walked around, looking at things. He looked at the queen's gold plate in her workroom for a long time. Will he steal it?"

"Of course not," Matthew said. "And you're not to leave your bed at night." La Faye was more likely calculating how much gold the queen could afford to give the French cause. No harm in that, though he still didn't like it.

"Why do you say Monsieur La Faye is nasty?" Cory asked Marcus.

"Because Samuel spilled a little wine on him as he was serving, and the frog cuffed him and called him a bastard. That's not right, is it?" Marcus said with a self-righteous air. "To hit someone else's servant or to call him that name."

"No, it's not," Cory agreed, her tender glance at Samuel's bent head reflecting her regret for the hard name and the blow.

"He'll be your adopted brother as soon as the legalities are concluded," Matthew cut in. "As his father, I don't want him called that by anyone."

Cory beamed at him like the noonday sun, sending a jolt of desire through him. He could barely restrain his wish to kiss her as she turned back to the children. "That's right. Samuel is not a servant anymore. Remember that, all of you," she said. Matthew noted the warning that flashed in her eyes as she gazed at each of the children, especially Marcus. So she could be stern with them if necessary. Perhaps they did agree on one thing.

Chapter 25

White roses in August? Where had Matthew gotten them?
W Cory inhaled their fragrance, along with the ferns and
marigolds lying in her lap, then gazed at his name scrawled on
the accompanying note. In mere minutes, she would be bound
for the rest of her life to Matthew Cavandish. He had comforted her at Moll's funeral, had offered to adopt her children,
had even sought late-blooming roses to please her on their
wedding day. More than any of these things, he set her blood
racing at a single touch.

She drew a deep breath, admitting he had shown her kindness, generosity, and a passion so rare, she would never know
it with another in her lifetime. But unfortunately, he would
show her one thing more. When Carew was older, Matthew
would take his son and leave her for years at a time.

The truth was, she couldn't imagine his settling down in
England. It was alien to his nature. Despite his promise to
Carew, despite her belief that he would honor it, he hadn't
stopped working on his ships. He intended to be off to some
destination soon, perhaps one close at hand, but he would
leave. He was an adventurer, first and last.

"Mama, you look beautiful."

Cory looked up, startled to find that Letty had slipped into
the maids' dormitory without her hearing. Her daughter was
the one who looked beautiful, Cory thought, as fine as a

princess in her first court gown of pale green brocade adorned with lace. She was everything right and proper, except for her flyaway curls that refused to be subdued. Those rebellious curls were like a symbol of her child's spirit, resisting things she didn't want.

Her own rebellious spirit resisted many things. She would not sit at home, alone and despairing once Matthew left her. She would fill her life with other people; she had her family. She would survive.

"Everyone's waiting for you, including Her Majesty," Letty whispered, touching Cory's silver-shot brocade skirts with an admiring hand.

Rising with determination, she took Letty's hand. Together, they walked to the chapel where the wedding party waited. Someone had decorated the great chamber with exotic sprays of wild ferns and flowers, reminding her of Matthew's cabin aboard *The Revenge*. As she paused at the door, she searched for him in the crowded chamber and found him at the altar.

Their gazes met and locked. His resolve to possess her burned in his gaze, which sent an earthquake shimmering through her middle. Despite being clean shaven, he was the pirate prince of her dreams, clad in midnight black touched with gold. The late-afternoon sun streamed through the chapel windows, bathing him in liquid fire. Or did the fire emanate from him?

She knew it did. He burned with a zeal to explore and subdue the unknown. She had been the unknown for a time, but soon she would be a known quantity and therefore boring. She could wed him and have her dream, but it wouldn't bring contentment. He was an untamed explorer and would never be hers.

Despite her lack of hope for the future, she walked down the aisle, irresistibly drawn to him. Standing at his side, she gazed into his molasses-brown eyes and felt the wild Caribbean in his restless soul. Suddenly, it was night by the Thames again; they had just met. She was touched by midsummer night's madness as he pledged her his troth. The heat of the tropics spoke at her center as, in his deep voice, he swore to honor her. His hand claimed hers to settle a gold band on her finger, making her his for all time. She was forced to close her eyes against the tears.

Made for love. The peddler woman's fortune-telling returned to her, clearly an error. She would have her dream lover and pay the price in sorrow. Yet she deliberately chose him, for she wanted Matthew Cavandish more than she wanted anyone else in her life.

The wedding was the event of the summer. It drove Matthew half mad. He waded through the late-afternoon ceremony, the wedding feast, and the serving of wedding cake, feeling as if he were slogging through sludge.

Bow over young women's hands. Thank them for their costly but useless gifts. Bow over old women's hands. Try to ignore their bawdy jests. He tried to smile as more wellwishers crowded in on him and Cory, but only managed to bare his teeth.

"Did you find a room for us?" Cory whispered in his ear between congratulations.

"I will," he muttered, bowing over another woman's hand. He meant it, too. She looked incredibly desirable in white shot through with silver.

The guests in the queen's green antechamber lingered forever over bridal cake and wine. Matthew bid each one god'den with undisguised enthusiasm, including the queen. Afterward, they had to get the children in bed. It seemed to take forever.

Marcus kept picking fights with Carew. The nine-year-old was clearly jealous of his new competition for Cory's attention. By the time they closed the door to his chamber on the boys and Toby, who would stay with them for the night, Matthew felt drained. Finally they were alone.

In a corridor. Not a romantic spot for a wedding night.

By the light of the wall sconces, Cory glittered in her white satin and silver-shot brocade. She looked like his Titania, which gave him an idea. He captured her hand and set off.

At the door to Giordano's chamber, Cory stopped him, laughing. "In here? You want to spend our wedding night with Giordano looking on?"

Matthew pushed the door open. "It's better than having half the court watch. And we'll be safe from our murderer. He won't think to look for us here."

Thomasine set off for home with a gold coin in her purse and a smile on her lips. Matthew shut the door on the good woman and led Cory to the narrow settle. "Sit on my lap." He struggled with the ties and bindings holding her overgown in place. He had hungered for days on end to possess his magnificent fairy queen.

Fueled by urges of her own, Cory removed the pearl-trimmed overgown for him. She rose and stepped out of her silver-shot brocade skirt, then removed her silver embroidered stomacher, followed by the white velvet and silver tissue bodice and sleeves. Discarding layers of petticoats and corset, she stripped down to her gossamer silk smock, then turned at last. He reclined on the settle, gloriously naked and ready for her.

The sight of firelight flickering on his body shot her through with shivers. Muscle, sinew, and taut flesh kissed by golden light.

She studied the rolling ridges of his abdomen and rock-hard thighs. Cradled between them, his arousal announced his desire for her like a royal standard.

She was his wife.

Anticipation hummed through her brain. The importance of this moment had built for weeks. The first time, she'd been confident she could bring him joy. Now, she wasn't so sure. . . . Her gaze traveled his body, enjoying the view of his wide chest and corded neck. His eyes intrigued her the most. They were dark pools full of passion . . . as well as something else.

Here were dragons.

She sensed the cruel, winged beasts crouched in the shadows of his past, waiting with their sharp claws. Tough, scaly skin was wrapped around his heart, a barrier to any touch.

Yet Carew had fought past Matthew's dragons. She must challenge them to battle, calling on her strongest weapon—the warmth of her caring heart.

From the first, she had touched him with her depth of feeling. Her power was like the best hand of cards fortune could deal. Yet she could lose everything. Her house of cards could come crashing down. Despite the terrible risk, she couldn't hold back. She needed him too much, for whatever short time was given to her. Stepping forward, she bent to kiss his lips.

With obvious impatience, he pulled her against him. Within minutes the welcome heat rose within her as he kissed her mouth and caressed her breasts.

Rough in his eagerness. Tense with longing. How she loved

the moist heat his skillful fingers churned awake between her
legs. As with their first time, mutual need drove them, and suddenly she too felt impatient at the long wait.

Full of jubilation, she explored his body, teasing his need
and her own to greater heat. As his lips traveled her neck on an
unruly path of kisses, the temperature rose in her body. His in-
creasing frenzy fed hers. Tired of waiting, she parted her legs
and invited him in.

As if unsure, he eased inside her to his full length, and they
lay still, locked together. She felt the tension of his desire, like
a power throbbing between them. Did he read the same hope
and fear in her eyes as she saw in his?

Pain didn't die overnight. When it finally eased, the innocence of first pleasure was gone forever. A more complicated,
even frightening response took its place.

The response of the cynic—the man unable to believe.

Could she wipe away his skeptical gaze? Could she heal her
own spirit as well as his? Or could they do little more than survive the shipwreck of their hearts?

"I'm not hurting you, am I?" he asked.

His concern melted Cory's ability to hold back. He was a
caring companion, for what little time he belonged to her. "Far
from it. I love the feel of you." She moved her hips against his.
Fire flared.

"And what is that feeling?"

She wanted to name a thousand desires, but they were too
intense to share. "I feel hot for more of you," she said simply.

"More of this?" He flexed within her.

At his subtle teasing, she tightened her muscles in response.
Pleasure rumbled in his throat like the growl of a wild beast.
Delighted, she tightened again. "Can you feel that?"

"Of course. As you can feel this." He tensed and flexed, and
she smiled as blinding sensations careened through her body.

So good. So complete. He filled her body, each movement
bringing mutual pleasure. What power she felt, knowing she
could drive him to his peak and her own as well.

She pressed against him, taking him deeper, then drew back.
He mirrored her movement, sliding in, then out. Like a
threaded needle that plunged into fabric, the motion bound
them together. The perpetual friction of his body, his ragged
breath betraying his excitement, brought her quickly to the

edge. With a cry, she mounted the last barrier to fulfillment and was swept upward toward a rainbow arch.

Behind closed eyelids, she saw a dazzle of colors. Her body shook with pleasure, and she felt him swell within her. But as she held him against her, eager for the hot fountain of his seed, he suddenly withdrew.

"Oh, Matthew, wait!" Bereft, she grasped his hips, but it was too late. Fear of abandonment flooded her. Pierced by the pain, she clung to him so he couldn't draw farther away. "Why did you do that?"

"Because I might get you with child."

"I hope you do," she cried, baffled. "I want a child so much. I hope . . ." She trailed off at his stricken look. "You don't want more children?"

He turned away, looking ill, and she realized what was wrong. "You're afraid I'll die in childbed, the way Joanna did," she said starkly.

"There's a chance you will," he rasped, as if he found it hard to breathe. "People at court think me a bold adventurer who laughs in the face of danger and hardship. But I'm a coward when it comes to childbirth. It's . . . horrible."

She touched his hand. "Thank you for caring enough to fear for me."

He averted his gaze. "You don't know what you're saying. You can't imagine . . ."

Reaching up, she smoothed back his hair. "Imagine what?"

"What it was like. All the blood."

"Tell me."

He drew a deep, shaky breath, as if it took great effort to do as she asked. Yet she hoped that by telling his story, she could find some way to convince him that not all births were the same.

"She labored for a full night and day, refusing to scream when the pains came. I still hear her tortured moans in my dreams." He fixed his gaze on the wall, his voice leaden. "When Carew was born and seemed healthy, we were ecstatic, but Joanna didn't stop bleeding. The midwife said the afterbirth was normal." His face was ashen as he relived that night. "My mother and sisters tried to help. They prepared a healing poultice of herbs, the midwife packed it in place and told Joanna she was to rest.

"I sat with her for a long time, but I was so tired. None of us had slept since her labor began, so when she fell asleep, I went into the next chamber and dozed off. Her cries and Carew's woke me. When I went in . . ." He paused. Sweat had collected on his forehead, and he kneaded the coverlet with restless fingers. "The room looked as if there'd been a slaughter. Blood stained everything. The white sheets. The floor. Joanna's night smock. I'll never forget her bloody footprints crossing the chamber. She had gotten up to go to Carew but never reached him.

"Since then, I've often wondered if she'd even wanted a child. We never discussed it. We were so young and eager for each other's bodies, we married, made love, and let the consequences come as they would." His self-deprecation was all too evident. "What came was all the blood. Even her smile was weak from loss of it. She died in my arms at dawn."

Wordless with sorrow, Cory caught his hand and carried it to her cheek. He turned slowly to meet her gaze, and she saw the horror of that night in his eyes. It explained his reluctance for her to conceive.

How could she fight against such overwhelming shadows? The tragedy he had endured seemed greater than any weapons with which she might fight.

Chapter 26

After his emotional wedding night, Matthew didn't want another confrontation, but he saw one coming as he and Cory left his chamber the next day. Monsieur La Faye came storming down the corridor toward them.

"Look at this," the Frenchman shouted, sticking a bare foot in the air. "I ask you, is there any excuse for this behavior? Can you think of a single reason why I should have to wake up to sticky feet because that little monster finds it amusing? I demand you thrash him in my presence. Now."

Matthew knew he ought to sympathize, but La Faye looked so ridiculous in his bare feet, his spindly knees poking out from beneath his short gown.

"What monster are you referring to?" he asked, "and what is it on your feet?" He glanced at Cory, who was staring with embarrassment at La Faye's bare, skinny calves.

"That ruffian you call your son," he railed. "If you won't thrash him, I will."

"Do you mean Marcus Hailsworthy?" Cory asked.

"Yes. The little worm poured honey on my feet while I slept. I awoke, stuck to the bed," he shouted in rage.

"Goodness, monsieur, you need not wave your foot in my face." Cory recoiled with well-bred repugnance. "Why do you think Marcus did this? Did you see him?"

"I did not see him!" La Faye roared, seeming at his wit's

end. "But it *was* him. Who else would pour honey on my toes? And it won't come off. I tried wiping it and it sticks."

"Of course it won't wipe off." Cory's calm was unwavering. "Honey must be washed away. I'll fetch a kettle of hot water and a basin and we'll have you clean in no time."

La Faye looked aghast. "You suggest I submerge my feet in water? It's bad for the health."

"No, it isn't." Cory moved toward him. "A good washing won't hurt you."

La Faye backed away, his horrified expression much like Toby's at his first encounter with a tub of hot water. This seemed to heighten Cory's resolve. She quickened her pace as he fled down the corridor. They were barely out of sight before Matthew exploded with laughter. He knew he ought to be getting to the bottom of Marcus's unacceptable behavior toward La Faye. He would, too, as soon as he stopped laughing. It was just that the unlikable Frenchman looked so absurd.

He laughed again when Cory said that rather than endure her washing, La Faye had locked his door and shouted for a coach to be readied. He was leaving for France as soon as he found a ship.

"He says he's had enough of our country where children are allowed to treat important guests with scorn and even the adults show little regard for the winning of a war that will affect our safety. He declines to be our guest at Graystock Manor." Cory held one hand to her mouth to hide a smile. "I'm sorry I laughed at him, but I couldn't help it. He looked so absurd."

"Let him go home," Matthew said. "We've seen enough of him, and he's finally realized there's a limit to English generosity."

They collapsed into each other's arms, laughing, but Matthew heard a note of hysteria in Cory's voice. The strain was affecting them both.

"Marcus, have you been in the honey?" Cory asked her son in the privacy of the bedchamber as Matthew waited outside the half-open door. He and Cory had arranged for him to hear what was said, though Marcus couldn't see him.

"Honey?" Marcus sounded his usual, innocent self. "Me?"

"Yes, you, Marcus, dear." Cory's tone was as sweetly coated

as La Faye's toes. "Did you fetch some from the kitchens during the night?"

"Umm, I might have," Marcus hedged.

"Well, you spilled it, so you're going to have to clean it up. All of it. And then you will personally launder the sheets."

"Very well, Mama." Marcus took his consequences astonishingly well for his nine years. "I will clean up the honey. But I want to show you what I found. You were asking the tirewomen about the painted box you gave your friend Moll. Monsieur La Faye had one, so I brought it to you."

"What do you mean, dear? What box?" Cory sounded surprised.

"I'll show you." Matthew stepped closer to the door and saw Marcus kneel by the bed. He pulled out an object and gave it to Cory.

Cory examined it. "Why, it's the painted box I gave Moll. The one I couldn't find among her things." She placed the box on a table, then came to the door. "Matthew, please come in." She gestured toward the table. "I pray you look at what Marcus found. Where was it again, dear?"

"Half buried in the ashes beneath Monsieur La Faye's grate. I don't think anyone's cleaned his hearth for months," Marcus said.

Cory frowned as she dusted away ashes from the flowers still visible on the charred box and popped off the lid. "I suppose Moll gave it to him as a keepsake. I'm relieved to know that it wasn't stolen, but I can't think how it was burned, unless someone other than La Faye did it." She bent over the remains of the box to examine it. "And the things I know Moll kept in it are gone. Except for this." She pulled a torn edge of paper from the joints of the box and studied it.

Matthew peered over her shoulder. *Dearest Moll* were the only words he could make out.

Cory looked at Matthew with sorrow in her eyes. "Here's our proof that La Faye wrote her love letters. But I still can't think why he would burn the box or not be angry if someone else did, although perhaps he was. It's all very upsetting. Poor Moll. She didn't deserve to have her things burned."

It was difficult enough to have Cory stirred up again over her friend's death, but several hours later, more trouble arose as Matthew entered Elizabeth's chamber and heard her shouting.

"Where is Essex! I want his head." The queen wore a wig that transformed her into a fiery redhead. Her contorted face matched her hair. "How dare he swear eternal devotion, then wed behind my back."

Cory stood with two ladies in waiting, not even trying to calm her.

"Who told you this? I'm sure it wasn't Essex." Matthew demanded.

The queen seemed more than willing to divulge the tattler's name. "That Frenchman told me, and though he's been an annoying scold about raising money for Navarre, I assure you he had his facts correct about Essex. And to think of the favors I did that betraying lad. He's just like his mother, a serpent in my bosom. I want him put in the Tower. Captain Wells, see to it."

Matthew raised his eyebrows, signaling to Cory, and she hurried over to him.

"This is the answer to our prayers," she whispered, her relief palpable. "I can sleep again, knowing Essex is locked in the Tower of London. Now if I just speak to Lord Burghley, and he impresses upon Essex the importance of obedience to his sovereign, perhaps he'll reform. Such a lecture will certainly make a greater impression on him in prison, within sight of the green where nobles are beheaded for treason, than here at court. I'll be safe, and although she doesn't know it, so will the queen."

Matthew wasn't so sure. Although he appreciated having Essex out of the way, he had a gut feeling that the murder attempts weren't over. Someone had put too much effort into them to give up now. But he would accept the turn of events at face value. "We must depart for Graystock Manor first thing on the morrow. I'll tell Her Majesty," he said. But before he could do so, the queen issued another order.

"I wish to speak to Baron Cavandish. Alone. The rest of you, out."

Matthew waited for the others to leave. He would hear what the queen had to say, but then he would bid her farewell and they would make their final preparations. He couldn't wait to reach the peace of Graystock Manor, where they would be free of danger and court intrigue. And now that he knew La Faye would not accompany them, he was doubly pleased.

The door closed behind the last person, and Elizabeth thrust a letter at him.

As he digested the contents, the urge to roar with rage consumed him. Elizabeth then gave him a short note from Margaret, his sister-in-law, which pleaded for his help. He brandished them at the queen. "How long have you had this letter from my brother? Margaret's is two days old."

"Your brother's is three days old, but I didn't want to ruin your wedding day."

It was the first time he'd ever seen her contrite, but it didn't help. "It's ruined now." He stalked from the chamber without even bowing.

His brother Jonathan had sent a garbled message to the queen. Despite a recent wound, he intended to enter the besieged city of Paris for a final confrontation with George Trenchard. The old family enemy had resurfaced, and his brother was in life-threatening danger.

Matthew knew that once his daredevil brother decided on a course of action, he was unlikely to forsake it. In his wounded condition, he would need help overcoming Trenchard, and Matthew was taking no chances that Jonathan already had it.

He wasn't entirely convinced their murderer was in prison, but with Essex in the Tower, François gone, and La Faye departing, Cory was far safer than his brother just now. He would settle her and her family at his brother's London town house, where he knew and trusted the staff. He would also leave a dozen men under Hugh's command to protect them. Even with those safeguards, he hated like hell to leave Cory, but he couldn't abandon his brother in a life and death situation. He had no choice but to leave for France on the next tide.

Cory despaired as she watched Matthew ride for his ship at Deptford. He'd taken her, Carew, Madam Henrietta, Letty, Marcus, and Samuel to Jonathan's London town house, where they were to stay with her sister-in-law, Margaret. With a hurried kiss and the admonition not to worry, Matthew had departed with Toby, leaving Hugh behind to guard them.

Their wedding journey was indefinitely delayed. Cory's hopes for the future were in ruins.

Grandmama patted her hand and tried to cheer her. "He's a resourceful man. He'll come back safely, never fear."

Cory knew he was resourceful, but she wasn't convinced Matthew would return safely. She felt like Carew, desolate and betrayed.

"He lied to me." Carew battled to hold back sobs as Cory tried to comfort him.

"He's just going across the Channel. It's not the same thing as going around the world," she tried to explain. "He's going to help his brother Jonathan in Paris, which is besieged."

"Why is my uncle in Paris if it's so dangerous?" Carew raised a stricken face to her.

"He wants to confront George Trenchard, who has a personal vendetta for the Cavandish family." The way Matthew and Margaret said Trenchard's name had struck terror in Cory's heart. "But your father is sure your uncle's recent wound makes him too weak to do it alone." She told Carew the story, related to her by Margaret, of how Trenchard had been betrothed to Carew's Aunt Rozalinde, and how he had betrayed both her and his country by working for enemy Spain. "Everyone thought he was dead years ago, but he was apparently still working for Spain. Now he intends to kill your uncle."

"I thought King Henri was friends with the English," Carew countered. "Why doesn't Uncle Jonathan ask him for help? How did Uncle Jonathan get inside a besieged city to begin with?"

Cory writhed in mental agony as she sought to justify Matthew's decision. "King Henri *is* a friend of the English, but he has his hands full already, fighting the Duke of Mayenne, whose troops are just strong enough to keep King Henri busy but not strong enough to drive him away and raise the siege." She had a good idea of the situation, having heard much about it from Monsieur La Faye. "Paris is encircled by walls or the River Seine on all sides. King Henri guards the gates from the outside. His enemies guard them on the inside. People slip over the walls at times, but it's dangerous. Anyone doing it could be killed by Henri's troops if he were thought to be an enemy, or by those inside for the same reason. Your uncle is taking a terrible risk."

Carew's tears returned. "Then my father will take a terrible risk too. I don't want him to do it alone. Why couldn't I go with him? He said he wouldn't sail again until I could too."

Cory explained that the situation was too dangerous, yet

pain stabbed at her core. Despite how she told herself it was rational for Matthew to go to his brother, she felt as abandoned as Carew.

Carew seemed to despair as well. "He said he would come back, but he may be killed. He always makes promises he can't keep. I hope he goes to the devil." With a cry, Carew fled. Cory saw the rift between father and son gape, an ugly wound reopened.

Worn out from the emotional farewell and the stormy session with Carew, Cory sought her bed. Jonathan's town house was so spacious that each of them had a chamber, private compartments to hold their individual confusion and pain. How ironic that when she and Matthew had wanted privacy, they couldn't have it; now that it was available, she was alone.

Cory dreamed of her pirate prince that night, but he came to her bleeding from a grievous wound, as copiously as Joanna's final loss. Blood was everywhere. On Matthew. On her hands.

She awoke the next morning, solitary in the great bed. Determined to rise and cheer the others, she sat up. A white square of paper lay on the bed near her feet. Her name seemed to leap at her from the sheet as she leaned near. Holding her breath, she ripped it open.

I'm going after Father, Carew had written. *I pray you will not worry, Cory. I'm old enough to sail with him. He'll realize that once we're together.*

Cory dropped the letter and began throwing together clothing for a journey. Her stomach clenched in fear. As an afterthought, she added the green silk scarf to her bundle—the one she had bought the night she met Matthew. It gave her courage to remember how he had sprung to her defense that night and ever since.

"What is it, Mama? What are you doing?" Letty hung on the door, her blue eyes wide.

"Carew has followed his father to France. I must go after him." Cory congratulated herself on managing to hide her trembling from Letty.

"I believe he took one of the horses." Letty twisted her apron with both hands.

"You knew he was leaving?" A reprimand for holding back such important information rose to Cory's lips, but she held it in as she saw Letty's face. "What else have you not told me, Letty?"

"He . . . he told me he was leaving last night," Letty faltered, tears welling in her eyes. "I should have told you, but he made me promise not to. I'm sorry, Mama. I didn't know what to do." She rubbed her streaming eyes. "He will be safe with Lord Graystock, won't he?"

"If he catches up with him, yes." Cory embraced Letty, anxious beyond words. Matthew's ship had left on the evening tide. Carew could well have arrived at Deptford after his father's departure. She dared not leave it to chance that Carew would reach France safely on some other ship and find Matthew. It wasn't safe for a boy to travel alone.

PART 4

Chapter 27

With Hugh at her side, Cory set off for Deptford, driving them at a relentless pace. Upon arrival, she learned that Matthew had departed for France, and no one at the docks had seen Carew. Based on the wording of Carew's letter, he had planned to stow away on *The Revenge*. He wouldn't take the chance of talking to his father before he sailed, Cory reasoned. If he did, Matthew would make him stay behind.

The trouble was, Carew might have arrived after *The Revenge* had sailed. Then he would have had to find another ship bound for France, which worried her greatly. She didn't like the idea of his sailing alone on a strange ship. She had no choice but to cross the Channel herself and look for him. As she prepared to ask after a ship to make the crossing, Hugh spied a pinnace called *L'Honneur*.

"It must be French, m'lady," he said. "Let me inquire if it's returning to France."

Cory waited at a respectable inn while Hugh made inquiries. He returned with good news. "The ship is bound for France, m'lady, and Monsieur La Faye is aboard. He's a-leaving for Le Havre shortly. He says as long as there're no children along, he'll take us both with pleasure."

Relieved to have an escort and a reliable ship, Cory arranged for the horses to be returned to Margaret. Then she and Hugh boarded *L'Honneur*.

*   *   *

The crossing wasn't rough, but Cory couldn't rest. She was too worried about Carew. They dropped anchor at Le Havre sometime during the night. At dawn, Cory leaned against the rail, planning her next move. "As soon as we are on land, Hugh," she said, "we must search for Carew."

"I will help you find him, my lady." Jacques La Faye appeared at her elbow, unfailingly polite.

"I am so sorry for the behavior of my children toward you," Cory said for the dozenth time. "And I'm terribly sorry I laughed about the honey. It was rude of me."

"Never mind. 'Tis forgotten," he assured her. "I will send my men ashore to look for Carew. We shall wait here for their report."

The men returned a short time later. *The Revenge* was in port, and Matthew had been seen departing for Paris the previous day. No one had seen a lad with golden hair. Not until La Faye personally went ashore and asked did they discover that a merchant who sold foodstuffs remembered such a youth. He'd set off for Paris with a man transporting food.

Relieved to know Carew had arrived safely in France but still anxious for him, Cory resolved to follow.

"As I am also bound for the environs of Paris, may I give you a place in my coach?" La Faye offered. "Allow me to warn you, however, that you must not go to Paris proper. I will take you to Meaux, a small town just to the southeast. You can send word to *monsieur le baron* from there. Surely Carew will have joined his father by then."

He seemed so willing to assist, Cory thought the opportunity too good to refuse. Hugh didn't much like the arrangement, for he had to ride a mule behind the coach. His wooden leg made balancing in the saddle awkward, but he agreed to do it. Once more, Cory felt relieved to have an escort.

The countryside near the coast showed few signs of war, but anxiety for Carew ate at Cory. How she wished she could send La Faye's servants racing ahead to search for the boy. They could undoubtedly find Carew faster than she could, with her poor French. If only she'd practiced more with Moll, so she could offer them extra coins to look for Carew. Yet her weak French kept her prisoner. Though she suggested the idea several times to La Faye, he seemed unwilling to act on it.

"We must stay together," he said each time. "It's safer, especially as we approach Paris."

That night, although La Faye found her lodgings in a comfortable private home, Cory couldn't sleep. She would rather have continued their journey, but La Faye insisted that night travel was unwise.

Not only did she want to find Carew, but she wanted to see Matthew and know he was well.

She must be patient, La Faye admonished with a smile.

But she couldn't be patient. The lives of people she loved were in jeopardy.

They reached Meaux by midday, and Monsieur La Faye found her new lodgings on the upper floor of a solid if unattractive home. The chamber she accepted had only a narrow bed, table, and stools, but she gave them barely a glance. She must contact Matthew and find Carew at once. Calling for pen, ink, and paper, she sat down to write to her husband.

She was startled by the sound of a brawl below stairs.

La Faye appeared in the entry, one hand on the door latch, a congenial smile on his face. His familiar crimson doublet reminded her of their many card games and pleasant chats.

"Is ought amiss?" she asked.

"All is well," he assured her. "I wanted to see how you were getting on. I will see your letter is delivered to your husband at once."

"I'm almost finished. I should like to see Hugh, though. Would you send him up?"

He held out his hand for the letter. "Just sign it. There is no time for delay."

"I'm not done." She glanced up at him, wondering at his urgency. He hadn't responded to hers before this. "I wish to see Hugh," she added more strongly. "I pray you, send him up."

"I have a man waiting to depart," he growled.

That seemed a reasonable excuse for his hurry, yet she hadn't been in the chamber more than ten minutes. And why shouldn't she see Hugh if she wished? She rose and headed toward La Faye and the door. "I'll call him," she said. "He's surely just below."

La Faye barred her way and instinct told her something was wrong.

"Hugh cannot come up until you sign the letter." He seemed unnaturally still, watching her, poised to block her attempt to leave the chamber.

Baffled, she stared at him. "Why not?"

She heard someone climbing the stairs and peered over La Faye's shoulder, hoping it was Hugh. But the man who appeared on the landing and stepped into the chamber struck her dumb with shock. It was François.

"The Duke de Mayenne is ready to hear your report, monsieur," François said with a bow.

His dark gaze slid over Cory, leaving her feeling as if a slug had passed over her flesh. Although he spoke French, she understood the duke's name, as well as the word for report.

"W-why is the Duke of Mayenne here?" she stammered as François departed. "You said you served Navarre, that he needed gold for his cause. And François. He tried . . ." She stopped, afraid to say what she believed François had done and why.

"The Duke of Mayenne is here," La Faye said calmly, "because Meaux is his headquarters. And I never told anyone in England that I served Navarre. I said I represented the true king."

She stared in horror as she realized he spoke the truth. He'd always referred to his master as the rightful heir to the throne or the rightful king of France. They had all assumed he meant Henri of Navarre, but he'd meant the Duke of Mayenne.

"B-but Francois. He was Essex's servant. He—"

"Francois is my loyal servant," La Faye said. "He always has been."

More horrifying realizations flooded Cory's mind. Because Moll spoke French, she must have learned La Faye's secret, which was why he'd had François kill her. La Faye had also been behind the attempt to kill her with the runaway coach, as well as the poison meant for Matthew. His decision to return to France, even his seemingly generous offer to escort her across the Channel and to Paris, had been more treachery meant to end her and Matthew's lives and protect his secret. "You're a liar and a murderer," she cried, backing away from him. "And the Earl of Essex never—"

"The Earl of Essex thinks he is clever at plots and political maneuvers," he cut in, his gaze as icy as the far north. "He was happy to pay François to help him with some of the more un-savory details and keep quiet about them. Now sign that letter." He took a threatening step toward her.

Incensed to know he meant to lure Matthew into enemy hands, Cory darted to the table and ripped the paper from end to end. "What have you done with Hugh?"

"You may find out after you rewrite the letter. Once your husband comes to fetch you, *madame la baroness*, you will see if Hugh is alive and well."

"I won't write it. You can't make me," she cried.

With a bound, La Faye crossed the room, grasped her arm, and twisted it behind her. Pain shot through her arm as he forced her into the chair, then released her and stepped back, smoothing his doublet. "Now write."

With a sob, she lifted the quill and tried to write, but her hand shook too much. Her first word was an illegible blur, and her clammy fist left a damp spot on the vellum. "I cannot."

La Faye backhanded her across the face, half knocking her from the chair. She burst into tears, seizing on her all too real terror as an excuse. "You must give me time."

She didn't see La Faye's fist coming until it connected with her ear. Hot sparks erupted in her head, and she cupped her throbbing ear in one hand. Bending over the paper, she scrawled an unintelligible series of sentences, then passed it to La Faye.

"That won't convince him you're well and eager to be re-united with him." He crushed the paper and flung it across the room. "I'm going to have my dinner, but you shall have noth-ing until you write that letter. Not even water." He swung out of the chamber and slammed the door.

Cory heard the key scrape in the lock as she sank back into her chair, trembling. By fortune, her kind heart had fooled her into thinking La Faye was her friend. Why hadn't she recognized his treachery? And how could she warn Matthew of the danger without letting La Faye know?

Cory labored over the letter for what seemed like hours. It had to be written. She just hoped Matthew would realize that something was wrong when he got it. Surely he would know the Duke of Mayenne held Meaux. But even if he did, he would still have to enter La Faye's trap to rescue her.

With a pang, she realized that La Faye's decision to return home had been no coincidence, coming just before Matthew announced he was sailing to France. Had La Faye learned that Matthew's brother had written to him? The queen had held Jonathan's letter for three days before she gave it to him. La Faye could have heard that a letter arrived and bribed a servant to see it. In truth, he might have arranged to see dispatches and letters from France regularly. Cory knew a half-dozen people who would take payment for something as seemingly harmless as looking at letters.

However it had happened, La Faye had taken steps to prevent her and Matthew from telling his secret. If he succeeded, their families and the queen might never learn the truth.

She shuddered. Marcus had sensed La Faye's dishonesty from the start. She would never disbelieve her son again . . . if she got the chance. Holding up the sheet, she reread the letter she had written.

> *Lord Matthew, I am here at the village of Meaux, only*
> *a dozen miles from your camp. Pray come in all haste,*
> *for I am starved for your presence. How eagerly I*
> *await the opportunity to be reunited with you, to touch*
> *you, to kiss you, which is why I did not do the*
> *easy thing and stay in London. Indeed, I have braved the*
> *discomforts of a Channel crossing, and it was indeed*
> *a rough one, unsettling to the stomach as well as to my*
> *nerves. Yet the trouble will be well worth it if I may*
> *greet you once more. I am starved for your voice, your*
> *every move. If you are not too engaged in your work, pray*
> *remember to make time for me.*
>
> *Until we meet again, I remain your loving wife, Baroness*
>   *Cavandish*

It was the most foolish letter she had ever written, but she could think of no other words to convey her message. "I've written the letter," she called at the door, hoping someone could hear her. "May I have something to drink now? Please?"

Footsteps crossed the wood floor in the chamber beyond. La Faye unlocked the door and held out his hand impatiently. "Let me see it."

She handed him the large piece of vellum and held her breath as he read. The letter was stilted and nonsensical where she'd stuck in words to suit her needs. She had tried drafting a better one on another sheet but had soon put it aside, sure that La Faye would guess what she was doing. Would Matthew even believe she had written it?

A sudden inspiration solved the problem. Fumbling in her sleeve, she drew out her green silk scarf. "If you put this with the letter, he'll know 'tis not a forgery. He'll recognize the scarf."

La Faye took the silk square without comment and continued to study the letter as if he didn't trust it. Afraid he would guess her subterfuge, she steeled herself for another cuff from his fist.

"Do you two always write to each other like this?" He grimaced with distaste.

So he saw the artificiality of the letter but not the reason for it. Cory nodded. "Always."

La Faye folded the paper. "And I thought the French were sentimental. But off it goes."

Cory nearly fainted with relief. He had accepted the letter. Now she must hope that Matthew understood the message hidden in her words.

Chapter 28

"Your brother says he intends to remain in Paris, Baron." Henri of Navarre tapped a message just brought to him by an aide-de-camp. Dressed in a simple linen shirt, leather jerkin, and worn galligaskins, the king was indeed a man of the people, disdaining regal fabrics and posturing, especially in battle. But he emanated a charismatic power that brought men flocking to his standard.

Tense with anxiety for his brother, Matthew sat with him and Henri d'Orléans, Duke of Longueville and one of the king's favorite commanders, in the abbey at Montmartre that served as siege headquarters. The king had received him cordially yesterday but said he had no way of communicating with Jonathan in Paris. Matthew had forced himself to wait one day, hoping Jonathan would send a message to Navarre, as he frequently did. The message had come, but the news was bad.

Matthew sucked in a breath, frustrated by his inability to act. There was so much to worry about—how Carew was reacting to his broken promise, whether Cory was really safe since Essex was in prison, and now, his brother's danger. "I need to talk to Jonathan or get him a message, Your Majesty. How did he get that message to you?"

"It was thrown over the Paris wall at my men guarding one of the gates," Navarre said. "Since it was bound to a rock, no one inside stopped the thrower. The leaders of the League of Sixteen are all too happy for the Parisians to throw stones at us. Or worse things," he added darkly. "We have an imperfect system of communicating with your brother. Since he knows where to find my men, he throws his messages over the wall and I pass them along to your queen. But I cannot get a message in to him." The king's usually jovial face distorted with anger. "When I think of my people inside Paris, starving and dying while the Leaguers eat, I curse them to hell."

"It *is* wicked," Matthew agreed, deeply aggrieved by the situation, made worse by the danger to his brother. "Does Jonathan mention George Trenchard?"

Navarre consulted the message again. "He says he's closing in on him."

"I know that name," Longueville said, coming to attention at the mention of Trenchard. "He contacted one of my officers not long ago, saying he was an English spy with information to sell. We bought it, then learned it was false. A number of my men died as a result."

Matthew tensed at this news. "You must not trust anything he offers. My family has an old score to settle with him, and my brother thinks to do it, but I'm concerned he's not strong enough. You say you saw Jonathan some days ago, Your Majesty? How was his wound?"

"Not good." Navarre pulled thoughtfully on his short, curly beard. "He almost killed Trenchard in a one-to-one encounter but sustained a rapier wound to the lower left thigh and barely escaped. He's insane to be on his feet so soon, let alone in Paris."

"It seems I must enter the city and find him if he won't come out." Matthew rose with determination. "I don't expect you to help me, but could you tell me the best time of day and place to go over the wall?"

Navarre rose and clamped a hand on his shoulder. "I admire your courage, *mon ami,* but you're not going in that way. You would be killed by Leaguers. They shoot anyone coming over the wall."

"Then how the devil did Jonathan get in?" Matthew demanded, pushed beyond endurance.

"A bit of bread can work wonders with the guard at the

gate, but you can't go in during the day. Wait until tonight," Navarre advised.

Matthew seethed with impatience. He hadn't left Cordelia and his family so abruptly to sit, twiddling his thumbs. He reached deep inside for the patience he'd built over the years, but the inactivity tormented him. He'd hated leaving Cory. The desolation in her eyes had hurt him, but it was only sensible when his brother was in danger and she was perfectly safe.

In the effort to school his emotions, he forced his thoughts along different lines. "Your Majesty, I all but forgot to convey a message to you from our queen. She hopes the assistance my fellow countrymen provided to your emissary, Jacques La Faye, was helpful." He wasn't going to wait another day for some expression of appreciation from Navarre. It really should have been tendered the instant he arrived.

"Who?" Navarre turned to accept a new dispatch brought by another aide-de-camp.

Matthew was annoyed with Navarre's inattention. "Monsieur Jacques La Faye," he said more loudly. "He spent over six months in England raising two thousand pounds from us. He returned to you with the money a day or so before I arrived."

Navarre looked up from his dispatch. "I know of no Jacques La Faye. What are you talking about?"

Matthew stared at him, filled with repugnance and disgust for La Faye. Could his worst suspicions about the man be true?

"Do you mean to say that someone represented himself as my envoy when I don't have one?" Navarre was incredulous and incensed. "What did he look like?"

Matthew described La Faye, from his red suits to his arrogant manner. "You didn't send an envoy?" he repeated, scarcely able to credit the idea.

"No." Navarre shook his head for emphasis. "I wondered to whom your queen referred in her dispatches when she wrote of my representative, but I thought she meant the man her people meet with over here. It seems this La Faye must also have intercepted my letters to your queen, perhaps altered them, for her responses were not always what I expected."

"This is shocking," Longueville joined in, his attractive face twisted into a snarl. "What other damage has he done to our cause, not to mention that of England?"

"This La Faye must work for the Duke of Mayenne." Navarre whipped a hunting knife from its scabbard at his waist and began to sharpen it on a whetstone. "What a hotbed of betrayal we live in when men impersonate my representatives." He tested the blade of the knife, looking as if he would like to use it on La Faye.

Another aide-de-camp appeared at the door, received approval from the guard to pass, and offered his communication to the king.

" 'Tis for you." Navarre handed Matthew the unopened letter and thanked the aide.

The folded vellum was addressed to Matthew. Wondering who could possibly be writing to him, Matthew slit the letter open with his dagger. A green scarf floated out, suspiciously like the one Cory had bought the night they met on the Thames. Disconcerted, he read the single page.

"Who is it from, *mon ami*? You looked troubled," Navarre said.

"It says it's from my wife." He tilted the letter and reread it. The handwriting certainly looked like Cory's, despite the odd wording. The green silk scarf confirmed its validity. He rubbed the fine silk between thumb and forefinger, still doubting what the letter suggested. "She says she's in Meaux."

"The Duke of Mayenne holds that town," Longueville said gravely.

Matthew tensed. In a panic, he reread the letter, searching for some clue that would explain. Cory wouldn't leave the children and follow him here . . . not unless she'd learned something vital or something terrible had happened. Even if she had, how could she be in enemy hands?

"Did she say anything about coming over before you left?" Navarre asked.

"Not a word." With his mind working in a dozen directions at once, Matthew studied the letter more closely as a vague memory shouted to be recognized inside his head. Some words were scrawled to take more space than was natural, as if she were trying to fill space. Yet if she had wanted to fill

the page, why not stretch all the words? Unless she had
wanted each line to start at a particular place . . .

Was there a message hidden in the letter? They had played
at writing acrostic verses in London before his departure. He
studied the first letter of each line and put them together. It
read, "lafaye danger."

Suddenly it all made sickening, ugly sense. "La Faye has
my wife at Meaux. I must leave at once." He lunged for the
door, blinded with panic for her safety.

At a signal from Navarre, the guard lowered his halberd,
blocking the exit. Matthew rammed past him and raced down
the corridor, but someone leaped on him from behind. He
curled his body as he fell, struggling to break free of the man
clinging to his legs. Cory needed him. He must go to her.

"You must first let me scout the area and hear the report so
you know what to expect." Navarre squatted beside them, and
Matthew stopped thrashing. "Listen to reason, Baron. You
can't help her if you're captured by Mayenne. She'll be safe
enough if they're hoping to lure you to her." He tapped the
man holding Matthew down. "Let him up."

"*If* they're hoping?" Matthew exploded, leaping to his feet.
"Damn it, they have my wife. I can't sit here and hope they
mean to use her as bait. They might just as well decide to kill
her." He turned to go.

"He's still irrational. Hold him," Navarre ordered.

Guards poured out of nowhere, many hands restraining
him. Matthew fought them. He wanted to tear the country
apart. To knock the king out of his way, mount the nearest
horse, and gallop for Meaux.

Navarre stood firm. "I will seek volunteers to assist you
and have them assembled in a few hours," he said. "By the
time you return, we may have heard again from your
brother."

"You can take your 'few hours' and hang them from the
nearest tree." A haze of fury clouded Matthew's mind, leaving nothing clear but Cory's need. He pushed and jerked his
captors to force them off balance.

"Baron, listen to me." Navarre grabbed his face, and
Matthew froze as his gaze locked with that of the king.
"Think of your years of experience. You must plan carefully
before taking action. You know it as well as I."

His reasoning slowly penetrated Matthew's fury. He wouldn't get anywhere behaving like one demented. He did neither Cory nor himself any good.

He took a deep, calming breath, and Navarre released him. "He's all right now. Go about your duties," the king said with a nod.

As men moved away, Matthew rubbed his face with both hands. He had to be calm and rational. Cory's life was at stake.

Despite the soundness of Henri's plan, Matthew's patience was stretched to the limit as he gathered supplies and weapons for the journey to Meaux. He prepared a sturdy length of rope, cleaned and loaded his calivers, and cleaned and sharpened two daggers and his sword.

From time to time, he glanced at Cory's letter and suffered a thousand nightmares with every moment that passed. He couldn't lose her. He wouldn't. Not if he kept his heart out of this and worked with his head. He had too much experience from raids with Drake to rush off like a blind fool. He must use what he knew and what Navarre offered, no matter how much he hated the delay. He must prepare and work for success . . . for Cory's sake.

Cory jerked awake for the third time that night, her tied hands numb from their bonds. Shifting onto her back, she rubbed them against her thighs to wake them up. As pins and needles tormented her flesh, she wondered what time it was. Would Matthew be here soon? At least her hands were tied in front of her, not behind her back. And although they were tied at the wrists, she could still pick up things. She might be able to help when Matthew arrived. And she had seen Hugh. He was tied up in the stable, La Faye had said, but at least he was alive.

Rolling onto her side, she swung her feet over the edge of the cot and levered into a sitting position, then rose and went to the window. Would she see Matthew when he came? Would he signal her somehow? Perhaps *she* should signal him. It didn't matter if La Faye heard her, although he might cuff her again. But making noise would help if Matthew were nearby.

She tried the window latch but it stuck tight. By fortune,

she wanted some air and she wanted to signal Matthew. Incensed to be at La Faye's mercy, she grabbed a stool with her bound hands and shattered the glass panes and mullions, one by one. "Damn you, Jacques La Faye," she shouted as she methodically beat glass and wood with the stool. "Damn you all to hell for keeping me, Cordelia Cavandish, prisoner."

Footsteps pounded on the stair after less than a minute of her shouting, and La Faye unlocked the door. "Stop that noise," he demanded in a rage as she paused at the window, stool in hand.

" 'Tis hot in here," she said calmly, daring him to object. "I needed some air and the latch would not give."

La Faye uttered a French expletive. "Not another sound or I shall make you sorry. And don't try to escape. You'll break both legs if you jump from this height." Slamming the door shut, he relocked it, and she heard him retreat down the stairs.

She was glad she had disturbed him, though he probably hadn't been asleep. He, too, would be awaiting Matthew, weapons at the ready. The thought of her husband walking into a trap set bile churning in her stomach.

She had to force her mind in another direction or be ill, so she gazed out the window. La Faye was right. The drop to the ground was too great from this height, nor could she reach the nearby tree. She would do neither Carew nor Matthew any good if she broke every bone in her body. She would have to wait. And while she waited, she might as well clear the window sill of all broken glass and wood.

Matthew froze as he crouched in the thick woods near Meaux, listening to glass shatter and female shouts—Cory's shouts. He sagged in relief, knowing that if she could shout and break glass, she was all right. For the moment.

He glanced at the five companions who had accompanied him. Louis and Blaise, the two who knew the area best, had identified the house on the outskirts of Meaux as the logical place to house a lady. The shouts from the top story left no doubt in his mind where Cory was, especially when she added her name to the curses she heaped on Jacques La Faye. It took all his willpower not to break from the trees and go to her. But to do so would be to walk into a trap.

"Damn you, La Faye." Her angry cry was punctuated by another explosion of glass. "May you roast in hell."

As Cory's shouts faded, then stopped altogether, Matthew gripped his sword. "Do you think they left the house unguarded?" he whispered to Blaise.

"Not a chance. They're waiting for you. Here comes one now." Blaise pointed to a lone figure as it slunk from the stable and scuttled toward the trees, its gait an odd limp.

"We'll capture him and learn who's waiting in the house. Don't use your knife," Matthew warned. "You trip him and I'll tackle him."

Blaise nodded and moved into position. As the man reached the trees, Blaise sent him sprawling. Matthew leaped on the downed man and struggled to pin him to the ground.

"Let me go, ye bastard, or I'll knock ye into next Sunday," his victim cursed in English. Matthew released his grip in surprise. "Hugh? What the devil are you doing here?"

"M'lord?" Hugh sat up and labored to catch his breath. "By God, I'm glad to see you. I came to protect her ladyship, but I done a sorry job of it. They had me trussed in the stable but I got loose. Her ladyship's upstairs, and Master Carew, we don't know where he is. When he followed you, her ladyship was worried to death. Is he safe with you?"

"Carew's not with me. Do you mean he followed me to France? Alone?" Matthew was staggered by Hugh's answering nod. The news hit him harder than a boulder flung by a siege engine. Carew was somewhere in France, alone and unprotected. Despairing, he turned back to the house, forcing himself to take first things first. "We must free Cordelia," he said to Hugh in English. "Then we will seek Carew." He switched to French. "Let us begin the diversion," he said to Blaise.

"I'll go with 'em. I know the downstairs of the house and where they're waitin'," Hugh said, taking the dagger Matthew passed him.

Blaise signaled the others, and the six left their cover to approach the house.

Cory paced the chamber, frantic with anxiety. She must do something to assist Matthew when he arrived . . . but what?

She stilled at the ping of a stone hitting the side of the house near the broken window. Hurrying to the opening, she squinted into the night. A shadowy figure waved at her from the tree. " 'Tis Matthew," he called in a loud whisper, filling her with relief. "As soon as Hugh and the others create a diversion, you must climb out."

"How?" She eyed the distance to the ground and her stomach wrenched.

"I'll help you when the noise begins," Matthew said. "I tied a rope to the tree and will throw you the end. You tie it fast, hang from it, and drop. It won't be far to the ground."

It would be hard with tied hands, but Cory had no choice but to manage it. "What do I tie the rope to?" She scanned the bare chamber, at a loss.

"Try the door latch."

It was the only reasonable possibility. The table was too light, as was the cot. The door wouldn't move since it was locked . . . unless someone opened it. She had to hope no one would.

Anxiously, she waited, fear pooling in the pit of her stomach. La Faye would be below with many men, perhaps enough to overpower whomever Matthew had brought with him. What if they were caught?

Violence erupted below her as Matthew's friends assaulted the guards.

"Now!" Matthew threw the rope.

Her breath caught in her lungs as she missed the first throw, and Matthew had to reel in the rope. *Hurry,* she prayed as he pulled it in, hand over hand. Below her, a caliver shot rang out amidst the cacophony of the fight. She leaned far out the window and held out her tied hands as Matthew threw the rope again.

She caught it this time, pulled it taut, and hurried to tie it. Sprinting back to the window, she sat on the sill, her legs dangling. The rope seemed far too fragile as she grasped it with her tied hands and leaned forward.

Footsteps pounded on the stairs behind her. Someone was coming.

Tightening her grip on the rope, she pushed off from the sill. The rope gave, and she plummeted toward the ground. The knowledge that someone had opened the door flashed through her mind as she crashed into Matthew, who waited for her on the ground. Every tooth and bone in her body vibrated from the impact. Even as they hit the ground, he was up and lifting her to her feet.

Caliver fire flashed from the window she'd just left, at the same time that a burly man hurtled from the house. He was on Matthew in an instant, bearing him to the ground. The two were a blur of motion as they struggled. Cory could scarcely make out which was which in the dark until she saw a dagger glinting mere inches from Matthew's throat and realized the man was La Faye.

No! He must not kill her love.

Spurred by terror, Cory darted forward and kicked La Faye's hand. The dagger shot into the air. With a groan of pain, La Faye scrambled after it.

Partially freed of La Faye's weight, Matthew twisted and struck. His dagger sank to the hilt between La Faye's shoulder blades as the Frenchman moved on all fours, a mere foot from his weapon.

Matthew turned to stone, silhouetted against the night. Watching. Awaiting death.

The world around Cory stopped. Numb with shock, she watched as La Faye's struggles diminished, then ceased. He collapsed on his stomach, wheezing through the dark liquid that bubbled from his mouth. His arms and legs twitched with a sudden spasm. Then he lay still.

The deception he had begun six months ago was ended. The false envoy of Henri of Navarre was dead. Stricken by the knowledge that she had helped take a human life, even if it was to save Matthew, Cory stood rooted to the spot.

Shouts from the house brought her back to reality and spurred Matthew to action. He pulled his dagger from La Faye's back, wiped it on the grass, and cut her bonds. "Run," he ordered, grabbing her hand. "Before it's too late."

Cory bolted for the woods with Matthew, knowing their lives depended on it. They crashed into the underbrush and pushed through without a pause. Ahead, she spied tethered horses.

"What of the others?" she gasped as Matthew boosted her onto the first horse and untied the reins. "Hugh?"

"They're coming. Hear them? Follow me." As Matthew

urged his horse forward, shouts rose behind them, along with the sound of men crashing through the underbrush.

Praying that Hugh was with them and safe, Cory snapped the reins against her horse's neck. La Faye was dead and would not rise again to deceive them, but the Duke of Mayenne's men were behind them, eager for their capture. With her heart in her throat, she rode after Matthew into the night.

Chapter 29

*H*er love. Matthew was her love. Hysteria bubbled up within Cory as they arrived at the King of Navarre's camp after a hard ride. It must be hysteria. Why else would she laugh at a time like this? The urge to giggle mixed with silent sobs as she recognized her feelings for Matthew. She had fallen in love, something she had sworn never to do.

Now it would hurt all the more when he left her.

Her eyes misted with tears as she watched Hugh, apparently unhurt but missing his false leg, eased from the saddle by Louis, who had ridden double with him back to camp. The horror of their close escape and La Faye's death had not worn off, and she hugged herself with both arms, trying to stop trembling. One of their party had died, but Matthew was safe.

Yet they still did not know where Carew was. And Matthew must help his brother defeat his old foe. Their troubles were far from over yet.

"Are you cold? You're shaking," Matthew was at her side, one arm around her before she realized it.

"N-no," she quavered. "I want to help Hugh." Knowing she would collapse if she stopped now, she pushed free of Matthew's embrace and went to the boatswain where he balanced shakily on one leg. "What happened?" she asked, knowing only that he had followed them to the horses, running on two arms and one leg like a monkey.

"One of them frogs tried to kill this fellow." Hugh jerked a thumb at Louis, who had dismounted behind him. "I blocked his saber with my leg. Blade stuck fast an' wouldn't come out, an' the blasted frog wouldn't let go his saber. It was either bring him along or lose the leg."

The urge to giggle overwhelmed Cory as she envisioned Hugh, unstrapping his leg and racing to safety on three limbs. Tears followed, and with a loud hiccup, she buried her face in her hands.

"Just sees I get a new leg soon," Hugh muttered as he accepted Matthew's support on one side, Cory's on the other. "And stop your laughin', m'lady," he hissed at Cory. "I practice movin' around that way, in case I have to get by without my leg."

"I'm sorry, Hugh. I'm beside myself with relief. I swear." She gripped his hand and placed it on her shoulder, knowing he was mortified to be one-legged before their hosts.

"You're hysterical," Matthew said roughly from the other side. "You need to lie down."

But she couldn't let the nightmare overtake her. She urged the boatswain to lean on her as he hopped forward on one leg.

"I am most grateful for your assistance, Monsieur Mannerly," Louis said as he followed them into the house Navarre had assigned them. "If not for you, I would be a dead man. As it is, one of our company was killed in the attack."

"Ye're welcome, monsieur," Hugh said with great dignity. "I know you woulda done the same for me."

Cory spent only a minute hugging Matthew and reassuring him that she was well. She couldn't bear to dwell on her feelings for him. Instead, she insisted on dressing a superficial wound on Hugh's arm, then searching for the appropriate craftsmen to make Hugh a new leg.

"Thank ye, m'lady," Hugh said as the man finished measuring and departed with his tools.

"You're more than welcome, Hugh. It's the least I can do in return for your loyalty and friendship to Matthew and me."

Hugh snorted and shifted his gaze. "We've still got to find Master Carew."

He was right. And there was also Jonathan and George Trenchard.

The knowledge subdued Cory. No remnant giggles threatened, for her hysteria had passed.

The King of Navarre sent word to every scout in his service to watch for an English boy, thirteen years of age, with golden blond hair. As the sun peered over the horizon, casting its rays on the land, Cory had to be content with that. She selected supplies for Matthew's venture into Paris. He was resolved to face the danger, and she was resigned. She would never have a husband who lived and loved with her in comfortable domesticity. Danger was a way of life for Matthew, and she must not shed tears over it.

Matthew worried about Cordelia. After only a brief rest during what remained of the night, after doing everything she could for·him and Hugh, she played cards with Navarre's soldiers. Matthew saw her pull a veil of pretended indifference over her anxiety for him and Carew, immersing herself in the play.

Within the span of a day, Matthew saw Navarre's men fall hard for his bride of hearts, but it wasn't just because she played cards. Despite her limited French, she found ways to communicate with them. Often she halted a game to minister to them, seeing to one's wounded knee, sewing up or washing their clothes, and soothing their troubled spirits. It was so pleasurable to be nurtured by the baroness that within the single day, men competed for the privilege. Soon, everyone was talking of her kindness and caring ways. So much so, that the king heard and sent a message that evening, asking Cordelia to meet with him.

Matthew accompanied her, guessing that Navarre considered it improper for a woman to take over the care and entertainment of his men. As they entered the chamber where the king sat with Maximilien de Béthune, Sieur de Rosny, another of his chief ministers and captains, he wondered what approach the sovereign would take in curbing Cory's enthusiasm for good deeds. Not that he thought she should be curbed. Knowing well the benefits of her tenderness, he was loath to refuse it to those who were strained to the breaking point by the duress of war.

"*Madame la baroness,* you are well met." Navarre bowed over Cory's hand and bade her be seated. "I have heard how you have captured my men's hearts and wished to meet you myself." He praised her lavishly, then they discussed the plans for Matthew to enter Paris the next day.

Matthew felt a twinge of jealousy as the king eyed his wife. By all reports, he was susceptible to pretty females, and despite her narrow escape from La Faye, not to mention her worry over Carew, Cory had never looked more beautiful to him. Navarre seemed of like mind.

"If you wish to play at cards, my lady," Navarre said gallantly, "I would pray you play with me. I'll not have it said that Navarre fails to entertain his female guests appropriately."

Despite his own anxiety over Carew and his brother, Matthew restrained a grin as Cory pulled out a pack of cards. So the king thought to restore propriety by insisting she play with him rather than his men. Little did he know that when it came to cards, Cory would take him literally. Although the king reportedly loved cards, he couldn't possibly know what was in store for him.

With regal motions, she indicated the table, and they took their places. "Shall we play for pleasure or compliments, *monsieur le roi*?" she asked.

"Compliments?" The king seemed baffled by this proposal.

"Yes. The loser must give the winner a sincere compliment that has nothing to do with physical looks." Cory blinked her long lashes at the king, and Matthew saw the monarch fall another degree under her spell.

"I think we had best play for money," he insisted, dredging some small coins from his pockets. "I may be unable to restrain my wish to follow a compliment of your gracious ladyship with something more."

Matthew sat down, annoyed with the king's interest in Cory's charms and knowing it was going to be a long night. Cory would be oblivious to the king's carnal desires and would refuse to stop at just one game of cards. She would willingly play hundreds. Seeing the way Navarre spread the cards expertly in his big hands, he realized that the same must be true of the king.

The pair sat over the cards late into the night. Navarre played with the same fervor as Cory, using the game to block thoughts of more troubling matters. He hunched over the table, seeming fascinated by Cory's speed as she skillfully manipulated the cards.

Let them find their own form of escape, Matthew thought, politely refusing every time they invited him to join them. He dozed on a settle, desperately needing sleep in preparation for the morrow. He sat up, though, when an aide-de-camp brought a message to Navarre.

Henri scanned it. "'Tis from your brother Jonathan, dropped over the city wall to one of my men," he said to Matthew. "Permit me to read from it aloud. 'I hear it said in the streets that the League is holding my nephew. On the morrow, toward evening, I will attempt a rescue. I pray Your Majesty to alert the command at the northwest gate of the city. If I succeed, I'll put Carew through the gate to your men at sundown tomorrow evening. If I fail, I will come to the gate alone before dawn the next morning. Bring bread.'"

"They have Carew? My God!" Fear drove Cory's voice an octave higher than usual, and Matthew wondered in alarm how his son had entered the besieged city. Yet given the way Carew was growing and changing, he realized his boy cared about him so fervently, he had wanted to be with him at all costs. Carew had evidently thought Matthew had entered the city ahead of him.

"Let us hope Jonathan will succeed in rescuing him," Navarre said gravely. "If he fails, I will personally assist your entry into the city, Baron Cavandish."

"Thank you." Matthew rose and shrugged into his doublet. "I wish to go to the gate now. If Carew comes out, I want to be waiting for him. I also want to speak to my brother."

"I wish to be there as well." Cory put down her cards.

"We'll all go," Navarre said, rising. "Nicholas." He motioned to his captain of the guard.

"I am at your service, Majesty." Rosny rose with some difficulty due to a recent hip wound at the battle of Ivry. Nicholas left the chamber to prepare a protective guard for the king.

"Bien. We shall continue the play whilst we wait," Navarre said to Cory, scooping up the pack of cards.

By the time the king's party took up its vigil near the gate in a home owned by royalist supporters, it was early morning. The minute they were settled, Cory and Navarre resumed their card game where they had left off. Both played with a quiet desperation that Matthew felt as well. The waiting was torturous. Restless, he paced as they played.

"I win." Navarre slapped down his last card.

"Your Majesty is having an unaccountable run of good luck." Cory didn't sound particularly appreciative as she shuffled the cards.

"*Mais non*, you have that wrong." Navarre leaned tiredly on an elbow. "As a card player, perhaps I have luck, but as a king, I have none. Especially not with this siege."

"Did you truly let three thousand women and children leave Paris in July?" Cory dealt the next game.

Navarre nodded heavily as he stared at the cards accumulating before him. "*Oui*. And a few weeks ago, I did so again. My advisors and my enemies say I committed political suicide, but I could not let innocents starve."

Cory finished the deal and stacked the remaining cards on the table, but she made no move to pick up her hand. "You wish to raise the siege, do you not?"

"My ministers and commanders advise against it. I would lose Paris." Navarre glanced reproachfully at Rosny and his other commander, Charles de Chatillon-Coligny, the Marquis d'Andelot, both of whom sat behind him. "As if I will have Paris when so many of my people are dead. The League of Sixteen does not suffer. I hear they feast on good bread and fresh vegetables, then unbuckle their belts a notch and let them hang, pretending to starve like the rest."

"That's terrible." Cory frowned. "They're using those with less as pawns against you."

"*Bien sûr*," Navarre agreed. "I ask you, what is the use of winning Paris if I am crowned king of the dead? They say thirteen thousand have died. Yet if I end the siege, the French throne is still empty. The people of Paris may eat, but civil war continues. They suffer in other ways."

"Your Majesty, if I may be so bold." D'Andelot spoke for the first time. "You have but to hold firm and you will win Paris. The Duke of Mayenne is not strong enough to drive you away."

"Ah, but you forget, the King of Spain is sending the Duke of Parma from the Netherlands to help Mayenne," Navarre barked without turning around. "Mayenne will reprovision

Paris while I fight Parma, though I doubt he'll be drawn into battle. He'll find an excuse to avoid it, but I care nothing for him. My fear is for my people." The king waved his arms as his anger grew. "I am killing them to subdue unruly nobles and clergy who do not suffer. In the city, the priests exhort the poor to die of hunger, even to eat their own children, rather than yield to a heretic king. Yet they sacrifice nothing. Is that not disgusting?" He spat into the bare hearth.

Nausea rose in Cory's throat. "I think you should raise the siege, Your Majesty."

Navarre threw his arms wide. "If I wish to be king, I cannot, but how in heaven can I do otherwise? My people suffer so. Earlier in the month, the bourgeois of Paris demonstrated, demanding that peace be proclaimed and that I be welcomed into the city, but the governor had them disbursed by armed monks and many hung for speaking out. If they could throw open the gates, I think the people would welcome me, but fanatics prevail."

"Your Majesty, I pray you be steadfast," d'Andelot repeated doggedly, "you will see—"

Navarre slammed both palms flat on the table. "I have been steadfast since May and look where we are," he roared. "Parma will be here in the flesh any day now, swelling Mayenne's army to twenty thousand. It will rival mine, despite the supporters who flock to my standard." He leaned across the table toward Cory and spoke in lowered tones behind a cupped hand. "Even those who join me cannot be trusted. I have heard they come only because they hope to pillage Paris when it falls, as a revenge for the Saint Bartholomew's Day Massacre in fifteen seventy-two."

"Forgive me, Your Majesty, but they flock to your standard because you are a superb commander," Rosny protested. "You will be victorious, I know."

Navarre straightened. "You see how it is?" he demanded. "Both my faithful commanders give me sage advice, yet I do not like the results. Nor do I like the results if I do the opposite."

Cory glanced helplessly at Matthew, than back at Navarre. "Another game, Your Grace?"

"*Oui,*" the King muttered. "Another game is what I need to keep me occupied. But if your son is not produced tonight," he said to Matthew as he took up his cards for the next hand, "I am prepared to support your entry into the city. 'Tis time to confront the worm in his lair."

Matthew's hopes descended deeper into the abyss as eight in the evening arrived and Jonathan failed to appear with Carew.

"Do you suppose Jonathan encountered George Trenchard?" Cory asked, her face drawn and pale from the strain.

Matthew shook his head, too weary to respond.

"That does it. You must enter the city," Navarre declared. He had departed to consult with his commanders, visit his garrisons, and sleep for several hours, but rejoined them to hear the news. He appeared as disappointed as they at Jonathan's failure to appear with Carew.

Cory stood at an open window, looking out at the walls of Paris as the sun sank in the west. "If only the city would give way," she said as she twisted and tugged at her handkerchief.

"It's an impossible situation." Navarre raised his hands to the heavens. "*Dieu,* what am I to do? I have word that Parma has arrived, yet I might still prevail if I hold this position. We command the entire enclave around the city. Paris is close to the breaking point. Yet who is left to welcome me in save people who love Spain?"

Cory slipped from Matthew's side and faced the king. "Your Majesty, I have a proposal. Why not let Dame Fortune decide the city's fate?"

"What do you mean?" He regarded her warily, as if one more empty hope would be beyond bearing.

"Yes, Cory, what do you mean?" Matthew moved away from the window, wondering what she was about to say. Yet even one of Cory's schemes might be better than this impossible siege.

"Your Majesty, I propose we play three games of Cent." Cory's upturned face was earnest in the light of the setting sun. "If I win two of them, you raise the siege and move your troops to meet Parma's. If you win, you stay where you are and the siege continues. What do you say?"

Matthew grimaced. By now, he'd seen the strength of Navarre's love for a wager. His pleasure in playing for stakes was second only to his love for his many mistresses. He would be helpless to resist what Cory proposed. "Cory, I don't think this is wise," he warned.

"Your Majesty, you cannot—" Rosny said as he joined them with a lantern.

"Silence, everyone!" Navarre ordered. He glared at Matthew and Rosny, then turned back to Cory, his gaze narrowed in thought. "I wish to consider *madame's* proposal. Do not interfere."

Matthew held his peace. The idea of thousands of bodies lying in the Paris streets made him ill. If the siege were raised, lives would be saved. He could also rescue Carew, and Jonathan could quit the city. Despite the unusual nature of Cory's proposal, he had to admit he favored it.

Navarre must have too, for his wide mouth curved into a smile. "I'll do it!"

"Your Majesty, I pray you consider. You're not going to let a mere game of cards decide your future, are you?" Rosny pleaded.

" 'Tis not a mere game of cards." The king paced before the window, gesturing in excitement. "Do you not see? Dame Fortune decides our fate in all things, regardless of what we do. I am merely asking her for a clear sign."

Matthew couldn't help but appreciate the way Cory let the king convince himself.

Rosny was not so easily persuaded, however. "This is not a good solution," he warned his sovereign. "You will regret this hasty decision to let Paris's fortune hang on the turn of a card."

"I will be relieved to know what Fortune has in store for us." Henri linked his arm with Rosny's and guided him across the chamber. At the entry, he let Rosny proceed into the corridor, then slammed the door and dropped the bar in place. "Are you next, Baron?" he asked Matthew as Rosny protested from outside.

"I enjoy watching a good game of cards." Matthew vowed to say no more. If his wife was going to determine the outcome of the siege of Paris, he wanted to be there.

Henri sent for his favorite physician and three captains of the guard. They would serve as observers and witnesses, he explained, in case a dispute arose. He then invited Cory to sit at the table and took his seat across from her, placing the lantern to one side. They settled to play, with Cory dealing from a fresh pack of cards. "I have thirty points in my sequence," he announced after exchanging the cards he didn't want.

Cory discarded her unwanted cards and chose replacements. "I have five and twenty points."

"*Trés bien!* I am ahead, *madame*." The king was jubilant. "I have the four aces as well."

Cory appeared downcast. "Your aces are higher than my four queens. None of mine count."

Navarre rearranged his cards. "Do not feel badly about it, *madame la baroness*. You are the queen of every heart."

"Princess of hearts," Cory corrected. "Where I come from, Elizabeth Tudor is the queen of everything, including hearts."

Navarre grinned over his cards. "Princess of hearts, lady of hearts, fishwife of hearts. Be whatever you wish, *ma belle*, but you will probably lose this game."

"Are you sure you don't *want* to lose?" Cory seemed entirely serious.

"When I play for a wager, I play to win," Navarre said. "The outcome shall be as it shall be."

Matthew held his peace as the play continued. Tension grew as cards were slapped on the table and called so swiftly, he had to concentrate to follow the score. He prayed that Cory would win.

Hope took a distinct downturn as she lost the first game. If the siege were not raised, he would have to enter Paris and risk being killed in order to search for Carew. But if she won, the siege would be lifted, making his chances of finding Carew much better. How could he not hope that she would succeed?

Navarre dealt the cards for the next game and put the remainder on the table. He motioned to Nicholas. "Fetch us something to drink, and don't let Rosny in."

The two played with an intensity that rivaled that of duelsmen, fighting to the death. Cory drew four knaves in the second game, and Navarre, only four eights, which moved her ahead. As they began the final play for tricks, Cory held the lead. She won the second game and took the cards for the final deal.

"Do you hope to win the third game, Your Majesty?" Matthew asked, unable to bear the tension in silence any longer.

"I cannot say. I put my own fate and that of Paris in Fortune's hands." Navarre locked his gaze on his cards as Cory announced she had the four queens.

Navarre had only the four knaves, so they didn't count.

Cory led the play for tricks with the queen of diamonds.

Navarre took it with his king of diamonds.

Cory played an ace. The king lost the trick. The play accelerated, with the number of tricks taken by each seeming equal. Matthew gave up following Navarre's score and added only Cory's. The cards held diminished in each hand. Cory snapped her last one on the table with a flourish.

Matthew squinted to see what it was. The queen of hearts.

"*Merde*," Navarre muttered, playing his last card. It was an eight of spades.

"I win!" Cory snatched up the pair of cards and waved them in triumph. "The siege is raised. Thousands will once again eat the bread of life."

Matthew slumped in his chair with relief. Cory had won the wager. They could rescue Carew and Jonathan . . . if it wasn't already too late.

Chapter 30

It was late, after midnight, and François was satisfied. When the Cavandishes arrived, he had a stratagem that would not fail. The opportunity to ingratiate himself with the Duke of Mayenne had arrived, and he intended to play it to its fullest. He would be rewarded with advancement and recognition. How opportune that he had heard the rumors of a blond English lad wandering the streets of Paris, inquiring after his relations. He had acted immediately and captured this nice little tidbit with which to bait a trap. Very clever indeed.

Elated by his certainty of what was to come, he cuffed the bound Cavandish boy tied to his chair and smiled at the child's struggles to hold back tears. Most amusing, a useless show to hold out against pain. Why not grovel? He had discovered with Moll Dakins that he liked it when people groveled.

George Trenchard entered the chamber, a substantial presence with thick, graying hair cut straight across his brow, a massive square jaw, and gray-green eyes. He wore a fine-quality short gown in green brocade and had an accent that sounded neither French, Spanish, nor Italian, but an odd mixture of all three.

Since La Faye's disastrous demise several nights ago, François's future had been uncertain. But the Cavandish boy, attempting to find his uncle in the besieged city, had been easy quarry. The lad had given him instant entrée into Trenchard's employ. "We will be rid of two more Cavandishes by tonight," François commented, hoping to elicit a positive response.

"Three Cavandishes." Trenchard's mouth rose in a wolfish grin directed to no one in particular. He acknowledged few servants directly, seeming to speak to the window or the wall.

François had decided this was due to his lofty position in the King of Spain's favor and did not feel insulted. He would reveal more of his plan, to ensure that Trenchard did not cut him out of the Cavandish confrontation, and thus the rewards. "If you would care to step into the next chamber," François said, "I should like to show you how I intend to kill Matthew Cavandish whilst you dispose of Jonathan Cavandish."

Trenchard brought his steely gaze to bear on François for the first time. "Very well."

Heartened by the response and eager to demonstrate his idea, François led the way into the next chamber, opened a cupboard, and withdrew a thick glass bottle. Pulling out the stopper, he offered the bottle to Trenchard.

Trenchard sniffed the contents and wrinkled his face as François replaced the cork. "Oil of vitriol. What will you do with it?" He still looked at François directly.

Gaining his new master's full attention was a heady experience. "I will simply dump it on him," François replied.

Trenchard nodded, seeming to approve the plan. Although his silence made it impossible to judge exactly where one stood with him, François hoped his nod boded well.

But he decided not to mention that if his proposed stratagem failed, he had an even better emergency plan.

"You cannot come. 'Twill be dangerous," Matthew told Cory as he prepared to meet his brother at the rendezvous. He and Cory had slept through what was left of the night. It was now close to dawn.

Nerves twisted his stomach as he composed his mind for what must inevitably be a fight to the death with Trenchard. The old family vendetta must end at last.

"But I should be there for Carew," Cory pleaded.

"Cory, please." Matthew set aside the caliver he'd just loaded and faced her, a hand on each of her shoulders. "If I know you are waiting for me here, in safety, I'll be able to do what I must. Jonathan and I will bring Carew to you, and we'll all return to England together." Suddenly he pressed her to his heart, overwhelmed by the feelings that accosted him. He had a frightening premonition that Dame Fortune hovered above him, holding everything he had ever cared about in the balance. It was a baffling feeling unlike any he'd ever had before a battle. "Cory, promise me that you will stay safe. I need to rely on that certainty."

She gazed up at him, her eyes alight with tenderness. "Truly? It matters to you?"

He could scarcely answer, his throat was so choked with foreign emotions. "It matters."

"Very well." She sighed and leaned against him. "The King of Navarre will be moving to his new headquarters as he prepares to raise the siege. He invites me to accompany him in his personal entourage. You must take directions from him so you can come to me at once."

Relieved that his declaration had somehow convinced her to remain in safety, he leaned to kiss her. The touch of her lips took his breath away.

"Go with God." She slipped from his embrace and stepped back. "Carew is waiting for you."

Carew nodded in his chair, hating the bonds that held him upright. If only he could lie down and rest properly, he would be stronger, more able to think of a way to escape. He studied François, visible in the next chamber, working on something by candlelight. Carew felt an urgent need to know what it was.

The man twisted to check on him, and Carew lowered his gaze. He must pretend to see nothing, to be stupid with fear and unable to help himself.

After what seemed like forever, François picked up the candle and left the chamber. Carew listened to his footsteps descend the stairs and was relieved. It was always better when François went away.

Carefully rocking his chair forward, Carew shifted his weight to his feet. Although the chair was heavy, perched on his back, he could move around this way, and that was worth a good deal.

Moving awkwardly, he inched across the chamber. He must not bump the chair legs against the floor, nor lose his balance and fall over, for he wouldn't be able to right the chair. But he intended to see what François had been doing. He knew enough French to understand that his father and uncle would arrive soon.

At the table, he stopped and squinted at a piece of wood. On it lay three darts with needle sharp tips. Several glass bottles stood nearby. One he recognized as the oil of vitriol François had shown George Trenchard last night. Carew hadn't understood the words, but he had guessed the bottle's contents. It would be the same acid that had burned him.

But François had not used the oil of vitriol. A smaller bottle sat near the darts. If he guessed right, François had dipped the tips of the darts into the contents. It must be poison. When the needles pierced flesh, the substance would enter the person's body and cause death.

With great care, Carew bent down and, using his teeth, picked up one of the darts by its feathered end. François wouldn't be back until after he broke his fast the next morning, and from experience, Carew knew he wouldn't hurry. He seemed to enjoy Carew's acute discomfort from being forced to sit upright all night, as well as his pitiful eagerness for the rare chance to be untied and allowed to eat, relieve himself, and move around. Carew hated him.

Carew worked with two of the darts, his movements slow but thorough. He returned each to its original place as he finished, but not the third. He dropped this one on the floor in the far corner.

Footsteps sounded downstairs. Carew returned to his original position in the next chamber. He was nodding with sleep, as before, when Trenchard peered in at him, then moved to inspect the darts. Good. When François returned, he would think Trenchard had tampered with them. He would be unlikely to suspect Carew, at least not until it was too late.

Cordelia's kiss had filled Matthew with a strength and inspiration that sped him to the gate Jonathan had named. Yet he also carried desperation in his heart. His concern for Carew and his brother had grown to astronomical proportions. He prayed Jonathan would be in the designated meeting place this time.

Navarre had sent orders to his troops to evacuate the suburbs of Paris during the night. At his signal, the retreat would be ef-

fected with lightning swiftness and the royalist army quit of the
vicinity and beyond danger before the Parisians even knew the
siege was raised.

Yet Matthew could see the Parisians suspected. Fighting had
halted without explanation, and a stunned silence seemed to
hang over the land. As he walked past a row of houses and approached the huge, arched gate, he saw the shadowy figures of
monks on the walls. He paused in the shelter of the last house
to watch.

An hour must have passed, during which Matthew fidgeted
with anxiety. Had his brother been killed or captured? Would
he fail to arrive once more?

As the sun peered over the edge of the horizon, the gate
opened for an instant and closed again. Matthew squinted in
the dark, unable to make out whether someone had passed
through. After a few moments, he spied a bent figure hobbling
down the road, leaning on a crutch, looking mangy and, when
he got closer, smelling worse.

Evidently the Parisians had let him pass through the gate to
be rid of his stench. Matthew recoiled into the entryway of the
house, but as the wretch drew parallel to him, he stopped,
standing as still as a statue in the narrow street.

"Well met, brother," the cripple said.

Matthew recognized Jonathan's voice at once and cursed
himself for not seeing through the ruse. They embraced in the
protective shadow of the house.

"I can't believe it." Jonathan dropped his crutch to clap him
on the back. "My little brother, come to my aid. As boys, 'twas
the other way around." Even in the darkness, Matthew made
out the twinkle in his brother's eyes. "I was invited to the house
where Carew is held but smelled a trap," Jonathan continued.
"As I suspected, they had a dozen starving wretches ready to
fall on me the instant I arrived. We require a strategy."

"Our strategy is that the siege is raised," Matthew said.
"Navarre is moving his army even as we speak." He pulled out
a packet that Cory had prepared and offered it to Jonathan.

"Navarre's raising the siege. Excellent." Jonathan wolfed
the hunk of cheese from the packet, alternately swilling water
from a jug as Matthew went on to tell him how Margaret fared.

"If your wound's too bad, I can find Carew while you stay
here," Matthew offered.

"No. I'll see this through to the end." Jonathan's expression turned grim. "Anyone with you?"

Matthew jerked a thumb over his shoulder. "Two men with extra horses at the end of the street."

"Good." Jonathan cast away his outer rags and the stench surrounding him lessened. "Did you bring bread?"

Matthew indicated the huge sack he'd lugged with him. "Let's get on with this."

The Parisians wouldn't know the siege was raised for several hours. Despite this, Jonathan indicated that Matthew should follow him, and they went boldly to the gate.

"Bread delivery!" Jonathan whispered in French to the guard inside.

The man yanked the gate open without any questions.

Matthew and Jonathan pushed their way inside, thrusting the huge sack of sweet-smelling bread into the man's arms. With a yelp of joy, he buried his face in it.

In response to the strong, unmistakable odor of yeast, a rain of men dropped from the walls and rushed to fight for the bread. With their sense of smell honed to a keen edge by starvation, they must have found the odor of fresh bread more heady than an aphrodisiac.

Forgotten by them during the feeding frenzy, Jonathan and Matthew moved through a maze of filth-encrusted alleys. As he stumbled over a stinking heap of refuse, Matthew felt bile rise in his throat. "What is all this—" He halted, suddenly realizing the heap was rotting corpses. "Horrible," he muttered, sick at heart for the waste of human life. "Thank God Navarre is raising the siege."

"Yes," Jonathan agreed, grasping his arm and guiding him forward. "Keep moving. If you stop, you can be set upon in some quarters. This is one of them."

Matthew moved faster as he noted the emaciated faces staring at him from doors and windows, their deep-set eyes seeming rabid with hunger. "God save them," he murmured, appalled.

"Yes, they wish Navarre would win and liberate them from the fanatical monks who hold their city hostage," Jonathan said.

"Do they, truly?" Matthew asked as they halted at a point

where an especially odoriferous alley gave way to a wider, more prosperous avenue.

"His people love him," Jonathan said simply. "How else do you think I survived? Navarre's supporters sheltered me, and I contrived to feed them." He pointed to a house down the street. "Carew's in there. They expect us to come the back way, so we'll go in by the front door. That will at least give us the element of surprise."

Matthew scrutinized the handsome, two-storied house set between its neighbors. "How do we get rid of the starving wretches waiting for us?"

"I'll deal with them." Without warning, Jonathan darted forward and entered a house. He returned moments later with an urchin child in his arms. Though thin, the child didn't look starved, and though still drowsy with sleep, he grinned up at Jonathan trustingly. "*Bonjour, El Mágico.* What have you brought me this morning?"

"*Bonjour,* Daniel. I regret the rude awakening, but I've brought you some bread," Jonathan answered in French.

The child regarded him gravely. "Not Madame de Montpensier's bread from the League?"

"No, not that stuff the Duchess de Montpensier, Mayenne's sister, had made from the cemetery," Jonathan assured him as Matthew grimaced at the thought of bread made from ground bones. "All you need do, after you eat, is run down the street shouting these words." Jonathan explained what he wanted the boy to say.

"Is it true, monsieur?" the boy asked.

"It will be in an hour or so." Jonathan handed the child a chunk of bread he must have saved from his meal.

The boy bolted the bread, then rose and trotted down the street. "The siege is lifted," he shouted in a voice ten times his size. "Food has arrived at the gates. I have just had a wonderful piece of bread. Hurry. Succors is come at last."

Matthew crouched in the shadows and watched in sorry fascination as people in all manner of nightdress stumbled from the houses and rushed down the streets. As if they'd been lying awake, awaiting this moment, a few serving wenches in scanty smocks footed it for the gates. But the majority of the people were men, as Navarre had let women and children leave the city. Men in flapping nightshirts raced down the street, attended by their lackeys. One carried a huge pot, as if hoping to fill it with edibles. Others, apparently having dressed before quitting their homes, emerged after the first wave, moving twice as fast to make up for lost time.

The house Jonathan had pointed out was no exception. At the urchin boy's first shouts, the door had burst open and a ragged pack of ruffians swarmed into the street to join the others. Soon the street was empty. The babble of excited voices receded.

"It's light enough to see now," Jonathan whispered. "And we've evened the odds. Two of us against Trenchard."

Matthew's heart contracted with violence as he and Jonathan burst through the chamber door and he saw Carew, his legs free but his waist and knees bound to a chair, his hands tied, his mouth gagged. He sent his son what he hoped was a reassuring smile, then turned to face the enemy.

"So, George Trenchard, we meet again." Jonathan adjusted the dagger in his left hand, the sword in his right.

Trenchard's mouth split into a grin above his sword. The wicked blade of Spanish steel gleamed in the early light. "I never expected you to remember me, Cavandish. You were but fifteen when you saw me years ago. Your brother here was still soiling his tail clouts."

"You've been plotting against England too many years." Matthew refused to be troubled by the insulting reference to his youth. " 'Tis time it ended." He brandished his sword at the malevolent, dark-haired François.

François scowled. "I cannot fight a man with a sword when I have only a dagger."

"I don't see a master of duels present to censure the impropriety." Jonathan took a broad stance and gestured with his sword for Trenchard to take his guard.

"There's not room for four to fight in here," Trenchard protested. "Let us step outside."

"No." Matthew assumed his own stance, unwilling to accept any changes.

Trenchard's gaze narrowed, but François shifted his dagger to the left hand and stepped forward, a glass flagon in his right hand. "Come now, I am no match for you with a sword. Why shouldn't we settle this peaceably?" he invited. "Have a drink and we will discuss things." He stepped closer to Matthew, offering the goblet.

Matthew backed away, realizing what the goblet must contain. He dropped his dagger and grabbed a stool, prepared to shield himself from the caustic acid. Even the smallest drop would burn him, but he might be able to avoid being drenched.

Behind him, Trenchard and Jonathan clashed. He heard steel meet steel and realized they would inevitably impede each other. The chamber was too small. Yet moving to another chamber or the street, where some advantage might await their opponents, made no sense.

Refusing to be distracted by his brother's fight, Matthew crouched, the stool ready, hoping to block the rain of acid about to hurtle his way. François sidled closer.

A sharp thud sounded, but Matthew kept his gaze locked on François. Time seemed to slow, every sound and movement registering sharply in his mind. The furious crack of steel on steel punctuated by his brother's and Trenchard's puffs and grunts sounded to his left. François advanced toward Matthew, the threatening goblet in his outstretched hand.

From the corner of his eye, Matthew saw something hurtle across the chamber from his right. As François raised his arm to fling the acid and Matthew sidestepped, Carew appeared, still tied to the chair, racing on legs free only from the knee down. With head lowered, Carew struck François square in the shoulder like a battering ram.

François fell sideways toward Trenchard, the goblet arcing from his hand. As the caustic contents sloshed from the container, Jonathan and Trenchard thrust at each other. Steel pierced flesh. Trenchard, goblet, and acid met.

François collapsed and lay stunned as Trenchard shrieked in pain and clawed at his face.

Reacting with lightning speed, Matthew discarded the stool and righted Carew, whose chair had fallen on its side after his attack. "That was amazing, Carew," he said, meaning it with all his heart. With his dagger, he cut his son's bonds. As he straightened, he saw with horror that Jonathan was leaning against the wall, clutching his left thigh. His lips were drawn back into a snarl as he gritted his teeth against the pain.

Sprinting to his brother, he pressed his folded handkerchief against the bloody flesh visible through his canons. Trenchard bled copiously from the wound Jonathan had given him in the chest, but in return, Trenchard had pierced Jonathan's old wound a second time. It bled fiercely.

"Water," Trenchard cried, writhing on the floor. "Water, for pity's sake."

"Father, watch out!" Carew cried from behind.

Matthew raised his gaze to that of François, who had risen without his noticing and slipped into the next chamber. He held a sword in his right hand. In his left was a feathered dart. During his travels, Matthew had seen such a weapon, and he knew the dart would have a poison tip.

Chapter 31

Matthew dropped to a crouch, readying his sword and dagger, but François seemed reluctant to fight. "If you two come with me," he said in his thickly accented English, "I shall let the boy go."

"Don't do it," Jonathan ordered, wincing as he spoke. "He won't keep his word."

"Why should we go with you?" Matthew demanded of François.

"The Duke of Mayenne wishes to meet you."

"So he can kill us at his leisure? No, thank you." Matthew ensured that Carew was well behind him, then took a broad stance. "I prefer to fight."

"As you wish." François matched his stance and they began to circle, each looking for an opening.

"What school are you trained in?" Matthew advanced slightly into François's striking range. As François struck, Matthew repelled and followed through with a lightning counterattack. François lurched backward as Matthew's sword tip nicked his stomach. "Ah, you studied in the Spanish school. I should have guessed." Matthew chuckled mirthlessly, a technique that he had learned would disconcert his adversaries.

François grunted as he recovered his stance after his narrow escape. "And you?"

He seemed to play for time, perhaps fearing he was the less

experienced combatant, as indeed it seemed he was. "Mine is more exotic." Matthew continued his dance, moving lightly. "Let us call it English-Italian-Spanish with a taste of the Orient."

"Formidable." Sweat had appeared on François's brow. "But perhaps irrelevant in this case." He raised his hand with the dart and moved forward.

"Indeed." Matthew took careful note of François's sword arm and chest position, then rotated his sword point away and turned his left shoulder forward, provoking an attack.

As he'd hoped, François forestalled use of the dart and drove for his shoulder with the sword, though he kept the dart raised. Matthew spun counterclockwise as François attacked, swinging his shoulder out of danger and his sword up, into François's right arm. His blade met bone.

With a shriek, François released the dart. Pain pierced Matthew's shoulder as he retracted his sword. He was hit. Incensed at François's success, he ripped the dart from his flesh and flung it away. How long did he have before the poison began to work?

Mouth open, François staggered back, clutching his wounded arm, which dripped blood.

Only then did Matthew notice Carew, advancing on François. He, too, held a dart. Racing into close range, Carew threw it. As it thudded into François's neck, Carew jumped back.

François turned ashen and yanked the dart from his flesh, staring at it in horror.

"Come, Father, Uncle." Carew gestured urgently.

Matthew felt a surge of hope. If he could get Jonathan and Carew to the gate and Navarre's men before he collapsed, they might be safe. And perhaps he could die in Cory's arms.

They moved slowly but steadily toward the gate, Matthew supporting Jonathan, arms looped around each other. The streets were oddly silent in the early morning, only a few people scuttling in the same direction, but as they neared the gates, they saw people had gathered.

"I knew I wanted you here for a reason, little brother," Jonathan panted as he leaned heavily on Matthew. "Bleeding's stopped, at least."

"Don't talk. Walk," Matthew ordered, surprised that no weakness had yet beset him. "I may not last much longer, myself." At Carew's questioning glance, he decided his son must not have understood the purpose of the darts. "That dart François threw at me was poisoned, son. Why do you think he was so pleased to hit me with it? And you hit him with one. Surely you knew."

Carew's face lit up with a sudden smile. "I wiped the dart clean earlier. The one I used on him was poisoned, but not yours."

Matthew stopped in the street, so amazed by his son's ingenuity he could scarcely credit it. "But how did you manage without François knowing?" he asked, incredulous.

"The same way I crossed the chamber with the chair on my back. I waited until he went downstairs, then cleaned off two of the darts and kicked the third poisoned one into the corner where he wouldn't find it. You don't think I was going to let him kill you, do you? I love you too much, Father." Carew's grin was both endearing and heart-wrenching, for Matthew saw in it both his son's love and his desperate wish for that love to be returned.

"Dear God, thank you for this wonderful son." Releasing his brother, Matthew caught his son in a fierce embrace. "I love you, Carew. I can't believe I sired you. You're a wonder." He laughed with sheer joy, knowing he was going to live. Elation swept through him as he realized the years ahead he would have to prove his love to his son.

Carew clung to him with savage intensity. "You love me, Father? Even if I'm a rascal and a rogue?"

"You're neither of those things, Carew." Matthew smoothed the wayward hank of hair from Carew's eyes. "I love you more with each day that passes. Will you give me a chance to prove it? I swore I was never going to leave you and I intend to keep my word."

Carew clung to him, apparently struck speechless, but Matthew saw the love in his son's eyes. The gap that had loomed so long between them narrowed, then closed like a crevice after an earthquake. The landscape was once more serene, yet beneath the surface, changes of great importance had taken place. Matthew intended to build on them in the future. His son had proved more than his love today. He had proved his mature progression toward manhood.

Daniel came around the corner at that moment and, eying the embracing Matthew and Carew with disapproval, went to Jonathan. "*Bonjour encore, El Mágico.* You're hurt," he said, concern in his dark eyes beneath the filthy hair. "Need help? Those two don't look too useful just now."

"Yes, Daniel, I could use help, thank you. You could tell folk at the gate that we carry a message from the Spanish ambassador to Henri of Navarre." Jonathan appeared to be struggling to stay on his feet.

"Indeed, we must keep moving." Matthew tussled Carew's hair affectionately and moved back to Jonathan. "Will the people at the gate believe Daniel?" he asked as he buttoned his doublet, thinking to look more formidable and official.

"Long enough to get us outside," Jonathan said. "Daniel? Are you ready?"

"*Oui,*" Daniel said. "And once we're out, can I meet His Majesty."

Jonathan assessed him with a glance. "Of course. Navarre likes quick, ready lads."

"Then *he*'d better help me," Daniel said, jerking his head toward Carew, "so it looks like we both work for you." The boy shot Jonathan a quirky grin, grabbed Carew's hand, and ran toward the gate. "Make way for the messenger of the Spanish ambassador. Make way. Make way," he shouted in that voice ten times his size. Carew quickly picked up the French for *make way* and shouted it as well. In the confusion, their party passed safely through the gate.

Cory waited in the cool interior of a church at Chelles, Navarre's new headquarters on the Marne River east of Paris. She was beside herself with anxiety, but she must be patient. Matthew had waited patiently as she played Navarre for the outcome of the siege. Now it was her turn.

"*Madame la baroness*, I believe they are come," one of the guards announced at the entry.

Cory rushed for the door, her heart beating like a tocsin, sounding the alarm. They must be safe. They must be safe. They must be safe, or she would . . .

All thoughts of what she would do failed her as she stood on the church steps, craning her neck to see past the bustle of soldiers moving about their business. At the far end of the street, three riders appeared. Or was it four?

At the first sure hint that this was, indeed, the party she awaited, Cory leaped from the steps and raced down the street. Matthew and his party apparently saw her coming, for they halted and dismounted. She hurtled into Matthew's arms, laughing and crying at the same time. "Matthew, you're safe. Praise fortune. I'm so glad." She opened an arm to pull Carew into the crushing embrace. Cory was so relieved to see him, for a moment she couldn't speak. She held him to her, glad to have him hug her hard in return. "Carew, my dear, I've been so worried about you. Thanks be to God you're well. How could you run away like that. Shame on you. You frightened me half to death. I've never been so happy in my life to see you whole."

"It's thanks to him that I'm not dead," Matthew laughed, holding her around the waist as she hugged him over and over. Despite being caked in dust, he was a welcome sight to her weary eyes.

"Thank you, Carew, for saving your father. What did you do?" she asked.

"I wiped the poison off the dart," Carew said with importance. "François got the bad one."

"I want to hear every detail," she assured him, not understanding at all and feeling close to hysteria, her emotions were wound so tightly. "But we must attend to your uncle. He's hurt. This is Jonathan, is it not?" Feeling selfish for her slowness in aiding her brother-in-law, she hurried to his side. He leaned against Blaise, who had just helped him dismount.

"I've been punctured," he said lightly, "but I'll survive. Nothing important was hit or I wouldn't have made it this far. By the by, I'm pleased to make your acquaintance, sister-in-law. If I were feeling better, I'd make you a bow and kiss your hand."

"Don't you dare do anything but let me put you to bed and send for the king's physician. You look white as a sheet," Cory scolded, looping his free arm about her shoulders so he had support from both Blaise and her. "I'm going to feed you and make you comfortable and see you on the mend. How dare you get cut up, Jonathan Cavandish, with your wife about to have a child."

"You must let me support him," Matthew insisted, gently removing his brother's arm and taking Cory's place. "Where are we going?"

"To that big house on the square." Cory pointed out a house with a blooming flower garden. "The mayor of Chelles is delighted to accommodate us. I have hot food waiting and hot baths and clean beds. Come, Jonathan, you shall be first in everything."

Jonathan smiled with an air of grateful resignation. "I'll do anything you say, sister-in-law, if you will first permit me a long rest on one of those clean beds."

"Of course! You must be drained." Anxious for him, Cory put an arm around Carew and led the way.

"Father was wonderful. He's an amazing swordsman," Carew said to her as they entered the cool house and servants responded to Cory's directions, helping Jonathan up the stairs.

"And you're an amazing ally, Carew," Matthew said as Jonathan disappeared from view and a lad ran to fetch Navarre's physician. "I was never so surprised in my life as when you said you'd wiped the poison from my dart. I had expected to die." He put a hand on his son's shoulder in a loving gesture. "You saved us more than once today."

Cory's eyes widened with amazement. "You were hit by a poison dart? You thought you were dying, yet you escorted your brother and Carew out of the city and back here?"

"But I wasn't dying, you see. I found out once Carew remembered to mention how he'd saved me." Matthew wrapped both arms around Carew and held him close, smiling down on his son. "I love you, Carew," he said, as if savoring the words.

"I love you too, Father." Carew's voice quivered. "I know you love me enough to die for me. I hope you know I would do the same for you."

"I'll never leave you again. I swear it. My ships and everything else can go to the devil." Their gazes locked, and Cory saw love and understanding pass between father and son that was so strong, she was warmed to the core.

Yet she felt left out as well. Matthew was finally able to love his son freely. She could only hope he might someday feel as much for her.

By the time Cory had heard the physician pronounce Jonathan's wound likely to heal nicely, seen her patient eat, and watched him fall asleep, Carew, Matthew, and their associates had devoured most of the lavish dinner she had prepared. Weary to the bone, she stood outside the dining parlor, watching her husband. As if sensing her presence, Matthew looked up and met her gaze. He excused himself to the others and came to her.

In the privacy of the chamber reserved for them, Matthew crushed her against him, showering her with kisses. Unexpectedly, tears burned her eyes and she let them come.

"What's wrong?" he soothed her. "Don't weep, sweetheart. We've come through safely."

"T-that's why I'm crying," she stammered, beside herself. "You're all safe. I'm so glad."

"Then you're crying for joy?"

"Yes," she sniffled, unable to check the tears. "I'm glad you won't be leaving. Carew needs you." She tightened her arms around him, grateful that he had rediscovered his love for his son, yet unable to suppress her loneliness.

"What of you?" he asked, all too perceptive of her sorrow. "Do you need me?"

"I suppose," she sniffed, not wanting him to know what she was thinking. "But Carew needs you the most." She buried her face in his shoulder, trying to hide her need. "You mustn't worry about me," she whispered brokenly.

Matthew rocked her gently. "That's one of the reasons why I love you, Cory. Your tender heart puts everyone else first, but you know we can't let that happen all the time."

She stilled, unable to believe what he'd said. "You . . . what?"

"I love you, Cordelia Cavandish." He smiled as he tilted up her chin. "Do you know, in the moment when François's supposedly poison dart hit my shoulder, I looked death in the face and knew that if by some miracle I survived, my love for you would rival yours for me."

She could only stare at him, afraid to believe his words.

"I've just realized that I can feel every bit as much as you do. I had just forgotten how," he said. "Life hurts us, but it also gives us joy to make us strong again. I love you, Cordelia. Won't you admit you love me?"

The sincerity of his words, his earnest expression, convinced her at last. He wasn't teasing. He was telling the truth. "Of course I love you!" she hugged him tighter than ever, scarcely able to believe it. "I realized I loved you at Meaux, when you almost died. I kicked away that dagger because I couldn't let you be hurt."

Matthew chuckled. "Quite a kick it was, too. I'm grateful for it." He leaned forward to nuzzle her cheek. "Now that we know the truth about La Faye, I believe he arranged for Essex to appear guilty in his stead. I'm rather glad that Essex is innocent. The queen's attached to him."

"I'm glad too, but I don't think he's entirely innocent." Cory responded to his caress with one of her own. "He may not have committed murder, but he has a bad enough temper to rise up in rebellion on impulse. I hope Her Majesty can control him."

"Knowing you, you'll help her. You're always stepping in when trouble brews."

"I didn't do so well with Jacques La Faye," Cory said with a grimace. "I cannot think why I believed he loved Moll or was worthy of her love. I was a fool."

"You're never a fool, Cordelia," Matthew consoled her. "Your kind heart blinded you to the truth. You wanted to think well of him for Moll's sake, and most of the time, people benefit from your trust by rising to the occasion. In fact, I knew the minute I heard you were in France that you would manage things and all would be well in the end."

"Liar." Cory wrinkled her nose at him. "You wanted to throttle me and bundle me back home, but that's one of the reasons why I love you, Matthew. You remind me of the ways I succeeded rather than failed."

Her sobs subsided, and then she sighed as she brushed against his hips and realized he was aroused. "Make love to me," she begged, wanting to experience the ultimate closeness with him. "I can never get enough of the physical expression of our feelings for one another."

"With pleasure, sweetheart." He kissed her long and passionately.

The physical expression of their feelings, of their faith in one another. It sounded so right, and for the first time he seemed to agree. It wasn't just lust. Not just bodies meeting and parting, but tenderness expressed in a way that went beyond flesh.

"You are braver than anyone I know," he said, pulling her down onto the bed.

She smiled despite damp eyes and reached to kiss him. "Let us concentrate on the joy and forget the pain."

"I would be delighted for you to arrange it," he grinned. "Shall we make a child? A being who will be a manifestation of our love for one another? Another person to cherish, along with our existing horde?"

"I thought you didn't like our horde?" She ran one hand down his chest, pretending to be coy.

Matthew grimaced. "I believe I must learn to appreciate them better. Marcus and Letty had an instinctive distrust of La Faye from the start. Marcus, especially. He's sharp."

"Are you still afraid I'll die in childbed?"

"Terrified. But my love gives me the courage to face it."

"That makes me very happy, Matthew." She leaned over to embrace him. "For I long to hold our babe in my arms."

Matthew pulled at her laces, loosening her bodice. "Enough drama, wife. I've been too long without you." He sat up among the soft linens and peeled off his doublet.

Cory shrugged out of her bodice and held out her arms to him. Let people like La Faye and Trenchard do what they would; she knew where the true power lay in the world. And she knew that although Matthew had once forced the strength of healing emotions from his heart and mind, he had at last welcomed their return. His courage had glowed within like a last live coal keeping its nightlong vigil on the hearth, except that now morning had come, and with the right fuel, the coal had blazed fully to life. It burned with a living flame, and her joy was complete. "Amen, to that, Matthew Cavandish," she said as she joined her passion to his. "Amen."

Epilogue

Marcus stuck two fingers in his mouth and stretched his lips into a hideous grin.

The babe on Cory's lap chortled with glee and batted at him, her hands wet with drool.

"Good gracious, Marcus, such a face." Cory laughed, a joyous sound.

Matthew pressed her hand. "Happy, love?" he asked as Marcus experimented with a dozen other ways to contort his features and the baby crowed with delight.

"Now that little Margaret is here, yes, very." She rubbed the laughing baby's back and gazed at her husband. "And now that we're bound for your island in the Caribbean, I'm happier still." She gestured toward the majestic sea beyond the railing of the sunny deck where they sat.

He returned her smile with satisfaction, and it occurred to him that her green eyes still reminded him of the promise of coming spring. Yet for him, the hopeless wait for the season of rebirth was over. It had arrived, and he had since entered the summer of his life, reaping the bounty of love he had longed for. With pride, he regarded his family, then the four ships following *The Revenge.* "Cory, I do believe Dame Fortune predicted correctly," he said, feeling in the mood to tease her.

"You mean the fortune-teller who said I was made for love?" Cory scoffed. "I should never have told you what she said. You tease me about it unmercifully."

"But she proved correct," he insisted, reaching up to play with her hair, which was whipped by the sea breeze. "We met immediately after she made her prediction, we fell in love, we married, and now you've successfully borne our second child."

"I do believe you have the order of events wrong." Cory wrinkled her nose at him. "We married, *I* fell in love, and you noticed. You were slow about doing your part."

"What I lacked in speed, I shall make up for with intensity," he vowed, stealing a kiss.

"Ugh, do you have to be kissing all the time?" Marcus glanced up from the baby.

"Yes, we do," Matthew said firmly. "We'll even kiss you. I've learned that such expressions of feeling are good." He grabbed for Marcus, but his adopted son dodged away with a yelp.

"Save me. I'm about to be kissed," Marcus bellowed, racing to hide behind Carew and Samuel, who had just sauntered up, looking ready for company.

"So? It won't hurt," Carew retorted. At seventeen, he let few things ruffle his composure.

"Look, I'll kiss Father." He dropped the caress on the top of Matthew's head.

Matthew caught his tall son's arm and kissed him in return, then captured Samuel, who was looking forlorn, and kissed him as well. "I still marvel that you helped me defeat La Faye and the horrible George Trenchard, Carew. Your Aunt Rozalinde was ecstatic."

"Wait 'til you see what else I do." Carew grinned. "I intend to go far in life."

Marcus grimaced. "Ugh. Come on, Samuel, race me to the poop deck. These folks make me sick." He crouched for the start.

"You always beat me," Samuel protested, refusing to move from Matthew's arms.

"I'll race you, Marcus." Carew dropped into a starting position. "Father, will you give us the signal?"

Matthew started them off, then followed them with his gaze as they tore past the sailors. "We've been most fortunate," he said to Cory, enjoying the way sunlight glittered in her ebony hair. "I was terrified when you went into labor the second time, but here's Margaret, and here you are—"

"And we already have our Charles, as well as our other children, so all is well with the world," Cory finished as Margaret whimpered and butted against her breast to nurse. She opened her bodice, and the baby nestled close. "Though I can't say I wish to bear another child right away."

"But I do wish to love you again soon," he whispered in her ear, his heart full as he feasted his eyes on his wife and nursing child. At the start of her protest, he patted her lips with one finger. "I have no wish for you to endure labor again soon either, so I will employ a method to prevent quickening," he assured her. "Leave it to me."

"Not horrid herbal potions, I hope," she said, looking skeptical.

"No, a flexible sheath made of animal intestine. We don't want any children born on my island when we don't have a midwife."

"Agreed." Contentment wreathed her face in a warm glow. "Oh, but I can't wait to see your island, Matthew," she said in sudden excitement. "I can scarcely believe we're sailing the Atlantic Ocean, bound for your land of perpetual heat. No more cold winters for you, and—"

"No more separations from my son," he completed the thought. "I thought you were mad when you suggested the idea."

"There will probably be moments ahead when we both think it's mad to live on a tropical island, cut off from civilization," Cory agreed, "but it will also be wonderful in many ways."

Matthew agreed wholeheartedly. It had taken him over three years to agree that they should use her money in this way. But at last she had convinced him they could decide together how to spend the money now belonging to them both. This voyage was something they both desired. And they would be within a short day's sail of several other port towns that welcomed trade with the English.

Cory started as a bell rang on the quarter deck. "Gracious, is it time for dinner already?"

"Indeed, it is." Madam Henrietta bustled up with young

Charles tucked under one arm and Letty in tow, a guilty expression on her face. "And this naughty child of yours—"

"This child of ours," Cory teased.

"Yes, she is our child, isn't she," Henrietta said in a tone that was half loving, half indignant. "Well, do you know I found this child of ours in the kitchens, bullying the cook into making trifle? Can you imagine anything so wild? The cows in the hold would have apoplexy if they knew what was happening to their cream."

"Grandmama, cows don't have apoplexy," Letty insisted, "and the cook was excited to learn an elegant dish. He *can* make something besides beans. Though it may not be perfect, we shall have trifle for dinner."

Matthew looked at Cory, and they both burst out laughing at the idea. Trifle on board ship? It seemed an extraordinary luxury, but if Letty had managed it, why not?

Madam Henrietta huffed, but it was good-natured as she plopped two-year-old Charles into Matthew's lap. "This one is into everything. I suggest you tie a rope to his ankle or next thing he'll be overboard."

"No rope." Charles stood on Matthew's lap, held his face steady, and looked him straight in the eye. "Charles hungwy."

"You have an insatiable appetite, dear, but it *is* time for dinner," Cory said, chuckling at her child's directness. She leaned over and kissed and hugged him lavishly.

After the family had dined, eating on deck because of the beauty of the day, Cory gathered all the crew not on duty and began the afternoon entertainments. There were cards, of course, as well as singing led by Hugh, and hornpipe dancing. All of the men gazed at Cory with adoring eyes as she walked among them, praising one's generosity for helping his fellow add up his cards, complimenting another for his fine voice and willingness to entertain them.

As he leaned against a mast, Matthew realized that the bride of his heart had done just what she'd threatened to do many moons ago. Not only had she created a circle of friends among his crew, but she had been right about encouraging Henri of Navarre to spare Paris.

"Just think," he said, catching her around the waist as she passed, "Henri was welcomed into the city as king last month by those very people whom Jonathan told me wanted him all along."

Cory smiled. "Of course they wanted him. His instincts are excellent. He couldn't bear to see his people suffer, and by raising the siege, he convinced them he would always put their interests first. So they crowned him despite those horrid Leaguers."

"Yes, and France will recover its prosperity at last. I must admit I feel rather satisfied with our part in it, though I'm still amazed how the end of the siege hung on the turn of a card."

"It didn't, really." Cory's remark was careless as Charles toddled up and she scooped him into her arms.

"Why, what do you mean?" Matthew turned, astonished.

"What I mean, dear heart," she said, her smile guileless, "is that I cheated in the last card game with Navarre. You don't think I would leave something as important as ending the siege of Paris to chance, do you? I made sure I had the four queens and most of the kings and aces."

Matthew stared at her, too stunned to speak.

Cory tossed her head and laughed aloud. "Matthew Cavandish, if you think to reproach me, pray do not. It was the first and only time I cheated at cards, though I am capable of doing so anytime I wish. Don't you agree I chose the proper moment to put my skill to work? It was for an excellent cause, for now Navarre is bringing badly needed peace to the land."

Slowly, Matthew's amazement ebbed as he realized she was right. His wife had chosen the right moment to manipulate the cards. In fact, the more he thought on it, the more he felt like . . .

A chuckle burst from his throat. The chuckle grew into a laugh, and the laugh swelled to a full-blown guffaw. "Great Neptune, you are amazing, Cory. You used your skill to ensure that his people would love him. You made them see him in the best possible light."

She sent him a loving smile. "I only nudged him in the direction he was already leaning. It was the right thing at the right moment." She caught him around the neck and kissed him, then moved on among the crew, helping one to reckon his score, the next with his hornpipe steps.

Matthew shook his head in wonder. Her love was so boundless, she seemed capable of accomplishing the impossible. She had ended the military siege of a great city. She had also reawakened in him emotions he had believed were long dead. But her best gift of all to him was the knowledge that his ability to love had never really left him. It had been lying dormant, waiting until he was willing and able to love again. Cory had helped him heal, but he had had to reopen his heart. And he had done it in order to love her.

The knowledge was a strong new power within him. With God's grace, they would have many years, but never again would he be spiritually mangled by the loss of someone he loved. She had taught him that life was full of many kinds of love, and that the purpose of living was to reach out to others in order to give and receive. As long as he held that knowledge in his heart, his world would never again be an empty void, as it had been when he lost Joanna.

That night, as he held Cory in his arms and made love to her until she cried out with joy, he knew that Dame Fortune had predicted rightly. She was indeed made for love, and he welcomed her into his life as his bride of hearts.

HISTORICAL NOTE

After years of civil war in France, Henri of Navarre finally changed his religion. It had become apparent that he would be crowned in no other way, as the French Salic Law states that the king must be Catholic. In 1594, he converted and was crowned King Henri IV of France. The question relevant to this story, however, is why did Henri of Navarre, the first of the great Bourbon kings and father of Louis XIII, raise the siege of Paris as he did on Tuesday, August 30, 1590? Some history books tell us only that the Duke of Parma arrived from the Netherlands with a large army and Henri was forced to move his troops to meet him, thus raising the siege.

I believe the situation was infinitely more complex. For one thing, Henri's skill in battle tactics was legendary. He certainly would have known to stay put if he had wished to continue the siege. In fact, he actually did leave part of his army in control of the suburbs and key neighboring cities while his main force met Parma. He retained the option of returning later to tighten the noose.

In either case, Parma would have been forced to initiate battle to draw Navarre away, and would have been too busy fighting to carry food to the beleaguered city. In fact, Parma refused to fight at all, as Henri had been warned he would. Why, then, did Henri raise the siege and go to meet an army he knew would not fight?

In the memoirs of Maximilian de Bethune, Sieur de Rosny, later Duke of Sully and chief minister to Henri IV, the edition published in Edinburgh in 1805, I found an answer that I believe explains it best and that I mentioned in the story. Many of Navarre's commanders and troops were Protestants whose

families had been destroyed at the bloody St. Bartholomew's
Day Massacre as they visited Paris in 1572. Navarre had heard
whispers that these factions intended to pillage Paris once it
was conquered. They would exact their bloody revenge for
their losses eighteen years earlier. Henri realized that if the
Parisians surrendered, they would be utterly destroyed by his
troops. As a man who loved his subjects, no matter their religion, Navarre refused to begin his reign with a gesture that
would go down in history as rivaling the St. Bartholomew's
Day Massacre. To his own detriment, he chose to raise the
siege.

In keeping with my practice of augmenting history with a
woman's touch, I allowed a woman, Cordelia, to be the driving
force that settled Navarre's indecision. Since the king frequently vacillated in political and battle plans, appearing unable to decide which course to take, he could well have been
influenced by a beautiful female. This is especially true since
we know his lack of decisive action was often precipitated by
his temporary abandonment of important affairs while he pur-
sued a woman. He was a notorious lover who had many mistresses, yet at the heart of the man lay a true love of his subjects
and a wisdom that put the health of the nation in a category
apart from his personal needs. In fact, the wisdom of his decision to abandon the siege of Paris was borne out when, in
March 1594, he was welcomed into Paris by the common people and the bourgeois who longed for the peace he brought.
They had no great love for the Duke of Mayenne, with his ties
to Spain and willingness to put Philip II of Spain's daughter on
the throne, nor did they appreciate the Spanish Duke of Parma
coming to the Duke of Mayenne's aid, despite the fact that he
appeared to be the reason Navarre raised the siege.

Under Henri IV's reign, a great tolerance for all religions in
France spread, as did the improvement in the country's eco-
nomic welfare. He ruled well until he was assassinated in
1610.

As for Elizabeth Tudor, Queen of England, I took great joy
in portraying her strong yet vacillating and manipulative per-
sonality as accurately as I could. The court could be a hotbed
of intrigue and gossip; certainly not a place to nurture intimate
relationships. Nor did the queen seem to encourage deep
friendships among her courtiers. In general, she was jealous of

most of the females who came to court except for the few who devoted themselves exclusively to her service, and she seemed to demand adulation from most of her male courtiers.

Yet having studied the life of Elizabeth in some depth, I believe I know a bit about her character. Though she formed few affectionate ties throughout her life, especially with women, she did have a few favorite female associates. One of these was Lady Bridget Manners, who came to court at age fourteen to serve as a maid of honor and swiftly captured the queen's heart with her loving ways. It is from descriptions of Bridget that I drew the character of Cordelia Cavandish. The queen's affection for Bridget was so great that when the girl married in secret, although the queen was furious, Bridget talked her into releasing her husband after only three months in prison. This was a record, by all reports. In comparison, Sir Thomas Shirley spent nine months in the Marshalsea prison when he married the maid of honor Frances Vasavour without the queen's permission, and although Sir Walter Raleigh spent only five weeks in the Tower when he married the maid of honor Elizabeth Throckmorton without permission, his poor wife spent five months as a prisoner. Three months for Bridget's husband was without question a deal.

As for the Earl of Essex, Elizabeth Tudor didn't actually put him in the Tower when he married Lady Frances Walsingham Sidney without her permission. However, Essex's hot temper did spur him to lead a rebellion against the queen in 1601, and he ended his life on the headman's block for his foolishness. Those of you who have seen the Verdi opera *Roberto Devereux* or the old Bette Davis and Errol Flynn movie *Elizabeth and Essex* probably know this well.

As for the character of Jacques La Faye, I found no indication that Henri of Navarre sent an envoy to England in 1590. This created the perfect opportunity for my story. Given the slow communications of the era, a false envoy could well have gotten away with his charade for a lengthy period without being discovered.

I must also explain my decision to have Matthew nickname Cordelia "Titania" and the references to *A Midsummer Night's Dream* in the opening scene. Historians guess that this play was written by Shakespeare around 1594. For this reason, since my story takes place in 1590, I referred to the play

Matthew saw as being "rough in its infancy." I am suggesting that Matthew read an early rough draft of a scene from this play, rather than the finished work. I consider this possible since Matthew frequented court circles and Shakespeare was, as far as we know, living and writing in London in 1590 and before. As I have often drafted scenes or openings to stories, then put them aside to work on something else, I thought it possible that Shakespeare might have begun work on this play, shown a scene to a potential patron (who shared it with others), then put it aside temporarily to work on something else. Somewhere in there, Matthew got a peek at it.

Finally, with regard to the game of Cent, if you're wondering how the players had so many face cards all the time, it's because Cent is played with only the 7s, 8s, 9s, 10s, jacks, queens, kings, and aces. The object of the game was to make points by counting your sequences, sets of four, and sets of three, then to play for tricks. The game was later called Piquet, and a variety of versions developed.

Finally, I must correct an omission from the acknowledgments in my last book, *Firebrand Bride*, by thanking Judy Peters of Columbus Emergency Veterinary Service for her advice about the early scene where a foal is born. Thank you, Judy, for your explanation of how a foal's leg could be bent back and so impede the mare's delivery, and my apologies for forgetting to express my thanks in the appropriate volume.

Don't forget to write and let me know how you liked *Bride of Hearts.* I can be reached by e-mail at jlynnford@aol.com. You can also receive my latest, free newsletter by sending a business-sized envelope to Janet Lynnford, PO Box 21904, Columbus, OH 43221. And do visit my web page at http://www.sff.net/people/JanetLynnford. And always remember, love *does* have the power to change the world.